Dear Reader,

I'm excited to share with you the second book in the Sweetblood series, *Embraced by Blood*. This world is a deadly and seductive one, where a team of vampire Guardians fights to protect humans from Darkbloods—vicious members of their race who kill like their ancestors and sell the blood on the black market. The rarest, called Sweet, commands the highest price.

When I first met Alfonso, it was through his brother's eyes. Naturally, I was intimidated to write about him. How could a man with a past like his ever redeem himself enough to be a hero? But the more I got to know him, the more I fell in love with him, and I began to see him as Lily did—a warrior, wounded in body and spirit, with a heart of pure gold hidden underneath.

That's not to say sparks don't fly be　　　　Alfonso. This is a reunion story—　　heart once and she's not about to　　again. Besides, you don't cross I　　　　s repercussions. I hope you enjo　　　　ow she took him to his knees and　　　　of the darkness, whether he though　　　　not.

Oh, and regarding the first　　　　　e to the students of Western Washing　　　　, my alma mater. Now you know what waits　　　in that dark corner near Haggard Hall.

All my best,

Laurie London

**Other Sweetblood titles
available from
LAURIE LONDON
and HQN Books**

Bonded by Blood
Hidden by Blood (ebook exclusive)

And coming soon
Holiday with a Vampire
Unbound by Blood

LAURIE LONDON

EMBRACED *by* BLOOD

HQN™

Recycling programs
for this product may
not exist in your area.

ISBN-13: 978-0-373-77586-6

EMBRACED BY BLOOD

ACKNOWLEDGMENTS

Writing a story may be a solitary process, but making it a book isn't. I am truly thankful for so many people.

In addition to my sister,
I'd like to thank Janna, Kandis, Mandy, Shelley,
Kathy and Barb for giving me invaluable feedback.
When I count my blessings, these women are
seriously at the top of my list.

Thank you to Cherry Adair,
who opened her heart and her home to
a bunch of fledglings and encouraged us to fly.

To my Romance University friends,
particularly Kelsey Browning, thank you for everything.
To Vicky Dreiling and Delilah Marvelle,
thanks for your friendship and the marathon phone calls.
To the Cherryplotters, thank you for the laughs
and the creative inspiration. Thank you to my agent,
Emmanuelle Morgen, my GIAM x4 buddies,
and my fellow GSRWA writers.

Thank you to my talented and thoughtful editor Margo
Lipschultz as well as all the hardworking people at HQN
Books who've been so enthusiastic about this series.

A giant thank-you to my mom for all her help
and to the rest of my family who've been so encouraging.
Thank you to my two wonderful children, who think it's
cool to have a mom who writes books even though
they're not allowed to read them.

And last but not least, to my sexy sidekick, my incredibly
supportive husband, Ted: thank you, baby, for holding
my world together. With every breath, I love you.

EMBRACED by BLOOD

To my sister, Becky,
because without you, there'd be no *this*.

CHAPTER ONE

GALE-FORCE WINDS BLEW IN from Bellingham Bay, funneling rain between the darkened lecture hall buildings like a raging river. Red Square in the middle of campus should've been deserted at this time of night.

A lone student dashed under the covered walkway of Haggard Hall and slipped off a heavy backpack. It hit the bricks with a splatter.

In the shadows behind her, a dark figure watched her movements with interest. He didn't bother stepping deeper into the doorway—the darkness rendered him invisible to humans.

Alfonso Serrano sniffed the air and let his pupils dilate with hunger.

Don't they tell students, especially the female ones, not to walk alone at night?

Fortunately, there were always a few who didn't follow directions.

Breathing hard, the student brushed off her rain-sodden hood and swiped her nose with the back of her hand.

Alfonso moved a step closer and reached for her.

But when she grabbed a cell phone from her pocket, he hesitated and dropped his outstretched arm. If she made a call, he'd wait. If she texted, he'd continue.

She brought the phone to her ear, and he retreated into

the seldom-used doorway, careful not to disturb the waterlogged pile of leaves in the corner. Stuffing his hands deep in his pockets, he clenched them into fists to stop the tremors. Her call had better be quick, otherwise he was likely to drain her dry when he struck. Four weeks between feedings was way too long.

She yelled into the phone and he bristled at her harsh tone. Fighting the urge to plug his ears, he rethought his decision to wait. He didn't know how long he could listen to this.

As she carried on her heated conversation, a blast of wind swirled around him, blowing his chin-length hair into his eyes. He pulled out a knit skullcap, stretched it over his head and tucked the hair beneath it.

But when the damp wind changed direction, it brought with it an odd smell. A sickeningly sweet odor, like that of rotting meat, and he froze.

Darkbloods.

He scanned the darkness and unzipped his coat with quiet precision. From a leather sheath strapped to his chest, he eased out two silver kunai and held them by their rope-twined grips. The custom-made weapons, small but deadly, were designed to be thrown. They fit perfectly in his hands, like the contours of a lover.

What were Darkbloods doing in Bellingham? The Alliance didn't normally set up cells in small northern towns like this. There weren't enough people and, given the low ultraviolet index, the residual energy level in the indigenous population was too low to make it worth their trouble.

Christ, that was why he'd moved here. To be far away from them.

Staying in the shadows, Alfonso crept to the next doorway, trying to pinpoint their location. The scent came from the far side of the square, but he didn't have a visual yet.

It shouldn't have surprised him they were here. Logic said they'd move in eventually. Expanding the DB power base among law-abiding vampires was one of the Alliance's primary objectives. However, it wasn't as if Bellingham was a hotbed of activity. Of the vampires who lived in the region, most were concentrated near Seattle and Vancouver. Not in small college towns.

And then another possibility dawned on him.

The smell might not be from an ordinary Darkblood.

It could be his blood assassin.

A glacial calm filled his veins as he fingered the handles of the identical knives and looked out into the night again. Puddles of standing water rippled in the howling wind, reflecting the light of the streetlamps scattered around the drained fountain. A paper coffee cup tumbled toward him and lodged behind his heavy work boots.

What a fool he'd been to think he was out of the Alliance's reach. You couldn't do what he did and expect to get away with it. But, Jesus, he thought he'd been so careful moving to this remote town.

The sound of the girl's voice drew his attention once more.

"Listen, Ryan, I'm not putting up with this bullshit much longer. Either you tell her or I will." Oblivious to the fact that she was surrounded by those with deadly intentions, she stepped away from the leading edge of the rain and slumped against the building. She popped a piece of gum into her mouth and let the wind carry away the wrapper.

Could she be the target, not him? Her blood type was relatively uncommon in this part of the country, he reasoned. He'd covered his tracks well and it wasn't as if this was a planned visit to the campus anyway. No one knew he was here.

Movement in the overhang of Old Main on the other side of Red Square caught his eye.

Two figures—darker than the shadows—hugged the ivy-covered brick. Like marionettes on the same wire, their arms and legs moved in unison. To a casual observer, they looked like well-coordinated Goths, but to a fellow vampire, they were remorseless killers who profited from the death of humans.

Alfonso relaxed. Blood assassins worked alone. They must be after the girl.

Adjusting the rope grips in his palms, he cursed silently. His fingers felt so weak. Hell, his whole body did. If it hadn't been so long since he'd taken the blood of a human, he'd be stronger right now. He couldn't confront them like this.

Besides, since he was marked for elimination, the average DB wouldn't hesitate to finish him off if they learned his identity. It wasn't like he wanted to rub shoulders with them on purpose.

He tucked the blades away and melted into the shadows.

As soon as he rounded the far side of the building, his

steel-toed boots began to feel like lead, each step more difficult than the last, and he stopped. The hollow pit in his stomach became too hard to ignore.

He had planned to take only a small amount of the girl's blood, leaving her tired and a little dazed, yet alive. But if he left, she'd be dead within minutes, her body completely drained of its life energy, her blood portioned out and sold in vials to the highest bidders. A perfect example of how supply and demand worked on the black market of the vampire underworld.

He didn't need much from her to regain his strength. Was there enough time to—?

Nope, too late now. He'd have to let them have her. Better her than him, he thought as he turned up his collar and took off again toward the empty parking lot across the street. The sound of his boot heels striking the pavement echoed loudly between the buildings. Each step seemed to be saying, "Loser, loser."

A Guardian would never stand by while a Darkblood took a human.

I'm not a Guardian, he wanted to remind his conscience. *It's not my job to protect humans from vampires.* But he hesitated anyway.

The Darkblood Alliance believed their kind belonged at the top of the food chain—they had no regard for human life. They didn't want to blend in; they wanted to dominate. These predators would either discard the body here to be discovered by the authorities, or they'd take her back to their den and drain her there. Regardless of what they did with her, every kill, every disappearance, risked exposing their secret to the human population.

That backward attitude may have been tolerated in the Middle Ages, but it wasn't acceptable today.

Even in his weakened condition, he realized he wouldn't be able to live with himself if he didn't at least try to prevent the inevitable. Goddamn guilty conscience.

He made his way back along the edge of Haggard Hall. When he got to the corner, he glanced quickly around. Driving rain fell at a severe angle, but he could still make out the Darkbloods moving on the other side of Red Square.

He sprinted across the narrow walkway over to Miller Hall, thankful the weather was so crappy. Chances were, even though vampires' senses were more acute than humans', the DBs couldn't hear him above the sound of the wind and rain. As he flattened himself against the brick facade, he formed a plan. He'd jump them when they got closer and hope to God he had the strength to pull it off. Retrieving the blades, he waited.

Within heartbeats, the two figures emerged like liquid darkness from the corner of Old Main and stopped on the far end of the same walkway, but they didn't advance farther.

Damn. Had they seen him? He doubted they smelled him. Not only was he downwind, but their all-blood diet dulled their sense of smell.

Although he couldn't make out exactly what they were saying, the wind carried snippets of their hushed whispers. They were trying to figure out what to do next.

Shit, they had seen him.

With his lack of strength, the element of surprise had been his only ally. He couldn't hope to fight them like this and win. His only hope now was for the girl to leave. Then he'd split.

For chrissake, he wanted to yell at her. *Would you get the hell out of here? Your voice is like a goddamn dinner bell.*

Unsure what to do next, he considered his options. Maybe he could stall the bastards.

Switching both blades to his left hand, he tucked them against his forearm to keep them hidden. He stepped from the shadows and ambled toward the end of the walkway in his best non-confrontational manner, a skill he'd honed to perfection as a double agent.

Side by side, with their hands on their hips, they waited for him. The tall, gangly one, a female with stringy blond hair whipping across her face like Medusa, fidgeted the heel of her boot.

A newbie maybe? Seasoned DBs were usually more stoic and controlled. Perfect.

The other one, a stocky male, stood silent beside her. Both wore matching ankle-length black coats, but because neither one had on the wraparound sunglasses common among DB pairs, he could see their coal-black irises and the lifeless gray of their whites. Along with that rotten meat smell, it was another characteristic of their all-blood diet.

"What's going on?" Alfonso asked as he got closer. He touched two fingers to his lips in a fang-slang greeting and dropped his hand. "Darkbloods, right?"

Wordlessly, they looked at each other, something passing silently between them before they relaxed their stances and returned the gesture.

Great. Just great. The female couldn't be as new as he'd first thought—the pair operated in tandem like most longtime DB partners who fed from the same hosts night after night.

The male cocked his head in the direction of the coed. "You taking her tonight?"

Relieved that it definitely was the girl they were after, not him, he flashed an apologetic grin, hoping they'd buy his discomfort. "Was thinking about it."

"Is she an A-poz or B-poz? We couldn't tell from over there."

"B-positive, I think." He tried to convey uncertainty, although he knew for sure that she was. "Why?"

"Excellente," the male said with a faux accent. "We're building up our stock and are short on a few of the less common varieties. More people are B-poz up in Vancouver than down here. Didn't want to head up there just for that, so this is perfect." He flipped open his coat and displayed his wares. His partner did the same. The inside was like a goddamn pharmacy with vials full of blood, syringes, a few nasty-ass knives and God knew what else.

"You a revert?" the woman asked, as she fastened her coat and scrutinized him. "Or just slipping." One of her eyeballs canted slightly off center, not quite moving in conjunction with the other one.

Glass eye or lazy eye?

He noted the whites of both her eyes had the same dull gray tint.

Better assume lazy and be pleasantly surprised if I'm wrong.

"Am I reverting back to the Old Way? Yeah, I guess you could say I've moved beyond the occasional slip-up."

"Well, good for you," the male said. "Got any kills under your belt?"

Alfonso shrugged. *More than you'll ever know.*

"You're in luck," the male continued. "Me and Sigred—" he indicated his partner with a jerk of his chin "—are settin' up shop here in Bellingham. We can save you the trouble of having to come out on a night like this looking for a little substinex."

The blonde leaned toward her partner. "Sustenance," she whispered.

"Don't go fucking college on me," he said through clenched teeth. "I know what I'm talking about. As I was saying, we're gonna save reverts such as yourself a lot of time and offer a delivery service of sorts. You call us, place your order, and we'll figure out where to meet. No more embracing the elements, if you know what I'm saying."

Sigred produced a plain white card with a single phone number printed in black. "As far as I know, no other Darkblood cells are offering this special service. Not even those fancy big-city ones. In Seattle or Vancouver, you go to them. You traipse through the clubs and alleys looking for a seller if you're in the mood for a little *substinex.* That, or take it off the hoof. We know most reverts aren't comfortable doing it old-school, at least when they're starting out. But here, we come to you."

Forcing another smile, Alfonso took the card and tucked it into his pocket, where he crushed it into a tiny ball. "You know what they say—you get better customer service in a small town." That got a hearty laugh from both of them.

"Since you found her first, how about we'll do her to save you the trouble and give you a couple of freebies." The male pulled out an empty syringe and displayed it with his pinkie lifted as if he had class. "Sound like a plan?"

Alfonso rubbed his forehead under his cap to make them think he was considering their offer. Maybe if he stalled them a little longer, the girl would leave and they'd all go home empty-handed. He glanced over, but she was still there on the far side of the square. Jesus, how long was she going to fight with her boyfriend anyway?

"I don't know if you've done it much," the male was saying, "but feeding off the hoof is a little tricky, although you did choose an excellent locale—dark, private—and your subject is alone. But the instant you strike and you taste the rush of fear in the blood, it can freak a guy out if you're not expecting it. If you're not good at mind manips, you feel what the human feels the entire time their life energy is waning. Not sure if you'd be into that or not."

Did he look like a youthling fresh out of puberty? Most of their kind did feed from live donors, just not as often as these losers did. Suggesting an alternate memory of events during a feeding was one of the first things a youthling beginning his Time of Change was taught. *This is perfect. They think I'm younger and less experienced than they are.*

He tried to keep the satisfaction from showing on his face, flashing them a nervous smile instead. "I wasn't planning to drain her dry."

"Old habits are hard to break." Sigred patted his arm. Although his first instinct was to jerk away, he didn't flinch, instead rubbing the pad of his thumb on the rope grip to control the impulse.

"Personally," she continued, "I adore it. Blood tinged with fear is sweeter than most. In fact, I love scaring them right before I strike for that very reason. But many reverts are uncomfortable with it at first. And we understand that. That's what we're here for. You can have your cake and eat it too. It's a service we're happy to provide. What do you say?"

A perfect regurgitation of the DB playbook. "How long have you been here? Any more D—Darkblood cells here in town?" He'd almost slipped and used Agency slang. He'd been out of practice too long.

"Not yet," she said. "But with the Night of Wilding less than a month away, we'll probably have a few new groups moving into the area. The new sector mistress is planning a huge event."

The pair started toward the girl, brushing past him a little too close—their stench always made him nauseous.

"So where's the party this year?" he asked, trying to stall them.

Originally, the holiday had been an all-night festival of eating and dancing as family and friends celebrated the longest night of the year, but for the past few decades Darkbloods had been using it as a means of attracting and recruiting new members. It had devolved into little more than a costume party of debauchery and violence, often held in a macabre location. The few humans invited rarely left alive.

"Keeping it secret for now," Sigred said as she watched the girl, eyes narrowed and focused like a predator. "Do you play HG?"

"What?"

"The online game, Hollow Grave?"

"No, I don't." He recalled some of the Darkbloods talking about a new online game, but that had been almost two years ago.

"As long as you're a registered user and get to Grave Crawler status, you can log in at noon the day before and the location will be posted in the forums. There'll be plenty of time to get there between sundown and midnight. It'll be on one of the islands this year."

Wasn't that interesting? He knew the Alliance was working on some new ways to attract the younger generation of vampires, but since that hadn't been his area of expertise when he was inside, he had no idea what they were up to. Online gaming? They must be using it to promote their agenda by romanticizing the violent past of their kind.

He fought to keep his expression blank as he recalled being a youthling in a Paris gaming house centuries ago, where less than candid recruiting methods had been used on him with devastating results.

"We should have an ample supply of Sweet by then."

How were they planning to get more? Last year he'd helped thwart the Alliance's plans to breed sweetblooded humans and had seen to it that all their research had been destroyed. Had he missed something? Were they starting up operations again?

There was a huge market for the extremely rare, highly

addictive type of human blood—the street price was astronomical. Sweetblood, Sangre Dulce, Devil's Elixir—it was all the same. It shouldn't be a surprise that they would be trying other methods to get their hands on it. If there was one thing he'd learned while spying on them from the inside, it was how tenacious they were. Like mongrels on a steak dinner.

"How does the mistress plan to get it?"

Sigred snapped her attention from the coed to him, her gaze narrowing slightly. Shit. He'd asked the question a little too quickly, or maybe the tone wasn't right, or maybe he shouldn't have been so confident in how he'd referred to the sector mistress.

Alfonso gave her his best sheepish grin and rubbed the back of his neck. Hopefully, her bullshit meter wasn't set too high. "I mean, isn't it difficult to find Sweet? I know if I had some, I'd have a hard time saving it. You guys must have some serious willpower to keep from draining a sweetblood."

"You got that right," the male replied. "Last time I ran across one it was with my old partner. Let me tell you, he had to pull me off the bitch because there'd be nothing left to sell. I went like fucking mad for a while—like a feeding frenzy—I couldn't stop."

Maybe he's the one who's new. Most DBs got pretty good at capturing their victims, bringing them back to their dens, then draining their blood there. This one's impatience and lack of control suggested inexperience.

The male continued. "The sector mistress is turning a Tracker from the Agency to help find 'em. Guess those guys can smell one from miles away. All we gotta do is follow the nose."

It was a sucker punch straight to the gut and panic flooded his veins like wildfire. He had to use every ounce of his training to keep the shock from showing on his face. Lily, his former lover, was a Tracker.

"We don't know that for sure." Sigred's laugh sounded forced. She was backpedaling; her partner had said too much. "That was just an idea someone bounced around. Everyone's trying to get a piece of the action, making promises to have more Sweet available, staking out their territories. So far, it's just been us here in Bellingham, but probably not for long."

Alfonso found himself thinking once more that he shouldn't be surprised DBs were moving into areas they'd never been before. With Lord Pavlos, whom the Darkbloods reverently referred to as "the Overlord," dead, the Alliance was going through a power struggle of sorts as potential leaders crawled out of the woodwork like rats, trying to make a name for themselves. The one who controlled the Sweet was the one with all the power, a fact he knew firsthand. A Sweet-laden Night of Wilding was sure to attract those living on the fringe of civilized vampire society and maybe a few who didn't realize they could be tempted like that.

"Ain't it a bloody shame that you've got to share this small town?" Alfonso was relieved to notice that the girl was finally leaving.

Should he try to take these two out? He wasn't Agency—these guys weren't his problem. The girl was safe.

He tucked the weapons under his coat and thrust his

hands into his pockets. Time to go home. He could last one more night without feeding.

The blonde halted, turned back around and pinned him with that lazy eye of hers. "What was that?"

"Huh?"

"Did you just say 'Ain't that a bloody shame?'"

"I don't know. Did I?" He didn't like the sudden change in her voice. He pulled his hands back out of his pockets and held them loosely at his sides.

"You know, it's funny," she said. "I rode a day transport from Southern California to Seattle last year with a guy who was high up in the Alliance ranks. Didn't get a good look at him, but that was his pet phrase. He must've said it a dozen times on the way up. Heard he turned out to be an Agency spy. The one responsible for the Overlord's death."

Shit, shit, shit. She must've been one of those recruits in the back of the bus.

"No kidding." With his heart pounding, he turned to leave. He reached under his coat and grabbed the rope-wrapped handles again. His slow, measured footsteps echoed under the walkway. One…two…three.

Keep walking. Don't rush. Act casual and they won't think anything of it. These two aren't familiar. They don't know me. Just keep going.

"The name was Alfonso Serrano, I think," Sigred called after him. "So tell us, friend, what's yours?"

Without hesitation, he spun around—they were drawing their weapons. He had one chance. With a flick of his wrists, the kunai cut through the air and landed simultaneously between their breastbones with a *thunk*.

The male fell to the ground. The silver had penetrated his heart; he'd be a pile of ashes in moments. But the female was merely wounded.

She dropped the blade in her hand and staggered sideways, away from the covered walkway. While the rain pummeled her face and plastered the hair across her cheeks, her fingers curled around the hilt of the kunai and pulled it from her chest. If he hadn't known for a fact she had silver weapons of her own, he'd have waited it out until she collapsed from the energy drain. But she had his blade and who knew what else. He was just as susceptible to silver as they were and he certainly couldn't outrun a silver bullet.

In one motion, he leaped forward and retrieved his stake from the rapidly charcoaling male. The exertion and sudden movement made him dizzy. He staggered and fell to the bricks.

"Fucking traitor," Sigred hissed through clenched fangs as she lunged at him, kunai raised above her head.

Summoning the last of his energy reserves, he scissored his legs, knocking her feet out from under her. As she fell, he aimed the tip of the retrieved kunai slightly to her left, several inches down from her shoulder. She landed on the blade, and with a little shimmy on his part, the razor-sharp tip scraped over bone, slid to the hilt between two ribs and hit home.

He pushed her dead weight off and lay flat on the ground, that putrid Darkblood smell lingering in his nostrils.

While the rain pounded his face, soaking his knit cap and jeans, he watched, completely spent, as her body folded inward and turned to ash, leaving behind only metal. From amidst the clothing rivets, zippers, coins, syringes, needles, a multitude of weapons and—oh yes— one glass eye, he fished out his other kunai and slowly pushed himself up.

Let campus security think this was the remnant of a drug deal gone bad. He kicked everything around and crushed the vials, blood washing away in the rain. Although drinking it would've given him the strength he needed, he wasn't about to consume blood taken from a killing. He was weak, but he still had morals.

He yanked off his waterlogged cap and made his way slowly across Red Square. Christ, that nip/tuck had just about done him in.

With a hand up to his face to block the wind, he finally made it back to Haggard Hall. His rig was parked nearby.

And there she was. Western Washington University's dumbest, most irritating student, a mere ten feet away.

Alone. With no one else in sight. Texting.

Yes, Virginia, there is a Santa Claus.

CHAPTER TWO

NINETY MILES SOUTH of Bellingham, on the rain-soaked streets of Seattle, Lily DeGraff was about to have a major panic attack. Problem was, that wouldn't set the best example for the Tracker trainee she was mentoring.

They dashed across First Avenue in Belltown and slipped into the shadows of an old brick building, pausing to make sure they hadn't been spotted. If a human witnessed them moving this fast, even though the few still out were wasted or high, they'd be forced to slow down and do a mind-wipe. But that took time, a luxury they didn't have. Their footsteps echoed on the sidewalk as they sprinted downtown again.

Just after the clubs had closed, a call had come in over the police band about a missing young woman. Lily and her trainee had made a routine drive past the Pink Salon to see if it involved their kind. The private, Vegas-style club was popular among both races, except the humans were clueless that they partied with a few vampires.

In the alley out back, she detected fresh blood. Not a killing amount, but she could guess what had happened. Like many other predatory animals, a vampire wouldn't carry his meal too far away. Once a revert crossed the line and went into feeding mode, he wouldn't have the willpower to wait too long for the blood and energy rush he craved.

But that had been thirty minutes ago. Now they were running all over the city trying to locate the bastard before it was too late and the woman was dead.

Although he hadn't said anything, Kip Castile probably wondered why his trainer was waiting so long to take over from him. At least that was what Lily assumed he was thinking. She'd be thinking the same thing if she were him. Only problem was, after that brief scent of blood in the alley, she hadn't detected anything more. All she smelled now was a muddy, dirt-like odor, as if everything was mixed together into one massive, indefinable lump. This weakening of her ability had been fluctuating off and on for quite a while now, but lately, it seemed to be getting worse. Tonight she could hardly smell through it.

"Let's hold up a minute, Kip. Take a deep breath and before you exhale, I want you to focus inward. Good." Her calm voice was a stark contrast to the rising knot of turmoil in her gut.

"I still can't smell the blood trail, Ms. DeGraff. I'm sorry." The kid was starting to panic.

She gave him a reassuring pat on the back. She'd already told him several times that he could call her Lily, but he kept slipping into formalities. Nerves, maybe.

"That's all right. Let's keep going. He can't have taken her far." She only hoped the woman was still alive.

"Maybe you should take over. I'm…I'm just not sure I can do it."

Normally, she'd have guided Kip closer and closer

until he could pick up the scent himself. Build up his confidence. Then they'd track the revert, take him down, call for a pickup and be back to the field office in time for corn flakes. After decades of being a Tracker and working for the Agency, these kinds of assignments were pretty routine. But not any longer, she thought, as she noticed the chalky grayness of the night sky. Morning wasn't far away.

There it was on the corner of Pike and Pine. The unmistakable smell of human blood. Finally. She drew in another full breath, processing all the ambient scent markers. It was the human woman from the club.

"Kip, do you have it yet?" She was eager for him to experience what it felt like to detect a blood memory. She'd never forgotten the first time she'd been out on patrol and mentally matched a scent to something she'd smelled earlier.

"I…I think so." The young man lifted his nose a little higher and blinked when a raindrop hit his forehead. His short brown hair looked almost black in this light, and his expression was wide-eyed and hopeful. God, he was young. Had she looked that fresh faced once? "It's pretty faint, though."

"Tell me what you're smelling. Close your eyes. It's easier to concentrate and focus your olfactory senses. An important part of the process is being able to match what you're scenting now to something you scented earlier."

"Okay." He did as he was told and took a deep breath in through his nose. "Sea air from the sound. Garlic and oregano from a restaurant."

"Good. What else?"

"I smell—" Kip gasped. "There it is! It's coming from over there."

"Describe it for me, please, as we head that way."

"It's coppery, of course, and slightly sweet. Not a sweetblood, though." His laugh was almost giddy, and his dark eyes glittered with excitement, the pupils expanding in response to the adrenaline and scent of blood.

Yeah, she remembered the first time she'd gone on a real assignment after spending countless hours in class and in the scent labs. It had been an exhilarating feeling. And even after all these years, it still was.

"The blood in the alleyway was a human female," he continued, a little breathless as they ran down the sidewalk. "Blood type AB, and I think it's the same marker I'm smelling now." He took another deep breath. "I can sense the warmth and her fear. I'm pretty sure she's still alive."

He smelled the victim's fear? Although this was a skill she'd mastered some time ago, she sure as hell couldn't detect any fear now. Gritting her teeth, she tucked away the nagging feeling that something was terribly wrong with her. She'd deal with that later. Right now, she had a job to finish.

They slipped under the Post Alley sign and she flattened herself against the brick wall on one side of the entrance, motioning for Kip to do the same on the opposite side. The erratic beat of her heart slowed with relief as she slipped into Guardian mode now that they had a lock on the bastard.

Okay, time to wrap this thing up.

She held up one fist, indicating Kip should stay where

he was. He hadn't gone through any hand-to-hand combat training yet, so she didn't want him to get much closer to the target. Agency rules were pretty specific in regard to what a rookie could do. The takedown was her responsibility.

She scanned the shadows and doorways as she edged closer to the smell, trying to get a visual. Careful not to touch the business end, she eased her red-tipped nails into a set of brass knuckles with silver spikes—not normally her weapon of choice, but she really needed to punch something—and crept around the iron railing of a stairwell. The coppery, slightly sweet scent intensified and her pupils dilated further.

The nagging voice of sensibility, her rule-abiding conscience that was never far away, told her she should've called for backup a while ago. But she didn't want to admit to anyone she needed help. There were plenty within the Agency who believed she'd made it to Tracker only because of her father's influence. She wasn't about to prove them right by admitting she couldn't handle a routine patrol call. No, she'd keep this matter to herself.

In the direction of one of the darkened doorways at the far end of the alley, she heard the scuffle of shoes on the wet pavement followed by a low, almost orgasmic moan.

Finally. You can run, but you can't hide.

Kip had been right. The human was alive, but just barely. There wasn't much time. After punching a code into her cell phone to request a pickup and a medic, she sprinted down the alley, not caring if the revert loser spotted her at this point. If he ran, she'd catch him.

But before she got to the far end, a side door banged open in front of her. She ducked behind a Dumpster right before the light from the doorway spilled out, spotlighting the alley as a train would a dark tunnel. An elderly woman in curlers and slippers shuffled out holding a plastic trash bag. But it was another figure, not more than ten feet away, that caught Lily's attention. Hunched over a body, he raised his hands to shield his eyes from the sudden glare. But he didn't cover his fangs, which dripped with his victim's blood.

"Oh, my word! What in the world is—" The woman dropped the bag at her feet and the door slammed shut, trapping her outside. "Hon? Hon?" she called, not taking her eyes off the horror playing out in front of her.

Great. Just great. Guess I'll have an audience.

Lily jumped over the trash bag, ignoring the woman's gasp of surprise, and launched herself at the loser. Grabbing a handful of his hair, she yanked him away from the body. Her fist made such a satisfying sound when it connected with his jaw that she had to stop herself from doing it again just for the hell of it. Instead, she flung him onto the cobblestones. He landed at the feet of the old woman, who tried to scream but ended up in a coughing fit instead. Thank God for tiny miracles. She didn't need any other human witnesses. One was enough.

The revert pushed himself up with one hand and defensively held up the other. Clearly, he wasn't a fighter, just a run-of-the-mill loser—of which Seattle had plenty.

She repositioned the silver knuckle piece to the inside of her hand, the short spikes facing inward this time, and grabbed him around the neck. He shrieked and clawed at her hand when the metal pierced his skin. But it didn't take long for the silver to do its thing and he became too weak to stand on his own. She restrained him with silver-lined handcuffs and dropped his ass to the ground.

As she took a step in the direction of the victim, the old woman's coughing reminded her she needed to deal with secrecy issues before attending to collateral damage.

"Ma'am, it's okay. I'm just going to—"

"Don't— Don't— Stay back." The woman's eyes widened even further in the dim light of the alley.

Lily ran the tip of her tongue over her fangs, which had stretched from her gums during the fight. Guess she couldn't pass for a regular cop now. "It's okay. I won't hurt you. I just need to—"

The woman screamed, and this time her voice found itself.

Lily was on her in an instant. She brushed a hand over the woman's forehead, silencing her. "You saw two drunks in the alley. Nothing more." Lily wrenched open the door as if it had never been locked. "Now get back to bed and stop this sleepwalking. Hon is waiting inside and wants a little lovin' from you."

The woman blinked a few times. A glassy, faraway look replaced the terror in her watery gray eyes. Clutching the front of her housecoat with a gnarled hand, she shuffled inside a little quicker than Lily had expected, a faint touch of pink coloring her cheeks. The door closed softly behind her.

Lily got to the victim just as two unmarked black-panel vans turned into the alley and screeched to a stop.

A medic with a crash kit and a member of the capture team stepped out and jogged toward her.

"Over here, fellas." She pointed behind her and strode out of the alley, thoughts whirling.

For God's sake, this was a simple assignment. What was going on with her? She glanced over her shoulder as Kip followed her into the night. She might as well be a trainee, too, not an elite Class-A Tracker for the Governing Council.

"Ms. DeGraff, why are you walking that way? Your car is parked down the hill over there."

She tossed him the keys. "Go ahead and take it back to the field office for me. I need the fresh air. Good job tonight, by the way. We'll review things in the classroom later."

IF THE GUY GOING POSTAL on him in the hardware store hadn't been Region Commander Tristan Santiago, Alfonso would've let the two-by-fours over his shoulder "accidentally" smack the asshole in the head. Instead, he threw the lumber onto a flatbed handcart and headed over to the flooring department.

"Look, I told you everything I know. DBs are after Trackers. Don't know how, don't know where, although I assume it's somewhere local since they mentioned the islands. Hell, I don't even know if it's true. It's not like I got the information from a reliable source. They were greenhorns and, for all I know, they could've been blowing smoke."

"And you wasted them before you got any real intel." Santiago's voice sounded like he'd just chain-smoked a pack of bare-ass Camels, although Alfonso knew he never touched the stuff. "What the *fuck* is up with that?"

A woman pushing a shopping cart covered her child's ears and flashed Santiago an indignant expression. For a moment, it looked as if she was going to scold him, but then she quickened her pace and sped down the aisle. That was nothing, Alfonso wanted to tell her. If they hadn't been in public, the guy would be cursing in three languages.

With his eyes narrowed to slits and his own anger barely in check, Alfonso glared at Santiago. "What are you talking about? I had no choice but to—" Why the hell was he sitting here justifying what he'd done? He looked around and lowered his voice. "Listen. I don't work for you any longer, remember? Pavlos is *finito.* My obligation to the Council has been met. I can show you the documentation if you don't believe me. They did it up real nice. Parchment paper, fancy lettering. Hell, it even came wrapped in a goddamn scroll. Figured I was doing you a favor letting you know what I stumbled across. Guess I was sorely mistaken. Why don't you go back to Vancouver and leave me the hell alone?"

Santiago's jaw muscle flexed over and over, like he was chewing on what he was about to say. Or more likely, he was pissed off and trying not to flash fang. "You know, I let you have your time after everything that went down last year. Recoup from your injuries—that leg of yours looks fine now, by the way. I wanted you to decompress in peace and quiet—"

"How terribly considerate and thoughtful of you." Alfonso threw a box of drywall screws on top of the lumber and resisted the urge to rub his knee. Maybe his limp wasn't as noticeable as he'd thought.

Santiago continued as if Alfonso hadn't spoken. "But that was a year ago—" more than that, but who was counting? "—and we could really use your help now."

"So you insult me, then you offer me a job? That's a funny way to conduct an interview. And why are you the one asking me, anyway? Why isn't Dom? Isn't he technically the Seattle field team leader?"

"Your brother's in Australia, helping with the opening of the new Carpentaria field office down there. He's not scheduled to be back up here until after the Night of Wilding. The baby's not due till after the first of the year."

Alfonso sighed. His brother's wife, Mackenzie, had just started wearing maternity clothes the last time he'd seen her. He'd commissioned a few paintings from her that depicted the hill country of his ancestral home in Spain. As soon as he finished building his house, a smaller version of his boyhood villa, he planned to hang her artwork in the entryway.

Not that he had any illusions that this tribute could atone for what he'd done to his parents. Hell, he probably wouldn't even be around long enough to enjoy it. Sooner or later his blood assassin was bound to track him, and he was far from confident that he'd survive that meet-up. Selected as youthlings by the Darkbloods' inner circle, these vampires were raised in the art of killing and torture. Strong, fast and lethal, they didn't make mistakes.

"If what you discovered is true," Santiago said, "we've

got a big problem on our hands. The Longest Night is only a few short weeks away."

"Don't you have a tech person who can break into that game forum to figure out what's going on?"

"I've asked Cordell to look into it, but frankly it's a wonder Darkbloods haven't overrun the city by now. With Dom and Mitchell out of the country, we're understaffed. We could really use you."

Alfonso shoved a hand through his hair. The guy was so friggin' dramatic.

"What part of no don't you understand?" Alfonso looked over the various diamond blades, trying to find one that would fit his particular wet saw. His current blade was dulled from all the tile-cutting he'd been doing and needed to be replaced.

"I understand plenty, starting with the fact that you have nothing going on. What's so important you'd turn this opportunity down? Tinkering on that house you're building? A man needs goals in his life. Something to work toward. He needs direction."

"Yeah, well, I do have goals. They all revolve around getting my house finished." And finished quickly. Since those losers had guessed his identity, it wouldn't be long until the assassin tracked him, too. Then he'd be on the run again. He'd always known it'd happen, that his assassin would eventually figure out he wasn't living in Europe, that those leads Alfonso had meticulously created were false. But he really hoped to finish the house before that day arrived.

Yeah, recreating *Casa en las Colinas* probably was a stupid dream. He'd been a fool to let his sister-in-law talk him into setting down some roots—even if it was tempo-rary. Give him a chance to meet his niece or nephew. At-tempt to repair his relationship with his brother. What had he hoped to accomplish by building this house, anyway? Impressing Dom? Earning his respect? Getting him to understand that he did honor their parents' memory, de-spite everything he'd done? *Maybe it's time for a reality check—forget about the house and disappear.* He could mail the keys to Mackenzie, and she could have it fin-ished. Or not.

"And then what? You gonna take up fly-fishing?"

"Fuck you."

"I'm serious, Alfonso. Your expertise on Darkblood matters is unequaled by anyone in the Agency here in North America. It's a shame you're pissing away that talent and knowledge while you swing hammers at a pipe dream."

Alfonso gripped the handle of the cart so hard he was afraid it would bend beneath his fingers. There was a reason he preferred talking to Santiago on the phone: so he could hang up on him. Good thing they were out in public or he'd have the guy by the throat right about now, even though Santiago was one menacing vampire with a hair-trigger temper and a Dempsey-like left hook. The black military shit inked on his neck was just icing.

"What would my brother say if I suddenly became one of his Agents? He'd go ballistic on your ass, not to mention mine. It's not like he and I are suddenly best friends. Centuries of thinking your brother is one of the bad guys isn't rectified in one short year. Besides, I'm tired of Darkbloods. I'm tired of the Council."

Santiago stared at him with those dark, piercing eyes, clearly not buying any of it. For chrissake, the guy never took no for an answer. How did Dom put up with this? What did he have to say to get through to him?

"Listen," Alfonso continued. "I worked for centuries on the inside, trying to redeem myself in the eyes of everyone I cared about, and for what?" He pounded a fist on his thigh and a sharp pain pierced through the dull ache in his knee. "I'm permanently injured and my family wants nothing to do with me."

Given that he'd been marked for assassination, it probably wasn't safe for them to be around him anyway, but he wasn't about to share that little tidbit with Santiago. Alfonso could hardly stand knowing what he'd pledged all those years ago.

And what it had cost him.

He sure as hell didn't want to admit it to the Council. They could very well revoke his pardon.

"I'm tired of everything, and it's probably time for me to move on anyway. You're right. Maybe the house is a stupid pipe dream."

"But—"

"Shut the—" He glanced around. Seeing an elderly man nearby, he lowered his voice. "You seriously think I'd want to come back? You wasted your time coming down here, Santiago. I've put in my time, so leave me the hell alone. Go find yourself someone who cares, because I'm done."

"So then it makes no difference to you that Lily is back at the Seattle office?"

Like a shot from an air compressor, his heart slammed

against his rib cage, and he struggled to keep the emotion off his face. He couldn't have been more surprised if someone had doused him from behind with a bucket of ice water. "I thought she transferred down to one of the southern regions," he said, his voice almost as gravelly as Santiago's.

"She did for a while. Guess it was too hard commuting back and forth with her daughter up here in the Horseshoe Bay region with her parents. Getting to British Columbia was no longer an easy three-hour drive over the border."

"But she and Zoe were together. I heard she was… trying to make a go of it with Zoe's father again." At least that's what his sister-in-law had told him. Part of him just wanted Lily happy, but another part of him desperately wanted— *Don't go there,* he reminded himself. *Don't do it.*

Santiago shrugged. "I don't get involved in my staff's love lives. I'd need a damn social secretary for that. I'm just glad she's back."

My God, given this new DB intel, he'd have been keeping tabs on her had he known she was back in the area. "Does she know about this new threat against Trackers? She's not going out alone, is she?"

"She's in charge of on-the-job training for the rookies coming out of Tracker Academy. So, yes, she knows about the threat and, no, she's not alone. Jesus, Alfonso, if I didn't know better, I'd think you still had a thing for her. Still wish she was your Agency contact? Your *handler?* I'm sure we can arrange to have her handle something of yours, if that's what it'd take for you to join the team."

Alfonso's gums ached as his fangs threatened to elongate. Santiago had no idea. The guy could laugh all he wanted, but he had no fucking clue. Not even Lily knew the truth about why he'd left her. He grabbed a saw blade off the shelf and shoved it into the cart.

"So what do you say? Can I count on you this time, Alfonso? Can we make an honest man of you yet?"

"On the contrary, I'm afraid you've given me the best reason of all not to come back."

Santiago raised his brows, clearly clueless.

Alfonso pushed the cart toward the checkout stands. "Lily."

CHAPTER THREE

"WHAT'S SO interesting on the other side of that window? You've been staring outside all night." Although Mel had first served the guy almost an hour ago, she'd not had the gumption to strike up a conversation with him till now.

Not that she was timid or anything—far from it—but he had that don't-mess-with-me vibe, and she did her best to respect that. As a bartender in this joint for years, with the gray hair to prove it, she'd learned who was approachable and who wasn't into chitchat. He fell into the latter crowd. But something about his expression made her ask tonight.

He pulled off his knit cap and ran a hand through his hair. Right now it was mainly dark blond, but some strands were much lighter. She'd be willing to bet that in the sun, it'd bleach out to a surfer's golden blond.

She cracked open the longneck—only his second since he'd arrived—and slid it toward him, the wisp of escaping carbonation evaporating into the air. The guy nursed his alcohol like a first-time mother did her baby.

Not really expecting an answer to her question, she wiped a small water spot from the polished oak bar and grabbed his empty. But as she turned away, she was shocked as hell when he replied.

"Just keeping an eye on an old friend."

She retrieved a fresh bar towel from the stack under the counter and flipped it over her shoulder. His leather bomber jacket, worn to a lighter shade of black around the wrists and neckline, creaked just a little when he lifted the beer and took a long swallow.

"Friend, as in friend? Or friend, as in an enemy you want to keep tabs on?"

"A friend."

Having just tossed the bottle into the recycle where it rattled with the rest, she wasn't sure if she'd heard him correctly. She lifted her eyebrows, waiting for him to say more.

Somehow he didn't seem like the type to be pining over some woman, nor could she picture him as a stalker. More like the other way around.

The guy was working-class handsome, with rugged hands that no doubt knew how to swing a hammer and a slight limp he tried to conceal. He definitely wasn't an accountant. A light stubble covered his jaw, and his eyes, despite their crystal-blue color, were intense and hinted at something a little frightening. Yes, his picture could seriously be in the dictionary next to *dangerously hand-some.* She prided herself on being a pretty good judge of character. No, the guy wasn't a stalker. But a heart-breaker? Oh, yeah.

He saw the question in her expression and tipped the bottle toward the window. "A woman I used to know is over there. In the Pink Salon."

Ah, but maybe he was jealous. The Pink Salon wasn't a place people went for a dart tourney with coworkers. "How long ago did you two break up?"

He narrowed his eyes. So her guess had been accurate. "Last year."

"And she's out with someone else?"

"No, working."

"Yo, Mel," called one of the guys at the far end of the bar. "Show us a little love down here."

She filled a couple drink orders, and when she returned, Mr. Not-An-Accountant was still looking outside. Several club hoppers stopped on the sidewalk in front of the window. He scooted his barstool a few inches to the left to get an unobstructed view of the garish pink sign across the street.

As she polished nonexistent water stains, Mel scrutinized him further without making it appear she was. She knew if you looked a reluctant guy in the eye, he'd clam right up. But keep your gaze focused elsewhere, and he'd yap like an ankle-biter when the doorbell rings.

"She a bartender like *moi* or a waitress?" she asked, somehow doubting his ex was one of the high-priced hookers who frequented the place.

The left side of his mouth twisted up slightly, revealing a fleeting dimple. "No."

"A cop then?"

"Sort of."

She was dying to ask him what a sort-of cop was, but didn't want to continue pressing her luck.

Noticing the time, she flipped the channel on the small flat-screen that hung at an angle on this end of the bar. One of the local stations replayed last week's high school football highlights at midnight. She was a sucker for anything that reminded her of being younger, and watching those fresh faces who thought they were grown-ups always brought her back. She took a drink order from one of the waitresses and filled two glasses with Jack and Diet, but when she glanced at him again, she couldn't resist another question.

"Some bad stuff went down over there the other night, but I heard they caught the guy." What kind of a twisted SOB would have the cojones to kidnap a woman in front of all those people anyway? "Your ex involved in bringing him down?"

"It's my understanding that she was. The main thing is, he's off the streets and won't be seeing the light of day for—let's just say a long time." There was that dimple again. But it disappeared as quickly as it had come.

Mel nodded and turned back to the TV, still listening.

"She's doing routine stuff tonight."

One of the kids on the highlight reel caught a flea-flicker, broke an almost-tackle, then ran it in for a touchdown. Beautiful. A little thrill shivered down her spine and the guys clustered at the other end of the bar cheered with gusto. Yeah, she wasn't the only one who vividly remembered those Friday-night games, although from the looks of it, those guys weren't going to be remembering much of anything tomorrow. She should probably consider cutting them off.

"That place sure gets its share of freaks. Seems like you're worried about her even though she's a cop. Can't she take care of herself?"

He picked at the label on his beer, tearing off little strips and piling them on his coaster like a mound of confetti. "Cop or no cop, it's no guarantee she'll be safe. But she can take care of herself. Or at least she thinks she can."

"And that's why you're here. Because you can do it better? Take care of her, that is?"

His bitter laugh surprised her. Clearly having had enough of the nursing, he drained the rest of his beer in one long guzzle. Unlike most of the yokels in this place, he didn't belch when he set the empty bottle down.

"No, definitely not." He pushed the stool away from the bar and stood. Peeling off a bill, he plunked it onto the counter and tapped it with his knuckle, indicating he needed no change. Holy criminy. She'd pegged him as a good tipper, but this was ridiculous. "She's much safer with me out of the picture."

A bad boy who knows he's not good for you? Oh, to be young again. "Why? You got loser friends?"

He nodded as he turned to leave. "I suppose that's one way of putting it."

THE RED DIGITS ON THE ALARM clock confirmed it was late afternoon, and Alfonso cursed.

A hell of a day this was turning out to be. He'd kept Lily under surveillance most of the night, making sure she did indeed have someone with her at all times. That she wasn't vulnerable to those responsible for poisoning his life. Not that it was foolproof, he reasoned, but there was safety in numbers. Sure enough, Santiago hadn't been dicking with him; the entire night, she'd been accompanied by her trainee. He'd watched them head for the field office, confirming with Jackson that she'd arrived safely before he left for home.

He flipped the pillow to the cool side and shoved the couch cushions back into place beneath him. After all these months, he hadn't expected that seeing her would affect him so profoundly. But hell, he couldn't stop thinking about her. And because the imported European tiles still hadn't arrived, he couldn't get his mind off of her by working on his house.

What had happened between her and her ex that had caused her to move back to Seattle? he wondered. A familiar ache formed in his chest as he thought about her living with another man.

He didn't begrudge the fact that she'd started seeing Steven again. After all, the man was her daughter's father. Almost ten years ago, shortly after he and Lily had begun dating, Alfonso's work within the Alliance had required that he move back to Europe. They'd called things off because, at the time, Alfonso didn't know whether he'd ever make it back to the States. A few years later, he had come back, only to learn that Lily had been engaged, had given birth to a daughter, and that her relationship with Steven had ended. She'd eagerly accepted the assignment to act as Alfonso's handler within the Agency and they'd begun their relationship again as if it had never even ended.

And it had been great. While it lasted.

The explosion changed everything.

At first he hadn't let her know—hadn't let anyone know—that he'd survived the fire. The Alliance needed to believe that he'd died trying to save the Overlord. His plan was to wait till he recuperated before going back to Lily. During that time, the Alliance would forget about him as various lieutenants vied to become the new leader. Battles would be fought, people would be killed, and he'd be just another vampire who'd sacrificed himself for the cause.

Deep down he knew that part of his decision not to tell Lily had also been motivated by pride. He didn't want her to see him until he was whole again. And he didn't want her sympathy, either.

But when he'd discovered that his blood assassin had been activated, that the Alliance knew he was alive, all his hopes for the future had been shattered.

He recalled in painful detail the phone call where Lily had demanded answers. For days, he'd been ignoring her calls and emails, hoping to find a way out of this mess, but he couldn't. After finally reaching that agonizing realization, he'd watched his phone light up over and over before he answered. He'd known what he had to say to her.

With this permanent knee deformity, he'd never be able to adequately protect her. The assassin would hunt him down and go after her as well. If he'd told her the truth, she would have tried to convince him that she could take care of both of them, that she was tough and a good fighter. But he couldn't let her take that chance, so he'd lied, told her he'd no longer loved her, and hoped she'd stay away.

And it had worked.

He sighed heavily and flung an arm over his face. Last night, he'd recklessly shadow-moved closer to her than necessary. But he couldn't help it. He'd decided that he didn't bloody care if she detected him or not. In fact, if she had, she'd have confronted him then and there. That was her style. Actually, maybe that was why he'd done it in the first place—to speak with her again, to see her up close, even if she wanted to kill him with her bare hands. He'd always loved provoking her.

Reaching down with his other hand, he cupped himself lightly and thought of how she'd looked last night.

With that trademark swagger and attitude that made confident men stand up and pay attention while weaker men shriveled, she had walked out of the Pink Salon, sauntered down the block and climbed into that red Porsche of hers. He'd held his breath, wondering if she'd scent him, but she hadn't. Her trainee barely had the door shut before she'd peeled away from the curb. He could almost smell the lavender scent of her favorite soap on the night air as her car had sped past him in the shadows.

In a hotel suite they'd shared once, she'd walked toward him in much the same manner. Her jaw set, her eyes determined, focused. Except then, she'd been naked and focused on him. He'd waited for her on the bed, positioned as he was now, a hand behind his head, one knee bent, and the other hand around the base of his erection. Her hips had moved the same way, back and forth, back and forth, her blond hair skimming her shoulders—although last night her hair had seemed longer, pulled back into a high ponytail, the ends reaching to the middle of her shoulder blades.

He closed his eyes and was back in the hotel again. Her breasts bounced as she climbed onto the bed, inviting him to come play with them. And he did, for hours, while they made love and he nestled his—

Oh for chrissake. His cock was as hard as a baseball bat. Again. Kicking off the sheets till they bunched at the foot of the couch, he got up and took a quick shower. No use dreaming about something that could never happen. Things with Lily had been good while they lasted. Period.

Ten minutes later, he grabbed his laptop. If he wasn't

going to make progress on his house tonight, might as well make some progress on something else.

After a few botched attempts at playing Hollow Grave, he came to the conclusion that he at least needed a game controller, if not a few other accessories. He wasn't about to ask Cordell because Santiago would find out and, if that happened, the guy would be all over his ass. He'd claim Alfonso did give a damn. No, Santiago didn't need to know. If Alfonso found the location of the party, he'd inform Jackson and deal with Santiago then. But if he didn't, at least he wouldn't be giving the guy any false hopes that he actually cared.

A short time later, with his laptop tucked under his arm, he entered the computer store and headed to the help desk.

"What do I need to buy in order to play video games on this thing?"

"That depends," said the kid behind the counter. He wore a name tag that said, I'm Kenny. Ask me, I know. "What game are you interested in playing?"

"Why does it matter? Just get me a game controller and a headset."

"Depending on your laptop's capabilities, it might not have the best graphics card for gaming. Or enough RAM. Or decent speakers. You might need a new computer in order to—"

Alfonso held up a hand. "No. I need to play it on this." The laptop had been configured to make his online movements virtually impossible to trace. He certainly didn't want to leave a trail; he worried enough about his blood assassin finding him without laying down a bunch of virtual bread crumbs.

"All right," Kenny said slowly as he scratched his head. "How much memory you got? Are you interested in playing first-person shooter games, strategy, RPGs…?"

Oh for chrissake. Alfonso opened the laptop and typed in the URL of the Hollow Grave website. The screen went black for a few moments before animated trickles of blood dripped downward, and the sounds of blowing wind and a pipe organ echoed through the tiny speakers. "This game. What do I need to play it?"

Kenny's face lit up as if he'd just stepped into Disneyland. "Dude, that's totally sick. It's like the forest in *The Blair Witch Project.* And the haunted house. What's this called—Hollow Grave? How'd you hear about it, anyway? I'm a gamer and I've never heard of it."

"From a friend. Now what?"

Kenny cracked his knuckles and excitedly rubbed his palms on his jeans. "Do you mind if I check out the system requirements to play the game?" With his fingers poised over the keyboard and his heart beating fast and loud enough for Alfonso to hear, he looked inquisitively at Alfonso.

"Go for it."

Kenny's hands flew over the keys and in a few seconds, he was smiling. "You're lucky. Your machine is totally kick-ass. With just a few add-ons, I think you'll be in business."

He soon had the laptop outfitted with a controller, a headset and a pair of external speakers. Anxious to get home to start playing, Alfonso quickly paid and threw Kenny an extra fifty bucks.

"Thanks, kid," he called over his shoulder.

Before he got to the door, Kenny ran around in front of

him, the money clutched in his hand, face flushed, eyes wide. "Want me to help you with the game? You know, set up your user name and stuff."

"Nope. I'm golden. Just needed this stuff to get me going."

"Are you sure, mister? I could show you some tips, get you started. It doesn't seem like you've played many games before and I've played a lot."

Alfonso took a deep breath and considered the offer. The tile delivery should arrive tomorrow, he reasoned, and after that, he wouldn't have much time to waste learning how to play Hollow Grave. Alfonso could just wipe the kid's memory clear of the website when they were done.

"All right then. Let's see how fast you work."

Soon they were situated in The Garage, the store's gaming lounge, the screen open on the table before them.

"You're going to need a screen name," Kenny began.

"How about BlackNight?" He had to devise a new persona, someone who was looking to party at the Night of Wilding.

"Lame," said Kenny. "Bloodsucker?"

Alfonso stifled a smile. "Too clichéd. There are probably many with that name."

"Yeah, you're probably right. SoulEater?"

"Maybe. BloodySunday?"

"Ooh, I like it. It's perfect." Kenny held out his hand. "Now, we're going to need a credit card."

Ten minutes later, BloodySunday was the newest user on the Hollow Grave website, complete with a skeleton avatar dressed as a military operative, three starter grenades and a full syringe of liquid power, also known as Bleed.

"Now what do I do?" Alfonso couldn't even get his character to move out of the foyer of the haunted house.

"Here, can I try?" Kenny twisted the laptop toward him slightly and with a few clicks, BloodySunday grabbed a knife inside a small cobweb-infested box sitting on a hall table, slit the throat of a zombie who stumbled out of the dining room, filled a second syringe with Bleed and headed down a long flight of stairs.

He glanced over at the redheaded kid sitting on the edge of the seat, his heart beating loudly enough to make Alfonso's mouth water. That kind of enthusiasm for adrenaline-induced excitement reminded him of when he'd been a spirited youthling centuries ago. He and his friends had sought out anything that produced crazy, mind-numbing thrills. Wild rides on horseback through Spanish hill country at night. Masquerading as swordsmen for hire. Tormenting human grave robbers, which in turn had sparked rumors about the existence of vampires. That stunt had landed him in all sorts of trouble with his parents. Too bad he hadn't obeyed his father, who'd been newly appointed to the Governing Council. Instead he'd chosen to frequent the gaming houses and brothels of Paris that summer, where nothing was more seductive than a pile of notes, the *écarté* tables and beautiful women well-versed in the art of male pleasures. He sighed and turned his attention back to the game.

They continued playing and a short time later, a message popped up in the corner of the screen, congratulating BloodySunday on his progress. Not only had he gotten past the Newly Anointed level, he'd achieved Grave

Crawler status, which gave him access to the forums where players shared special tips and tricks, and could make teams. He was on track to learn the location of the Night of Wilding party.

Which meant it was time to go. He'd post something in the forums about wanting to party when he got home. He pushed back from the table and faked a yawn. "I don't know how you guys do it, playing all these games, staring at a tiny screen all day. My eyes are about to pop out of my head and my ass is numb. Thanks again, kid." He'd have flipped him another fifty—he really couldn't have gotten this far on his own without getting completely frustrated—but didn't want to draw more attention to himself.

"If you ever get stuck or need more lessons or anything, I'd be happy to help," Kenny said.

Not knowing whether Darkbloods used the game to troll for human victims, Alfonso didn't want to risk it. He gripped the kid's outstretched hand firmly. "Thanks for helping me restore my computer. When it crashed, I thought I'd lost everything." The kid's eyelids fluttered a moment as the altered memory took hold.

"Uh, sure." Kenny blinked. A confused look flashed across his expression, and then it was gone. "If you continue to have problems with that hard drive, bring it back and I'll see what else I can do."

In a half hour, Alfonso was back at the estate. He right-clicked on an icon Kenny had shown him and memorized all the screen names currently logged on, noting the ones highlighted in red. They were the forum moderators and, quite possibly, Darkbloods. He wasn't sure if the whole game had been created by the Alliance or if they only moderated the forums.

He scanned the thread topics but saw nothing out of the ordinary. Taking a deep breath, he created a new thread asking if anyone knew of some good parties in the Bellingham area. Then he logged off and strapped on his tool belt.

AN AIR-CONDITIONED CHILL blasted Lily in the face when she pushed open the heavy double doors at the end of the tunnel that connected her condo to the field office facility. Housed several stories beneath the city, it occupied a large but secret portion of Underground Seattle. The city had been damaged by fire over a century earlier, but instead of demolishing and rebuilding the structures, city planners at the time had elevated the roads and constructed new buildings above the old ones. The Council had wanted to establish a Guardian presence in Seattle anyway, so they took advantage of the unused space. They blocked off areas, did their own excavating and eventually located the field office in the heart of the city, right under everyone's noses. Later, when tours of the Underground started, no one had a clue what was on the other side of the charred brickwork.

She'd been getting ready for bed but didn't think she could sleep until she'd seen what Kip had put in his online log notes about tonight's capture. In his last few reports, he hadn't mentioned anything about her inability to track, but it was the third night in a row things had gone badly. First the alley with the human witness, then the nightclub, now tonight in the SoHo district. Recalling the look on Kip's face a short time ago when she'd passed him the car keys again, she knew she couldn't keep up the charade much longer.

Would anyone take note of the large chunk of time that had passed between when the original call came in and when the capture team was dispatched? She'd take a look at the capture team's report as well in order to prepare herself for possible repercussions. Better to know now than to be blindsided later. And then she supposed she'd have to discuss her waning abilities with Santiago—if that's what was really wrong with her.

She got to the security checkpoint and smiled at Francesca, who was sitting on the other side of a glass partition. The young woman looked up from her crossword puzzle and her face brightened.

"Forgot to tell you, but I finished that book you loaned me last week," Francesca said. "Loved it."

Lily smiled and placed her thumb on the reader. They often traded books, but with everything on her mind lately, she couldn't remember which one she'd loaned her. "Awesome, that's great," she said generically.

Three tones sounded. She removed her thumb, inserted her key card into the slot, and Francesca buzzed her in.

"Got any free time?" Francesca tucked a pencil behind her ear. "It'd be fun to get together and discuss it. Someone told me about a new coffee shop nearby that caters to book lovers. Maybe we could check it out."

"I'd love to, but I'm booked solid. Heading up to see Zoe and the fam. Can you wait till I get back?" Maybe by then she'd feel back to normal, and she could concentrate on something other than her problems.

"Yeah, sure."

She waved to her friend, tucked the lanyard back

inside her zip-up hoodie and strode down the hallway, apprehension growing with each step.

She didn't want to speculate about what might be going on if her lack of abilities couldn't be explained by a simple sinus virus. But then, what kind of virus lasted for this long and kept getting worse? Being a Tracker was much more than just a job. It meant that for the first time, she'd been respected for her talents and her brain, and not because she was Henry DeGraff's daughter or because she looked good in a miniskirt. Sought after by other field offices, she'd located vampires and humans that no one else could track. But if she couldn't get rid of that muddy scent clouding her ability to delineate smells—much like a filmy cataract lens obstructing one's vision—she'd be worthless as a Tracker.

Which basically made her...worthless.

She poked her head into the gym and looked around. On the far side of the huge room, just past the juice bar, Cordell Kincade worked out on one of the rowing machines. *Okay, perfect,* she thought as she headed toward him. Since she only had access to the Tracker system, she'd get him to pull up the capture report, then she'd check out what was on the official record. If she was lucky, the long time-gap wouldn't be noted and Kip's report wouldn't mention anything out of the ordinary. She'd be able to relax for now, and head up to British Columbia this evening. Maybe that and a few nights off were all she needed to get back on track. She was eager to see her daughter again.

She smiled at how far she'd come since finding out she was going to be a mother. At first, she'd been horrified. Hooking up with a player like Steven had only been meant as a fun distraction. It wasn't supposed to get her pregnant. Not to mention that her job as a Tracker, with its unpredictable schedule and the frequent travel it required, was extremely demanding and very important to her. How could she possibly do that and be a mother as well?

God knew her parents had been excited about her pregnancy, even if Steven hadn't, and they offered to do anything they could to help. But when she'd held Zoe for the first time and seen her chubby face, none of that had mattered any longer. She'd vowed to figure out a way to work as a Tracker, with or without Steven. As the mother to the most beautiful child on the planet, she was determined to make a good life for both of them.

"Hey, Cordell, when you're done, can you get me into TechTran? I want to take a look at the capture reports from a few assignments."

"You bet. Give me…a minute." Eyes forward, concentrating on his workout, he spoke only when he exhaled as the seat slid backwards. "Last night's report?"

"Yeah, that and a few others."

His gaze flickered in her direction but he kept rowing. "You think…they entered…it yet?"

Damn. He did have a point. She'd already filed her activity summary, but had everyone else? Trying to act casual, she shrugged, but the knots in her shoulders tightened anyway. "Hadn't thought about it."

A few minutes later in the computer lab, with a white gym towel around his neck, Cordell pulled up the TechTran system as Lily leaned over his shoulder. She held her breath while he scrolled through the various field divisions, finally clicking on the capture team button.

"Nope." he said, pushing back in his chair. "Nothing for last night yet. Protocol may dictate everyone file timely reports, Lil, but you're one of the few around here who actually does it."

She exhaled slowly, unsure whether she should be relieved or not. Maybe it wasn't all bad, she reasoned. The longer they waited to submit the summary, the less detailed it was likely to be. But she'd still need to keep checking, which meant involving Cordell each time. Unless it was filed today, she probably shouldn't head north tonight. Her heart weighed heavily in her chest at the thought of not seeing Zoe. With her piano recital coming up, Lily's daughter had been practicing daily and was eager to play for her mom.

A shitty Tracker and a shitty mother. What a combination.

"Hey…you mind if I log into my account?"

"Knock yourself out. I'm hitting the showers."

She waited until he'd left before she clicked into the Tracker section. *That's funny.* She double-checked that she was on the correct page, but she was. All of Kip's other reports were there. Neat, organized, just the way she'd taught him. The only one missing was last night's. Surely he wasn't slacking off already, was he? Was she the only one around here concerned about the rules?

Irritated now, she logged off and exited the computer lab. Kip had obviously been hanging around Jackson too long. His poor habits had rubbed off onto her very conscientious trainee. She ground her teeth together. All the screwups in the office seemed to revolve around Jackson. Well, things were about to change.

A fresh, vaguely familiar scent caught her attention

when she stepped into the hallway. She inhaled, couldn't quite separate it from the muddiness, and that too-familiar swell of panic gripped her stomach again. In an enclosed environment like this—undisturbed by the elements—a scent should be easy to identify.

Knowing that smell was closely associated with memory, she closed her eyes and pressed both hands on the top of the foyer table, careful not to lean in too close and get speared by one of the pointy orange flowers that looked like a crane's head.

She took a deep breath and held it for a moment, focusing inward on the mental images and emotions stirring in her mind as she tried to pry loose the scent memory.

Apprehension. Disrespect. Inadequacy.

Then it dawned on her. *Of course. Gibson's here. I should've known.* He'd assumed she'd gotten the job as a Tracker because of her father, not because she was qualified, so he'd never respected her.

Angry with herself for letting an ass like Gibby get under her skin, she squared her shoulders. Catching sight of herself in the reflective doors of the elevator, she made a quick appraisal. Not bad, but not perfect either. Much as she loathed being judged for her looks alone, around men like Gibby, her image was her armor.

"Good, you're here," said Jackson, startling her, his heavy footsteps beating a loud rhythm behind her. Subtlety was not one of his character traits. "I need to talk to you."

Three boxes of sugary cereal balanced precariously in his bulging arms, along with spoons, a half gallon of milk and two bowls large enough for popcorn. Without waiting, he brushed past her and headed toward the game room.

"Listen," she said, following him. "I'd appreciate it if you'd try to be a good example for the new guys. I know it must be hard, but for godsake, you're the acting field team leader. They look up to you. The least you could do is encourage them to follow procedure. They're in place for a reason."

"What are you talking about?"

"Kip, that's who I'm talking about. He used to be so responsible, but hanging out with you, he's—"

"Hold on. All this…it's slipping." The snake tattoo on his biceps, with its open mouth, fangs and forked tongue, looked eager to be eating Tony the Tiger as Jackson juggled everything.

She grabbed the bowls from him. "And why didn't you give me a heads-up that Gibby was here? You know I can't stand him."

"What? I figured you knew. Sensed him or smelled him or something. Sorry." With a snap of his head, Jackson flicked his hair out of his face, blond and gold highlights mingling with the brown, the splayed-out ends settling back along the top of his shoulders. Ever since he'd dated that chick who worked at one of Seattle's top hair salons, the guy had been addicted to funky highlights. Two weeks ago they'd been various shades of blue.

"I did, but…not soon enough. I've got a head cold. I would've changed into something else before I came over."

He gave her a quick head-to-toe. "What are you talking about?"

How could she explain it to someone so obtuse? No

use beating around the bush with him—he'd never get it. "Because you're all used to seeing me like this, eh? We hang out together and have a good time. But the guy's a total Richard. Sorry, he is. It makes me uncomfortable when I know I could look better."

"That's dumb. You look hot."

Oh man, why had she even bothered?

She followed him into the game room, half expecting to see Kip inside. Without looking up, Val Gibson leaned over the pool table and took a shot. He didn't bother to acknowledge her, so she returned the favor and stayed silent.

After setting the bowls on the wet bar, she leaned against the doorjamb and absently flicked the tiny chain hanging from her navel while her annoyance grew. *This better be fast. I'm sick of him already.*

Jackson held up two boxes and looked at the cartoon characters on the front as if trying to decide which was more worthy. Evidently he couldn't make up his mind because he dumped some of each into his bowl.

She cleared her throat. "Jacks, you had something you needed to—"

"You gonna take a shot or not?" Gibby asked Jackson, interrupting her as if she'd never spoken.

Her skin prickled. She plucked a stray blond hair from her sleeve as she counted backward from ten to one.

"In a sec," Jackson said to him. "Lil, did you hear DBs might be looking for Trackers to help them locate sweet-bloods? Wanted to make sure you watch your back when you're out."

"Yeah, they want to bring you over to the dark side," Gibson said in a faux announcer's accent, like the whole thing was a joke. He dumped at least a half box of cereal into his bowl, then held up the carton of milk and poured it in a slow, steady stream.

Oh please, did he need to make sure each piece was coated? She gladly tore her eyes away as Jackson continued.

"They're looking to convert Trackers. Use them like, well, bloodhounds—tracking and finding sweetbloods. They're branching out to places not previously popular with Darkbloods. Building up their blood inventory levels, I guess."

Gibby had discovered that? It sounded way too covert for a musclehead like him to be in on. "Converting Trackers? How'd you get that intel, Gibby?"

"Ah, he didn't." Jackson kept his head down and stuffed a large spoonful of cereal into his mouth. "Alfonso called."

"Alfonso?" The blood drained from her face and she felt light-headed for a moment.

Why should it be surprising that her former lover didn't want to deal with her and went straight to Jackson with this news? Acutely aware of a sudden ache deep inside, she folded her arms tightly across her chest and kicked at the carpet nap with the toe of her flip-flop. She most definitely didn't have feelings for him any longer—just anger at herself that she'd been gullible enough to ever believe he felt the same way about her. She may have thought she loved him once, but not any longer. Not after what he'd done. "How did he hear that?"

Jackson stirred his cereal. "He ran into a couple of DBs who told him right before he wasted them. But Gibby says a Tracker disappeared just last week down in the San

Diego office, so it could be happening all over. Maybe
it's a new tactic they're trying."

Gibson took a bite and wiped a trickle of milk from
his chin with the back of his hand. "I thought you guys
were friends with benefits since you were his handler in
the Agency for…how many years? You guys broke up,
huh?"

She was not about to discuss her failed love life with
Gibby. Especially not after those nightmarish few months
with Steven in San Francisco—what the hell had she been
thinking trying to start something back up with Zoe's
father? Clearly, she had poor taste in men. She was ready
to call it quits in the relationship department altogether.

It was her turn to ignore Gibby. Flexing her fists, she
directed her question to Jackson. "How do DBs think
they can get an Agency-trained Tracker to work for
them?"

"Probably by getting them addicted to Sweet," Jackson said. "Gorge on enough of it and it's as difficult to
kick as a meth or heroin addiction. You'll do just about
anything to get more. Alfonso said they do that type of
coercion a lot."

He should know. That's exactly what they did to him.

With the cereal bowl in one hand and his thumb on
the spoon to keep it from slipping inside, Jackson approached her. "He was really worried about you, Lil,"
he said, keeping his voice low. "I think if I hadn't told
him you're training someone—that you haven't been on
patrol alone lately—and that you're off the schedule for
the next few days, he may have come here himself. He
asked if you were going up to your parents' house to see
Zoe."

"And what did you tell him?"

"I told him I thought you were. He chilled out a little after that."

Alfonso was worried about her? She highly doubted it. He was aware she had a black belt in Krav Maga and, as far as he knew, she was still one of the Agency's top Trackers.

"What's Gibby doing here then?" The guy worked out of the San Diego office most of the time, and she wished he would've stayed there.

"He flew up for the MMA fights. We've got ringside seats. It's gonna be on HBO. You should watch it and see if you can see us."

"So what do you say, princess?" Gibson called from across the room, raising his thick eyebrows. "Wanna hook up? I'll show you what a real man is capable of."

"If you're the definition of a real man, then I'm going to bat for the other team. Jacks, for the life of me, I can't figure out why you're friends with a guy like him."

"The other team? Now you're talking," Gibson said, rubbing his hands together. "I haven't had a threesome in ages. My body could be your wonderland."

"Oh, please." She held up her middle finger to Gibby and left.

JACKSON SET DOWN the empty cereal bowl and caught up to her at the elevators. "Lil, wait up. I didn't mean to stir up old feelings. Should've just told you we got the information through some intelligence in the field without mentioning who the source was."

"I can assure you," she said coolly, "there's nothing

to stir up. Any feelings I may have had for him are long gone."

He wasn't so sure, but he wasn't about to argue with her. "Listen, I know this is going to sound out of left field since you and me—well, we haven't gotten together in forever. But...are you going straight to sleep when you get home or do you need a little company?"

Well before she'd met Alfonso, Lily and Jackson had rolled around in the sack together a few times just for fun. Like all modern vampires trying to control their naturally aggressive tendencies, they needed the tension release that only sexual activity provided. He'd never considered it serious, and neither had she. Just a fun way to work off the edge. And right now she looked like she could use a little tension reliever.

"Wow, out of left field is right." She smiled. "Jacks, you know I love ya, and the shagging was fun." She knocked him on the arm and he knew the *no* was coming. "But that was forever ago, like you said. We hang out now, have fun. You tell me about the women you date, and I try to keep them all straight. I'm afraid you've become more like the little brother I never had. A little brother with giant muscles. Jeez, what are you feeding these things?" She smacked his biceps again with the back of her hand. "It'd be weird now. Sorry, love."

He hadn't really expected she'd take him up on it, but it never hurt to try. And it wasn't completely altruistic on his part either. After all, she was hot and had a smoking body.

After glancing at her watch, she pressed the elevator button and twisted the cord of her hood around a finger.

What was she anxious about? Did she have to get back home for something?

Then it dawned on him. No wonder she seemed anxious and in a hurry. Kip was probably waiting for her back at her place.

"Sorry to have kept you from your boy toy," he said. "I'll let you get back to him."

A confused expression flashed across her face. "What are you talking about?"

"Kip. Isn't he waiting for you back at your condo?"

"*Kip?* Why would you think so? For one thing, he's totally not my type. Too young and probably way too inexperienced."

Jackson gave her a skeptical look. Since when was being the more experienced partner in a sexual relationship a bad thing?

"I'm serious. He's probably crashed in the bunk room by now. It took us a little longer than normal to track down a revert and I think he was pretty tired when we finally did. Go check if you don't believe me."

"I don't think so. Xian just made up one of the beds for Gibby and mentioned that Kip wasn't there. I just assumed you and he—"

"You're way off. Hey, there's Xian now," she said, looking behind him. "Let's go ask." She brushed past him and strode down the hallway.

As they got closer to the kitchen, the smell of warm chocolate nearly brought Jackson to his knees.

"I'm glad you're here," Xian said to Lily. "I wanted to get these to you before you left for Willow Run." The small, dark-haired man offered her a bundle wrapped neatly in brown paper, tied with a frilly pink bow.

"Brownies. No nuts. I promised Zoe I'd send some with you the next time you headed up."

"Oh, Xian, that's very sweet of you," she said, taking the package from him. "She adores your brownies. Thank you."

Brownies? Jackson's mouth was watering already.

For a moment he forgot why they needed to talk to Xian as he scanned the granite counters, first the large island with some frou-frou wicker basket arrangement, then around the perimeter, looking for a pan, a platter or the friggin' plate that held them. He was about to ask Xian if he'd made any extra when he spotted a lidded plastic container. *Bingo!* He beelined to the far side of the kitchen.

Lily started asking Xian a bunch of questions, but Jackson was only half-paying attention. He removed the lid and— Holy cow, they were frosted.

"I put nuts in the batch I made for everyone else," Xian called over his shoulder as he touched the wall-mounted Comm screen.

"Is there anything you can't do, Xian?" Grabbing the container, he shuffled back to the other side of the kitchen, trying to decide which one to eat first. The biggest brownie or the one with the most frosting? *The biggest,* he decided, and fished it out, smearing chocolate all over his fingers.

"Yes, get you to approve the latest expense sheets. I've got Guardian and trainee credit card bills due soon. Dom never makes me wait this long."

"Oh shit, sorry. Remind me later, okay?" Jackson stuffed the thing in his mouth and crunched down. Not surprising, it was fan-fucking-tastic. Moist, chewy and very chocolaty. "Xian, you know it'd really suck if you Van Helsinged and teamed up against us. I'd miss all the food."

"Jackson!" Lily's eyes narrowed.

"What? I'm joking. Kind of." He sat on the counter and crossed his legs. "Sorry, Xi, if I pissed you off."

"No worries. But if you don't get your feet off my clean granite, those will be the last brownies you ever eat." The man's eyes sparkled with amusement as he punched a few more buttons on the screen.

Jackson obeyed and crooked his pinkie, which was covered with frosting. "See, Lil? Xi and I are tight."

Not that Jackson actually thought Xian would sever his loyalties to their kind, deciding instead to hunt and persecute vampires as a handful of humans had done over the years, but he liked to tease the guy anyway. When Darkbloods had slipped into the family bakery late one night, targeting them because a few of them were sweet-bloods, Xian and his sister would've been dead if it hadn't been for Guardians. They hadn't arrived in time to save his mother, but because he and his younger sister were not sweetbloods, the Darkbloods hadn't gotten around to killing them before the Guardian showed up

Grateful and insisting he owed the team his life, Xian eventually became the administrative manager for the Seattle field office, where he did a little of everything, including occasionally volunteering as a blood donor. And making some kick-ass desserts. Although Jackson could do without all the fish and healthy shit the guy loved to fix.

"No, it appears Kip is not in the field office," Xian said. "His badge has not been scanned since—" Xian touched the screen again "—since eleven forty-three last night."

Lily's face paled. "That's the time we left for our shift. I assumed he was entertaining one of the women. Are you sure?"

"I am certain of it."

Jackson licked his fingers one by one. "I don't understand. Weren't you working the shift together, Lil? I thought he was shadowing you." He grabbed another brownie and held it out to her.

Glancing at his hand, she cocked an eyebrow and shook her head. He shrugged and shoved the piece of heaven into his mouth.

"He was with me on second shift, but I had him drive my car back to the office while I walked home. I…I wanted to clear my head after a somewhat difficult capture."

He considered taking yet another brownie, but decided two were enough. Any more sugar and he'd never get to sleep. Then again, as soon as the others saw the brownies, the container would be picked as clean as a chicken leg in a tank of hungry piranhas, so maybe he should take a third.

"That's your very own container," Xian said, obviously following his train of thought. "Didn't you see your name on the lid?"

Jackson flipped it over and saw his name printed neatly on a piece of masking tape in Xian's perfect script. "Xi, dude, if you were a woman, I'd kiss you." To Lily, he said, "Is your car here? Did he even come back?"

"I'll go see," she said as she sprang toward the door.

"No, wait. I can check the parking garage cameras

from here." Xian swiped his finger over the screen several more times, then made a clucking sound with his tongue. "I am afraid your red Porsche is not parked in the garage."

"Maybe he stopped by the Pink Salon and is spending dayside with a human woman somewhere." Jackson popped the lid on and held it on his lap.

"With my car? Without calling or asking? No, Kip's not the kind of guy who would do that."

From the pocket of her sweatshirt, she pulled out her cell, punched in a number and held the phone up to her ear. She waited a few moments, a worried look creasing her brow, before she snapped it shut. "He's still not picking up."

"Come on," Jackson said as he jumped from the counter and jogged to the kitchen door, the container of brownies tucked under one arm. "Let's have Cordell pull up your car's GPS system to see where it's located."

Lily followed closely on his heels. "Tell me exactly what Alfonso told you about Darkbloods looking for Trackers."

ALFONSO SET A HAND-PAINTED tile flush against the edge of the wet saw, lined up his black Sharpie mark, and grabbed the handle of the blade. Just as he was about to flip on the power switch to make the cut, his phone rang.

Not Santiago again? Few others had his number. He checked the screen and his gut tightened. Damn. The Seattle field office.

He pressed the green answer button. "Yes?"

"Alfonso, it's Jackson. Lily's partner is missing."

Alfonso's heart flipped in his chest and he stripped off his protective eyewear. "Lily. Where is she?"

"She's fine," Jackson said.

Alfonso leaned on the wrought-iron railing and sank to the bottom stair as his heart kick-started under his ribs again with the force of a jackhammer.

"Your intel was accurate," Jackson continued. "We're thinking Darkbloods kidnapped Kip because he's a Tracker. It happened to a Tracker Agent in San Diego as well."

"Isn't Kip the new guy? He hasn't gone through all the training yet, has he? I thought you said Lily just started working with him."

"Yeah, she only had him out on patrol a few times."

Alfonso grabbed the handrail and leaped to his feet. "Then it's her they wanted, not him."

"Could be a possibility."

"Where was she when he disappeared? Wasn't she with him? Tell me everything."

"She decided to walk home last night at the end of their shift and Kip was to drive her car back himself. Evidently, she's done it before."

"Walked home alone?"

"Yeah."

Alfonso groaned, rubbing his temples.

She hadn't walked home the night he had watched her. What was she thinking? He was a fool to assume she'd carry out her duties the same way every night.

Jackson continued, "But this time, he never made it back to the field office. The car was found only a few blocks from where they'd originally parked it."

My God, it could just as easily have been her. "Didn't

you tell her what I told you? That she shouldn't be out on patrol alone with Darkbloods actively looking for Trackers? What was she thinking?"

"Of course I told her, but you think that made a difference? She's not gonna change shit just because someone doesn't think she can handle herself. Besides, we don't have a lot of Agents here. Not really enough personnel to double up on patrols."

"Oh, for godsake. They were probably after her in the first place and took the trainee by accident." The thought of Lily walking unprotected through the streets of Seattle made him want to throttle some sense back into her.

"Thing is," Jackson said, "she's taking Kip's disappearance really hard. Thinks it's her fault. That if she'd been with him, DBs would never have been able to kidnap him. She's going out at nightfall to track him."

"And who's going with her?"

Jackson hesitated. "No one. We can cover more ground if we split up."

Not if I can help it.

Alfonso sprinted upstairs. "Was this decision discussed with Santiago? Does he know you've got a missing Tracker? I've already told him that they're being targeted by the Alliance. Does he know you plan to allow one of the Agency's finest Trackers to go out alone?"

There was an icy pause before Jackson replied. No man wanted to be questioned about whether or not he'd checked with his superior for permission. "He's in complete agreement with me. Lily isn't just a nose. She's an awesome fighter. Hell, she's kicked my ass a few times."

Yes, but these guys had no fucking idea what she might be up against. "Fine. Then I'm going with her."

He retrieved his army-green duffel bag and began jamming a few things inside.

Jackson laughed. "Dude, you better plan on telling her yourself because I sure as hell don't want to. She'll rip me a new one thinking we don't believe she's strong enough to do the job without help."

Alfonso paused. If she heard he was coming, she'd leave before sundown and deal with the resulting energy drain, rather than deal with him. "Don't tell her I'm coming. It's imperative you stall her as long as possible. That woman is not to go out alone, understand? When she goes, she goes with me."

"Wait. You're not coming now, are you? It's still daylight."

"I'm leaving in five minutes."

Jackson swore and muttered a few things under his breath. "You'll be a friggin' mess when you arrive."

Yeah, maybe, but he was willing to take that chance. "My rig is outfitted as a pseudo Daytran vehicle. It came in handy a few times while working undercover. I'll manage." With his heavy weapons bag in one hand, he took the stairs two at a time.

"I need to clear this with Santiago, since you're not technically an Agent."

"You do that," Alfonso said and slammed the phone shut.

CHAPTER FOUR

LILY PUSHED OPEN THE STEEL door at the far end of the parking garage with a bang, her heart thumping madly in her chest. She was angry, she told herself. Angry and pissed off, and not at all excited.

There he was. Just where she figured he'd be.

Alfonso leaned against the hood of her red Porsche, his long legs stretched out in front of him, one large boot crossed over the other, looking like he owned the whole damn place. The warm smell of leather and pine filled her nostrils as she marched toward him, her heels pounding on the pavement with every crushing beat of her heart.

An hour ago, while she'd assembled her weapons bag, the little hairs on the back of her neck had begun to tingle and thoughts of Alfonso kept filling her mind, despite her attempts to shut them down. And now, of course, she knew why. Her sensory abilities had detected him, knew he was nearby, whether her conscious self was completely aware of it or not. At least her scent memory wasn't totally fried.

Shoving the duffel bag behind her, she stopped in front of him, feet squared, hands on her hips. "What the hell are you doing here?"

Calm as always, he shifted his weight to the other foot and examined his fingernails for a moment before he lazily lifted his gaze to meet hers. The clear blue of his eyes used to remind her of the color of truth, but all she saw now was icy deception. What a fool she'd been to trust her heart with someone like him.

A hint of a smile sat on his lips, his dimple appearing on one cheek. "What's it look like I'm doing?"

"Listen, Alfonso. Don't play games with me. My intelligence quota has increased exponentially since you last saw me and I'm not nearly as gullible. Why are you here? And I want the truth."

His brow furrowed and he studied her face as if she were a science experiment that needed to be weighed, measured and cataloged. Then his gaze traveled slowly down her body, tickling every traitorous nerve ending. "You miss the latest Agency directive? Until further notice, all Trackers shall be accompanied by another Guardian while out in the field."

"I'd have heard if the rules had changed." Jackson hadn't said anything about it a few minutes ago.

"It was just faxed to all the field offices in the region."

How the hell would he know? He was obviously trying to trip her up, make her think it was official so she'd agree. "And last I knew, you're not a Guardian. How'd you even get in here? The place is cloaked. Did Mackenzie tell you what was going on? She did, didn't she? Or wait, Jackson!"

During the lame-ass emergency briefing that had cut into the precious time she should've been out searching for Kip, he hadn't made eye contact with her. Not once. It totally was him. Next time she saw the guy, she was going to fry his ass.

"Nope." He looked down, flicking something off his thigh. As he picked at the frayed edges of a small hole in his jeans, his thick lashes rested against his cheeks.

His nonchalance fanned her anger and every muscle in her body went rigid. How could he be so calm and act so totally uninterested? They hadn't seen each other in over a year. The least he could do was shake her hand or give her a hug. Tell her she looked good or something. Like normal people would do. Normal people who'd once shared something special. God, she was so stupid for thinking he'd ever cared about her.

A tiny voice inside told her she wasn't exactly welcoming to him either, but she shut that down instantly. She needed to keep her exterior shell as hard and rigid as possible in order to protect her too fragile heart. Love was a candy-coated fairy tale whose sugar high didn't last long in the real world.

"Sorry to break it to you, but you're not coming with me." She poked a finger toward him and the loaded duffel bag almost slipped off her shoulder. She elbowed it behind her back again. "In fact, you've got a lot of nerve showing up like this. What do you mean *accompanied by another Guardian,* anyway? You're not Agency."

"Santiago okayed me coming on board temporarily to help you track down the missing trainee."

It felt as if someone had slapped her. The Region Commander didn't think she had the chops to handle this assignment on her own? Santiago must think she'd slacked off because Kip had disappeared under her watch. Despite the chill in the air, her internal temperature cranked up like a furnace and the stiff collar of her jacket suddenly became too tight.

She clenched her jaw and pressed her lips into a hard line. "Well, news flash for you. I don't report directly to Santiago. I don't need your help or anyone else's, so get away from my car. It's new and I don't need any scratches or fingerprints."

"He got the okay from Roxanne Reynolds. Does that make a difference?"

She had started to step over his legs, but that stopped her in her tracks. Roxanne was in charge of all Tracker Agents and her word was law. If you valued your job, you didn't cross her. Unlike Santiago, her bite was much worse than her bark.

"Yeah, I thought it would." He stood up, straightening to his full six-foot-four frame, taking full advantage of the fact that he was almost a full twelve inches taller than her. She had to crank her head back to keep eye contact with him and it made her feel even smaller. Damn. She should've worn heels.

A piece of his tousled blond hair fell to the middle of his cheek, and when he absently pushed it off his face, it slid back down anyway. The soft color of his eyes and the tiny wrinkles around the corners belied the hard planes of his square jaw and the rough texture of his unshaven face. Those large hands, with fingertips callused from playing the guitar, were incredibly dexterous, and that powerful body could be surprisingly tender. He was a mass of contradictions, wrapped up in a package too attractive for her own good.

She shouldered past him, the corner of her duffel

smacking against his hip. Too bad it missed his balls. Yanking the car door open, she threw the bag inside, angry with herself for still being so physically attracted to him. He angled himself around to the side of the car, and leaned against the front quarter panel as if he was the one calling the shots.

"You wasted a lot of time driving down here," she said. "Despite what everyone must think, I am perfectly capable of tracking Kip on my own. Now, step aside." But he didn't budge. Fine. He'd move his ass as soon as she hit the accelerator.

"I realize that," he said. "You're one of the best Trackers in the Agency. That's not why I'm here."

She crossed her arms and raised a skeptical eyebrow. "Then why *are* you here?"

"Despite what you must think, Lily, I worry about you. With this new Darkblood strategy, if they even so much as catch wind of you while you're looking for your little trainee, they'll ditch him in a heartbeat. He's not who they wanted in the first place. I plan to be your temporary assistant. No, your bodyguard."

"You? My assistant?" She lifted her chin and laughed. "That's the most absurd thing I've heard in a long time. Wait. I think I understand. You're feeling nostalgic and want to screw again, eh? You want to do it for old time's sake because—" she lowered her voice to a caricature of him "—*I can't find anyone who shags like you do, baby.*"

"Gimme a little credit here."

Something flashed in those glacier eyes. If she didn't know any better, she'd have thought he looked hurt. But that wasn't possible. He was the one who had hurt her.

"Yeah, nothing says you care like a year's worth of… of…nothing. I was much too naive, thinking you'd be back after things settled down. But I guess it was just an assignment to you. A long-term assignment, and once it was over, we were over."

"Jesus, Lil." He opened his mouth as if he were going to say more, but snapped it shut. The square corners of his jaw flexed over and over.

She'd struck a nerve. Good.

"When Mackenzie thought she saw you in the lab moments before she saw flames, I thought you'd been trapped inside. I spent the next few nights sifting through the ashes looking for your remains. I looked for that medallion I gave you for luck, but then you probably only wore it when you knew we were getting together anyway."

He reached into his shirt and pulled out the gold pendant that swung on a leather cord around his neck.

She stared at it, stunned. He still wore it?

"I'm sorry," he said, "but it couldn't be helped. They had to believe I died along with Pavlos."

She swallowed and tried to regain her composure. He'd probably put it on knowing he was coming to see her. "And you didn't see fit to inform me of your little deception."

When she'd thought he had died in the fire that day, a huge part of her had died as well. But when Mackenzie told her later that he was very much alive, she wasn't sure what to think. Then, in one fateful phone conversation, when he'd told her he no longer loved her—even after all they had shared—it just about sent her over the edge. She'd sworn she'd never be such a sucker for romance and a handsome face again.

"For your sake, it was better if everyone thought I was dead. It still is." He examined the medallion, its interconnected links with no beginning or end, as if he'd never seen it before. "I was hoping you'd moved on by now."

"And what makes you think that I haven't?"

His expression went suddenly blank as the implication of her words sank in. She could've sworn his pupils widened for a moment. Yeah, let him ponder that. Her gaze languished down his powerful body to make her point, over his lean hips and muscular legs, then back up to meet his icy-blue stare again. There was no way in hell he'd been celibate this whole time. No way. God, she didn't want to even think about him lying between the legs of another woman.

With a sniff, she flipped her long ponytail to the other side, smoothing it over her shoulder, in order to keep her thoughts grounded in the present. And in the present, he pissed her off.

"You're not tracking him by yourself, Lil. You're clearly the original target. Santiago and Jackson are idiots to let you go alone. I told them both that, so I went around their authority. And if I were on speaking terms with my brother, he'd no doubt agree with me."

She had to admit Alfonso was right about one thing. If Dom wasn't on assignment in Australia, he would insist she have backup as well. They were cut from the same mold. Stupid, overprotective Serrano brothers. She scoffed and rolled her eyes.

He smacked his hand on the roof of her car and she

jumped. "You are not. Going. Alone." As he stepped around the open door and into her personal space, his jaw muscles tensed below his earlobes, the black of his pupils expanding against the blue.

Not wanting to touch him, she stepped backward, flattening herself against the back door of her car. In this position, his scent was stronger than ever, filling her head and activating memories that were too dangerous for her heart. He rested a hand on the roof, just inches from her face, and leaned in close. Her breath caught in her throat, and for a moment, she couldn't remember if she had been breathing in or breathing out. He wasn't going to try to kiss her, was he? Because if he did, she'd—

She stared at his full lips, recalling how they'd felt moving against her own, brushing over her neck, tickling the delicate skin beneath her chin and along her jaw.

Shit. He was talking. She blinked, tried to concentrate.

"I thought about forcing you to stop—I can and you know it." He enunciated each word with deadly precision.

Her pulse quickened and the chain of her belly ring flickered on the sensitive skin of her lower abdomen. Their relationship had always been passionate; sometimes she'd been the one in charge, and other times he had. Clearly, he was taking the dominant role tonight, and although it pissed her off, it excited her on some level as well.

"I'd find him myself," he said, "but my ability to track is a fraction as strong as yours. I can't do it without you. My only choice is going with you and that's what I intend to do. Give me your keys. I'm driving."

No one ordered her around. Gritting her teeth, she pushed him away, thinking if she wanted to, she could grab him by the shoulders right now and plant a knee or an elbow in a number of tender spots. *Force me? My ass.* She'd taken down bigger men than him just for the sport of it.

"There is no way in hell you're coming with me. I don't need you or want you. Now get out of my way."

"Lil, please." The brittle planes of his face softened just a little. "If you're driving, how do you expect to concentrate on tracking your friend's scent? You'll be faster, more effective, if all other stimuli are eliminated. Come on, let me drive. You just close your eyes, concentrate and tell me which way to go."

She examined her fresh manicure and pushed back a cuticle. Her goal was to find Kip as soon as possible and she supposed it would be easier if she didn't have to drive.

"My way is much more efficient," he continued. "Come on. We don't have time for this." He snapped his fingers, as if she were an insolent child.

She was about to acquiesce—he did have a point— when this arrogance of his slipped under her skin again like a newly sharpened dagger. Digging her nails into the palms of her hands, she drew in a breath to calm herself. She was about to tell him to go to hell, but then Kip's eager, young face, flush with excitement over his first few tracking assignments, flashed in her mind. Finding him, getting him back safely, was the most important issue. Not her past relationship with a man she used to love.

Fine. She'd table her emotions and put up with Alfonso temporarily for Kip's sake. But one thing was for sure. Despite their past and the fact that he was still so damned attractive, she would not allow him to get into her heart. He'd played her once. She would not let her guard down again.

She fished the keys out and threw them at him hard enough to make a mark. With lightning-fast reflexes, he snatched them out of the air and gave them a jaunty little toss before he turned his back and grabbed the door handle.

"Let's get one thing straight," she called over her shoulder. "I'm only agreeing to this because of Kip."

"Fair enough."

The leather squeaked as he slid his large body down into the seat, and he scanned the interior of her new car. By the time she'd jogged around to the passenger door, he'd reached over and cracked it open for her from the inside. As she climbed in beside him, the Panamera's engine roared to life, a deep, rumbling, powerful sound. His fingers caressed the top of the dash as if he were familiarizing himself with an exciting new lover that he couldn't wait to bed. She had to admit, he did look pretty hot behind the wheel.

"Ever drive a sport-mode dual clutch?" Her voice sounded a little too scratchy, so she cleared her throat.

He adjusted the seat and mirrors in such a precise, preoccupied manner that she wondered if he'd even heard what she'd said. "How hard can it be?"

Oh, this should be interesting. She leaned over, pressed

a button on the console near his thigh, taking care not to touch him, and popped the gear shift back to center.

"What was that?"

"Turned off the sport mode and put it back into automatic. The dual clutch takes some getting used to."

He quirked an eyebrow at her in a flippant, you-don't-know-what-you're-talking-about look. Figured. All men thought their DNA made them better drivers.

"I don't have time to give you a lesson," she said. "And I can't be distracted wondering when the hell you were going to shift."

As if his mere presence just inches away wasn't distracting enough.

CHAPTER FIVE

"THIS IS IT." THE MAN TAPPED a knuckle on the taxi window. A small, unadorned prayer box dangled from a hole in his thick pinkie nail and clinked against the glass. "Wait for me around the corner."

"For how long?" the driver said, his nicotine-graveled voice sounding more like a growl. "I'm scheduled for a pickup in an hour."

The passenger slipped him a hundred-dollar bill, the pads of his fingers brushing against the cabbie's outstretched palm, and he repeated his command. "Wait for me. I've got another one marked for you when I return."

The driver's eyelids fluttered a few times and his worn expression softened. "Sure, I'll be right up there."

After navigating past a line of young palm trees and stepping over the uneven pavement of the walkway, the man stood on the front porch as sounds of a TV blared through the half-closed door. Noticing a scuff on the toe of his shoe, he stooped to brush it off, irritated when it didn't disappear. He straightened up, realigned his black jacket and rang the doorbell.

He waited, then rang it again.

"Brice!" a female voice called from inside. "The pizza guy's here." Footsteps shuffled on the fake Spanish-tile floor a moment later.

"I didn't order any damn—"

The door was flung open with gusto, creating a slight breeze across his forehead. He smoothed his slicked hair back in place as a man in a stained college sweatshirt appeared at the other side of the screen. The smell of cigarettes, fried food and beer-laden blood filled his nostrils. He pulled a handkerchief from his inside pocket, folded it carefully and dabbed his upper lip.

"Oh, Jesus. Ah, Father, what can I do for you?" The man pushed the screen door and held it open. "Would you like to come in?"

He touched the mandarin collar of his jacket. It wasn't the first time he'd been mistaken for a man of the cloth, and it probably wouldn't be the last. "Heavens, no. I'm tremendously sorry I did not call first. I don't wish to trouble you, but I have a simple request that had to be made in person."

"Yeah, sure, what is it? Father…Father…?"

"Rejavik. The name is Rejavik." With his hands clasped at his waist, he held a smile in check and tried to look pious. "You take on boarders from time to time, is that correct?"

"Not really, Father Rejavik. My old lady used to, but not anymore. Why? You looking to rent a room?"

Rejavik held back his contempt. He'd rather lie on a beach at noon, have the sunlight leach every ounce of energy from his body, than spend one night in this filthy shit hole. "I'm trying to locate a member of my congregation who may have stayed here several years ago. His name is Alfonso Serrano. Tall fellow, blond hair, blue eyes."

"Hey, Marge," the man yelled over his shoulder. "You remember a renter named Alberto?"

"Alfonso," Rejavik said quietly. *Idiot.*

"Why does the pizza guy want to know?" she yelled from the other room.

"Oh for Chr—" Brice clamped a hand over his mouth and hiccupped through his fingers. "Sorry, Father. A few years ago?"

Rejavik nodded.

"I haven't lived here that long but I know Marge had a long-term renter for a while. Maybe he's your guy."

"Let me speak with her."

"Hey, Marge!" No answer. The television laugh track, prompting the desired proletarian response, blared from the other room. "Marge!"

Enough of this. Rejavik placed his palm on the man's shoulder. "Take me to her."

The man jerked away and eyed him warily. "What the hell was that? It felt like an electric shock or something."

Not quite the intoxicated simpleton I'd assumed. "I'm terribly sorry. With the cooler air, I sometimes conduct a little more electrostatic energy this time of year. There—" he touched the doorjamb "—it's dissipated. Forgive me." He held out his hand to the man and gave him a benign smile.

Tired of these pathetic niceties, he silently counted to three, at which point he'd spill this fool's blood and get the answers from Marge himself. Either way, it didn't really matter, although he just picked up this suit from the cleaners and didn't want to get it soiled again so soon. He was hungry, but not desperate.

Thick, sausagelike fingers gripped his hand and the human's energy flowed into his body like an open spigot. *Ah, yes, very good.* Palm-on-palm was much more effective than contact through clothing anyway, making thought suggestions harder to resist. Although palm-to-forehead was best, he didn't think he could bear touching the man's sweat-stained face.

"Take me to Marge, then lie down and go to sleep."

Within a few minutes, the man was sleeping on a ratty couch, the television was turned down and Marge's hands were clasped between his.

"He has eyes like Paul Newman," she said, "and he's tall. Had to duck under the attic beams and couldn't stand up all the way. He pays in cash, six months in advance, but like I said, I haven't seen him in a long time. Don't remember his name being Alfonso, though. Do you think he could be the same guy?"

"He stayed in your attic room?"

"No, he didn't like it there. Said he needed to come and go at weird hours and didn't want to disturb us, so he rents the outbuilding at the back of our property. Not sure why 'cause he's hardly ever there, but, hey, I'm not complaining. Don't think he's into drugs or nothing."

"When was the last time he was here?"

She shrugged. "Six months. A year, maybe more. Like I said, I don't keep track. Pays like clockwork though."

Wedged against the rocky hillside a half acre from the rear of the house, the wooden shed looked largely forgotten. Tumbleweeds lay among the rusted-out garden tools, empty paint buckets and other assorted junk that leaned against the outside walls. Some idiot—probably the one who'd answered the door—had parked a dented blue car, now up on jacks, so close to the shed that it blocked the small door. The woman unlocked it and stepped aside to let him pass.

The interior should've smelled stale and dusty, a perfect environment for black widow spiders and scorpions, but it didn't. It had obviously been cleaned more recently than the house, but then, that wasn't saying much.

She pulled the cord of a light fixture near the door, and the bare bulb swung from the ceiling, casting moving shadows over the room. Pushed up against the far wall was a cot with a floral comforter tucked in at the edges and a small nightstand.

What kind of man would stay in a place like this? he wondered as he looked around the neat and tidy surroundings. Maybe the lead he was following up was wrong. Surely someone with Serrano's means and lineage would never surround himself with such flea market squalor, even if it was simply used as an occasional hideout.

He opened the nightstand drawer with his handkerchief and found a flashlight, an unscented candle, a book of matches and a well-worn bible. He grabbed it, flipped through the pages, and when a guitar pick fell out, he couldn't help smiling. Serrano took his guitar everywhere.

This was promising after all.

When he picked up a pillow and drew in a deep breath through his nostrils, something lingered in the back of his scent memory and almost—

"How can you tell if your guy is my renter?" The woman's voice broke his concentration and his shoulders stiffened. "I mean, we really shouldn't be in here without his permission. It ain't right."

"Wait for me outside near the blue car."

"Why—"

He leveled a hard stare at her and noticed the loose skin of her jowls hung in parallel cords from her chin to the base of her neck. The soft tissue would tear easily, he thought as the tips of his fangs poked through his gums.

"I'll be right out there if you need me," she said, suddenly wising up.

Good. He didn't want to flood his system with her blood right now anyway. It would dilute his senses too much and he needed them keen at the moment.

As his fangs receded, he turned back to the cot. With a fingernail, he lifted the lid of the prayer box and held it to his nose.

He recalled the Oath of Loyalty ceremony when the item had been placed in his possession centuries ago. In the dimly lit caverns beneath the city of Madrid, he had watched as the Overlord drew a blade over the palms of each of the inductees. They were to dip a square of muslin in their own blood, place it inside a prayer box and present it to their assigned blood assassin as a sign of their undying loyalty to the Overlord and the Darkblood Alliance.

Something about Serrano's demeanor had nagged at him that day, and he'd checked inside the tiny golden box before placing it into the vault. Maybe it was the way Serrano had looked at him, almost glaring at the Overlord, eyes full of defiance, with no trace of the reverence visible on all the others' faces. It was, after all, an honor to be asked to join the inner circle.

Maybe it was the slight sheen of sweat he'd noticed on Serrano's upper lip. Rejavik couldn't be sure what it was that hadn't seemed right, but it was a good thing he'd checked—the tiny box had been empty. The blood-soaked piece of cloth had somehow fallen to the dirt floor.

Serrano had acted surprised, as if he thought he'd placed it inside the box, but Rejavik wasn't so sure it hadn't been intentional.

When he'd learned Serrano had been identified as the insider responsible for the death of their great leader, that he'd been feeding intelligence to the Governing Council's Guardian unit for years, Rejavik hadn't been surprised. He doubted Serrano had ever been loyal to their cause. It would be his pleasure and honor to kill the traitor.

A quick death would be too kind. No, he'd make sure to draw it out as long and as painfully as possible. And if there was anyone special in Serrano's life, anyone he cared enough about to share blood, Rejavik would find her and make her suffer as well.

He inhaled deeply and held his breath, the remnants of Serrano's blood inside the box reactivating his scent memory. He visualized the defiance in Serrano's eyes, which shone brightly beneath his hooded robe, the slight flare of his nostrils and the rigidity of his shoulders. Ah, yes. It was all coming back to him now.

He closed the lid and ran his fingers lightly over the bed, leaning his face close to the surface. Yes, the scent patterns matched. Although the smell was old, Serrano had definitely been here.

But there was something more.

He pulled back the comforter and sniffed again.

Although faint, the smell of sex still clung to the sheets. Serrano had fucked someone in this shit hole? A whore? Did he drain her as well? Rejavik didn't detect any blood scent, though.

He was about to leave when his hand alighted on a lump near the foot of the bed. Flipping back the comforter entirely, he spotted a tiny, wadded ball of black string and lace forgotten on the sheets, kicked off in the heat of the moment.

With just the tip of a finger so as not to disturb the scent, he lifted the flimsy material to his nose.

A woman's scent. Yes, but—

He inhaled again, letting the top notes dissipate as he processed all the markers.

Not just a female. A vampire female. And Serrano's scent was almost as strong as hers.

A pleasant thrill ran over his skin like a tropical breeze. He could hardly believe his luck.

Carefully, he removed a small plastic bag from a pocket and tucked the lace inside. He stood, his cock now painfully hard.

It wasn't just two separate smells he detected—semen and the female's scent. The semen was mixed with her scent, which only meant one thing.

Serrano had taken the vampire female's blood.

This was perfect. Now he had two targets to hunt. If he couldn't find Serrano, maybe he could find the woman.

Rejavik wanted to laugh out loud. What a fool. It wasn't the first time Serrano's whoring had gotten him into trouble. Some people never learned from their mistakes, no matter what the consequences were.

He examined the panties through the plastic. They were the impractical kind worn by a female who knew they'd be seen at some point.

He was half tempted to relieve himself right here. He'd mark this spot with his own scent—his own potent scent—and drown out the smell of that betrayer.

As he slipped a hand into his trousers, he heard a rustle outside the door and paused.

Ah, yes. The woman. She was waiting for him outside.

He pulled his hand from his pants and smoothed the front of his jacket. No use wasting his seed just to grandstand. It might as well serve a purpose.

Outside, although the night was still young, the light in the sky was gone; it was ink-black now. The jagged outline of the San Bernardino Mountains looming to the east had disappeared into the darkness.

He loved when night fell earlier and ended later. Soon, the hours of darkness would exceed the hours of daylight. It was truly a magical time of the year for his kind. The human advantage was lessened, because vampires ruled the night.

Since he'd clicked off the bulb as he left the shed, the only illumination now came from one stark floodlight on the far side of the property. Cicadas and other night insects buzzed from the bushes as he slipped past the old car, careful not to brush up against the rough siding of the shed and snag or soil his clothing.

Several coyotes howled in the foothills, their crazy,

wild yapping signaling that they had surrounded their prey. All that was left was the thrill of the kill.

Indeed.

With his hands clasped together, he slipped around the corner of the car and didn't bother to conceal his elongated fangs. The woman sat on the front bumper, her back against the grill, as she sucked in a long draught of her menthol cigarette. He watched as she exhaled two smoky columns from her nostrils, like a dragon.

He willed himself not to disappear amongst the shadows when he stepped in front of her. It was important for her to see him like this.

He *needed* her to see him like this.

Fear-infused blood tasted so much sweeter on the tongue.

CHAPTER SIX

WHEN LILY OPENED ALL THE VENTS and rolled down the windows, cold gusts of air circulated around the interior of the car. Although tracking a target while inside a moving vehicle was difficult to do, Alfonso knew that Lily wasn't your ordinary Tracker.

With one hand, she held her honey-blond bangs out of her eyes, while the rest was clasped into a sleek, thick ponytail, wrapped by a thin coil of hair. God, she looked great. Maybe a little thinner though, which bothered him. Her curves were perfect before. Her breasts had always been—

Shit, they'd better find Kip quickly because he had to stop thinking like this. Her feisty, she-cat attitude had always turned him on, but when she'd gone off on him in the parking garage, it made him acutely aware of how much he missed her. His leg ached and he rubbed his palm on his thigh, trying not to remember the feel of her hips under his hands as he held on and pushed himself deeper into her warmth. Not once had he made love to her without taking her blood, and now that he was marked for assassination, he'd never risk her life like that again. Unlike before, this short-lived assignment would be strictly platonic.

"Take I-Five North." Her head was slightly turned away from him as she gazed out her window.

Had she moved on and found someone else? As much as it killed him to think about it, he hoped she had. She deserved someone whose love didn't put her in danger, who would be a good role model for her daughter, someone whole and unbroken. Not some former Sweet-addicted member of the Alliance's inner circle who'd made evil promises long ago and was now too weak to defend her.

He gripped the leather-covered steering wheel tighter and jerked the car around the corner a little too quickly. The low-profile tires squealed on the wet pavement. Her scent didn't seem to be mingled with anyone else's, but he sure as hell didn't have the courage to ask her.

"How far did you track Kip? Jackson told me you went out in the early morning as soon as you discovered him missing."

"Jackson, the shit," she mumbled to herself. "I got as far as the North End before I had to turn around at sunrise. That's not happening again."

"Why? Are you confident we'll find him soon? Is his scent that strong?"

"I'm not heading back until I find him, that's all. Regardless of whether his scent is strong or not, I'm not coming back without him."

"Tell me what you know about his disappearance."

In the same slightly husky voice that he knew so well, Lily recounted what little she knew. He could listen to her talk forever, he thought wistfully, recalling the times he'd made her read to him aloud. Books, newspaper articles, advertisements. It didn't matter. He was mesmerized by the silky sound of her voice and could listen to her forever.

Aw, Jesus, he had to knock this off.

Since when did Lily have a problem tracking someone? Especially someone she'd been working with, whose scent memory should be familiar to her. It wasn't like she had to conjure the memory from an object. He had the distinct impression she wasn't telling him everything.

"So even after you heard DBs were looking for Trackers, you set out on your own? What would possess you to do something so idiotic?"

Her eyebrows pinched together and her caramel-brown eyes flashed darker. "You don't need to remind me that I screwed up, Alfonso. Don't you think I know that? I shouldn't have left Kip alone. Period. He's not had any formal hand-to-hand combat training. If I had been with him, he wouldn't have been taken by DBs."

"I'm not talking about Kip. I'm talking about you. Do you think I give a shit about some Agency trainee I've never met? If you had been with him, they'd have taken you. They wouldn't have bothered with him."

She crossed her arms and settled back in her seat. They drove north on the freeway, the silence almost tangible.

Finally, she cleared her throat. "This is it. This is as far as I came this morning."

At the top of the exit, he pulled the car off to the side of the road and left the engine running, waiting for direction from her.

"Pick up his scent yet?"

Without looking over at him, she pursed her lips tightly

together and shook her head. Something was clearly bothering her. He didn't need to be a pop-psychology guru to figure that out.

"Well, it rained last night, which always makes tracking a scent more difficult, right? Come on." He turned off the ignition. "Let's walk around and see what you detect outside."

They climbed out of the car and gravel crunched under his footsteps as he came up behind her. She held her shoulders stiff, bit her bottom lip between her teeth as she looked around.

"May I?" When she didn't answer, he slipped a hand under the collar of her jacket, touching the skin on the nape of her neck as he had done so many times before. He had loved to kiss her there from behind, precisely where his thumb was rubbing, feel her quiver beneath his lips as she waited for him to trail along her shoulder blades and down the center of her back. Now, though, she tensed up at first when he touched her, but he kept rubbing until she relaxed and dropped her head slightly.

God, she was all knotted up, with kinks on top of kinks. He knew from experience that she kept her tension in her neck and shoulders, but this was ridiculous. Only a long soak in a hot tub and a deep-tissue massage would begin to loosen her up, get her to truly relax. Maybe that was her problem. She was too keyed up.

"So who is this Kip? Are you…ah…seeing him?" He forced himself to say the words as calmly as he could. Although he'd not been with another woman since he'd left Lily, he doubted she'd been celibate, given her sexual appetite.

"No, he's the son of my mother's best friend. Gorgeous, but way too young for me. I promised her I'd take care of him. Gave her my word."

Aware that his relief was completely self-centered, Alfonso continued with both hands now, massaging tiny circles on either side of her spinal cord with his thumbs. Out of habit, he found himself pushing a little of his energy into her body before he slid his hands over her coat to rub her shoulders and the tops of her arms. Looking down, he saw that her eyes were closed, her lips slightly parted. He desperately wanted to kiss her, drag her into his arms, but he knew that she'd never let him. Besides, as much as he wanted to, he was a selfish fool to even think about going down that path. Kissing led to fondling, which led to sex, which led to blood sharing. It was easier not to start, rather than trying to shut things down midstream. With Lily, he'd never had a good track record of stopping himself once he got going.

"Better? Is this helping any?" he asked.

When she took a deep breath, he thought she might launch into him again. Tell him she could take care of herself. That she didn't need his or anyone else's help.

Instead, she straightened up and her eyes blazed with excitement. "Got it!" She pointed down the street. "He was taken somewhere in that direction."

They jumped back into her car and for the next few hours they wound around the city, each road and neighborhood seedier than the last. Chain-link fences surrounded many of the run-down houses, keeping *in* the pit bulls and keeping *out* unwanted guests. Grass lawns were nonexistent, choked out by crabgrass, dandelions and blackberry bushes long ago. And none of the junkers lining the streets had seen a showroom floor in decades.

"They must be using some sophisticated scent-masking techniques," Alfonso said.

"I'm...ah...not sure."

They had to be. Lily was the best Tracker with the Agency and wasn't easily stymied.

She finally directed him to a dilapidated house with a red Condemned sign stapled to the front door. "His scent is strong, but it's not active," she said when they pulled up to the curb. "In fact, I can tell the place is empty."

"Maybe they held him here while they waited for instructions. Let's check it out anyway. We might find something inside that shows where they took him."

They crept around to the back of the house, stepping over huge cracks in the driveway and avoiding the trash piled up inside the carport. Alfonso wasn't surprised to find the back door kicked in, hanging on its hinges. It was totally in character for this neighborhood. He poked his head inside and looked around.

"It's not insulated well enough from the sunlight to make a decent place to hole up dayside," Alfonso said as he eyed the living room's caved-in ceiling, "and I don't think it's got a basement. They must not have held him here for long, since he was kidnapped shortly before dawn."

An overturned chair and a few empty vials of blood were the only signs of recent activity in this pit.

"Come on. There's nothing here," he said. Without thinking, he grabbed Lily's hand to lead her back to the car.

Instantly, her uncorralled energy blazed into his palm,

causing his cock to slam against the crotch of his jeans. Fuck. He let go of her as if she were on fire and stuffed his hands into his pockets. She'd always been so free in sharing her energies with him, whether she meant to or not. Obviously, things hadn't changed. Not wanting to see the longing he felt for her mirrored in her expression because he was liable to do something stupid if he did, he stormed ahead of her and climbed into the car. The memory of her elegant fingers clung to his skin and his thumbs ached to caress them again. He rubbed his hands on his thighs, trying to eliminate the compelling sensation.

She slid in next to him without saying a word, the only sounds the creak of the leather seat and the click of the door as it closed. As he swung the car away from the curb, he glanced over at her, but she kept her face turned away. She had to have felt it too. It couldn't have been just him.

"It's getting stronger," she said, once they'd driven around for a while.

He turned onto a five-lane roadway dotted with billboards in both directions advertising car insurance for drivers with a DWI, lawyers to help avoid child support, and loans for those with bad credit.

She angled her head out the open window. "Yes! It's strongest over there," she said, pointing to a windowless strip club. "Do you think they could be holding Kip there?"

That was odd. Shouldn't she be able to determine that from the strength of his scent? She'd always been able to do that before.

"I'd say it's a good possibility." He turned the car around and headed in the opposite direction.

"Where are you going? His scent is coming from over there."

"I'm parking this fancy car of yours elsewhere. It's clearly out of place. When you work undercover, every-thing someone sees or hears from you needs to be a re-flection of their expectations. And as much as I love this car, it does not fit the expectations of someone who hangs out in that kind of an establishment. It'd need to be at least ten years older and sporting a few dents to belong out front." He turned down a side street and parked under a burned-out streetlight. "Wait for me. I'll go in and see if I can locate him."

"You can't be serious. You want me to wait here, while you go in and take care of things? Do I look like a damn shrinking violet to you?"

He hadn't thought she'd stay, but it sure as hell was worth a try.

LILY CALLED IN TO THE FIELD office that she had a lead on Kip's whereabouts, but Jackson and another team were dealing with some rowdy youthlings just south of town and wouldn't be able to get here for a while. Maybe it was a good thing Alfonso was with her, but she'd never admit that to him.

Alfonso led the way as they jogged along the back side of the next block, his boots pounding out a don't-fuck-with-me rhythm on the pavement that made her nerve endings sing with excitement. From her vantage point slightly behind him, she found herself admiring his tight butt, which was accentuated by the design on his back pockets. His broad shoulders stretched the leather of his jacket; he moved in a way that was at once powerful and lithe, as if he could ricochet himself in a different direction at the blink of an eye. With his arms bent as they were, his fists clenched, would his biceps be flexed as well? Yes, they probably were. Her fingertips tingled at the thought of what they'd feel like under the leather of his coat. Strong, masculine, athletic. Whenever he made love to her on top, she delighted in running her hands along those arms and shoulders, feeling the pronounced definition between the two muscle groups as he strained to keep his weight from crushing her…too much…while he moved inside of her.

Oh God, she had to stop thinking of him like this. He'd left her and proved that he was no different from Steven. She didn't need to revive another doomed relationship. Reluctantly, she dragged her gaze away from him and focused on where they were going and what she hoped to find there.

Out on the main drag, they slowed their clip to a fast walk. As they passed a sandwich board advertising late-night psychic readings and a secondhand clothing store with barred windows, Alfonso grabbed her arm and yanked her inside.

"What are you doing?" she said, as the doorbell jangled loudly over their heads. The smell of stale clothes and old furniture reminded her of all the times she and her mother had gone antique-hunting.

"Since you wouldn't stay inside the car, we need to disguise your scent in case they recognize it. Muddle it up. With their all-blood diet, a Darkblood's sense of smell isn't all that acute, but I don't want to take chances." He sifted through the rack by the door, the wire hangers clicking together with purpose, as if he was on the hunt for something in particular.

"But we don't have time for—" She eyed the long fake fur vest he held up in front of her. "That's hideous. With all the bare spots, it looks like it's got mange. Who knows where it's been?"

"That's the point."

He took it to the counter where he grabbed a bent straw cowboy hat.

"Turn around."

"What? Why?"

"Just do as I say."

When she didn't, he spun her around anyway and started to loosen her ponytail.

His fingers in her hair sent shock waves echoing through her system. "What the heck are you doing?"

"Just finishing the job."

Before she could stop him, he pulled out her hair band and plunked the hat on her head. He turned her to face him again, smoothing her hair behind her shoulders with what seemed to be a little more care than was necessary, an odd, unreadable expression creasing his face. She caught his eye and, in an instant, the look was gone, replaced by icy determination.

"You're going to make me wear this getup while you get to waltz in looking normal?"

"Fine." He grabbed a blond afro wig still sporting a price tag and pulled it over his head. "Happy?"

She laughed, holding her cowboy hat in place to keep it from falling off. "You can't be serious. You're going to attract attention looking that way, not deflect it."

He shrugged. "You'll see."

"Well, you look ridiculous."

"Thank you," he said as he tucked his hair inside.

He paid the shopkeeper and within minutes they were standing outside, the club a few blocks away. Its giant neon sign, a flashing arrow and caricature of a bikini-clad woman, lit up Alfonso's wig as if it were rainbow-colored.

"You'd better be right about this." She flicked the length of the vest behind her hips to have easy access to her weapons, and tucked her fingers into the front pockets of her field-ops fatigues to avoid touching the matted fur too much. "Halloween is over," she grumbled, feeling like a weird version of a cowboy with the hat and duster. Either that, or a female pimp minus the gaudy jewelry.

"Trust me. We'll fit right in."

Sure enough, a group of young human men dressed in psychedelic seventies attire piled out of a car and got in line. Three of them wore afro wigs and at least half the people waiting were in costume.

Two vampire bouncers—drug-addict skinny with so many visible piercings that they probably had hidden body parts pierced as well—flanked either side of the door. They smelled like fresh blood and Lily stiffened. Reverts, definitely, but probably not DBs. Their pores didn't exude the same stench, although it didn't make them any less dangerous. If these losers decided to frisk them, all their weapons would be discovered and the

DBs who had Kip would be alerted. Mind manips only worked on humans.

For a moment she wondered if maybe they should wait till Jackson's team got here. They could storm the place then. Kip's scent was strong, but, damn, she couldn't tell if he was on the premises or not.

Alfonso laced his fingers between hers, stroking his thumb along the side of her forefinger while they waited in line. A warm current of energy traveled up from her hand, along her arm, lodging deep in her core and making the tender skin inside her thighs tingle, despite her wishes to the contrary. Energy sharing wasn't unheard of between two vampires, but it wasn't all that common either. Her traitorous body seemed to have a mind of its own whenever he touched her.

When they got to the front of the line, the two guys took a half step back and cranked their heads up at Alfonso. He was an imposing presence, even to fellow vampires. When he touched his first two fingers to his lips, they relaxed slightly and nodded an unspoken acknowledgment. His hand moved so quickly that, if she hadn't been paying attention, she'd have missed that he slipped a bill to the closest guy. The bouncer stepped aside, the chain in his nose swinging against his upper lip, and she found herself wondering if it got in the way when he fed from a human host. Probably, she decided.

"Okay, follow my lead," Alfonso whispered as they entered the club, his breath hot in her ear, the synthetic strands of his wig tickling her cheek. "We're just part of the crowd here. You concentrate on tracking the scent and let me know when you detect something. Come on, let's get drinks and we'll canvass the place."

Although it was early by party-going standards, the place writhed with activity. Mainly humans, Lily noted, but a few vampires were scattered throughout the crowd, probably trolling for someone who suited their tastes. Techno-noise, called music by some, blared out from all corners of the black-ceilinged room, while flashes of seizure-inducing lights made everyone's movements robotic. It'd be a miracle if she didn't vomit tonight.

Given the tracking problems she'd been having, how would she ever be able to detect Kip with all these different stimuli? She held on to Alfonso's hand, inhaling deeply, and his thumb continued to absently stroke hers. Unimportant details began to fade into the background, his touch, his energy somehow helping her focus and center herself amidst the chaos and stress.

The muddy, dusty smell which had been so familiar began to dissipate, as if the veil covering her abilities was lifting. She was finally starting to get a read on the scents. Cigarettes, stale sweat, and blood. Lots of it. Maybe all she'd needed was a little energy boost.

"What can I get you?" Alfonso asked her, the curls of his crazy wig sticking out everywhere.

She tried not to smile. Under any other circumstances, she'd be laughing her ass off. But tonight, not so much.

"Your usual? Hefeweizen with a straw?"

"Just ice water." She tapped her nose. "Gotta keep things clear."

As he sipped on his microbeer, she readjusted her cowboy hat and crunched on a piece of ice. Did he know he still hadn't let go of her hand? Probably not. Because it felt so natural, she'd just noticed it herself.

On the center of the stage, a dancer wrapped her leg around the pole and arched her body backward just as a drunk human sat down on the barstool next to Lily. She scooted away from him but as she did, he tried to catch a glimpse down her shirt. His buddy took the opportunity to push him. The guy would've planted his nose in her cleavage if Alfonso's hand hadn't shot out and clamped around his neck.

"Get the fuck away from her."

"Buzz off. It's a free country." The smell of stale alcohol and fresh weed lingered on the guy's breath.

"Not when it comes to acting like an asshole."

"I don't see her complainin'."

"Well, I am, so get lost."

When his buddy got a good look at Alfonso, his eyeballs bulged and he staggered backward. Although he couldn't know what Alfonso was capable of, humans instinctively sensed danger when they saw it wrapped in such a menacing package.

The drunk started to say something else, but before Lily knew what Alfonso was doing, he'd yanked her over onto his lap, her legs straddling his heavy thighs, and he kissed her. Hard.

"What do you think you're doing?" she said against the crush of his lips, her hands pressed against his shoulders trying to keep some semblance of distance between them. She had to remain detached and try to—

God, he tasted good. Just like he smelled. Minty, with a hint of warm leather. Like he always had. She wasn't sure why she expected him to taste different—maybe she'd hoped he would be less enticing, but he was exactly as she remembered.

"They need to know you're unavailable," he said against her lips.

"But—"

"Shut up and kiss me back." He grabbed a handful of hair at the back of her head, almost knocking off her hat which she grabbed just in time.

She was about to protest again when he pushed his tongue inside, making heat pool deliciously low in her belly.

She was virtually immobilized, pinned against his body as his other hand slid possessively up her thigh. A snap of energy sizzled her nerve endings, weakening her resolve, and she almost moaned before her brain thankfully kicked into gear.

Okay. I can do this. It's just an assignment.

They were playing a role, complete with costumes.

But his scent, his touch, his taste intoxicated her senses and numbed her reluctance until she found herself wrapping her arms around his neck. In response, he gripped her hips and pulled her bottom closer. As she slid across his thick, powerful thighs, the seam of her pants rubbed into her now highly sensitive core.

Oh dear Lord, help me.

No. She couldn't do this, feel him like this as if their past had never happened, and keep her heart out of it. Maybe he could—but she couldn't.

She pushed against his shoulders, but it was like bench-pressing a house.

Without loosening his hold, he broke the kiss and for a moment, she thought he was going to pull her hair back, expose her neck and slide his lips to her throat.

But he didn't.

He kissed her again quickly then dropped his hands.

Keeping her eyes averted so that he wouldn't see her dilated pupils, an obvious sign she was still so damned physically attracted to him, she climbed awkwardly off his lap.

She was pissed. If only her body would listen to her mind and acknowledge that it was just madness to succumb to him again.

"What the hell was that for?" she asked, settling onto her barstool again.

"The guy left, didn't he?" Alfonso took a long drink from his beer, probably to wipe the taste of her from his lips.

"Gimme a break. He was on his way out of here the moment you let go of his neck." Was this just a game to him now, was that it? "I'll take a Hefeweizen after all," she called to the bartender. "Two lemons. One straw."

Alfonso chuckled and draped his arm over her shoulder, like it was a habit or something. Her heart continued to race, her body's intuitive reaction to this powerful, possessive male.

She took a few quick drinks and soon acclimated herself to the wide variety of smells in the club, in spite of the added distraction. The muddy odor wasn't quite as prominent now and she filtered out each scent, eliminating them one by one. Several couples heading to the dance floor brushed past them, the waft of air from their passing tickled at her nose. She inhaled again and—

Kip!

She jerked her head in the direction from which the group had come, searching the crowds. "He's here. Somewhere." Not seeing Kip, she took another deep breath. "Or at least he was recently. I can't quite tell. I think it's coming from back there."

"I knew you could do it, babe." Alfonso squeezed her shoulder and helped her off the barstool.

Leaving their drinks at the bar, they threaded their way through the crowd and stopped at the opening of a long, dimly lit hallway. There weren't many people hanging out here; the bathrooms must be on the other side of the place.

"Doing okay?" he asked, dipping his head around her hat brim to whisper in her ear.

She nodded. With Alfonso's arm positioned tightly around her waist, forcing her shoulder into his chest, it was easier to just put her arm around him as well. He cast a quick glance behind them, then ushered her past the velvet rope and into the hallway beyond.

In the first door well, a human female dressed as a cat—complete with ears, spike heels and a long wire-wrapped tail—knelt in front of a young vampire male. Her face was buried in his crotch, her tail bobbing up and down with every movement of her head. The guy couldn't have been more than a few years past his Time of Change, when a vampire's cravings got stronger and the aversion to sunlight set in. No longer was a diet of food sufficient—human blood and energy were also needed.

The youthling flashed them a fanged smile, shaking the ice in his glass in a wordless greeting.

Alfonso led her quickly past the happy couple.

She approached the next door and sniffed. Shaking her head, they continued.

A Do Not Disturb placard hung redundantly on the next door marked private. The pungent scent of blood—human blood—emanated from inside. And it wasn't just a drop or two. From what she could tell, it was a killing amount. Either that, or someone had just developed a serious case of anemia. She cursed herself for not being able to discern the difference.

She started to whisper to Alfonso when voices boomed out from the other side of the door. The handle twisted and the sign dangled back and forth.

In a flash, her back slammed against the opposite wall and Alfonso covered her body with his. She gasped, and his lips came down over hers, capturing the sound in his mouth.

For a split second, she was completely shocked again, all her senses overpowered by him. But then she realized it was all for show, just like at the bar. They didn't belong in this section of the club and Alfonso was just playing a part.

And so could she.

Her hands slid down over his tight ass and she brought her leg up to graze his hip. He grabbed her knee, hitched it higher. When he kissed her hard, her body responded as if this were for real and heat trickled between her legs. If they had been naked, with her open to him like this, all he'd need to do was lift her a little higher and she could have settled herself down over him, her body eagerly taking in every inch of his thick girth.

They'd done it this way many times before. Never knowing how much time they'd have together whenever they met, they'd become experts at quickies. It was just an act now, but God, how she'd missed this.

The door opened behind them, and the heavy stench of blood permeated the hallway. Not sweetblood, but it was one of the rarer blood types that would command a fairly high street price.

"Hey, you can't be down here," a male voice said. "This area is strictly off-limits to club-goers."

Alfonso was kissing her throat now and his hand slid up her shirt. Every nerve ending tingled with delight as his thumb brushed over her lace-covered nipple.

"So sue me," Alfonso told the guy without moving his lips from her neck. The tip of his fangs grazed the skin over her artery and she recalled the last time he'd taken her blood. He'd surprised her in the early-morning hours at the martial arts studio where she occasionally taught a class. They'd had sex against the wall during a water break while her students were right around the corner. That had been well over a year ago, but it seemed like only yesterday because everything about him was still so achingly familiar to her.

"I don't think you heard me. I said you can't—"

Alfonso turned his head away from her, but not before she saw his black pupils had completely overtaken his irises. Anger was hard to hide among their kind. She knew her pupils had expanded as well, but in her case, it was due to sexual desire.

"Oh, hey. I didn't recognize you." It was the multi-pierced bouncer from outside. "Half the guys tonight are wearing wigs. We got a couple of rooms if you want, but unfortunately you can't stay here."

How much had Alfonso tipped him? she wondered. His large hand was still at her breast, his thumb absently caressing her nipple, making it hard for her to concentrate on much else, the aching need between her legs almost painful now.

"Where are they?"

"Got one out front—more like a little alcove—or you can see if one of the viewing rooms is available. They're usually not all taken until later in the evening, but I could be wrong. I haven't been out front in a while to see if they're all full or not."

"Viewing rooms?"

"Yeah, they're up the stairs and around the corner." The guy nodded his head toward the dark end of the hall-way, and that chain swung from his nose like a pendulum.

Kip's scent was strongest down there. "What's a viewing room?" Lily asked, her curiosity piqued.

"Didn't you see them when you were out on the floor?" He pointed a thumb behind him. "This must be your first time here, right?"

She nodded.

"Depending on your luck," he continued, "when you're using one of the rooms, the curtain may open and people on the dance floor can look up and watch you. It's like the ultimate rush, if you know what I mean. Well, other than a hit of Sweet." He threw his head back and laughed, light catching on the stud in his tongue.

"Is the curtain on a timer or something?" Alfonso's brow pinched together as he was obviously considering the parameters of their track-and-grab mission.

"No, the DJ monitors the video feed from the rooms. If something looks good, she hits the button and the curtains open for our patrons' viewing pleasure."

The fur vest was suddenly conducting her body heat like a furnace. She started to reach for her hat to fan her face, but Alfonso gave her a slight shake of his head. Oh yeah, she didn't want to advertise her own scent. Who knew if Kip's kidnappers were here and if they'd really been after her or not.

"Don't worry. Once the act is completed, we give you back your privacy. The curtains close and you can get dressed or whatever. Just knock on that door at the end of the hallway and tell Robert that Mo-Cash sent you. That's me."

Lily pulled away from Alfonso and the reluctance in his face was as clear as if he'd verbalized it. This might be their only chance to figure out where Kip was unless they waited for Jackson to arrive.

She pleaded to him with her eyes. It wasn't as if they were reviving their relationship, but surely he could pretend in order to get past this loser. She had no intention of actually doing anything in one of those rooms; she just wanted to use it as a pretense to get access to that part of the club.

"Wanna, baby? It might be fun." Without thinking, she sidled up to him and was shocked when her hip grazed his erection. Holy crap, he was brick-hard. What happened to this being just for show?

She could've sworn she heard a low growl in his throat before he dropped his hand from her breast.

"The guy's name is Robert?" Alfonso asked.

"Yup. Second door on the right."

JESUS, HE HAD A BAD FEELING about this.

Alfonso slid his hand around Lily, pulling her close as they stood before a man sitting in a metal folding chair.

"...the rules," the guy named Robert was saying. He ran a finger down a paper on his clipboard before he looked up at Alfonso with a bored expression. "If I assign you a room, you better be usin' it. No drugs, no blood hits and no sitting around talking, if you know what I mean. You're up there for a reason, and that reason is our patrons' entertainment. If and when that curtain opens, there'd better be some action going on." Stifling a yawn, he checked his list again. "Oh, and absolutely no jacking off. None of the males here want to see your johnson unless you're using it on her. Got it?"

The asshole addressed none of these comments to Lily. It was as if she were just eye candy to him. An empty vessel. Alfonso ground his teeth together. He should just drop it, but an attitude like that just pissed him off. "So, no rules for her?"

The guy flashed him a pathetically confused look. "What the hell are you talking about?"

Alfonso didn't know what was worse: an idiot who had no idea he was condescending or a sexist fucker who didn't give a shit.

"She heard what I said, didn't you, darling? All I care about is that she spreads her legs. You can do that, can't you?"

Fucker. Alfonso flexed his fist. Guys like him had more brain matter in their dicks than between their ears, and he seriously wanted to do some rearranging. But before he could lunge forward, Lily's hand tightened around his biceps and she made a low shushing noise to calm him down. *It's okay, love,* he imagined her saying, and his body relaxed just a touch.

"Do you want a room or not?" If Robert's attitude wasn't enough to thoroughly piss him off, his nasally voice was.

"Yes, we do," Lily said quickly. Her eyes told him to chill out. They needed to find Kip, and this loser was not important in the whole scheme of things.

She threaded her fingers through his hair, pulling his head down. When he saw how her lips parted just before she kissed him, his cock swelled impossibly harder beneath his jeans. "All I care about is you," she mumbled against his mouth.

Oh God, if he wasn't careful, he would totally get used to being with her again. Everything about her was perfect, and still so permanently etched into his psyche. When his hands had slid over her curves, they'd done so automatically. When he'd dipped his head to kiss her, first at the bar and then in the hallway, she'd lifted her chin to him, tilted her head just so, in order for him to easily fit his mouth over hers. Like practiced lovers used to the nuances of each other's bodies. But he had to remember that she couldn't be a part of his world, just as he couldn't be a part of hers.

"No biting either," the guy said. "Keep your fangs to yourself and save it for later. Most of 'em watching are humans and now's not the time or place for a horror show. You're in room number four. At the top of the stairs, take a left."

Alfonso guided Lily up the narrow passageway. Okay, they could do this. Although he couldn't get a lock on Kip, Lily was fairly certain he was up here. They'd rescue him, then get the hell out of here. Being around her was hard enough, but being in a sex club with her was sheer torture. He wouldn't be able to stand much more of this before he did something both of them would regret later.

"Wait," the guy said behind them, and Alfonso hesitated, every muscle on high alert. He slid a hand into an interior pocket, where his fingers touched the handle of one of his kunai. He cast his best nonchalant look over his shoulder.

Robert's lascivious gaze lingered on Lily. Even wearing that ugly fake-fur vest and ridiculous hat, she was hot. It shouldn't surprise him, because she often had that giddy effect on men—humans and vampires alike—but Alfonso gritted his teeth and wanted to wipe the grin off the dude's face with a blow to the head.

"Make it good," the fucktard said. "I'll be watching."

"I…I CAN'T TELL IF KIP'S still up here or not." Lily struggled to keep the quaver out of her voice as they made their way around the corner at the top of the stairs.

Oh for godsake. What a blubbering fool she was. She

needed to snap out of this asinine display of weakness and fake her way through until she came up with a scrap of something. Clenching her fists, she dug her nails into her palms, and hoped the pain would help her narrow her focus.

"He was definitely here at some point. All the scent markers are present."

Alfonso was looking at her way too intently. "But…"

Damn. He knew something wasn't right.

"But I can't get a lock on him. At this moment. But I will."

Wordlessly, Alfonso slipped a hand under her hair and cupped the back of her neck. She leaned into him as she had near the freeway, her eyelids flickering involuntarily as warm, soothing energy filtered through her skin. With just his touch, he'd always had an uncanny ability to dissipate her tension, infuse her with confidence, making her feel as if she could accomplish anything. Her shoulder blades relaxed from their pinched position.

"I don't know what's wrong with me. Normally, this should be a piece of cake, especially in an enclosed space. But now—" Admitting her failings to herself was one thing, but saying it aloud to someone who'd once had a lot of respect for her abilities was even worse.

Then her concern for Kip trumped her ego, wore down the tight restraint on her control. She couldn't go on like this, pretending, when Kip's life was at stake.

Alfonso brought his face close to hers until his forehead rested against the brim of her hat. In this light, his eyes were a soft, pale gray. Strong, concerned and at the same time strangely empowering. As he breathed out, she breathed him in and imagined she was gaining his strength.

"You can do it, babe. We'll be methodical, just like we were earlier, okay? We'll go room by room. Open up every closet, cubbyhole and storage area, if we have to."

God, he had such confidence in her and her ability. It made her stand a little taller.

And then he kissed her.

Not long and slow, as she would've wanted had they been anywhere else and the circumstances different, but quick, as if to emphasize his point, and she managed a weak smile. Although Alfonso's unwavering faith in her ability did boost her spirits somewhat, she still had plenty of doubt. A problem like hers wasn't fixed overnight, if it ever was.

"We don't have much time. They're going to expect us to be in that viewing room in the next few minutes."

Alfonso glanced at the TAG Heuer he wore on the inside of his wrist. "We'll either locate him now, or, if we need more time, we'll comply with their rules and then find him."

Comply with their rules? What a clinical way to describe having sex. But then again, he always was practical, never forgetting the purpose of a mission.

"There's no time for that," she said. "We need to find him now."

"Believe me. If it comes down to it, I'll be quick." She could've sworn she saw the crease of his dimple as he turned away from her.

Rooms one through three were occupied. A quick check at the doors revealed the thick scent of sexual activity behind each one, along with the noises to prove it. She continued past room four, stopping at the last door in this part of the club. Kip's scent was strongest there.

"Is this it?" Alfonso reached for his weapons. "Is he inside?"

"Um, not quite sure," Lily whispered. "He was at one time."

With his weapons drawn, Alfonso tried the handle. The fact that it wasn't locked could only mean one thing. Kip definitely wasn't here. Disappointment carved a hollow pit in her stomach as they slipped inside.

Crap was piled everywhere, making the window-less room seem smaller than it was, almost a closet or a cage. Stacks of plastic lawn chairs stood next to pallets of glasses. Half-empty liquor boxes were piled next to a rack of costumes. Alfonso headed toward a desk in the far corner scattered with papers, ledgers and magazines. Lily slid her hand over the back of a folding metal chair in the center of the room and squatted down next to it. A roll of duct tape sat on the seat. She leaned close and inhaled. Finally—finally—the muddiness had cleared enough for her to detect Kip's strong scent. A rush of relief buoyed her spirits.

"He was definitely in here. The scent is strongest in this part of the room—" she grabbed the tape and brought it to her nose "—and especially on this."

"That's where they restrained him."

"With what? The duct tape? The guy may be new to the Tracker program, but he's no ten-pound weakling."

"Normally, you'd be right. But if he was tired and

weak, a few meters of tape would be enough to keep him strapped in one place."

"But he shouldn't be weak. He and I fed from a couple of humans just a few nights ago and last night, I saw him take energy from at least three different individuals."

"This chair is from that house."

She hadn't really noticed. It looked like a flimsy metal folding chair to her. What did that have to do with anything? "I don't follow you."

"I'm guessing they duct-taped him to this chair and exposed him to sunlight all day back at that house, as well as touching or cutting his skin with silver." Lily cringed and he continued. "They weakened him at that secluded location, away from the temptations of blood, then they brought him here."

He did have a point. Even with fresh blood and energies, a day exposed to ultraviolet light would make even the strongest vampire as weak as a human.

"But for what purpose? Why not take him back to one of their dens?"

"This was probably the drop point. Where they handed him over to the sector mistress."

Lily almost choked as she tried to quell her rising panic. "When they find out he's just a trainee, they'll kill him."

"I doubt they'll figure that out for a while. From what Jackson tells me, Kip is very capable. Even if they discover he's not a fully certified Tracker, they might still find him useful."

"Why do you think it could take a while? Aren't they desperate?"

"Kip went through standard Guardian training before being accepted into Tracker Academy, didn't he?"

She nodded.

"Then he's been taught to resist the enemy. Breaking an Agent takes time, Lily. Usually more than just one day in the sun. They wear you down and eventually, you'll be so weakened, they'll get you to go against everything you believe in."

She clamped a hand over her mouth and spoke through her fingers. "Are you talking…?"

"Unfortunately, yes. They'll torture him, until he's too tired to continue resisting, then they'll either ply him with Sweet from a vial or—" He turned away from her.

"Or what?" She had to hear him say it.

He didn't answer right away, just sifted through the papers on the desk before he finally spoke again. "Or bring him a live donor. A live sweetblood donor. In that weakened, worn-down condition, a sweetblood is impossible to resist."

Without thinking, she silently approached him and slipped her arms around his waist. Although he didn't move away from her, his arms stayed stiffly at his sides.

"That's what they did to you, isn't it?"

"Yes." His voice was piano-string tight. "And I killed her."

His pain hacked through her heart like a jagged-edged knife. "You can't blame yourself, Alfonso. You'd have never done such a thing if you'd been stronger."

"The suffering she—"

"I'm sure it was quick. That it was over before she knew what was happening."

He stiffened and tried to push away, but she held on tight. His chest expanded as he took a breath, then he blew it out slowly.

"No, you're wrong. She knew exactly what was coming and what I was capable of doing. They drank from her first, sparing none of the gory details of feeding, not bothering to blur her memory. She was terrified, of course, but even more so when she saw my face. Even as I drained her, I knew I was killing her. Felt her life energy slipping away. But I couldn't stop, no matter how much I told myself I had to. The dark nature of our kind had a powerful hold over me and I was powerless to resist the call of her blood."

Lily couldn't trust herself to speak. Her heart felt like it would shatter into a billion pieces if she uttered so much as one word.

The pull of a sweetblood was strong—she knew that firsthand, having dated one for a while herself. She'd taken his blood once, but because she hadn't wanted to risk the temptation to take too much, she'd never tried it again and had broken up with him soon afterward. Most of the time vampires were able to resist the blood's potent allure, as diabetics avoided candy, but mistakes were made, especially when a vampire's willpower was at its lowest point. As Alfonso's had been.

He loosened himself from her grasp and walked to the far side of the room. Not wanting to force herself on him, she stayed put, and gave him his space.

Taking a deep breath, she opened her mouth to speak, to tell him that it wasn't his fault, that she didn't think he was awful or a monster, but the fog in her head cleared even more, and her scent memory of Kip reactivated.

"Alfonso, I got it," she said as she mentally cataloged what she detected. "The scent here is slightly stale. Several hours old. I can track it now—I've got a lock."

"Then let's get out of here."

In a flash, they were back in the hallway, the air thick with the smell of many vices, sexual activity the most potent one. She hesitated outside room four. A male in a neighboring room grunted out what was obviously an orgasm. Almost instantly, a muted sound of applause filtered up the stairway.

Alfonso cursed under his breath.

Room four might be next. "Wait. They'll know something's wrong if we never go in there."

A strange expression crossed Alfonso's face, then was gone. "What does it matter now? We got what we came for. This little charade of ours is over."

"We can't afford to arouse any suspicions, otherwise they could alert Kip's captors that we're onto them. They can't know that two Guardians have been here. So far, they think they've got the only Agency Tracker in the Seattle field area and that's probably what's keeping him alive. Come on. They're probably getting ready to open the curtains now, or at least they're checking in on us to see if what we're doing is worth watching."

His brow furrowed at that last comment and when he spoke, his tone was hard and callous. "I'm not going into that room, Lily, and having sex with you. It's not happening. Period."

Her skin prickled instantly beneath that stupid vest,

eroding any lingering sympathetic feelings she had for him. At first, he'd talked as if sex with her would be clinical, just part of the job. But if that weren't bad enough, now he spoke as if the thought wasn't even mildly interesting.

Of course, they had no time for sex or even a little foreplay, but she thought they'd shared an emotional connection back there. She flexed her hands, longing to punch something.

Chill out. Consider who you're dealing with. Why should anything he did or said surprise her after all he'd put her through? It really shouldn't.

Fine. Two could easily play this game.

"Let's get the hell out of here then," she said.

Without waiting for his reaction or to see if he followed, she took the stairs two at a time and barged out the door. Robert jumped up from his post, his clipboard and cell phone clattering to the floor.

"What the hell is going on? You two haven't been on yet. You were supposed to—"

"Ask him," Lily indicated with a thumb over her shoulder, not slowing. "Apparently he's not into the exhibitionist scene after all."

Robert looked confused as he stooped to pick up the stuff he'd dropped.

"Performance anxiety," Lily explained. "Things didn't quite work out."

She marched down the corridor and didn't look back.

CHAPTER SEVEN

THEY DROVE NORTH ON THE FREEWAY in relative silence, Lily only barely nodding when Alfonso asked if they were still heading in the right direction. A few times they stopped for her to double-check the scent trail, but it never deviated away from the interstate.

His insides churned with a thousand tiny knives when he considered how pissed off she was. He hated knowing that he'd hurt her. Teasing and irritating her was one thing, but this was different. He'd hoped she would have cooled down by now, but she'd not said two words to him since they left the club.

She stared out the windshield into the night; he doubted she was seeing anything but the twin beams of light cutting through the darkness. What was going on with her abilities anyway? He'd never seen her as unsure of herself as she'd been tonight, and it gnawed at him. He'd always admired her self-confidence. She had a strong sense of who she was and what she was capable of. Normally, a task like this should've been a piece of cake for her. They would've headed straight along the scent trail, having plenty of time to locate the particular Darkblood den where her trainee had been taken. But instead, he'd driven the speed limit and pulled over a few times for her to reestablish scent contact, putting them way behind.

He recalled the first time she'd wowed him with her scent-tracking skills. They'd been together down in San Diego when Lily had received the call that Darkbloods had kidnapped a sweetblood child and taken the girl into the desert. None of the other field agents could pick up the scent and time was running out. Lily's tracking ability was so acute, so finely tuned, that they'd driven straight to the hideout without needing directions or a map. If she hadn't been working out of the San Diego office on a temporary assignment, the field team wouldn't have been able to locate the child in time. Alfonso had disposed of the Darkbloods, while Lily whisked the sobbing child from their filthy den.

Alfonso would never forget the drive back to the girl's home. It had changed him profoundly. Through the rearview mirror, he watched as Lily held the child, gently rocking her, stroking her hair, whispering reassuring words into her ear, until eventually the girl's whimpering cries faded and she fell asleep in Lily's arms.

Their gazes had met through the mirror. Her tear-stained lashes had made her eyes even bigger. God, she was beautiful. She'd smiled at him and mouthed the words *thank you*.

It was then that he realized that even the toughest, most capable people could be tender and emotional inside without compromising anything. For the first time, he had wondered if he could be like that too.

He rubbed a hand over the back of his neck, still itchy

from the wig. He felt like shit. He'd been too abrupt with her. She had a soft place in her heart for those who couldn't defend themselves and she wasn't afraid to do whatever it took to help them. That was all she'd been doing tonight. As much as he would've loved to fool around with her, he just couldn't risk it.

"That comment back at the club was brilliant, by the way," he said, trying to break the tension.

"The one about performance anxiety?"

"Yes. It was a clever and creative way to get out of that situation without arousing their suspicion. Bravo."

She swore under her breath and took an unnecessarily long time to smooth her hair back into a ponytail again. When she used her teeth to open the hair elastic, he could've sworn he saw a flash of fang. "I figured you'd be pissed off," she said.

"If I had problems in that area, then maybe. But I found it amusing. You should've seen the look on his face as you strode down that hall. No one would ever question something like that." He glanced over at her slightly pouty expression, surprised to find she didn't seem impressed by his compliment. "What? Does that disappoint you?"

"Hell, yeah. I didn't do it to humor you."

For a moment, he imagined what it would've been like if he had gone into that room with her. Made love to her again after all this time. He ached to lose himself inside her and forget about the problems in the outside world. To pretend that they were just two ordinary people enjoying the pleasure of each other's bodies. To feel her inner muscles constricting around him as she pulled him closer, encasing the most intimate, vulnerable part of who he was in her welcoming warmth. To smell the intoxicating scent of her skin.

His erection strained against the crotch of his jeans. He shifted position, the leather of the seat squeaking as he tried to casually alleviate the discomfort, but it didn't work.

He glanced sideways at Lily. She'd turned slightly in his direction, no doubt sensing his restlessness. If only she weren't so observant, he'd tug on his jeans to loosen them. But he couldn't. She noticed every damn little thing. Nothing got past her. Better for him to weather the discomfort and have her think this whole thing was just an unemotional assignment to him than for her to know the truth about his feelings for her.

He could control himself with other women, but rarely with Lily. She seemed to bring out the most primitive, uncontrollable part of him, leaving little doubt that if they had sex, he'd take her blood. And if he did, her scent would be combined with his for who knew how long. He would have no idea when the effect would wear off. Which meant that if his assassin got close and picked up the change in Alfonso's scent, he'd know there was a woman, and Lily would be vulnerable to him.

Plus, the thought of being intimate in a strip club was almost nauseating. While a quickie with her was definitely appealing, it wouldn't have felt right in a place like that. She deserved to be cherished, worshipped, rather than screwed in a dive for other people's entertainment.

Not to mention that he'd want to savor every glorious moment without any distractions.

LILY KNELT AT THE SIDE of the road trying unsuccessfully to get a lock on Kip's scent. His captors must've transported him in a tightly closed vehicle. Although that normally wouldn't have made a difference—she'd tracked targets under more difficult circumstances before—it severely hindered her efforts tonight.

She walked to the edge of the pavement and onto the shoulder, fairly certain Kip was still traveling north on the interstate—otherwise she'd have noticed a stronger scent marker where they'd turned off. Because she and Alfonso had stopped to check virtually every exit, their forward progress slowed to a crawl. But she couldn't risk missing the scent leaving the freeway. Backtracking took too much time and that, she thought, noting the light gray sky to the east, was one thing they didn't have.

Leather squeaked behind her and gravel crunched under a boot. She half expected to hear a heavy, impatient sigh. Alfonso had been leaning against the hood of the Panamera, waiting for her, but he was getting restless. She didn't blame him. The sun was about to crest the mountains and they'd been at this since they'd left the club hours ago.

"We can't stay out here much longer," he said. "The energy drain will be too great. I feel it already."

"Did you bring a Daysuit?" With a hand on the stop sign, she looked down the lonely country road. She was almost positive Kip hadn't been taken in that direction, but her stomach soured because she didn't know for sure.

Okay, they'd simply get back on the freeway and continue north. "Why don't you change while we're stopped?"

"I didn't bring one."

"Then stay in the car next time. It's got UV coating on the windows."

His caustic laugh made her cringe. What now? "This isn't a Daytran-equipped vehicle. And you shouldn't be out here, either."

"Unlike you, I came prepared. I'll change into my Daysuit in a sec."

"No. We're calling it a night. Get in."

She snapped her head around and glared at him. He thought they should stop looking for Kip? That her trainee should have to suffer longer in the hands of their enemies? Anger, outrage and a heavy dose of self-doubt twisted the sourness in her gut. Something was definitely wrong, yes, but there was no way she was quitting on Kip. Giving up. All she needed was a little more time. "You don't think I have the ability to find him, is that it?"

"The scent is gone."

"No, it isn't. I'll pick it up. It's out there." She knew it was—she could almost taste it.

"I don't know what's going on with you, Lily, but staying out in the daytime isn't going to help matters. In fact, it's the last thing you need. Let's go."

"What kind of an executive decision is that? This isn't your mission—it's mine. Who knows what they'll do to Kip if they have him another day? We've got to keep going."

With a determined set to his jaw, he marched over to the passenger side and opened the door for her. "And with the energy drain from the coming sun, if we found them, we'd be completely worthless in a fight. Darkbloods would have themselves a much better Tracker—you— and they'd have no more use for your Agent-in-training. Your guy would be dead. You're letting your emotions drive your decisions, rather than logic."

Her emotions? She balled her hands into fists and felt her nostrils flaring. "Kip isn't just some anonymous person, Alfonso. He and his family put their faith and trust in me and no matter what it takes, I don't intend to let them down. You of all people should know what Darkbloods are capable of doing when you're vulnerable. I need to find him now, not wait till it's convenient. By then, it could be too late. When I pinpoint his location, we can assess our energy levels and decide what to do."

His expression softened. "I know you're worried about him, Lil, but you're clearly having troubles. Being out in the sunlight—Daysuit or not—would be detrimental. It'll strip you of any ability you have left. Ideally, you need human energy, maybe even blood, but at the very least, you need to nix the UV rays. We'll continue when the sun dies tonight, after you've had a chance to rest."

She started to protest again—he had no business ordering her to do anything—but the genuine concern in his eyes caused the words to evaporate in her throat. A Daysuit wasn't designed to protect against long-term exposure. As much as she'd like to deny it and prove him wrong, she did feel the tug of the sun on her energies, and that damn muddy smell wouldn't go away.

"It's a waste of time to argue with me, Lily. I've made my decision."

"You know, when you order me around like that, it makes me want to do the opposite just to spite you."

His I-told-you-so smile and that dimple made her cheeks heat. Man, she wanted to punch something right now.

On this little knoll above the freeway, she could see the miles of pavement stretching out in front of them. The sight made her even more exhausted than she already was. Tracking was hard work. Each of her senses had been on high alert for hours.

Okay. Alfonso was probably right, but she'd never admit that to him and feed his ego. He already thought he knew what was best. No need to encourage him. "And where do you think we're going?"

"To a safe house nearby. I've called ahead. They're expecting us."

THE WOMAN REACHED across the large oak desk that was scattered with papers and handed Alfonso the room key. "Go back out the main door, take a left, and the unit is straight ahead at the end of the brick path. If you need anything, just dial zero on your phone. I'm Niva."

Unit? As in one single room? "What kind of a place is this? When I called, I said I needed two rooms."

"You did?" Niva bit her lip and examined a few of the many sticky notes on her desk. "I must've misunderstood. I'm so sorry, but it's the only one I have available."

Staying in the same room wasn't an option. He didn't want to sleep anywhere near Lily. Well, he did, which was exactly why he couldn't.

He was half tempted to walk out and find a more accommodating place, even though the next closest safe house was thirty minutes away. Hell, if he did that, he might as well take Lily to his own house. It wasn't much farther. But the thought of her sleeping underneath the roof he'd built was way too intimate.

A confused look crossed Niva's face as she stared first at Lily then at Alfonso.

Clearly, she had assumed they were a couple. Or at least friends with benefits.

If only things could be that simple.

"We…ah…work together," Lily said. "Nothing more."

"The room does have a pullout couch," Niva offered hopefully.

With heavy steps, he paced to the shuttered window and wished he'd brought his guitar. It'd be sheer torture sleeping in the same room, even if they were in separate beds, and it would have given him something to do. Jamming his hand into a pocket, he rubbed his thumb over the rope grip of a kunai until his skin burned.

Lily turned away and tried to hide a yawn.

Ah, Christ, she needed to sleep now, not an hour from now. And she needed to get out of the early-morning sun.

This place would have to do. He'd camp out in her car if he had to, cover himself with the Agency-issued space blanket that resided neatly in her Agency-issued emergency pack. Or play Hollow Grave all day with the headphones on to distract himself.

"Fine," he growled through clenched teeth.

Niva brightened, unaffected by his lingering bad attitude. "The refrigerator is stocked with a few vials of blood if you need any. Also, there's a frozen pizza in the freezer and extra sheets in the closet. The shutters are on a timer and will open again at sundown, which is—" she consulted a chart on the desk "—at 4:28 p.m. I'll make the Hide-A-Bed up for you, if you'd like."

"No, we can manage," Alfonso said, eager to just get on with it. No use dragging things out. "The sun's coming up. You don't need to go out."

She gave him a grateful smile. The weariness in her eyes made him wonder if she worked this place alone.

"You two Guardians? Reason I ask is that most people who call a safe house for last-minute accommodations are Agents who are too far from the field office to make it back before sunrise." At Alfonso's curt nod, she continued, "Chuck Cartwright still the Region Commander?"

Lily shook her head. "He retired. You know Chuck?"

"My husband was a Guardian a long time ago, until he was injured and couldn't work any longer. That's when we bought this place, although he passed on a few years back. He used to report to Chuck."

"I'm sorry, ma'am," Alfonso said, his hand on the doorknob. So she probably did run things on her own. He felt a little guilty for being such an ass.

"It's okay. Dutch was in so much pain at the end that it was for the best. Darkbloods had gotten their hands on that highly potent Mexican-mined silver and made a few weapons before Dutch's team raided their facility. Skewered him with a blade that barely missed his heart. His body never did regenerate correctly and he was plagued with chronic pain for years because of it."

"Wait, this sounds familiar," Lily said. The two women continued talking while Alfonso brooded in silence. Apparently, Lily knew Niva's daughter. "Your husband didn't go to a regen clinic, did he?"

"No, unfortunately not. He was a brave man but stubborn as an ox."

Lily sighed, shaking her head. "My mother is a physician up at Region and treats regen problems all the time."

Alfonso reached down and absently rubbed his thigh, suddenly aware of the throbbing in his knee. He knew Lily's mother practiced up there. After the explosion, he hadn't been able to risk having anyone find out he'd survived, so he'd sought out treatment far away under an assumed name.

Niva twisted her wedding band. "So who's Region Commander now?"

"Tristan Santiago," Lily answered.

"Santiago?" Niva clapped her hands and laughed. "That hothead? For crying out loud, whose decision was *that,* putting him in charge?"

Alfonso bit back a smile. Santiago's temper certainly was legendary.

Amusement lit up Lily's eyes as she glanced over at him. She tried to cover a smile by sucking in her lower lip, but she wasn't very successful. The corner of her mouth turned up anyway, making her look impish and much too desirable.

"So you know Santiago?" she asked Niva.

"That's one way of putting it. My husband was his mentor. He trained him. And it was Santiago who saved his life."

"IT'S ALL YOURS." With her hair wrapped in a towel, Lily stepped out of the bathroom, a cloud of fragrant steam billowing out behind her.

He almost choked.

She wore the same kind of pajamas she had when they'd been together—well, when she chose to wear anything to bed, that is. Oftentimes, she'd climb between the sheets with nothing on, sidle in next to him, skin to skin.

Unable to drag his eyes away from her as she dug into her duffel, he noticed the flimsy tank top barely covered the creamy skin of her cleavage. The neckline would probably stretch far enough, and if it didn't, it could easily be ripped. Then her breasts would sit heavily in his hands, soft and pliable beneath his fingertips. She'd draw in shallow, ragged breaths, waiting for him to pull a nipple into his mouth. And when he did, she'd arch her back and make tiny moaning sounds as he suckled.

Stop. This was madness. He needed to—

With her back to him now, she rubbed lotion over her bare arms, her movements slow and deliberate, like she knew he was watching. Her tank top rose above her waistband, exposing several inches of her skin.

He drew in a ragged breath.

Those drawstring shorts. They would easily slip down over her hips to give him access to the dewy sweetness that had always awaited him. He could either dip a finger inside her first or rub her silky nub with his tongue, tasting her excitement. Then, with a hand on her knees, he'd spread her legs wide and—

What the hell was he thinking? He grabbed the empty pizza box and stuffed it onto the trash so hard that the small garbage can tipped over. He needed to get control of himself if he had any hope of making it through the night without touching her. Seeing her like this brought back all sorts of memories he'd be better off forgetting.

"Food's over there," he said gruffly. In three strides, he marched into the bathroom before she could notice the bulge in his pants or his fully extended fangs.

Once inside the shower, he turned on the water and wasted no time.

If only he could rip those flimsy clothes from her body and toss her onto the bed. He'd be on her in an instant, pushing himself into her warmth. Then, at that precise moment when her muscles tightened around him, he'd let himself go, climaxing along with her as he plunged his fangs into her vein. A beautiful circle of giving and taking.

His hand was a poor substitute.

When it was over, he rested his head on his forearm, closed his eyes and concentrated on the spray of water on his back. Although the pressure had been released, he felt empty and anything but sated.

LILY LAY ON HER SIDE and kept her breathing steady. Though Alfonso was on the couch near the shuttered window, it could've been the River Styx between them. When she'd thanked him for cooking the pizza, he'd said nothing. All she'd heard was the rustle of sheets and the creak of coiled springs when he stretched out onto the Hide-A-Bed.

When she'd emerged from the shower, she'd been almost certain he was going to come up behind her and slip his hands under her pajamas. Lord knew she had wanted him to. The heat from his stare had practically lit her skin on fire. Although she'd been pissed at him most of the night, it wouldn't have taken much coaxing on his part for her to allow that. She'd never been much good at resisting him.

But who could blame her? she reasoned. Not only was he the most gorgeous man she'd ever seen, with those icy-blue eyes hiding countless secrets, well-defined muscles that her hands needed to touch and golden-blond hair that tickled her nose when he kissed her, his skill in bed was unparalleled among her previous partners. It was as if he sensed what she wanted even before it became a conscious thought in her mind. He knew her body better than she did.

Goose bumps formed on her arms and she rubbed them unconsciously.

After they'd become lovers, all it had taken was a look from him or a whisper in her ear for heat to begin pooling in her belly at the knowledge of what he was going to do to her. Sometimes he'd make her wait, and other times he'd take her so hard, so fast that she could hardly catch her breath before she climaxed around him.

But he didn't come to her tonight, and it felt as if a hole had been punched through her heart. He'd rejected her again.

And she was foolish enough to want him still.

CHAPTER EIGHT

HER DRY SPELL WAS OVER.

Or at least partially so.

Kip's scent was heavy in the damp air as they crept through the forest. Finally, she'd tracked him.

Alfonso's even breathing on the other side of the room had finally lulled her to sleep that morning. Though she'd wanted him in a bad way, she hadn't held out any hope that he'd join her in bed. But his presence had been strangely calming. She couldn't remember the last time she'd slept so well.

At nightfall, they'd left Niva's place and begun their search again. Slowly and methodically she worked, just like they had the night before. And although that muddy smell was still messing with her tracking ability, it wasn't nearly as strong as it had been and she was able to pick out Kip's faint scent. Hours later, she and Alfonso had driven almost to the Canadian border when it became a little stronger. They'd turned east, and after losing it only a few times, she'd tracked it to this remote, wooded area off the North Cascades Highway.

A quick call to the Vancouver and Seattle field offices confirmed a backup unit wouldn't get here until just before dawn. She wasn't about to wait till then to make a move. Kip had been held captive by Darkbloods long enough—they'd go in alone.

With Alfonso at her back, Lily plastered herself against a huge cedar and peered around the trunk to a run-down cabin about fifty meters away. One of the support beams on the front porch leaned precariously outward, threatening to collapse part of the moss-covered roof. Another winter of heavy snowfall would do it, she thought.

"There," she whispered. "He's inside along with a few Darkbloods and—" she sniffed the air "—a sweetblood female. She's alive, barely. I just hope we arrived before they've gone too far with him."

"How many are inside?"

With her hand lightly on his arm for support, she closed her eyes and concentrated. Even through the layers of clothing, his muscles felt hard and powerful as he towered over her. "Three—no, four. I think." She breathed in a few more times and filtered the smells. "Also, there's another one outside somewhere."

"So that makes four inside and one outside. Is that correct?"

"Yep."

He squeezed her hand. "Come on. Let's move closer."

Without letting go, he whisked her toward the next clump of trees, hardly disturbing the undergrowth. Good Lord. This was crazy fast. The wind whipped through her hair and whistled in her ears. She'd thought that she was adept at melting into the night, moving like their kind had done for centuries. Joined like this, they shadow-moved as one cohesive entity.

What a friggin' rush!

When they stopped, she stifled the idiotic urge to laugh. Her hand tingled in his while her heart pounded madly in her chest. It took a moment to collect herself again.

"Over there." Alfonso nodded his head.

Lily caught a movement on the opposite side of the clearing at the precise moment she heard a shovel striking the earth.

Then she smelled it.

Fresh dirt and a fresh kill. A sweetblood.

They were too late for someone.

"Did they make Kip do that?" Her voice was scratchy, the words difficult to verbalize. "The body— I can— It's been drained."

His fingers tightened reassuringly around hers, his thumb stroking the tender skin on the back of her hand. "Maybe, maybe not. They want to turn him, but they also want something to sell. Like a spider, they'll suck out every last drop from their victims before casting them aside."

She shivered at the thought.

He continued. "It could've been Kip, but then again, it could just as easily have been one of them."

An arctic breeze whispered through the fir boughs, churning the waxy leaves of salal into a frenzied dance around them. She froze. If the wind changed direction now, the Darkblood might detect their presence. Then their plans of a stealthy attack would be thwarted. Outnumbered as they were, that wouldn't be good.

Alfonso pulled her close, fitting the contours of her body to his. "Shhhh." His voice so low, it was as if it came from inside her head. "Wait till the night air settles again."

Not needing any more convincing than that, she relaxed against him. The smell of warm leather invaded her nose, and the powerful beat of his heart thundered in her ear. In the darkness, she'd always felt a part of him. With her cheek pressed to the thin fabric of his shirt, she felt the cord of his medallion.

That's right. Why is he still wearing that thing?

When she'd bought it for him years ago, she wasn't sure he'd even wear it because he wasn't a man-jewelry kind of guy. Whatever the reason, she liked that something she'd given him rested against the bare skin over his heart.

The wind gust quieted just as the Darkblood finished tamping down the soil.

"Wait here," Alfonso said. "I've got this one." And before she could say anything, he was gone.

Not dropping her gaze from the Darkblood, she palmed her favorite handgun, a Glock 27 .40 caliber with a smaller, customized grip and a magazine of Agency silver-tipped rounds. Alfonso's shadow-form separated from the dark forest and slipped in behind the DB. There was a flash of silver and, before she could even comprehend what was happening, the guy staggered forward as if he'd been pushed. He collapsed to the ground just as Alfonso wiped off his blade.

Watching the body charcoal at Alfonso's feet, she was both exhilarated and slightly unnerved. In an instant, he'd gone from calm and protective to cold and lethal. Although he'd spent many years working inside the Alliance, she'd forgotten what an efficient killer he was.

When he slipped behind a car parked in the overgrown driveway and motioned for her, she holstered her gun and joined him.

"That was— You were—"

He held a finger to his lips. "Can you make out the individual locations of the DBs inside?" he whispered.

She flipped the ends of her ponytail as she glanced toward the cabin, but didn't know if she could get into that level of detail.

"I'm not sure."

He grabbed her hand and forcibly pushed some of his energy to her. It sizzled up her arm and into the center of her chest before she jerked away.

"What are you doing?" They were about to engage these assholes. He needed to conserve his own energy, not donate it to her.

"Just giving you a boost. Trying to up our advantage."

This part of the forest was devil's-mouth dark. They easily shadow-moved to the overhang of the long, narrow cabin. His thumb absently stroked hers as he pressed his ear to the moss-covered siding. She inhaled and was surprised to find the muddiness all but gone. The jumble of smells around her untangled, each one crystallizing and becoming more precise.

She squeezed his hand to get his attention and whispered, "Two at this end with Kip and two at the far end. Probably a bedroom."

"What time do you have?" he asked, glancing at his TAG Heuer.

She passed a hand over her own Agency-issued watch, which wasn't nearly as handsome. The movement made the numbers glow just enough for her to see them. "Eleven forty-one."

"Okay, at a quarter to the hour, we go in. You take this door. I'll take the rear." Then he disappeared around the end of the cabin.

Crickets and other night insects chirped in the bushes, oblivious to the horror taking place on the other side of this wall. But when a female voice cried out from inside, the cricket noise stopped, and the night felt suddenly heavier. Lily's patience waned as the minutes ticked by.

A male voice protested. "Not again."

It was Kip.

A surge of anger heated her veins. Bastards. It wasn't enough for Darkbloods to live by their own set of barbaric rules; they had to coerce an idealistic young vampire like Kip to help them carry out their plans. She vowed to see them all dead before the night was over.

The clock ticked down.

Three, two, one. Go.

Stepping in front of the shabby door, she easily kicked it in with her booted heel.

Even though she'd taken a deep breath outside, the thick smell of Sweet hung like a heavy sickness in the air of the cabin. Having led many raids on Darkblood dens, she was prepared for the scent and didn't let it affect her judgment.

However, she wasn't prepared for what she saw.

Kip was hunched over a woman on the floor, his dark head at her throat. She struggled futilely against his chest.

Two DBs flanked him, holding on to tethers at his wrists and neck, watching the display like eager spectators at a cock fight.

For a split second, she hesitated, unsure whether to pull Kip off the woman first or to go for the DBs, and in that moment of indecision, she was shocked when the two of them fell to the ground in unison.

Alfonso.

With his mouth pressed into a determined line, he leaped forward and retrieved his blades. She hadn't heard him enter the back door, nor had she seen any movement or flash of a blade. Figured. As she'd already witnessed, he was wicked fast with his knives.

She jumped to Kip's side and tried to pry him off the bare-breasted woman beneath him. But with his fangs buried in her neck, he didn't want to let go. Lily couldn't rip him away for fear it'd tear out the woman's throat.

"What the hell is going on down there?" a voice called from down the hallway. "Need any help?"

Alfonso pointed in the direction of the others. "I'll take care of them." And then he was gone.

"Kip, you've got to stop. You're killing her."

His mouth stilled. And although he stopped swallowing, he didn't pull away.

"You're stronger than this, Kip. Let go. It's me, Lily."

When he lifted his head to look at her, Lily shoved him away, sending his body flying against the far wall, separating him from the woman. Most vampires feeding from a sweetblood wouldn't have had the willpower to stop as he did. Before he came at the woman again, she quickly tied his tethers to a length of chain on the wall, vaguely aware of crashing sounds coming from the back room.

The whites of Kip's unfocused eyes were grayed out and his black pupils completely covered his irises. They must've force-fed him massive quantities of human blood to get them to change that quickly. A thin red trickle ran from the corner of his mouth, while the tips of his fangs indented his lower lip.

"Jesus H, what did they do to you?"

His jaw worked back and forth, as if he were trying to speak, and the smell of Sweet was thick on his breath. She leaned in close anyway, his voice barely a whisper.

"Keep...her...away...from me."

Lily turned to the woman and knelt beside her. She pulled the bloodied shirt back over the woman's bare shoulders, but it was so tattered that it was almost pointless. Uneven steps, one heavier than the other, echoed on the dirty pine floor.

Lily jumped up and leveled her weapon.

"It's me, Lil," Alfonso said.

Relieved, she lowered the Glock. With a thick lock of hair covering one eye, he limped into the room. "Did the other two make out better or worse than you?"

"Much, much worse." A touch of sweat gleamed on Alfonso's upper lip. "Here, let me take Kip. You deal with her."

The woman trembled violently, no doubt a combination of cold and shock from the blood loss. After licking her thumb, Lily ran it over the puncture wounds on her neck and the holes quickly healed. She scanned the paltry room and spotted a ratty blanket bunched up on the cushion of the threadbare couch.

She grabbed it, shook it out, and a large brown wolf spider fell from the folds. It skittered over the ashes of one of the Darkbloods and disappeared into the blackness under the couch. Lily flicked the blanket away. God, she hated those things. Where there was one, there were more. Darkbloods she could handle—spiders, not so much. She removed her own jacket and cocooned the woman inside.

"How's he look?" she asked Alfonso.

"He's drunk on Sweet. It's a bad high. One that will take a while to wear off."

But at least they'd found him. She'd get Kip to her mother's clinic, where he'd be put through detox. Hopefully, since not much time had passed, the addiction wouldn't have had a chance to take hold.

The sweat on Alfonso's forehead captured a piece of his hair. He pushed it out of his face and appeared to stagger slightly as he hovered over Kip.

"And you?" she asked him. "Everything okay?" He hadn't been in the back room for long. Was he having trouble being around the woman and all this blood? She got a glimpse of his face. His irises were still blue, not black with hunger, but the pain was evident. He *had* been hurt back there.

"Quite an operation they have," he said, changing the subject. "They'd been portioning the Sweet into vials. Or at least that's what they *were* doing."

That wasn't what she'd asked him. Her eyes narrowed when she noticed him putting most of his weight on one leg.

"When the rest of the crew gets here," she said, "they'll have a team comb through the cabin for any usable intel, then dismantle everything else."

"Or just burn it down. Nothing like a little fire to destroy what shouldn't be saved." The brittleness in his voice told her he wasn't only referring to this place. "Hey, get her out of here, okay? We need to keep them apart. He's likely to lose control and attack her again. From what I counted back there, she's had three units of blood taken already, and who knows how much he took from her. She won't be able to withstand much more."

Lily tried to help the woman to the door, but she was so unsteady that Lily scooped her up and carried her outside instead. She managed to dig out her cell phone and called the local Vancouver field office.

Thank God. Backup was already on the way and would be here shortly. Given Kip's present condition, they couldn't risk transporting him and the sweetblood in the same vehicle.

Cradling the injured woman as gently as she could, Lily shadow-moved through the forest toward where they'd parked the car. She opened the trunk one-handed and removed the emergency kit. The space blanket crackled as she spread it out on the dirt road and set the woman down.

Thankful for the Agency's desensitization training, which all Agents were required to go through, Lily tried not to inhale too much of the sweet-smelling bloodscent as she tended to the woman. That training, which Kip had recently completed, was probably what had prevented him from draining her dry. Not many vampires in that weakened condition would've been able to perform a Stop and Release on a sweetblood. It was too seductive. The call too powerful.

She'd see about putting a letter of commendation into his file.

A sob hiccupped from the woman's lips, her terror-filled eyes wide and unfocused. Damn. She'd thought the woman was still unconscious. Things had just gotten a little more complicated.

"Where…are they? Those men? Please…say they're gone."

Lily placed a reassuring hand on the woman's arm. "You're safe now. They can't hurt you any longer."

Twin rivulets of tears streamed down the sides of the woman's face and into her tangled brown hair. "Their eyes… I'll never forget. They made…the scared one in the chair b-b… Do terrible things." She covered her face in the crook of her elbow.

"The main thing is you're safe now. The medic team will be here any minute, and they'll take you to a medical facility. You'll be as good as new, I promise."

"I…I feel so…weak. This sounds crazy…but they were…vampires. You know—" she crooked two fingers "—with…fangs. They killed…that other girl. I…saw it. Cut her wrists…and threw her…at the one who was tied up."

So Kip had killed the other girl. Lily let out a slow sigh when she thought about the psychological damage he'd suffer. He'd be forever changed, knowing a human had died from his bite. How could she forgive herself for letting this happen to him? If only she could've killed at least one of the assholes responsible, but Alfonso had gotten them all.

Lily decided to be truthful with the human. She wouldn't remember anything after the memory wipe anyway, and it only seemed fair.

"Yeah, honey, I'm afraid they were."

The young woman balled up into a fetal position, silent except for a few sniffles. Lily noticed several dripping puncture wounds on her wrist.

Where was the medic team anyway? She'd rather leave stuff like this up to them.

Through the trees, she glimpsed Alfonso sitting on the front porch of the cabin, a fatherly arm around Kip. The display of protectiveness tugged at her heart. Maybe he was sharing some of his own experiences, recounting the horrible things DBs had forced him to do. Unfortunately, he and Kip now had a lot in common.

She turned her attention back to the woman. "What's your name?"

"Elisabeth." The woman dropped her arm from her tear-stained face. The circles under her eyes were so dark that Lily wondered when she'd last slept or ate.

"I'm Lily." She flashed her most disarming smile, hoping to calm her down before she proceeded. "I wish we could've met under better circumstances. Listen, I'd like to take a look at your wrist. See if they—"

Elisabeth examined her hands as if they were a stranger's, but Lily knew it was the blood she saw. "Oh…my God," she whispered.

Lily couldn't wait any longer. She licked her finger, reached over and quickly swiped it across the puncture wounds. The torn edges of skin began to heal upon contact, the holes getting smaller and smaller.

"What did you…do? It's tingly—" Elisabeth's eyes blazed with the realization that something strange had just happened. With surprising strength, she scrambled backward, elbows and knees pumping, until she slammed into the Panamera's back tire. "You're one of them… aren't you?"

Lily thought about lying, giving her some lame explanation for what had just happened. It certainly wouldn't be the first time she'd been less than forthcoming with a human. It'd sure be easier to deal with her in the short term, if Lily did lie. But when she glanced in Alfonso's direction again, she decided not to. Honesty, however painful, seemed the better choice today. "Yes, I am the same as them. A vampire."

The young woman clutched her wrist to her chest. "What did you…do to me? Are you going to…kill me now?"

"I stopped the bleeding. I'm a vampire, but I'm not going to hurt you. God knows you've been through enough. What those men did to you was very wrong. They won't be doing that ever again."

Elisabeth's shoulders visibly relaxed, although the wary look on her face didn't change.

Resisting the urge to taste the sweetblood on her finger, Lily ripped open an antiseptic package and cleaned off her hands. "Our saliva helps with the natural healing process, that's all. In a short time, your wounds will be gone."

Elisabeth's eyes narrowed to slits. "What...are you then? Either you are...or you're not...a vampire."

"Among my kind, there are a few who choose to live as our violent ancestors did, sustaining themselves only on human blood and energy. Unfortunately, you met several of those individuals tonight. However, most of us live peacefully, secretly among the human population, like we have for centuries."

Elisabeth's eyes widened at the thought and Lily continued, "We could be that person standing next to you during a late-night trip to the grocery store. Or that mysterious guy who moved into that house down the street. Or, in my case, the occasional martial arts instructor at your local gym. I work for a small, global organization, and it's my job to see that this peaceful coexistence between our kind and yours stays that way."

"You...you drink blood?"

Lily rummaged around in the emergency kit and handed her a small bottle of water and a granola bar. "We require only small amounts of human blood every few weeks, so we never need to kill. If the person feels anything as a result, it's merely a mild fatigue, like when you donate blood or don't get enough sleep. Many of us prefer blood from a vial anyway, not a live host, and we supplement our energy requirements with smatterings of human energy every few days."

Elisabeth frowned. "Energy? What...are you talking about?"

"Here, take my hand." When she didn't, Lily added, "It won't hurt. Promise. I just want to show you how it works."

Elisabeth reached out and tentatively touched her fingers to Lily's palm. When she took the woman's hand, Lily pulled in a minuscule amount of Elisabeth's energy through the skin contact. "Did you feel that?"

Elisabeth nodded, opening and closing her fist. "I think so. It made my skin…a little prickly. Look…the little hairs on my arms are sticking up."

"That's all there is to it. I took just the smallest amount of energy. Normally, we take more. Enough to make you tired and feeling like you need a good night's sleep."

Movement near the cabin drew her attention. For a moment, Lily forgot where she was and what she was saying because Alfonso had stripped off his shirt. Mesmerized, she watched his powerful muscles ripple in the moonlight, he shoulders flexing, his arms bulging. He tore the shirt, wrapped a piece around his hand and concentrated on Kip's forearm.

Silver spikes? It had to hurt like shit, but Kip didn't flinch as Alfonso worked on him. But then again, that powerful man could be amazingly gentle.

"Thanks…for telling me." Elisabeth's quiet voice snapped Lily out of her daze.

"Figured we owed you that much."

What Lily didn't have the heart to tell her was that because she was Sangre Dulce, most likely this wouldn't be the last time she'd meet up with a vampire. Being a sweetblood made her a target. Humans with standard blood types who unwittingly became donor hosts probably thought they were slightly anemic and prone to seasonal affective disorder. If they visited the doctor for any of these symptoms, they'd no doubt be given a prescription for iron pills and high-potency vitamin D, and told to sit under a light box for thirty minutes a day. But for a sweetblood, a chance encounter with a vampire usually was their last.

"So, are you in school or do you work?" Lily asked.

"Both. I go to school during the day…and wait tables at night."

She looked to be in her early twenties, which was typical. Most sweetbloods died young, because sooner or later, they'd run into a vampire, whether a Darkblood or not, who wouldn't be able to control the urge for their special blood. "Let me guess. One of these losers had been hanging around the club."

"I don't know…when I got into my car after work, they were there." Her voice broke as she spoke. "They seemed to come out of nowhere. The bouncer walked me to my car…and waited until I got the door open. The car was empty and…I waved him back inside as I climbed in. Next thing I knew…one of them was in the front seat… and the other one was right behind me in the back."

"Yeah, we're able to move pretty quickly in the dark. My advice? Get a different job. One that doesn't require you to be out at night alone."

Lily would make sure to put the woman into the database as a known sweetblood. That way, when the local field office had time, they'd send a routine patrol to keep an eye on her. Unfortunately, they didn't have the manpower to do sweetblood patrols more than a few times a month.

"What are you going to do with me?"

"Most likely you'll need a blood transfusion."

Elisabeth grimaced. "I hate blood." After wadding the granola bar wrapper, she twisted off the water bottle lid and took a long drink. When she looked at Lily again, a wary look was plastered to her face again. "So…why are you telling me all of this?"

Lily took a deep breath and let it out slowly, not particularly eager to tell her why. If the girl freaked out, Lily'd have to do a mind manip before she was questioned about any important details she saw or overheard. "Because we'll wipe your memory when it's all over. You won't remember what happened from the time you were kidnapped outside your work."

"You're going to…steal my memory?"

"Yep, I'm afraid so. You'll have no recollection of the horrible ordeal you've just been through."

"But that's just wrong. You can't just…take people's memories away."

"We're not really taking it. We're changing it." Seeing the incredulous look on Elisabeth's face, Lily added, "It may seem unfair to you, but it's vampire law."

"You guys…have laws?"

"Yeah, quite a few of them."

"Like what?"

"'If a human learns of our secret, a memory cleanse must occur.' Item Two of the Governing Council Charter. Item Three says to feed from a human host only when absolutely necessary."

"So what's Item One?"

"Do not kill."

After backup arrived and Elisabeth was put under their care, Lily approached Alfonso just as a medic was rolling his pant leg back down.

"Is he going to live?" Lily asked jokingly.

The young woman looked exasperated as she gathered up her things and snapped shut her medic bag. "Yes, but I'd like him seen by Dr. DeGraff at your earliest convenience, whether he wants to or not. I'd like to be sure there's not more damage than I can tell from this cursory examination." She glanced at the lightening sky through the treetops. "The human needs immediate medical attention, but we can't risk transporting her and Agent Castile together—his condition is too volatile. Can you take him to a safe house for the day where he can sleep off some of the effects of his ordeal, then take him up to Region tomorrow?"

Lily was about to answer when Alfonso piped in. "Absolutely. I'll take care of it."

"Niva doesn't have the room," she said. "Remember?"

"I've got somewhere else in mind."

CHAPTER NINE

THE SKY HAD LIGHTENED to a chalky gray by the time they turned off the main road and onto a gravel driveway. Lily glanced sideways at Alfonso's stoic features. The hard set of his jaw. The strong but slightly crooked nose that suggested a fight or two. He'd put on his leather bomber jacket but hadn't bothered to zip it up. Having taken off his shirt earlier, his muscular chest was exposed, and there, sitting between his nipples, affixed to a leather cord, was the medallion she'd given him.

She sat back against her seat and tried not to think about that.

Okay, so he liked it. That was all.

Instead, she concentrated on the fact that he'd seemed far more at ease back at the Darkblood cabin. Now he just looked...irritated. He must be pissed off that his involvement wasn't over, that Kip couldn't be transported directly to Region, allowing Alfonso to wash his hands of the situation and go back to his normal life. One that didn't include her.

If that was how he felt, then she wasn't particularly eager to be spending more time with him, either. It was the last thing she needed.

She thought about Zoe and the promise she'd made to herself about not getting involved with any more men.

Trying to make things work with Steven again had been a huge mistake. The longest six weeks of her life. The parties, the clubs, the women. To him, being a father was an afterthought. He had an agenda and it didn't include them. Which was fine—she'd never loved him. No, she couldn't subject Zoe to another one of her doomed relationships again.

The bumpy road began a steady incline. Surely there had to be a suitable safe house closer to the freeway.

Just as the slope leveled off, Alfonso hairpinned the car around an enormous stump covered with hanging moss, and the road narrowed considerably.

She eyed the encroaching blackberry bushes, their thorns lying in wait for anything that got too close. If he scratched her car, she was going to be pissed. "How much farther is this place? It's not like you're driving a four-wheeler."

"Perimeter coming up," he said, braking. "Does it bother you to go through or would you rather I disengage it? The remote control is in my bag."

"No, I'm fine, but aren't they expecting us? Shouldn't the cloaking system be down?"

The car lurched forward.

Wait. Why would he have the controls to a safe house anyway? Usually you call ahead and they have it turned off for you—if the perimeter was even camouflaged. Up here in the Northwest, not many vampire families bothered with that precaution.

Now that she thought about it, she didn't remember him making a call. "Whose place is this? I'm not aware of a safe house in this area."

"It isn't. It's my home—I mean, the house I'm building."

Before the shock of his words could completely settle in, they passed through the perimeter with a snap of electricity. Her skin tingled, setting her hair on end, and she absently rubbed the back of her arms. Good God, that was set high. She glanced at Kip lying on the backseat, but he was still so out of it that he hadn't reacted.

Alfonso was building a house? It didn't make sense. He could almost be classified as a drifter. A restless soul, he'd never been comfortable staying in one place for long. Always moving or needing to do something, he never seemed to fully relax. He would tinker with things or pick the strings of his guitar just to keep his hands from being idle. It was like he didn't know what to do with himself otherwise. She'd assumed it was because he'd been a double agent for most of his life, constantly on edge and never able to truly let his guard down. Obviously her assessment of him had been dead wrong.

A huge wrought-iron gate loomed about twenty feet ahead of the car, and the headlights cast grotesque shadows on the trees beyond it. Alfonso rolled down his window, touched a control panel she hadn't noticed until they were stopped, and the heavy gate slowly eased open.

Knots of apprehension brewed in her gut. Was he making his home here because he'd settled down with someone? She hadn't detected a female's scent on him, and yet—

She lifted her nose to the window. Although she didn't smell anyone, considering her tracking problems she could've easily missed the scent marker. Not having an item to lock in a scent memory didn't help, either.

Could that be the real reason why he hadn't come back to her last year? He'd found someone else and didn't have the balls to tell her? It was so unlike him to have a permanent residence, but it made sense if there was another woman involved.

She felt a little sick. At some point, she knew she'd need to deal with that knowledge, but she wasn't at all excited to be doing it face-to-face. Taking a deep breath, she willed herself to stay calm. If there really was another woman here, Lily already knew she was going to hate the bitch.

The forest opened up onto a large clearing on a bluff. Nestled into the side of the mountain was a majestic stone manor house with a red-tiled roof, arched doorways and windows and a breathtaking view of the water. In any other circumstance, she'd love to admire everything, but right now she just wanted to get things over with.

"Welcome to *Casa en las Colinas,*" he said flatly. "The House in the Hills."

He parked the car next to a battered blue work truck. Her legs felt heavy as she hauled herself out, but a strong updraft blowing in from the edge of the cliff almost lifted her off her feet. Another storm was definitely on its way. With this wind, no wonder she couldn't detect the other woman's presence. It'd be whisked away before she ever smelled it.

"You all must lose power a lot out here," she said, trying her hand at small talk in an attempt to keep her mind focused on trivial things. Talking about the weather was always a safe subject.

He shrugged. "I've got a high-efficiency generator that kicks in automatically and can run for weeks on its own."

She went to retrieve her bag from the backseat before helping Kip out, but Alfonso beat her to it. Resting her forehead on the doorframe, she knew she had to ask him, especially before they went inside. If there was another woman waiting for Alfonso, a lover who would drag him into her arms and welcome him home, Lily wanted a heads-up to prepare herself. Surely he'd have told her. Wouldn't he?

They'd been apart for more than a year—what did she expect? God knew she'd wanted to move on after it was clear he wasn't coming back to her. And if he had found someone special who had finally gotten him to settle down, it really shouldn't be that surprising. After all, she'd tried. Why couldn't he?

"Are you—" She closed her eyes for a moment, unable to form the words. "Why are you building a home clear out here? I mean, it's very beautiful, don't get me wrong. But it's so far away from everything. Don't you feel isolated?"

"No."

"But you've never been one to stay in one place for long. Building a house seems contrary to that." She steeled her shoulders. "Are you living here with someone?" She tried to keep the emotion from seeping into her voice, but she wasn't sure she was successful.

The car door on his side closed with a *thunk* and he

peered over the roof at her. The lively blue of his eyes had dimmed to a steely, unemotional gray in the flat light.

"I live here alone, Lily. I am not seeing anyone."

Relief flooded through her. Was that a flash of regret in his expression? She couldn't be sure. He opened his mouth, the words so close that she could almost see them forming on his lips.

Yes. The word popped in her head—the answer to an unknown question. Was he going to ask her something? *Tell me. Please.*

If he was, he evidently changed his mind, for he snapped his jaw closed and turned his attention to Kip in the backseat.

She straightened up and smoothed out her ponytail, a tactile reminder to herself to remain aloof and indifferent. "Good. I won't need to suppress the urge to scratch out some chick's eyes then. Old girlfriends and new ones don't exactly mix."

She heard the low rumble of amusement as he headed toward the front entrance, Kip's arm slung over his shoulder. Like any job site, the landscaping came last, and the place was a total mud pit during this rainy time of year. She followed him, trying to step exactly where he had. A few narrow boards had been placed strategically across the worst parts. Without slowing, he strode across them, obviously having done so many times.

With her arms out for balance, she tentatively stepped onto the first board. It tilted, but she was ready for it. As if walking a gymnastics beam, she put one foot in front of the other and kept her eyes straight ahead.

When she got to the far side, Alfonso clapped from the front porch. He'd set Kip down and was watching her.

She curtsied. "Piece of cake."

When she stepped onto the next board and took a few steps, it rocked her back on her heels. Overcompensating, she shifted her weight forward and promptly lost her balance. With a gasp, she stepped calf-deep into the mud.

Laughter erupted from the covered porch. "Hold on, Lil. I'm coming."

She lifted her foot, but the muck held tight and she ended up stepping in with the other one as well.

Alfonso jogged adeptly across the boards. "Here," he said, reaching for her. His large hand dwarfed hers. When he hauled her up, the mud made a sucking noise, refusing to let go, and, sure enough, both boots stayed behind.

She couldn't help but laugh as she stepped onto the board in her socks. "My God, I had those things laced up tight."

"Yeah, it's like quicksand. It hangs on and won't let go. At least you didn't fall all the way in. I've done that once or twice."

He freed her boots and, before she knew what was happening, he swept her up, piggyback-style. Her arms and legs went instinctively around him as she let out a whoop of surprise. His warm scent invaded her nostrils and every step jostled her body against his. She rested her chin on the hand that grasped his shoulder, rather than on the bare skin of his neck. If she weren't careful, her fangs were likely to elongate, being this close to his vein. She'd been this close to him at the club, but back there, they hadn't been alone. Kip was so out of it, she doubted he even knew what the hell was going on.

For all intents and purposes, it was just the two of them. In Alfonso's own home, surrounded by his own personal things.

Lord help her.

He traversed the rest of the way with ease and set her on the base of the steps. As he stepped away, she immediately missed the warmth from his body

"Here, let me take those from you." She reached for her muddy boots.

"I'll clean them up."

She started to protest but he interrupted.

"Remember, I'm an expert in cleaning mud off boots, clothing, whatever. They'll be as good as new before we set out again at nightfall. Speaking of clothes," he said, eyeing her pants, "you can take a shower and I'll wash those, too."

"Thanks." She couldn't look at him, didn't want him to see the emotion on her face. Her eyes stung as she recalled how he'd always taken care of seemingly insignificant things for her. Changing the oil in her car while she slept because he noticed it was overdue, making sure her cell phone was charged, fixing her coffee the way she liked it, even though it was a little high maintenance.

They climbed several steps and passed through an archway onto the large covered porch. Lined with stone pillars, it stretched from one end of the home to the other. Noting the infrared heaters in the ceiling and a single Adirondack chair, she wondered how often he came out here and played his guitar. Did he still tinker with that tune he was always working on?

An empty glass sat on the armrest, no doubt filled at one time with a finger of Maker's Mark and two ice cubes. He dropped her mud-covered boots before helping Kip to his feet.

The young man staggered, but Alfonso held tight.

God, the kid looked terrible.

"Kip, how you doing?" she asked.

He stared blankly at his hands and didn't answer.

"You didn't tell me why you moved out here," she said to Alfonso as he unlocked the front door.

He pointed toward the water. "The property reminded me of where I grew up. If you take a look at the coastline, it has the same rugged, undeveloped look as my family's home overlooking the Cantabrian Sea."

"How long have you owned it?"

"Couple of years, I guess."

So he'd had this while they were together. Why had he never mentioned it?

Stacks of lumber and boxes of tiles were piled against the exterior walls, along with a wide array of power tools. "So you're building the whole thing yourself? I knew you enjoyed working with your hands, but I had no idea you were so talented."

He laughed. "If I did it myself, I'd never have it done on time. No, I'm just doing the jobs I enjoy—tiling, painting, some of the finish carpentry. If I'm lucky, I'll have it done and furnished before the year's out. I'm getting pretty close and don't have a lot left to do. Come on. Let's get Kip situated."

He pushed open the heavy double doors and held them open for her. "Careful, I'm not done with the tile work in the entryway."

She stepped in and could hardly believe what she was seeing. The grand foyer opened all the way up to the roof, with a mammoth carved-wood chandelier hanging down over a floor tiled in an ornate mosaic pattern of azure blues and Spanish reds. On either side of where she stood, a galley ran the length of the house, much like the deck outside, with arched doorways leading to various rooms. The walls were made of some sort of stone that looked as if it had come from a medieval castle. She followed Alfonso to the right. On the floor between each window, brightly colored, whimsical landscape paintings waited to be hung.

"Oh my God, Mackenzie did those."

He looked pleased that she recognized them. "I know they're not really in keeping with the feel of this place, being that they're a modern take of the Cantabrian land-scape, but when I saw her work, I had to commission some pieces."

"They're perfect. They add a lighthearted spirit to the place. Has she been here to see what they look like?"

"No, you're actually my first guests."

A thrill rippled through her at the thought of being his first guest, the first woman invited into his dream home.

After getting Kip set up in a guest bedroom with its own private bath, she and Alfonso returned to the foyer.

"Will he be okay?"

"Yeah, what he needs most right now is sleep. We'll take him up to Region at nightfall."

She recalled what Alfonso had said earlier about having the house done on time. He'd made it sound like he had a deadline. "What's the rush getting the house finished? The end of the year is only a few weeks away."

He pulled off his cap, tucked it into a pocket and ran a hand through his hair. "I'm not sure how long I'm staying. I'm thinking it's time to be moving on soon."

A hollow, empty sensation gnawed inside her belly, reminding her of how she'd felt after that horrible phone call last year when he'd said he had fallen out of love with her.

Okay, this is silly. He's got some redeeming qualities, but clearly, commitment is not one of them.

She seriously needed some sense knocked into her. He hadn't even been back in her life for twelve hours yet and now she was sad to learn he was moving away. She examined the intricate tile work beneath her foot. "But why start a huge project if you didn't think you'd stay to enjoy it?"

"At one point, I thought I would be staying. At least I hoped I would. I…I wanted to make some changes in my life and thought building this house would help. Mackenzie talked me into sticking around for a while. You know—see the baby, try to patch things up with my brother, things like that. It was stupid really, thinking I could build a house like this, put the past behind me, lead a normal life."

She didn't understand. Hadn't he received a full pardon from the Council with an invitation to join the Agency as a Guardian? He had a future here, if he wanted it. "Why did you change your mind?"

He shrugged. "I got realistic."

Ahead stood a grand, uncarpeted staircase that curved up to the right. She could almost hear the swish of seventeenth-century silk skirts brushing against the stairs. To the left of the staircase, a long hallway led to more rooms.

She examined the exquisite tile work in greater detail. Although she'd never been to the part of Spain where he'd grown up, she imagined this was authentic to the region. "It looks like you're almost done with this."

"I'm ripping it out."

"Oh my God, why?"

"Not happy with the color."

"What are you talking about? It's lovely."

"I'm trying to recreate my parents' country estate. Although I imported these tiles from the same centuries-old tile maker in Spain that my parents used, it's still not right. And it's the third batch I've tried."

"Maybe this is as close as you're going to get. It might be impossible to create what exists in your memory. The composition of the clay wouldn't be the same after all these years, and the color dyes would be different too. You might be able to get close, but it won't be exactly the same."

"No, it must be perfect."

"Why?"

He didn't answer her right away, just looked at the floor in all directions with a critical eye. "Because I'll know it's not right," he finally said. "And so will Dom. If he ever sees it."

As she tried to see things the way he saw them, it

suddenly became clear. Alfonso was trying to prove something to his brother. If things were perfect with the house, Alfonso hoped that Dom would see that he did treasure what they had with their parents, and that his brother might forgive him. Although she didn't know the details, she knew Dom blamed Alfonso for their death.

"And you think that's the key to reconciling with him?" she asked quietly.

He shrugged.

"He's not like that, you know. He's not hung up on details like you seem to be. He's much more 'big picture' than that. You have to be to effectively run a field office. He'll see your efforts with this house for what they are. An honor to your parents' memory."

He huffed out a loud breath and headed through the first arched doorway to the left of the stairs. She followed him into a sparsely furnished room with a fireplace.

"You don't know my brother like I know him." He tossed his duffel onto a cordovan leather sofa next to a pillow and folded blanket.

In this huge house, he chose to sleep here? Why? "I know your brother well enough and I think he'd be impressed by all of this. I certainly am."

His laugh was cold. "He lost his faith in me long ago. I was foolish to think it could be restored."

"Maybe so, but that doesn't mean it's gone, that he doesn't want to have a relationship with you again. After he found out that you were my contact within the Alliance and that I had been sworn to secrecy by the highest levels of the Council, I was afraid he'd not be able to forgive me. But he did. Yeah, he was pissed off at me for a while, but he got over it. Although he should've been thrilled that Pavlos was dead and that Mackenzie was safe, he almost went into a mourning period when he thought you had died in the fire. No one saw him in the field office for days."

Alfonso looked unimpressed.

"Have you talked at all?" she asked quietly.

His jaw muscles worked back and forth. "If you knew your brother was responsible for the death of your parents, would you still want him in your life?" He brushed past her and headed back around to the staircase.

"When he found out you'd survived that fire and were in the regen clinic, he had Mackenzie check with your doctors for a progress report."

Alfonso stopped, one foot on the bottom stair. "She told me that, but…"

"But you didn't believe it."

He didn't answer.

"He cares about you, Alfonso, but whether either of you can admit that verbally is another thing. Both of you are cut from the same stubborn mold. Everything you've done—" She swept her arm wide. "Sacrificing a normal life and your own happiness in order to destroy the Alliance from the inside is pretty amazing. You deserve to be happy now, and if building this house does it, then I think that's wonderful."

Before she knew what she intended, she slipped her hand into his and gave it an encouraging squeeze. An electric energy passed between them, stretching outward to the top of her head and down to her toes, making her heart race. Without warning, he pulled her into his arms.

She expected his kiss to be more of a peck, but he shoved her against the wall of the stairs and his mouth came down over hers, stealing the breath from her lungs. With even more ferocity than she'd felt back at the club, he pried her lips open in an almost bruising fashion. It was raw and laced with pent-up emotion, not just a superficial game to be played out for others.

Stay calm, she told herself. He'd come to his senses in a moment and realize this was a terrible mistake. She braced herself, expecting him to abruptly release her as the realization dawned on him.

But he didn't.

The feel and smell of him diluted any further rational thought.

She slipped her hands up his chest, over the muscular definition of his pectorals, and wrapped her arms around his neck. His hand cradled her jaw as it often did when he kissed her, caressing the tender skin below her ear with his thumb. It was as if he were keeping her under his influence until he decided to let her go. She couldn't help but moan softly.

The amount of control he had over her body was an aphrodisiac, which was ironic considering she hated being told what to do. His iron-hard erection pressed against her hips, separated from her by only a few millimeters of fabric. She ached to feel him inside her; she needed to feel it.

"Lily, we can't," he said, his lips now against her throat, but it was more like an admonishment to himself. She was the one pinned against the wall; he was the one in control.

"Yes, we can," she heard herself say. Positioning one foot on the step above them, she gripped his ass and pulled him closer.

A low sound, almost a vibration, came from deep inside him, igniting a warm need all over her flesh. He hooked a thumb inside her waistband, slid it around to the front. The movement tickled, sending tiny goose bumps of anticipation along her arms and up her spine. For a split second, she thought he was going to unfasten her pants.

God, how she wanted him to.

But he pushed away from her instead and gripped the banister with white-knuckled hands. "Lily, I'm sorry. I can't."

The foyer was mausoleum-silent as she followed him up the stairs, trying to make sense of what had just happened. Or hadn't happen. Why had he stopped? He'd seemed to want it as much as she had. In fact, he was the one who'd started it.

Her heart continued to beat madly inside her hollow chest. What had happened to make him change his mind? She'd certainly given him every indication that she wanted it to go further, so why hadn't he? The fervent way he kissed her wasn't something she'd imagined. Maybe he was worried she'd get the wrong idea and want to rekindle their relationship if they had sex. That she wouldn't be able to consider it just a fun romp.

She ran her tongue along her teeth, relieved that her fangs had retracted.

Relationship? Yeah, right. That was the furthest thing from her mind. Sure, they were sexually compatible. Lots of people were. Just because he had the ability to give her several mind-blowing orgasms in the length of time it took to brush her teeth, didn't mean she was going to fall for him again.

Fool me once, shame on you. Fool me twice, I'm an idiot.

Given that his home was still under construction, she was surprised when they got to the upper hallway. Several groupings of elegant swords were displayed on the burgundy walls. From the crown molding and the antique furniture to the Savonnerie carpets, the upstairs appeared to be completely decorated. Were the rooms behind these doors finished too? Something about a nearby antique table caught her attention. Running her fingers along the top as she walked by, she could tell the piece was quite old. Made of walnut, the design was trestle-style with distinctively carved legs and two iron stretcher bars.

"It's a Spanish refectory table," Alfonso said without turning around, as if he knew she was admiring it.

Although he continued down the hall, she stopped to inspect it further. "What a beautiful piece, and in such pristine condition for its age." The thing was sturdy too, with hardly a scratch to mar the surface. "Seventeenth century?"

"I believe so."

"Where did you find it?" she asked.

"I didn't. It's been in my family for years."

He came back and towered over her, his breath ruffling the tiny hairs on her neck. He leaned in close and she felt the heat emanating off his body. At first she thought he was going to touch her again—she wanted him to. Instead, he jammed his hands into his pockets.

"My mother found it at a monastery that had been ransacked repeatedly by marauders believed to have ties to the Spanish government. Rome decided to close it down, so she took us along to see what pieces they couldn't take with them."

He stared at the table, a faraway look in his eyes as he recalled those old memories.

"I remember Dom and I riding all the way home— three hours on an uneven road—in the back of the cart with this and several other items. And in those days, the roads through the hill country were hardly more than cart paths. Our mother was afraid the furniture would get damaged if we boys weren't in the back keeping an eye on everything. It was one hell of a miserable ride. I remember Dom and I complaining for many nights about our sore muscles and aching arses until our father, who was sick of the whining, told us he'd give us something to really complain about if we didn't stop."

He laughed then and so did she. It felt good to loosen up after being so tense.

"And what about Catalina? Was she there too?"

Alfonso rubbed a hand over his stubbled jaw. "As I recall, my sister was just an infant, and thus she was spared the agony."

"Lucky her. When was the last time you saw her?"

"The last time I *saw* her? Several months ago. When I was in the U.K."

The way he phrased it, he made it sound as if he'd only *seen* his sister, not that they'd actually spoken. Did

Catalina harbor the same resentments toward him as Dom did? Lily didn't recall him ever saying that, but she didn't want to probe any further.

At an arched doorway, he rested one hand on the ringed, wrought-iron handle.

"Give me a minute to straighten up." Then, without waiting for a reply, he entered the room and closed the door behind him.

Heavy footsteps sounded on the wood floor as he rustled around inside. Several times, she heard a drawer or door slam shut. What on earth was he doing in there? He was tidy—she couldn't imagine clothes lying around, if this were indeed his bedroom. She crossed her arms and waited, studying the decor as she did so.

Several fan-shaped groupings of swords hung on the wall across from her. Lily whistled softly as he stepped out of the room. "I knew you were fond of swords and knives, but this is an amazing collection."

"Thank you."

She walked over and examined the first group, then took another few steps and examined the next one. "I'm curious, though," she said, turning to face him.

He raised his brow. "About what?"

"They're all considered to be common man's swords, aren't they? Made for cutting *and* thrusting, rather than a single purpose."

He smiled. "You never cease to surprise me, Lil, the things you notice. Yes, they're all *espada ropera*. But why do you find this curious?"

"I guess I'd expect you to have many other types of swords displayed, given your fondness for them."

"While I do own rapiers, sabers and a host of other blades, the *espada roperas* are particular favorites."

"Why do they appeal to you? With your father's position on the Governing Council, you were hardly a common man."

He walked to the first grouping of swords, reached up and touched the hilt of one. As he lightly brushed his fingers over the Toledo-steel blade, she found herself wishing he were paying attention to her body like that, running his hands over her skin, admiring how she looked, remembering the beautiful history they shared.

"Yes, but being the black sheep of the family, I was always different." His voice sounded clipped, but tired. "My father raised high-strung Thoroughbred horses on his English estate, so I preferred the sturdy Spanish Andalusians. My father hated the French, so I kept a flat in Paris. Dom became a Guardian, and I—" He abruptly turned away. "Well, you know what I did."

She followed him through the arched doorway into a large bedchamber and gasped as she tried to take in all the details. Dark Gothic paneling covered the walls, heavy draperies hung from the windows and a curtained bed with a massive walnut headboard and bedposts the size of tree trunks stood in the center of it all. She wasn't sure what she had expected, but this certainly wasn't it. "You did this all yourself?"

"I did have a little help, but fortunately, they don't remember a thing."

Why go to all this trouble making everything perfect, when it appeared he slept downstairs on the couch? Is that all he felt he deserved? she wondered.

"It's gorgeous, down to every last detail." She approached the bed. The ornate headboard stood a foot taller than her. It was some sort of carved relief. Pushing back the tassel-edged curtains, she examined the depiction of a countryside with soldiers on horseback, swords drawn, racing toward some unknown enemy in the distant hills.

It wasn't an old piece, but she recognized the workmanship and attention to detail. "You carved this, didn't you?" she asked, running her fingertips over the piece. The wood was so smooth, she couldn't imagine the amount of time he must've spent on it. Even the cracks and grooves were finely sanded and varnished.

He cleared his throat. "Yeah."

When she leaned over the pillows to get a closer look, she suddenly became aware of a faint throbbing between her legs that seemed to coincide with the beating of her heart. It was as if her body's cravings for Alfonso were making themselves known and they had an interest in using the furniture for its intended purpose. The interlude on the stairs hadn't sated her desire in the least; it had merely whetted her appetite for more. Being near a bed with him so close was definitely not a good idea. She backed away quickly.

"You don't mind if I take a shower?" she asked, knowing he'd already told her she could but unable to think of anything else to say.

"The room is yours. Make yourself comfortable. I'll be back with something for you to eat."

Again, she was touched by his attention to her needs.

"But this is your room. I can't take your bed. As long as I have a blanket, I'll be happy anywhere."

A strange expression that she couldn't quite decipher crossed his face for a moment. "No, it's not my room. I've never slept in here."

DOWN IN THE DRAWING ROOM, Alfonso was picking at the strings of his guitar when he heard the water running upstairs again.

Why would she be taking another shower? Then it dawned on him. She wasn't showering. Christ. She was taking a damn bath.

Closing his eyes, he rested his head on the back of the couch. She'd be slipping out of her silky pajamas right about now—if she wore them. There was a time when she would've raided his closet. What if she were wearing one of his shirts now? She'd have run her fingers along the edges of the hangers as she selected the one that had the most concentrated smell of him. Or at least that's what she'd always done before. The sleeves would be rolled up and the hem would hang midway down her thighs, making it easy for him to run his hand underneath and encounter nothing else but her. First, he'd feel the roundness of her bottom as it curved at the top of her leg. Then he'd move to the front, past a thin, neatly waxed strip of curls, slip a finger inside and listen to her moan.

He rolled over, fluffed the pillow again. Didn't she know he was trying to get some sleep down here? And these pipes... For godsake, they sounded like a flimsy, 1940s Rambler.

He grabbed his guitar, hoping to drown out the sound

and occupy his mind with something other than thoughts of that woman in his tub upstairs. A few empty chords not belonging to any song in particular echoed in the air as he played.

Then the water stopped. He pressed his fingers on the guitar strings to silence them.

She'd be stepping into the bath now—slowly, because the temperature would be hot. First one manicured toe, then the whole foot, a shapely leg—

Damn. He had to knock this off.

He set the guitar aside, grabbed the laptop and put on the headphones. With the volume cranked, his fingers stabbed the keys. If BloodySunday could kill a bunch of zombies, maybe his memory would take a hike.

He wasn't sure how long he'd been playing when the blood in his veins stirred for no apparent reason.

Lily?

He pulled off the headphones. Hit Pause.

Except for the crackling fire, the house was quiet. Perhaps he was mistaken. They hadn't shared blood in over a year—surely this unusual effect she had on him had worn off after all this time.

When they'd been together, sharing blood regularly, he'd always been able to discern her presence. If she told him to meet her at a hotel, he could locate the room without knowing the number. At a crowded festival, he'd walk right up to her as if he knew her precise GPS coordinates. He imagined that this innate ability would be like following a scent if he were a Tracker—the stronger the sensation, the closer he'd known he was getting.

A moment later, faint footsteps padded down the stairs. He set the laptop aside.

Why could he feel her now? He'd assumed it had something to do with the blood sharing, but it had been well over a year since he'd last taken her blood. In the parking lot of the field office, the sensation hadn't been apparent, but here, where it was just the two of them for miles, it was obvious.

If this ability hadn't worn off, what about the other ways she affected him? He shoved that thought from his head. What he thought may have happened a long time ago was just his overactive imagination. It simply wasn't possible. He'd been drinking that night, so nothing about those odd recollections made any sense.

Glancing through the doorway at the staircase, he first saw her feet, then her legs, then the rest of her as she descended. She had on pajama shorts. Holy shit. And one of his shirts. She was using it like a robe.

"Can I get you something?" he called out.

She leaned over the banister. Her hair was no longer flat-iron smooth, but tousled. Bed-head sexy.

"Just checking on Kip. I wanted to see how he's doing."

"He woke up enough to drink some weak broth, but he's sleeping now."

"I'll just peek in on him then."

As she stepped into the foyer and padded away, he pulled up the HG forums and halfheartedly clicked on a few threads. Nothing. No one had responded to his messages about looking to party. He didn't feel like posting a new one.

Five minutes passed. Then ten.

What was keeping her? He tightened his brace and pulled himself to his feet, cursing under his breath. His knee was always stiff when he'd been sitting for a while, but after the scuffle last night it had gotten worse. Ignoring the lingering pain, he flexed his leg to limber it up, then strode through the doorway and crossed the foyer.

In the hallway outside Kip's room, Lily sat huddled on the floor, her hands around her legs, her head tucked into her knees.

"Lily, what's wrong? What happened?" He was at her side in an instant.

She turned away, swiping a hand over her face. "Nothing. Just relieved, I guess."

Had she been crying? "I told you he'll be fine. They didn't have him long enough for the addiction to take hold."

"Yeah, I know."

He had a distinct feeling she wasn't telling him everything. "Then what's wrong?"

She didn't answer.

It gnawed at him. He needed to know.

"Come. Sit with me," he said, holding out his hand.

After just a slight hesitation, she slipped her hand in his. He was careful not to push or pull any energies as he led her to the drawing room.

Her skin and hair smelled of lavender. Warm. Fresh. Clean. She'd used the bath salts he'd set out for her. Why he had them in the first place, he wasn't quite sure. He'd bought the crystal bottle months ago, long after he'd made that fateful call to her telling her he no longer loved her. The scent had reminded him of her.

He motioned for her to sit, but he didn't join her on the couch. Instead, he threw another log on the fire.

"If it's about me taking advantage of you earlier, then I promise it won't happen again. I'll do a better job controlling myself."

She shook her head. "It's not that at all. I...I wanted that just as much as you did. I'm just sorry it didn't go further."

A sudden relief washed over him. Despite everything, she still wanted him, just as he wanted her. For once, he wasn't the cause of her pain. Somehow he resisted the urge to go to her. "Then what, Lil?" Although she didn't answer him right away, he sensed her resolve slipping. "Tell me," he prodded.

Her breath came out in a slow exhale. "It's my fault Kip is suffering. When I make my TechTran report, noting the time it took to track Kip as well as the distance and location, it'll be obvious that I've got problems. I had hoped to keep that information to myself, but I'm afraid I can't keep hiding it. This is all my fault."

"How long has it been like this?"

"Months. But it seems to have worsened lately."

"What about last night? You were fantastic."

"Yeah, after many hours of tracking. It shouldn't have been a hard find. Since he and I had been working together for the past few weeks, the scent memory should've been strong. I should've been able to go straight to him. When I was at the top of my game, I could've tracked him whether we'd been working together or not. I would've been able to find him that very first night."

"Why don't you let Santiago know? Or Roxanne.

Maybe you've just been working too hard and need a break. When was the last time you took any energies? Or blood—from a live donor? Hell, when was the last time you took a vacation?"

"It's not that." She drew her feet up underneath her, grabbed his pillow, and hugged it to her chest. "Once this decline in my abilities gets out, my career, which I've spent years building, is over. Everyone will find out it was only through my father's influence that I got the position with the Agency in the first place."

"Bullshit. I don't care who your father is and what calls he may or may not have made. That has nothing to do with it. No one qualifies for Tracker Academy without demonstrating an aptitude far above what others have."

"Well, my ability has been severely hampered," she said huskily. "And what good is a Tracker who can't track?"

A Tracker who can't track.

It suddenly became clear to him. This wasn't strictly a matter of guilt or a little self-doubt. This was an issue threatening her whole identity.

He examined her more closely. Her shoulders looked stiff. Her face was pinched with worry. He felt the tension roiling off her body in waves as if it were his own. She was wound so tightly, no wonder she was having troubles.

"Lie down. On the sheepskin rug. You need a massage."

CHAPTER TEN

INSTEAD OF LYING DOWN, Lily settled cross-legged on the floor between Alfonso's powerful thighs. She didn't want to be quite that vulnerable to him. Caving to him on the stairs had been bad enough. No, she'd stay strong this time.

Looking around the room to keep her mind occupied on more than just him, she saw his acoustic guitar leaning against the sofa. He still took the thing everywhere. Therapy, he'd once told her. Playing it calmed his nerves. And hers—she loved listening to him play. Was that what had woken her in the first place?

With businesslike efficiency, he went to work on her shoulders.

His thumbs kneaded expertly into her muscles, and when she winced at a particularly painful knot, he stopped. "Take off my... This shirt. I need the skin-to-skin contact."

She started to protest, but he wouldn't listen. "Just do it, Lil. I can't get at all these knots if I have to work through this thick material."

A little surprised that his demand didn't set her on edge, she shrugged out of the shirt and swept her hair to the front, ready for him to start working on her shoulders. He was right—her muscles were aching and sore.

She could use a deep-tissue massage, and he was so good at them. He'd always been able to find knots she didn't know existed.

Without warning, he stood up. "Let me get you something to eat first."

"I'm not really hungry," she started to say, but he was gone without turning around.

He returned a few minutes later carrying a cutting board with two apples, a hunk of cheese and a knife. Although she wasn't hungry because of the sandwich she'd eaten earlier, her stomach growled in anticipation. Secretly, she loved that he fixed her food, but she wasn't about to make a big deal about it, drawing attention to that fact. He was just being considerate to a houseguest. "That looks good. Thanks," she said casually.

When he sank down beside her, she caught a brief glimpse of pain on his expression.

His knee? It was clearly bothering him more than he let on. She didn't say anything about it, though.

Using his thumb against the apple, he cut a few paper-thin slices and offered her one. "Hold on. You need to eat it with a hunk of cheese," he said, handing her a piece. "It's really good paired together."

He was right. The bite was delicious. She'd never eaten them together before. She smiled as he sliced off another piece.

"Thanks for being so supportive of what's been going on with me," she said. "It…it means a lot."

He nodded but didn't look up from the cutting board. He'd showered recently, she noted. Not only did he smell of fresh soap, but his skin smelled damp and his hair was still wet near his scalp, although the ends were curling up haphazardly from the heat of the fire.

When she grabbed another hunk of cheese, her bent knee settled more firmly against his thigh. If she were smart, she should move it, but she didn't want to.

He speared a chunk of apple with the point of his knife and lifted it to his lips.

Suddenly, she felt the need to tell him more. "Back when you and I were together, I felt as if I was at the top of my game. People paid attention to me for something other than my looks. For once in my life, my father seemed truly proud of me. Talked to me like I was an equal, included me in conversations with my brother. But without my tracking ability, I'm nothing. I go back to being just a pretty face, and those within the Agency who suspected I got the job only because of my father will think they were right all along."

"I'm sure this downturn is only temporary. Honestly, Lil, I've never met anyone with tracking skills as strong as yours." A shadow passed across his face, darkening his features for a moment, but then he blinked and it was gone. "You've got your whole identity wrapped up in being a Tracker, and, while I admire your ability, it's only one aspect of you, Lily. Just one. You're so much more than that."

Neither said anything for a few long moments, both watching the flames flicker in the fireplace. It felt so natural to be sitting with him like this. And so easy to ignore the worry. Crunching down on a slice of apple, she realized Alfonso infused her with a confidence in herself that she'd forgotten. It felt good to open up to him.

A relief, actually. No one seemed to really understand her the way he did.

Spotting the open laptop with a controller and speakers, she asked, "So what's with that getup? I didn't know you were into video games."

He rubbed the mouse pad, and the words *Hollow Grave* appeared on the black screen. As she watched, the crimson font morphed to look like dripping blood. "I'm not, really," he said.

He went on to explain how Darkbloods were using the forums to target younger vampires and invite them to the Night of Wilding party. The Seattle field office had been busy tracking down the possible locations of the various parties, but this sounded like the one they needed to worry about the most.

"That's pretty damn clever on their part." She scooted closer in order to get a better look, somehow resisting the urge to rest her chin on his shoulder. It wasn't easy when he smelled so good. *Focus,* she told herself. *On the game. Not him.* "So for you, it's an RPG then, right? You're role-playing the part of BloodySunday, a wannabe partier."

"Exactly." He traced his finger over the mouse pad and the cursor spiraled on the screen. "It's the story of my life. Pretending to be someone I'm not, but this time, I'm not having much luck. The non-gamer in me is apparently invisible to the hard-core players, and—" he made a fake sad face that made her laugh "—no one wants to be my friend."

"Poor thing. The game looks creepy in an oddly compelling sort of way." He looked bemused by that. "What?

Don't look so surprised. You know how much I love scary movies."

He moved the laptop to the floor in front of them, and she leaned forward eagerly.

"Then you'll love the game, although, frankly, it's pretty damn gory."

"A little blood never hurts."

There was that dimple again, as if he were trying to hold back a smile but forgot to tell all of his face. He unplugged the headphones and handed her the controller.

"No," she said. "I'll watch you do it."

"Okay, but I'm warning you, I'm pretty terrible. In fact, I suck."

She smirked, thought about making a joke, but decided not to say anything. She wouldn't have thought twice about it if she'd been talking to Jackson, but with Alfonso, she wasn't ready to be that lighthearted with her sexual innuendos.

"Seriously," he said, "you should've seen the kid at the store who walked me through it. He made it look easy. Good thing this game gives you a lot of lives. If not, I'd be spending the majority of the time dead."

"Food for zombies?"

He laughed and his eyes crinkled up, his dimple punctuating one cheek. The sound filled the room and she found herself laughing along with him.

"Yeah, just wait and see. It's not pretty."

Like a couple of youthlings, they sat cross-legged on the floor with their backs against the sofa. The only things missing were the beanbag chairs and a bag of chips. While he navigated BloodySunday through an apocalyptic cityscape with overturned buses and burned-out cars, she rested her arm on the couch behind his head in order to see the small screen better and didn't realize until later that her breast was pressed against his biceps. It'd draw more attention to move, so she stayed where she was.

"Careful, there's a zombie hiding behind that corner. Oh no, run!" She clapped her hands when he found another vial of Bleed and staved off another attack.

After expending an inordinate number of lives—yeah, he definitely wasn't a gamer—BloodySunday successfully made it through the zombie horde hiding in the catacombs beneath the city and advanced to the next level.

"You're right. That's pretty gory." She rubbed her hands together. "But I love it. Can I try? I love killing zombies. Just promise me there aren't any clowns popping up anywhere. I *hate* clowns. And spiders. Oh, and talking dolls."

He chuckled as he handed her the controller. "Go for it. As far as I can tell, no clowns or spiders. Just various kinds of killer zombies who want to eat your brain. But then again, I haven't gotten far." He lowered his voice for effect. "Maybe the clowns come in the next level."

She knocked him playfully on the arm. "Don't say that."

"And what's the deal with the dolls? I thought all girls loved dolls. Dressed them up and played house."

She groaned. "Not me! They freak me out. I only buy Zoe stuffed animals. And Hello Kitty things."

BloodySunday walked to the wrought-iron gate of a cemetery and paused. Through the bars, past several leafless trees that looked like tangles of long-legged, knobby-kneed spiders, a mausoleum sat ominously in the distance.

"Dolls freak you out? Why?"

She put the controller in her lap and angled toward him. "A few years before my Change, a friend of my father's brought me and my brother gifts from his travels. I don't remember what Will received, but I got one of those porcelain dolls from France. I can still see her. She wore what all the fashionable girls were wearing in Paris that season—a purple skirt with a black lace overlay, tiny black boots and a large black velvet bow on the back of her head. But her eyes..." Lily shivered. "She had these eyes that used to follow you around the room, and, I swear, I'd find that doll in a different place each time. Like she had moved there herself. I used to imagine her with a silver knife in her hand leaning over my bed when I slept. My mother finally had to keep her in a locked glass curio cabinet in the sitting room on the first floor because I couldn't sleep. I kept asking her to get rid of it, but she wouldn't. She said it was too valuable to sell or give away. Given her love of antiques, I'm sure she still has it somewhere."

"I'll bet you money that your brother was behind it."

She looked up at him, bewildered.

"It's what brothers do. It's in our DNA."

"No, Will wouldn't— Oh God, you're probably right." She narrowed her eyes. "It'd be just like Will to have done something devious like that. I can't believe I never thought of that before. Or that my mother didn't figure it out."

"Boys are devious. Trust me."

She laughed. "You sound like an expert. What did you do to your poor sister?"

He stretched his arm across the sofa behind her and his hand grazed her shoulder. He didn't move it away. "Well—and this wasn't my idea but Dom's—I was simply the one who carried out his evil master plan."

"Oh no, this doesn't sound good."

There was that mischievous dimple again. "For the longest time, I used to sneak into Catalina's room and hide in a trunk at the foot of her bed, waiting for her to fall asleep. Then, when I was sure she was sleeping, I'd start making these scratching noises. Sometimes I'd growl."

"No, you didn't." She slapped his arm. "That's awful. Your poor sister."

"I know," he said, laughing. "Terrible, huh? I'd hear this whimpering sound, and sure enough, she'd shoot out of bed, run into our parents' bedchamber like she was being chased by a ghost and climb into bed with them. By the time they got around to returning her to her room, I was back in my own bedchamber, where Dom and I laughed our asses off."

His voice had an easy, carefree quality to it when he spoke of his family. She could listen to him all day.

"My God, you two traumatized her. How long did that go on?"

"It stopped as soon as the governess started sleeping in her room. So, yeah, I'm betting your brother had something to do with that doll."

The ends of his hair flared out playfully around the

edge of his jaw. She absently reached up to brush away a thick strand that curled on his cheek.

He moved the computer and game controller away and twisted his body to face hers.

"I didn't mean for you to stop talking. I love hearing about your—"

When his lips came down over hers, it took her breath away, although they were soft and undemanding. She didn't have to tell her arms to slip around his neck; they just did.

He kissed her with the gentle familiarity of a longtime lover, slowly, easily, stretching each second into an eternity. When he finally pulled back, the painful fissure in her heart, which had never really gone away, reopened like a fresh wound.

"You know, you could've made love to me and taken my blood back there," she said, her voice a little huskier than normal. "I wouldn't have minded. Unless, of course, you didn't want to." She prayed that wasn't the case, but prepared herself nevertheless.

He held his cheek against hers, his breath ragged and heavy in her ear as he seemed to gather his thoughts. "God, Lily, that's not it. Not at all. My needs, my desires have nothing to do with my decision not to make love to you. God knows I've wanted to. I've never wanted to stop."

She felt the tension in his face, in the muscles of his arms as they wrapped more tightly around her. "Then why, Alfonso? Why didn't you? It feels as though I've been rejected. Again. And I'm really getting tired of that feeling."

He pulled away from her until his eyes peered straight into hers, the warmth from his breath heating her lips. "My refusal to take your blood has nothing to do with how much I care about you. In fact, it's because I desire it from you so much that I broke things off in the first place."

She didn't understand. He was talking in circles. "Do you think it makes you vulnerable or weak to want something that much?"

He took a deep breath and let it out slowly, his dimple and lighthearted expression gone, replaced by something dark and wounded. "Not vulnerable or weak. The opposite, actually. With your blood, I always felt…stronger, better. I couldn't be around you because I couldn't trust myself not to take your blood as much as I had been."

"So what changed? We used to share blood often. I…I loved that part of our relationship, loved how it made me feel knowing I had a part of you inside me when we weren't together. It's been hard since we've been apart. Did I…do something to make you change your mind about me?"

He cupped her face in his hands. The vivid blue of his eyes drew her in like iron to a magnet, until she imagined she was looking straight to his soul.

"God, no."

He still cared about her in that way? "Then why did you tell me we couldn't be together? That you didn't love me?"

Hurt shadowed his eyes, tiny lines forming between his brows. With an agonizing slowness, he lowered his head and his lips came down over hers, as if he wanted to savor every sensation as much as she did. Although the kiss was tender, she felt the passion, the hint of urgency beneath it. The sadness.

A year and a half's worth of pain began to slough away. He had spoken the truth. He did still want her. Her heart felt lighter, making room for the dozens of butterflies in her stomach. But why had he ever left?

LILY'S HAIR FELT LIKE SILK in his fingers as he kissed her, trying with every ounce of willpower he had not to get carried away. He could lose himself if he wasn't careful.

His heart ached with the knowledge of how much he'd hurt her, how he'd caused her to doubt herself and his feelings for her, when all he had wanted to do was protect her from a fate she didn't deserve. What had he expected? Of course, she'd be hurt. Of course, she'd be angry. God, how he wished things could be different. Then, now and in the future.

He pulled her to his chest.

Face-to-face, he couldn't completely lie to her, feed her the same bullshit he had when he'd said he'd fallen out of love with her. But she didn't need to know *all* the details. Hell, he could barely accept them himself. He'd rather see her expression turn to anger than loathing and disgust. Anything but that. He'd seen that look on his father's face as well as his brother's, though even they didn't know the whole truth. He didn't know if he could bear to have Lily think that way about him, too.

But holding her, hearing how much pain he'd caused her, tore at the rigid walls he'd constructed around his heart. It was one thing to torture himself, but quite another to torture her.

"I wanted to come back, Lily, start a life together like we'd talked about. It needed to appear as though I had died in the fire, because only then could I live without my past catching up with me."

"We all thought you *had* died. Your plan worked. What changed your mind?"

"I didn't change my mind about you, Lil, but it became clear to me that we didn't have a future."

She pushed away from him, confusion and anger in her eyes. "Are you saying that you lied to me about ever loving me?"

Hell, he'd been lying his whole life. The only time he'd ever been truly honest was with Lily. Until he had to lie to her.

He stood and walked to the fireplace, refusing to limp even though his knee was killing him. Blue flames hovered deep inside the tangle of logs, barely moving yet burning hotter than the rest of the fire. Although the warmth from her body lingered on his hands, he felt cold. Absently, he rubbed his palms on his jeans.

"The Alliance discovered I was the mole, and for a short time, they thought I *had* died in that fire. But if word got out that I'd survived, everything would change. I had to be very careful."

"You could've at least told me."

"I didn't want to talk to you then. I didn't want you to see me like that—my knee shot and in need of a complete regeneration."

She marched over to him and got in his face as if there

wasn't such a large height difference. Her eyes blazed with such anger that her fangs had to be coming down. She jammed her finger at his chest.

"And you thought that would've mattered to me? After all we'd been through? That I was that damn shallow?"

No, he didn't think it would've mattered to her, which was exactly why he hadn't wanted her to come. Shit. She'd have seen right through him then, just as she was doing now. But how could he admit that he was worried about being able to defend her? She would've argued that she was able to take care of both of them.

"It matters to me," he said.

There was no way in hell he was going to let her take that chance.

Not then and not now.

Not when it involved his blood assassin.

That was why he had to lie to her then and that was why he had to continue lying to her now.

"I was and still am broken." He clung to this truth as if it was all he cared about.

"Bull. You're lying."

"You think I'm joking?" He tore away from her. "You think I'm exaggerating about what happened to me?" He yanked up the leg of his jeans, ripped the Velcro straps off his knee brace and pulled the bandage with one sharp jerk. Although the silver blade had been made from a weak alloy, the DB had managed to stab him right in the middle of the angry red skin, through the weakened part of his knee still trying to regenerate. Despite the butterfly bandages, the wound gaped, revealing white tissue.

Lily sucked in a breath.

"Yeah, it's fucking mess, isn't it?"

She dropped to the floor to examine it, but he turned away and covered it up again.

"My God, Alfonso, that's not a nick. The whole thing is messed up. Why didn't you let on it was so bad?"

"So now you know what I'm talking about. And I don't mean the little jab I got at the DB cabin. You deserve someone whole. Not someone like this. Not someone damaged beyond repair."

"You're so full of shit."

He jerked his head to look at her. With her eyes narrowed to slits, he could see that she was working through everything he'd told her in her head, combing over every little nuance, checking and cross-referencing the knowns and unknowns. Goddamn it. That was why he hadn't wanted to confront her face-to-face like this in the first place. He was a hostile witness and she was the skeptical prosecutor.

"You said you originally wanted to come back after you were hurt, and that they needed to know you died in the fire."

"Yeah, so?"

"At first, Darkbloods did think you were dead. You could've come back or called at that time, but you didn't. I want to know why. And don't give me that bullshit about your knee. An injury like that can take months to regenerate, but it's not impossible, especially when you follow the treatment. A knee injury isn't a head injury. Knees regenerate. Heads don't. Something else prevented you from calling me and I want to know why."

A noise sounded from the doorway. Alfonso turned

to see Kip stumble into the room. "What is…going on in here?"

"Oh, Kip." Lily rushed to the young man's side. "I'm sorry. Did we wake you?"

Thank God. Let her focus on her trainee for a while. Alfonso brushed past them, patting Kip's shoulder. "Good to see you up and about, my man. You're looking better than the last time I saw you. Let me get you something to eat. We'll leave for Region at sunset."

THE BLAST OF COLD AIR that blew into the bar should've felt refreshing.

Mel shivered despite the fact that less than an hour ago this place had been a virtual sauna, jammed wall-to-wall with football fans. Given the last few dismal seasons—pro and college alike—a home team win had deserved some major celebrating.

For Pete's sake, she thought she'd locked the door. She needed to finish up and get home to let out Hogan. He'd been cooped up all evening.

"Sorry, we're closed," she called over her shoulder as she removed the last of the glasses from the steam washer below the counter and stacked them on the shelf. "You'll have to come back another time."

"I am not looking for a drink."

She spun around to find a man of medium build, with slick coal-black hair and a prominent, aristocratic nose, standing near the waitress station. How did he get here from the door so quickly?

At first glance she thought he was a pastor, given the black jacket and mandarin collar, but something about his flat, unblinking eyes and granite expression told her that he wasn't. Besides, she doubted a religious guy would come to a bar this late at night and stand in a power position, blocking her exit. Something wasn't right.

Apprehension pricked at the little hairs on the back of her neck. She glanced toward the back room, hoping Arnold was still there, but the light was off.

"What can I help you with? If you're looking to save a few souls, we're fresh out for the night. They've all gone home."

He paused a beat, then laughed. It sounded forced and didn't reach his eyes. Like a robot preprogrammed to give a specific response, he clearly was going through the motions and had another agenda.

Panic snaked its fingers around the passageways of her lungs and tightened. No. Not an asthma attack. Not now. She sucked in a wheezing breath and tried to remain calm. He probably just needed something simple. Directions maybe. This was a confusing part of town, with one-way streets, roads spiraling out every which way. Seattle's infrastructure wasn't built on a grid system, confusing many people visiting from out of town. Although she couldn't put her finger on it, she got the impression he wasn't from the area.

The man's arms hung stiffly at his sides, and in the dim overhead lighting, something glinted in his hand. Oh Lord, a weapon?

Casually, she flung her towel over her shoulder and slipped a hand under the counter, her fingers desperately searching for the silent alarm button.

"Can I get you an Irish whisky or maybe a shot of

bourbon, Father?" She didn't know what priests drank, but he obviously wanted people to think he was one. And she sure as hell wasn't about to call his bluff. "Although technically we're closed, I suppose I can bend the rules a bit for you. I was raised Catholic, you know? Haven't been to mass in a while though, I'm sorry to say. Or maybe you'd like a glass of wine?"

She was rambling, but as long as she talked, she was alive and functioning. Where was that damn button anyway? The tips of her fingers splayed under the counter, but all she felt was the roughness of unfinished wood. Her mind drew a complete blank. Was it on the other side of the cash register? Damn. She had even been here when Arnold had it installed a few years ago. *Think. Think.*

Sweat formed on her upper lip, while the back of her neck sweltered underneath her hair. The air inside Big Daddy's Brew/Pub became as thick as it had been an hour ago, but this time it wasn't due to a hot flash or a bunch of raucous sports fans.

"I am not here for a drink. Just some information." His voice had an odd, almost lyrical tone, the vowels drawn out, each word perfectly enunciated with the cutting precision of a brain surgeon. American English definitely wasn't his native language.

That was all he needed? Seemed pretty late to be coming into a bar after closing just for some information, but she continued to play along. "What can I help you with?"

"I am looking for an individual I knew a long time

ago and with whom I wish to become reacquainted. He has been in your establishment recently."

Mel tried not to wrinkle her nose at the formal way he spoke. Intellectual people pissed her off. "Yeah, so what's his name?"

"Alfonso Serrano."

Relieved, she shook her head. "Sorry, don't know him." She couldn't wait to watch him walk out that door. One thing was certain—the damn lock would get double and triple-checked tonight.

But he didn't head toward the door.

Instead, he advanced a step closer. Licked his lips. His penetrating gaze fell from her face to her shoulders.

No, wait. Her neck.

Instinctively, her hand flew to the collar of her shirt, and her heart rate skyrocketed. There was something terribly wrong about this man. He looked at her not as another person, but as something to devour. His eyes were dark. No color. Just pupils.

She backed up, but the counter stopped her from going farther.

She was trapped.

"You sure he's been in here?" Her vocal cords strained tighter, making her voice higher than normal. "Maybe you're thinking of the place across the street. The Pink Salon is a popular dance club. It's trendy, edgy. Attracts all sorts of people. We mainly attract people who want to watch the games. I know the manager over there. I could call him and ask. Or you could just pop in. Unlike us, even though it's after last call, they stay open for a while. It's that neon-pink sign. See it?"

She pointed out the window, hoping he'd look in that direction so she could do something—anything—but he didn't. He simply stared at her as if he wasn't listening to a word she'd said.

Then he did something so strange that, even though she didn't understand it, she was utterly horrified.

His eyes flickered closed and he lifted a hand to his face. Long, clawlike fingers drew her attention, and she unwillingly fixated on a small object dangling from a grotesquely thick fingernail. He sniffed at the tiny square, sucking it partially into his nostril. While holding his breath, he dropped his hand and cupped it to his chest like an actual priest cherishing a religious relic, concentrating. After a few long seconds while she wished she could look away, he exhaled, angled his nose up and inhaled again.

When he opened his eyes, they were meat-locker cold and viciously intense, reminding her of Hannibal Lecter.

Blood rushed away from her fingers and toes.

Her teeth chattered.

She had to pee.

"No," he said. "I am certain he was here."

He actually smelled the guy? Oh Lord, she had to get out of here. Maybe she could duck under the counter at the far end of the bar and lock herself in the back room. She'd call the police, hide behind the owner's huge wooden desk and hope he couldn't get through the door.

"What's this fellow look like?" She asked, her asthma making it difficult to ramble. "Short, medium, tall? Blond, brunet, redhead? Jeans, suit, or—"

"Tall. Blond. With eyes like Paul Newman."

She blinked. Wait a minute. Paul Newman–blue eyes? Could he be referring to that guy who was an awesome tipper?

"There was someone in here the other day who matches that description."

Like a bored barn cat that suddenly spots a mouse behind the grain bin, the man's eyes brightened. Had she made a terrible mistake admitting that? She'd do anything to make him stop staring at her. With his full attention, she'd never be able to make a run for it.

"Describe him for me."

She gave him a lengthy description of the customer, down to his leather jacket and workman's boots. As long as she talked, she was stalling whatever he was planning to do. "Oh, and he had a slight limp."

"A limp?" His mouth curled up smugly as if it pleased him to know this. "Did you speak with this man?"

"Briefly. But he wasn't really the talkative sort. Just sat right over there and drank his beer. He said maybe a dozen words to me. That's it. Didn't tell me his name and he...paid in cash."

"Was he alone or—" his eyes glittered with excitement "—accompanied by someone else?"

"Alone."

"Are you absolutely certain?"

He took a step closer, and at that moment, she decided her own welfare meant more to her than a stranger's. "He was keeping tabs on a woman at the Pink Salon. Does that help?"

"I knew it," the man said almost to himself. "I knew

he was involved with someone. This is very good. Does the female work there?"

Female? Who talked like that, anyway? "I…uh…I'm not sure." Then she remembered and blurted out, "I think she's a cop." Maybe the mention of the police would scare him off.

Instead of being surprised as she had hoped, his charcoal eyes glittered with amusement. He lifted his chin and laughed at the ceiling. "A law enforcement officer? Oh, what wonderful news. I must know more."

He advanced closer. For some ungodly reason, her gaze fixated on his mouth. His teeth looked unusually long.

She felt light-headed. The room spun. His voice sounded distant.

"Tell me everything you know about him."

When he reached for her, she was pretty sure she screamed, but it happened so fast that she couldn't be sure. Given her asthma, she may have just wished she'd screamed.

His hands were smooth and cold, like a snake's belly against her cheek. Obsidian eyes didn't look in her face, but were trained slightly lower. Her skin tingled under his touch, and the ligaments in her knees suddenly felt nonexistent. She got the vague sense that she was talking—telling him something, but the words didn't stick in her mind.

When he lowered his head to hers, she didn't try to escape. At that point, she knew it was futile. In her mind, she saw images of the Discovery Channel—lions leaping at gazelles, crocodiles attacking zebras, snakes striking at rodents. Once the prey was caught, it didn't struggle much.

But she did worry about Hogan. Who'd let him out when she didn't return home?

CHAPTER ELEVEN

"Mom, is he going to be all right?"

Lily's mother tossed her latex gloves into the trash can outside the O.R. and turned toward her daughter. "Who?"

Oh for godsake. "Alfonso! Who did you think I meant?"

"Well, let's see, I might have been thinking you were concerned about the Castile boy."

Her mother knew damn well who she was asking about. Why did even the simplest question get a convoluted and roundabout answer from her? Yes, Kip was Lily's responsibility. Yes, it was her fault that he'd gone missing. Yes, she should've found him earlier. But her mother didn't need to provoke her like that.

"Mom, please. I care about Kip, but I'm asking you about Alfonso first."

"Kip's going to be fine. And so is Alfonso." A huge weight lifted from her shoulders. "Come with me," her mother continued. "They're taking Alfonso to recovery."

When they'd delivered Kip to the Region's medical facility several hours ago, Lily's mother had taken one look at Alfonso and admitted him as well. The medic must've alerted her last night about Alfonso's condition. Maybe her mother could bully him into taking better care of himself.

Motioning with her hand, her mother headed down the hall, and Lily followed. When they got to the corner, her mother stopped to consult with a young man in green scrubs about another patient. The conversation was fast, but not fast enough. Lily wanted all the details on Alfonso's condition.

"Very good then." Her mother turned her attention back to Lily. "Turns out Alfonso's injury yesterday was little more than a nick. It'll heal, but it's the old one I'm focused on now. I'm running a few tests to see the extent of what I'm dealing with, but I've started the first regen treatment anyway. He's going to be a little groggy."

"And Kip?"

"He'll be fine, too, although he's going to be completely miserable for another few days."

"What about Elisabeth, the human girl they brought in yesterday?"

"As soon as we finish this last transfusion, we'll clear her mind of the ordeal and take her back home. She'll be fine…for now." They both knew this meant until she ran into another vampire, but it was the best they could do, other than keeping a tight rein on Darkblood activity.

Her mother stopped, her dark eyes narrowing, and she put her hands on Lily's shoulders.

"This Alfonso—he means a lot to you, doesn't he?"

Lily nodded, not sure where her mother was going with this. Alfonso's position as a double agent was a closely guarded secret within the Agency.

"How long have you felt this way about him?"

Lily shrugged. "For a while."

"Then is he why you left Steven?"

Horrified, Lily pushed herself away. She'd have expected that comment from her father, but not her mother. Her dad still hadn't forgiven for breaking up with her ex. Both times. Right after Zoe was born when she caught him cheating and again a few months ago. Her father had said it was her duty—God, that pissed her off—her damn duty to stay with him because they'd conceived a child together. Marrying for love had never been a necessity in their culture, but producing offspring was. She'd thought her mother was less old-fashioned than that.

"I left Steven because he's a jerk, not because I was cheating on him. He's the one who screwed around on me, if you want to know the truth. Besides, I've known Alfonso much longer than I've known Steven, and Alfonso is nothing like Steven. Nothing."

"I'm not saying you should've stayed with Steven, honey. I was curious, that's all. Alfonso seems nice and quite…taken by you. I like him. So…do the two of you work together often?"

Okay, that was a little better. The wind slowly, but not entirely, slipped from her sails. She was used to her mother's prying questions. Lily's being a single mother seemed to give everyone the license to ask about her love life, concerned that she needed a man and that her daughter needed a male role model.

"Um, not really. Not now. He was just helping out with this assignment."

They continued down the corridor again.

"Is he new to the Seattle field office? I've not seen him around before."

She really didn't want to get into any of these details. The less her mother knew, the better. No use giving her anything more to worry about. "He's not with the field office."

"Is he from one of the other Regions?"

How was she to answer that? Then she remembered the cover story Alfonso told other people. "He owns a private security firm and was doing some contract work up here." Her mother started to ask another question, but Lily interrupted her. "Mom, please. It's classified, so I really can't say much else."

Her mother glanced away, looked hurt. "Fine. I've been privy to many Agency operations, but if you don't want me to know more, that's fine."

"It's not that," she lied. What she had with Alfonso was too raw, too emotional to share. If she did tell her mother how much Alfonso had once meant to her, she'd get the twenty zillion questions about him every time they talked. And since he probably wasn't going to be in the area for much longer, it would make dealing with her mother a little easier. Plus, their history was so convoluted that trying to explain everything would only emphasize her inability to sustain a relationship. "It truly is classified. I can't say anything about what sort of work he does for the Agency. You can ask Santiago. He'll back me on this."

"No, that's fine," her mother said. "I'm not going above your head. It was just a simple question that I thought would get a simple answer. Speaking of Steven, did you know he's coming up for Zoe's recital?"

"Oh great." Lily rolled her eyes. "Just the person I'm dying to see."

"Come on. He's not here that often. You can at least be civil."

"Yeah, he's not here often because he's a crappy father and couldn't give a sh—crap about his own daughter and what she has going on in her life." Her mother hated her bad language, so she tried to control her mouth when she was up here.

"He's not winning any father-of-the-year awards, that's for sure, but at least he's here. He's trying. You can at least try to be cordial with him. For Zoe's sake."

"I'll be nice to him, but I don't have to like it." That sounded childish, but she didn't care. She had a right to be immature when talking with her mother.

"So, you've known Alfonso for quite a while?"

"Yep."

"He's not the one you used to talk to your grandmother about, is he?"

Lily shot her a surprised look. Her conversations with her grandmother were private. "I don't know what you're talking about."

But she recalled those long talks she'd had with her grandmother when her grandfather was dying. Lily would sit with her at his bedside, hold her frail, thin-skinned hand, look into her faded eyes that had seen and experienced so much and listen to stories of how her grandparents had met and fallen in love centuries ago. A very private person, her grandmother had told Lily things she'd never shared with anyone else.

"We are *Enlazado por la Sangre*," her grandmother

would say. "Joined body, soul and spirit. When he dies, I die, for I cannot bear to walk this earth without him."

It was an uncommon bond between vampire couples who were connected through blood on a much deeper level than most, able to sense the thoughts or emotions of the other person. Lily felt honored that her grandmother had told her about it. Unlike her own parents' business-like marriage. When Lily witnessed her grandmother's deep love for her husband, especially when he was dying, Lily had told *her* about meeting Alfonso, this amazing man whom she'd felt so unusually close to, rather than telling her mom. Although she couldn't read Alfonso's thoughts, she did feel connected to him on a more emotional level sometimes, and because they had the ability to share energies, an unusual trait in its own right, the starry-eyed romantic in her dreamed she and Alfonso were *Enlazado por la Sangre* as well.

Just like her grandparents were.

Which was why, when he'd left her, she had felt as if she were going a little bit crazy.

"I know the two of you became very close before she died, and I did overhear you telling her once about someone special you'd met."

"You listened in on us?" Lily's face heated up.

"No, that's all I heard." Her mother readjusted the stethoscope around her neck. "Although I suppose I was a little jealous that you seemed to have a closer relationship with my own mother than what I had with you or with her. That's all. Relax, I didn't listen in. I was walking into the hospital room to check on Daddy when I heard just the briefest mention about someone you'd met. I left immediately because I knew it was a private conversation between the two of you. If you wanted me to know, you'd have told me."

Lily relaxed, although she felt guilty that she hadn't shared any of this with her. Her mother was many things, most of them wonderful, some of them annoying, but a liar was not one of them.

She hadn't realized her mother felt that way about the relationship she had with her grandmother. She hooked her arm into the crook of her mother's arm, suddenly needing to tell her a little about Alfonso. "We...ah... have the ability to share energy. Although I'd love it for things to work out between us, I'm afraid that's not possible. You know. His work and everything."

They stopped outside a patient room. Her mother smiled, brushed the hair back from Lily's face as if she were still a small child. The color of her eyes reminded Lily of stuffed animals, hot chocolate with a dollop of ice cream, and electric blankets on a chilly night. Comforting and perfect.

"He's inside. The structure of that joint is really fragile at the moment. If he heals as quickly as I'm hoping, I'll get him started on some physical therapy tomorrow. But first, in order for that to happen—" her mother gave her a pointed look "—his body will be needing blood... and energies."

Lily stiffened. It was one thing for her to bring up the topic of sex to her mother, but not the other way around. "Mom, are you saying...?"

"Love is not something you should let slip through

your fingers, Lily. You need to grab on to it while you can. He needs what only you can give him. Now, go."

UNSURE OF WHERE HE WAS or how much time had passed, Alfonso's recollection of hushed whispers and the stab of needles faded with the here-and-now sensation of soft female flesh under his hands.

Long, silky hair tickled his face and chest. The smell of lavender gave him a vague sense of numbness, making his body function on rote memory. His mouth sought out and found an aroused nipple, and he circled his tongue around the tender nub. Even if she hadn't made that soft gasp of surprise, he knew it was Lily who straddled him. He'd recognize her body by feel alone.

Cool fingers cupped his balls, gently stroking, massaging. A singular, primal need—like the instinct for food or water—suddenly became his driving focus.

But before he could roll her over, those same fingers gripped the base of his erection. Then, with minimal effort on his part, a tight sheath of warmth slid down over his cock, sending shock waves through his body. He groaned, arched his head back into the pillow as every nerve tingled with pleasure.

"My God, woman, what are you doing to me?" His words were slurred, but he was too consumed by this glorious sensation to wonder why.

"I need to be on top because of your knee. Just lie back and enjoy it. I fed from a human while you were being treated—both blood and energy—and I'm transferring it to you. That nick of yours turned out to be a little more serious."

Knee? Treated? Energy transfers? He was too groggy to figure out what to say or ask, especially when he was completely consumed by what she was doing to him.

She took his hands and positioned them along either side of her face. An unseen electrical shimmer passed from her body to his, sizzling along his thumbs and fingertips, up his arms and into his core, making him feel more alive. With his eyes closed, he reveled in this very intimate contact, absently stroking her temples with his thumbs. As he took in what she offered, he pulled her close, felt the press of her breasts as they flattened against his chest. He kissed her softly, undemanding, so as not to disrupt what flowed between them.

After he'd taken enough from her, he removed his hands from her face and ran them over her shoulder, along the narrow channel of her spine, and down to her backside. She trembled beneath his fingers. His cock swelled impossibly harder inside her.

"Thank you. Although I'm still…I'm still…" He wasn't sure what he was, his mind was hazy and the words wouldn't come to mind. "I hope you're prepared for the consequences."

"My goal from the start," she said against his lips.

With the most powerful thrust he could muster, he began moving again, her warmth tightly hugging him. God, this was heaven. His loud groan echoed off the walls and floor.

"Shhh," she whispered playfully. "Do you want everyone to hear?"

What was she talking about? The darkened room was quiet. They were alone. "Everyone?"

"The clinic staff. I hung a Do Not Disturb sign on the door, but I can't do anything about people walking down the hallway and hearing what's going on in here."

Of course, the hospital.

Wait. A hospital? He'd been thinking they were in a hotel room. He always made love to her in hotel rooms or various hideaways he kept.

"What am I doing in a hospital?"

"Your knee, remember?"

My knee? Aware now of the bandages around his leg, he remembered the bright lights of an O.R. and a female in a surgical mask asking him questions. Oh yeah, he'd had surgery. "You're having…sex with me…in a hospital room?" That didn't make sense, did it? Surely he had to be dreaming.

"You're so amazing, love," she whispered breathlessly in his ear as her body moved over his.

His chest swelled with masculine pride. He opened his eyes, planning to tell her he felt the same way about her, but when two plump breasts bounced inches from his face, teasing him, taunting him, he forgot about saying anything coherent. Reaching up, he lifted one with his fingertips, quieting its movement and feeling the weight in his hand. Then he rubbed a thumb over an aroused tip.

As if on cue, she stopped moving her hips. Her whole body trembled, waiting for him to continue. He lifted his head and guided the dusky pink flesh into his mouth again. With a quick intake of breath, she arched toward him, making his task even easier, and he leaned back on the pillow. On top, she probably thought she could control him, but in reality, her body responded to him like a finely tuned instrument, waiting for him to strum the right strings.

Lubricating each nipple with his tongue and delighting in her little sounds of pleasure, he softly pinched them between his thumbs and forefingers, and although he'd closed his eyes again, his tongue told him they'd peaked even further. He angled his hips up and pushed the tip of his shaft even deeper inside her.

Oh, she was almost there. He could feel it. Almost soft enough, but not quite. Wait for it, he told himself. Wait until she was totally ready. It will be so worth it.

He tried to ignore the pressure building in his loins, the highly sensitive nerve endings igniting along his length, but his willpower was running on fumes. He could feel this steady friction was bringing her to climax. Would she make her soft moaning noise that matched the rhythm of his hips?

Oh God. Yes, she did.

Just as he had hoped, she cried out, her voice throaty and so damned sexy.

"Alfonso, I'm…I'm…"

Her internal muscles tightened around his erection in successive waves of pleasure.

Ah, yes, it was time. Her body was signaling to his that she was ready.

Pressure surged instantly in his balls, and his fangs

stretched out to their full length. The primitive call became too powerful, too urgent to ignore any longer.

Using his tongue to guide him to the place on her neck where the artery was the closest to the surface, he quickly found what he was looking for. Her pleasure had given her blood a sweet, intoxicating scent—it pulsed beneath his lips, beckoning him like a siren's call.

Something tickled at the back of his mind. He tried to retrieve it, but it was like driving in a heavy fog, with indiscernible shadows just beyond his consciousness that he couldn't quite make out.

However, all that really mattered right now was this.

He placed one broad hand on her hips, halting her movement. With the other hand, he pulled the back of her hair, maybe a little too roughly, he realized, when he heard her gasp.

Two tiny thrusts were all it took as he sunk his fangs into her flesh.

And the universe collided behind his eyelids.

Time stood still as he released himself into her, his body functioning on autopilot, marking what rightfully belonged to him. The past and the future had no meaning—all that mattered was this precise, beautiful moment when he claimed her as his woman.

Lily mumbled something, but the words were mere vibrations against his lips. For when he swallowed that first sip of her lifeblood, the magnitude of this simple act overwhelmed him. Something inside him moved, thawed, his brittle edges becoming smoother.

Being with Lily defined who he was. She made him

want to strip away the shield, the hard exterior he'd lived with for so long, and discover who he was inside. He wasn't a killer, a traitor or an Agent. He was simply a man looking for a home, and he knew he could find it with her.

JACKSON PAUSED WHEN HE SAW the handwritten Do Not Disturb sign on the patient room door. Was Alfonso asleep? He really didn't want to come back later. He wanted to get this over with as soon as possible.

Why Santiago thought Jackson could talk Alfonso into coming to work for the Agency when none of his own arguments had worked was beyond him. If you asked him, it was a giant waste of time.

Besides, Dom would be less than happy. It wasn't like the two brothers were buddies. When he mentioned this to Santiago, his boss came unglued, saying Dom would just have to deal with his decision to bring his brother on board whether he liked it or not.

One thing was certain, if Alfonso did agree to come work for the Agency, Jackson was going to make sure he was nowhere near Dom when he got the news. The field team leader had a habit of taking out his aggression on Jackson.

Guess he'd come back later.

The muffled sound of a woman's voice came from inside the door. Oh, so Alfonso was awake after all.

Jackson ripped off the note and grabbed the handle. He wasn't sure what *he* was going to say to convince the guy, but, hell, who was he to argue with the Region Commander?

But when he heard the rumbling noise of a man groaning with ecstasy, he jerked his hand back as if he'd been burned. It definitely wasn't the sound of someone getting a sponge bath.

Shit. With his condition, that was the last thing he needed to hear. He was barely holding it together as it was.

Crumpling the paper into a wad, he did an about-face and strode down the hallway, determined to get as far away as possible from the activity going on behind that closed door.

He leaned over a water fountain, took a few gulps, then splashed his face. What if he'd opened the door and seen Alfonso banging some chick? Or Lily? Hell, it really didn't matter. The guy could be humping that hot nurse Jackson had spotted earlier, for all he cared. The point was, someone was having sex and it wasn't him. Despite his efforts, he felt his pupils expanding, and his gums began to ache. His control was slipping through his fingers like this water.

Come on. He needed to get himself together. What his body craved wasn't possible right now.

When he'd arrived at the clinic a short time ago, he recalled how the little redhead had given him a welcoming smile with those perfect white teeth. Although she wasn't quite his type—he preferred them edgier-looking and a little less wholesome—he wouldn't let that stop him if she wanted to hook up.

As she'd escorted him to the urgent care wing, she kept glancing sideways at him, sizing him up, taking stock.

Being used to such female attention, he was confident he'd be having sex with her before nightfall.

God, he sure as hell hoped he'd read her right and that she was nearby. Otherwise he'd have to approach someone else, and he wasn't in the mood for flirting, nor did he have the time. Stuck here in Region headquarters during the day, without the ability to get any human blood or energy, made him feel even more trapped. A poor substitute, yet more socially acceptable, having sex was the only thing that would help relieve the pressure he was feeling right now.

Surrounded by those who could figure out that his energy requirements were way above what they should be was not at all comforting. Scarier than shit was more like it. He knew what they did to those who were slipping, and he wasn't about to let it happen to him. The only relief he could hope for, now that his cravings had been triggered, was to have sex.

The sound of female laughter came from somewhere around the corner. The nurses' station? He hastily retied his ponytail, securing the leather band just around the upper portion, leaving the rest of his newly highlighted hair to fall loosely to his shoulders. Women loved the blue streaks, he thought confidently as he strode toward the voices. He was glad he'd changed them to blue again.

Would Little Red be there? Maybe they could hook up in some supply closet.

He felt his pupils dilating further, but thankfully, his fangs hadn't broken through yet.

The clip of his boot heels echoed off the sterile tile floor. Too bad nurses didn't wear uniforms any longer.

He could really go for a chick dressed as a naughty nurse, clad in a garter belt and hose with no panties underneath. After he had sex, he'd make himself scarce until dusk, then he'd troll for a little human energy on the way back to Seattle. Yes, the perfect plan.

He turned down the hallway, but it was empty. Christ, where was that nurses' station? He must've taken a wrong turn in this catacomb-like, underground facility. He tugged at his pants, trying to give his erection a little more room, and hurried back the way he'd come.

In his haste, he rounded the corner too quickly and didn't see the person in scrubs until it was too late. A clipboard and stethoscope went flying. He caught the woman by the elbow before she hit the floor, too.

Oh shit, Lily's mother.

"So sorry, Dr. DeGraff. Wasn't looking where I was going." Keeping his gaze averted, he hastily stooped to pick up her clipboard. Would she notice the change in his eyes? She could probably tell just by looking at his expanded pupils that something was wrong.

"No worries, Agent Foss. I was reading some test results, not paying attention, either. But I'm glad we ran into each other. I'd like to have a word with you. Got a minute?"

Fuuuuck. What did she want to talk to him for? He was in no condition to be chatting with the head of the Region's medical facility, let alone the wife of a Council member. Sweat beaded on the back of his neck, threatening to run between his shoulder blades. He had a feeling this wasn't going to be good.

"Yeah, sure," he said reluctantly.

With quick, efficient steps, she led him to an alcove furnished with uncomfortable-looking chairs, a small flat-screen tuned to a nature channel and a too-large aquarium that he didn't want to look at. With his back to the fish tank, he slumped in a seat and pulled out his ponytail so the hair would partially cover his eyes. Was this going to be a come-to-Jesus meeting? An I've-noticed-something-strange-about-you-that-concerns-me meeting?

He grabbed a magazine and flipped through the pages as she took a seat across from him. The possible explanations he could give her flashed through his mind. All of them lies.

I'm just slogging, that's all.

I haven't had any human energy in days because I've been working a lot and haven't made the time.

I haven't fed from a live host in ages, but guess I'm overdue.

My last feeding was cut short and I haven't had a chance to get more.

My girlfriend broke up with me, so it's been a while since I've had sex to burn off my excess energies.

Yeah, right. His excuses were endless.

"What can you tell me about Mr. Serrano?" Dr. De-Graff asked. "I know he and Lily worked together and that he's Dom's brother."

This was about Alfonso? Not him? A rush of relief washed over him and doused the panic. He kicked his feet up on the coffee table and crossed his legs. "You'll need to talk to Santiago about him. I'm afraid it's classified."

Few individuals inside the Council knew the identity of the Agent they had on the inside, so he was sworn to secrecy. In fact, some didn't even believe there had been someone on the inside. He recalled the times Gibby had given Lily shit about her so-called contact. Jackson had only become aware of the guy's identity when the Seattle field team's operation had come to a head last year, and Santiago had thought the guy had been killed in the explosion. Until then, even Dom hadn't known it was his own brother who'd been working for years as a double agent, supplying the Council with intel.

"Very well." Using the eraser on the end of her pencil to help turn the pages, Dr. DeGraff scanned through the chart she held on her lap. "Can you at least tell me how long they've been working together?"

Jackson stretched an arm along the back of the chair and gazed up at the ceiling, still not wanting her to look at his eyes too closely. "I think they've been working together since he moved to the States. Not long. Five, ten years maybe. Why?"

She tapped the eraser on her clipboard. "Curious, that's all. My husband and I knew she'd been involved with someone, but she's been reluctant to share much. Seeing them together, I just wondered."

Although Dr. DeGraff seemed pretty involved in her daughter's life, maybe too much, at least Lily had a family who cared enough about her to get all up in her business.

"Thanks for the information," she said, rising from her seat.

Relieved that the interrogation was over and that he could now resume his hunt for Little Red, he turned a few pages of the magazine and wondered if the nurses' station was to the left or to the right. "Sorry I couldn't tell you more."

"No, you told me enough." She paused at the doorway. "By the way, you're pretty talented."

He gave her a quizzical look.

With a tilt of her head, she indicated the magazine. "Don't know many who can read upside down."

CHAPTER TWELVE

ALFONSO SLIPPED A PIN into the next weight slot down and leg-pressed another set. Sounds of his loud groaning echoed off the walls of the physical therapy room. It was a good sound, one he'd missed for quite a while, and although weight machines were for women and old men, it was part of his therapy, so he didn't let it dampen his mood.

His knee still hurt like a sonofabitch, but it was definitely getting stronger. He hadn't been able to lift this much since before the accident. Despite his initial skepticism, Dr. DeGraff's regeneration treatment must be working.

After he finished his prescribed workout, he flipped a towel over his shoulder and sauntered into the steam room. Another part of his therapy. At least this one didn't hurt. Thank God the place was empty, he thought, as he splashed water onto the hot rocks and heard the sizzle. Small talk with some guy from Region wasn't on his agenda today. He climbed to the upper bench, rested his head on the cedar paneling and closed his eyes.

Breathing in the eucalyptus-scented steam, his thoughts drifted to Lily. He couldn't believe he'd been so delirious that he'd taken her blood the other day. It was foolish and reckless. And now that he had, he couldn't chance things by staying around much longer. Despite how much he wanted to stay with her, as soon as this knee healed, he knew he'd need to leave. Maybe he'd head back to Europe, strengthen those false leads again. Or maybe he should go somewhere else entirely. Anyplace to keep the assassin off track until Lily's blood faded from Alfonso's system and she could no longer be linked to him.

He took a drink of water and thought about how she'd walked through his house, admiring the work he'd done and taking a genuine interest in everything. They shared so many of the same interests. Like him, she seemed to connect to the history and significance of the objects he chose to place in his home and to the effort he was making by building it. She had even admired the headboard. He'd spent countless hours working on it, painstakingly carving every detail. A knight leading his soldiers into battle. He'd never been able to sleep in it and he doubted he ever would, although it warmed him to know Lily had. That would need to be enough.

But God, his heart ached thinking of being apart from her again. At least she'd know the truth this time when he left. That if things were any different, he'd want to spend the rest of his life with her.

He flexed his knee again. God, it felt strong.

Maybe, just maybe, he'd be able to confront the assassin—far away from Lily—once it fully healed.

The door banged open, bringing with it a whoosh of cold air. Annoyed at the disturbance, he cracked open an eye and checked the timer on his watch. Great. Another six minutes. Maybe the guy wasn't a talker.

"How's it going?" The bench on the opposite side of

the steam room creaked as the guy sat down and groaned. "Man, I love this place. It's been way too long." The guy coughed a few times. "Holy hell, it's steamy in here. You got this place cranking. Mind if I turn it down for a sec?"

"Knock yourself out." Nothing like an interloper coming in, thinking he could call all the shots, but whatever. Alfonso wasn't planning on sticking around for long.

The hissing sound of the steam quieted a little.

"There. Much better. Thanks."

Alfonso lifted his hand in a wordless reply. Maybe he'd get the hint that Alfonso wasn't interested in idle chitchat. He kept his eyes closed and flexed his knee. The joint moved freely, easily, without the pain and creaking noises he'd become accustomed to. If he didn't know better, it seemed almost as good as the other one already.

He had to admit, in addition to his surgery and treatment, Lily's blood and energies were also helping.

He felt…great. Better, physically, than he had in a long time.

"So what are you in for? The knee? You a Guardian? You don't look familiar."

Alfonso tensed, his fingers automatically curling around nonexistent kunai. Like a security blanket, those little blades had come in handy more than once, but right now they were sitting inside his gym locker. Damn. The last time someone had recognized him it hadn't been pretty.

But when he saw how the guy was lounging, he relaxed and somehow managed to suppress a chuckle. Unless the idiot was a magician, he was unarmed. Spread-eagled on the bench, he was buck naked, knees open, arms stretched out. With no place to stash a weapon, it was hardly what you'd call an offensive position.

He didn't recall seeing a sign that said Clothing Optional.

"Yes, my knee," Alfonso said, ignoring the other questions.

"Bummer. I'm just using the facilities while I'm up here. Gotta take advantage of the perks, you know?" He laughed and held out his hand. "Steven Hastings. And you are?"

Alfonso's chest constricted. This immodest motherfucker was Lily's ex-boyfriend? Zoe's father? The man Lily had recently been living with? What the hell was he doing here? He thought the guy lived in California.

With slitted eyes, Alfonso scrutinized him. He had dark hair, but maybe just because it was wet and slicked back—mafioso-style—a square, too-angular jaw and a lithe runner's body. His laugh was the kind you'd hear in a German pub during Oktoberfest, when tourists became bawdy and loud with too much beer, and you were totally and completely sober.

Yeah, Alfonso hated every single thing about him. He reluctantly shook the guy's hand and introduced himself.

"Good to meet you, Alfonso." Steven rested an ankle on his knee, giving Alfonso an even clearer view of what hung between his legs.

Oh, for the love of God, he did not need to see that.

So Lily hadn't mentioned Alfonso to her ex. He wasn't sure whether to be relieved that she'd kept their relationship confidential or disappointed that she had. He turned his attention to his watch as the seconds ticked down until he was out of here.

"So, where you from? You live around here? I'm up visiting from San Francisco. Like to take advantage of the Region's gym facilities. Makes the trip a little more bearable."

Bearable? He knew Hastings was some sort of fund manager for the Council, which was evidently why he was allowed access to the facility. Was the guy here on Council business or was he here to see his daughter? Fuck, he'd probably be seeing Lily as well.

Alfonso told him the same half truths about himself that he'd been telling others for years. He had another minute or so of the prescribed steam therapy, then he was out of here. The last thing he wanted to do was get all chummy with this guy. In fact, Alfonso thought as he clutched the edge of the wooden bench, what he really wanted to do was beat the shit out of him. From what Lily'd told him, Hastings was an ass. Just looking at him, Alfonso had to agree.

"God, you're lucky, you know that?"

"I am?" Oh, this was going to be good. Alfonso closed his eyes and wished the guy would just shut the hell up.

"You travel the world. Stay in an exciting city every week. No worries or responsibilities."

Excuse me? Alfonso mopped his face with a towel and gave him a what-the-fuck look. "What I do is very stressful. I've got plenty of worries."

"Yeah, but you're living the life *you* want to live. No one to tie you down. God, what I wouldn't give for that. To call all the shots. You can sleep with whoever you want to, wake up to a different face each evening, rather than the same one day after day. No one is nagging you to perform in a tough economy—as if I can pull a carrot out of my ass—to set a good example for so-and-so, to attend this or that social function, or reminding you that you have a kid to support and family obligations to meet."

Alfonso ground his molars together to keep from saying something he'd regret later.

"Don't get me wrong," Hastings continued. "I love my daughter. But being a father wasn't something I wanted at this point in my life. I wanted to see the world, lead an exciting life like yours, you know? But instead, I'm stuck in an office—granted, a nice one with mahogany furniture and a smoking-hot secretary—but every day those walls feel like they're coming in a little bit closer, snuffing out my dreams. It's stifling and I feel trapped sometimes. You know what I'm talking about?"

No, he honestly didn't know. This fucker had everything Alfonso had ever wished for, yet he was pissing it all away. The guy thought he was trapped? Trapped was when you had no choices. "You think living out of a suitcase sounds glamorous? Not setting down roots, not having a place to call your own? Sleeping in a different location all the time? Having no one to care about but yourself? Sorry, it's not."

Hastings scratched his belly and laughed. "Need some toilet paper to go with your shit? Don't give me that grass-is-always-greener speech. People who say that are always the ones living the life, trying to make those of us who are stuck feel better about ourselves."

What the hell was he talking about? From what

Alfonso understood, the guy had never let something as trivial as a relationship stand in the way of being a player and sleeping with anything that had a pulse. He'd had enough.

"You're a moron, you know that? You had a beautiful woman to share your life with and you have an amazing daughter. I can't think of a better way to go through life than with them."

"What the hell are you talking about? How would you know? She left me."

Yeah, Alfonso wondered why.

"Besides, I stay involved in my daughter's life. I flew all the way up here for her dance recital."

Alfonso stood and rewrapped the towel around his waist. "It's a piano recital." What a loser.

Something continued to bother him as he took a quick shower and dressed. Like a face he couldn't recall or a word he couldn't put his finger on, it was a thought just outside his consciousness. He barely remembered walking out of the locker room and had to go back for his gym bag. The conversation with Steven kept replaying in his head until he finally figured it out.

He wasn't any different than Steven. An asshole was an asshole. Although Alfonso hadn't cheated on her, he had left Lily, and he hadn't fought for their future either.

As he passed the rec area, he heard the sound of a piano being plunked rather unsuccessfully. The same melody played over and over, with the same note missed each time. He could tell the player was getting frustrated, because the tempo got progressively faster and louder until what was probably a fist came crashing down on the keys, squelching the melody altogether.

He popped his head in the door and saw a young girl perched on the edge of a piano bench, her feet barely reaching the pedals. He was about to turn around and head back to his room when she pounded on the keys again.

Dropping his gym bag, he approached her. "You're very close to getting it right. Need a little help?"

The girl looked over her shoulder at him with caramel-colored eyes that seemed a tad too large for her heart-shaped face. Alfonso's heart skipped. Despite the fact that her braided hair was a mahogany-brown, she looked just like Lily.

Oh Lord. Zoe.

She was even more adorable in person than in the photos he'd seen. Lily's mini-me. Was she here at the Region office waiting for her mom or her grandmother?

She shrugged. "I don't need help. I can do it myself."

He hid a smile. Definitely Lily's daughter. "It's a tricky song to play, that's for sure. I never was able to master it, myself."

"You play the piano?"

"Not much anymore, but I used to."

"Really?"

"Yeah. I had to play that same song in a recital in front of many of my parents' friends when I was about your age. You're actually doing much better than I did. Don't tell anyone, but I don't care that it's considered a classical piece of music. I've always hated it. I think it was that song that made me switch from the piano to the guitar."

Her eyes went wide. "You know how to play the guitar too?"

"Yeah. I enjoy it much more than the piano. But don't get me wrong, knowing how to play the piano does help you learn to play other instruments."

"I hate the dumb songs they make you play. They're boring and none of them have words. I have a recital and have to play this song in front of a bunch of people. It's just so hard. No matter how much I practice, I can't reach C-flat." She stretched out her fingers. "They don't go that wide."

He tapped his injured leg. "Yeah, I know the feeling when something doesn't work the way you want it. Mind if I try? Maybe I can help."

She shrugged. "I guess so, but I'm the one who has to play it."

He sat next to her on the bench, and for almost an hour, he watched her struggle with the melody and offered encouraging words and suggestions when he could.

"You play really well for an eight-year-old."

"I'm not eight," she said angrily. "I'm eight and a half."

"Oh, sorry," he said, trying not to laugh. "My mistake. You play really well for an eight-and-a-half-year-old."

Heavy footsteps sounded at the door. "Alfonso, when the fuck are you—"

Alfonso clamped his hands over Zoe's ears and glared behind him toward the doorway. Santiago. "Can't you say anything without cussing?"

Santiago looked a little sheepish when he saw Zoe. "We need to talk."

"I'll be with you in a minute."

He waited for the guy to leave before he turned back to Zoe and nudged her with his elbow. "Nice job. You nailed that tricky part. I think you're going to be ready for the recital."

Looking dejected, she twisted her hands in her lap, not buying his encouragement. "I don't know. I'll probably get up there and forget everything."

"Try to remember that many of the people listening to you don't even play the piano. They'll see what you can do and be amazed, whether or not you make a few mistakes. And if you do mess up, then you muscle through it anyway. That's what all performing artists do. No one's perfect. The only difference is they sell it with their confidence. Tell you what." He reached into his shirt and pulled the cord from around his neck. "Want to wear this?"

Zoe examined the intertwined gold pendant that had neither a beginning nor an end. "What is it?"

"A Gordian knot. Your mom gave it to me a long time ago, and it's always given me good luck."

"You mean it's a lucky charm?"

"Yeah, I guess you could say that. It signifies how even the trickiest of problems or situations can be overcome if you're bold in your efforts and confident in your abilities. Sometimes the biggest obstacles we face are the ones within ourselves."

She looked at him with glazed-over eyes as if she didn't know what the heck he'd just said, but he slipped the thin leather cord around her neck anyway. Many times he'd felt the presence of the pendant, its warmth against his chest and how it had given him that little extra something to keep going, whether he had faith in himself or not. Lily had given it to him before he'd left for Europe, when he didn't know if he'd ever return, and she'd told him not to forget her.

"My mom gave this to you?" Zoe turned the pendant over in her hand and traced the unbroken line with her thumb.

"Yes, she's…very special to me." He didn't know what Lily had told her about him or what the protocol was with children and ex-lovers. Feeling a little awkward, he cleared his throat. "If you want, you can tuck it inside your clothes, so you don't have to wear it on the outside."

The piano bench shook as she swung her legs. She'd forgotten about the necklace already. "You're coming, aren't you? To my recital?" When she looked up at him with her big doe-eyes, so similar to Lily's, his heart nearly flipped over in his chest.

How could he say no to that? But he had to. He couldn't get involved in Zoe's life, no matter how much he wanted to. He'd be leaving soon and it wouldn't be fair to her. "I don't think so, honey. Your grandmother is discharging me from the hospital soon, so I'll be heading back to my home. You're playing at the Longest Night celebration, right?"

With a pouty expression she probably used a lot, she stilled her legs and dropped her hands to her lap. "But I want you to come. I won't be able to play it without you there."

"Sure you can. Just remember what we practiced and you'll be fine. And don't forget about your lucky charm. If you believe in yourself, you'll do great. I promise." He kissed her on the top of her head. "Hey, I think I heard Jackson saying something about brownies in the Region's kitchen."

Alarm flashed in her eyes. She shot from the bench and ran toward the door.

"He better not eat all of 'em."

Alfonso laughed as she darted from the room without a backward glance, her problems at the piano now forgotten in favor of focusing on more important things. He could still hear the sound of her footsteps when Santiago entered the room again.

The Region Commander strode in wearing a pair of black dress slacks with a crisply ironed crease, a pinstripe shirt—no tie, and a sport coat with the sleeves shoved up to his elbows. Meeting attire, and given that perpetual scowl on his face, Alfonso figured it was his bullshit attire too.

"Listen," Santiago said. "Cordell's taking a leave of absence right before the Night of Wilding—his wife's been sick and he's worried about her—and we're still no closer to finding out the location of that goddamn DB party."

Oh God, not this again. "That's a bloody shame. What does it have to do with me?" Although he really didn't need to ask. He knew exactly what the guy wanted. A tiny part of him had to admit, it jacked his ego knowing Santiago wanted him on the team so badly.

"You've gotten further along in that video game than Cordell has been able to do. Yeah, don't give me that look and act like you don't give a fuck what goes on around here. I know you've been playing it and I know you care. You've gotta be on the verge of finding out the location."

Alfonso shrugged. "That's not really how it works. But if I do find out, I'll be sure to let you know."

Santiago leaned an elbow on the piano and crossed one leg over the other. "What'll it take for you to come on board and help? Just till the party's over. A fancy little sports car? I've seen you blowing your wad over Lily's wheels. A signing bonus? A private office? Wait. I got it!" He clasped his hands together in an overdramatic show of excitement. "You want a blow job."

"Oh good God."

Santiago pinched the bridge of his nose in an effort to keep from laughing, but it wasn't any use. The guy was grinning from ear to ear at his own joke. "I'm not really into that, but, hey, I'm desperate and willing to do just about anything, if that's what it takes for you to change your mind. You've been giving it to me up the ass for so long. How much worse could that be?"

"Stop." Alfonso laughed. "You'd do that for me, really? Honestly, Santiago, I'm touched."

"Like I said, I'm desperate." Santiago rubbed a hand over his closely cropped hair and got all serious again. "Listen, Alfonso. We could really use you."

"I'd like to help you out but…" The laughter died in his throat. Once Santiago learned he'd taken the Blood Oath, Alfonso was sure he'd change his mind about wanting to bring him on board anyway.

"But what?"

"You wouldn't want me if you knew the truth about me."

"I know quite a lot about you, in case you're wondering."

"Yeah? You think?"

Why was it so much easier lying to people when you weren't face-to-face? He scrutinized the guy. Sure, Santiago was a ballbuster, but the guy didn't always play by the rules either. You didn't get to the position he was in by coloring inside the lines. Maybe Santiago wouldn't run to the Council when he learned the truth. And if he did, most likely it wouldn't matter when this whole thing was over anyway. Who cared about a Council pardon if you were dead?

He was tired of this facade. Tired of pretending to be someone he wasn't. Could he trust Santiago not to say anything?

"Did you know that I took an actual Blood Oath of Allegiance to the Alliance and the Overlord?" His whole body stiffened as he continued, expecting Santiago to interrupt him at any moment with a tirade. "You can't tell me the Council would want someone in their ranks who had ever done something like that."

Santiago didn't appear surprised or even disgusted. "Like I said, I know a lot about you."

Incredulous, Alfonso stared at him. "You mean you knew that I'd taken the Blood Oath? That I swore my allegiance to them?" How was it possible that Santiago wasn't freaking out right now? The guy wasn't exactly the calm sort.

"You think we're stupid enough that we wouldn't fully vet out your background beforehand? Yes, of course we knew."

He'd said *we*. The Council? They knew, too? Alfonso could hardly get his mind around that.

Santiago continued. "Why do you think we made you the offer to work for us in the first place? We knew that since you took the Oath, you'd be above reproach within the Alliance and privy to all sorts of intel we'd been unable to attain otherwise."

"You didn't think that deep down inside I still had a Darkblood agenda? No one takes the Oath without agreeing to die for what they believe in or suffer the consequences, which are pretty fucking awful. No one ever denounces the Oath. Ever."

"Why did you think we assigned Lily to be your contact? Dom told us that he and your father suspected you'd taken the Oath."

"Dom knew?" He rubbed his eyes. His head felt like it was going to explode.

"Yeah, but we didn't tell him about our plans to bring you on board as a double agent. Thought it best that he be kept out of the loop in case Darkbloods got suspicious about anything you did or said and started digging around."

No wonder his brother had never trusted him, despite anything Alfonso said to the contrary. It explained so much. If the roles were reversed and he'd heard his brother had taken the Oath, he'd have felt the same way. Then, of course, he'd really fucked up by bringing Pavlos to their parents' home, thinking he could mediate a truce between the Council and the Alliance.

"But how did he find out? I didn't share that with anyone. It's not something I'm proud of, you know?"

"Dom said you told him."

"That's impossible. I'd have never told him that."

"Well, evidently you did. I'll bet there are a lot of things you didn't know about during that time. Addicts have shitty memories."

He recalled that back then, in the early days of his involvement with the Alliance, there were many days when he had no recollection of where he was or what he'd done. High on Sweet. High on opiates. Who knew what he'd done or said? Could he have admitted to Dom at some point that he'd taken the Oath?

Oh God, maybe he had.

He rested his forehead on the cool wood of the piano, his temples aching, his brain pounding. He felt like puking. The black sheep of the family had demonstrated just how different he was. No wonder Dom hated him.

"And you assigned Lily to me because of this?" he managed to choke out. "Why?"

Santiago scoffed at him. "I'm surprised you even have to ask. There's nothing that gets past that woman. If she detected even the least bit of sympathy toward them from you, smelled any sort of deception on your part, we'd have pulled the plug on our little arrangement immediately. When you approached us with your offer to spy on them from the inside, of course we checked you out. And part of that included talking to Dom."

He stared unseeingly at the piano keys and plunked

out a couple of familiar notes. "Since you know about that, then you know the problem I face." He lowered his voice until it was barely above a whisper. "I am tied in blood to a member of the Order of the Red Sword and he knows that I am the betrayer and that I'm alive. He carries my blood with him at all times to help activate my scent and track me down. And you know what that means, don't you? He will not stop until I'm dead and, since I've taken Lily's blood again, she's not safe from him either."

He went on to tell Santiago about the intricate steps he'd taken in Europe to throw the assassin off his trail, knowing that sooner or later the killer would catch up to him.

"You do know that our offices over there have the Order of the Red Sword under watch, don't you?"

"What?" His elbow landed on the piano keys, the sound filling the room. He had no idea. The thought of this secret order of killers being watched by the Council sent a thrill down his spine. Maybe the order wasn't as powerful as it appeared to be.

"Yes, in fact, let me give them a call now."

Within fifteen minutes, Santiago received confirmation that the Prague field office had Rejavik under surveillance where he'd been for the past two weeks. The ORS had a training facility located in an old monastery in the region. The Council had been watching it for years.

"So you see? He's over there. You're over here. We need your help. It's a simple equation. What do you say? Can you at least stay on until after we bust this big Night of Wilding party and deal with the aftermath? Dom will be back by then and we'll be able to limp along like we always have."

Holy shit. Alfonso took a deep breath and let it out slowly. Incredibly, his elaborate false leads must still be working. Maybe he did have more time than he thought. And even if the assassin had followed him to the States, he'd probably be tracking him down in San Diego, for a while anyway. He'd been so careful when he'd decided to move up here.

Relief washed over him as every muscle seemed to loosen. He felt light, free, more at ease than he had in a long time. Not since his wild days back in Paris, before he'd ever laid eyes on Rejavik, had he felt the absence of this heavy burden he'd carried with him all these years, weighing him down, stifling every decision he made.

Santiago cleared his throat, pulling Alfonso from his thoughts.

Alfonso reached out his hand and his arm felt strangely lighter. Santiago grasped it with gusto.

"Sounds like a fiesta I won't want to miss," Alfonso said.

"So you'll do it? You'll join the team?" Santiago's face erupted into a huge grin.

"Only temporarily. Just to get you past the Night of Wilding. The assassin may not be looking in the right place now, but that won't last forever."

"Fair enough."

"Oh, and that blow job?"

Santiago's head snapped up, his eyes narrowing.

"I think I'll pass. But thanks. I really appreciate the offer."

CHAPTER THIRTEEN

THE STREETS OF SEATTLE AT THREE in the morning were quieter than what Ventra Capelli was accustomed to, being from Mexico City. This was the only reason she heard that strange sound.

She'd been checking messages to see if any member of her Darkblood cell had turned up a sign of the scent Tracker's whereabouts. They needed to be extremely careful in how they conducted themselves, and she wasn't entirely sure they understood the gravity of the situation. Not only did they not want the Tracker woman to detect their presence, but the city wasn't their turf. If they were caught by the Darkbloods who worked this area, things could get messy. However, if things went according to plan, Ventra's status within the Alliance would skyrocket. Everyone would want her; she'd have her pick of sectors. The big prestigious ones, not the shitty little areas that were more like outposts. It was worth the risk.

The blinking crosswalk sign cast an orange light onto the touch screen of her phone when she heard a faint rumbling noise, like a heavy stone being dragged on the pavement. She jerked her head up and scanned the damp streets. It seemed to be coming from somewhere on the next block. Although some companies in this industrial area near the port were working second and third shifts, which could explain the sound, something about it seemed out of place.

She stowed her phone, slipped into the shadows and scanned the night to see if she was being watched. A few cars drove past, including a slow-moving Seattle police cruiser, but they were all humans. Hardly a threat.

With the Night of Wilding a few days away, she couldn't afford to miss anything, especially since things had gone wrong the other night. When she heard Guardians had raided the hideout and destroyed everything, she wasn't as upset as she might have been. The guy turned out to be a dud, not who they'd thought he was. Just some kid in training. But what did piss her off was losing a bunch of Sweet in the process. That was never acceptable.

At this time of night, darkness was at its deepest point, so moving within the shadows was relatively easy and took very little energy. She hugged the brick building facades and moved like liquid tar, careful not to make a sound. Up ahead, a streetlamp illuminated the cracked sidewalk in the mouth of an alley, removing the darkness in her path.

She stopped. She'd either go around or—

Inside the alley, behind a Dumpster, the shadows seemed darker than normal, more concentrated. She flattened herself against the side of the building and held very still, not making a sound. Out of habit, she sniffed the air, but as expected, she didn't pick up anything unusual—the only downside to an all-blood diet—although her sense of smell was still more acute than a human's.

Could another vampire be hiding inside that small sliver of darkness, watching her? It wasn't large enough for more than one. If so, what was his intention? Report her movements to his local cell and then what? Although she'd be long gone before others arrived, she'd be outed, raising suspicion among local Darkbloods that something was up. She wouldn't be able to move about as freely next time.

She'd take him out. Let them think Guardians had done it.

Raising her hand in a mock greeting, she cautiously approached the Dumpster. If he didn't recognize who she was, she'd tell him she was from out of town, just looking for a little liquid refreshment. No one ever expected someone dressed like this to be deadly. Soccer-mom chic didn't translate into skilled fighter. It caught them off guard every time.

Her eyes didn't waiver from that dark spot. That was odd. She sensed no movement whatsoever. When she got closer, she saw why, and let down her guard. It was no vampire hiding in the shadows, just a passed-out drunk, lying in a heap underneath a black blanket. Oh well, it was better to err on the side of caution than to be caught off guard. She hadn't gotten where she was by being careless.

The inside of her mouth still tasted coppery from her last feeding. Although she wasn't hungry, vampires were opportunistic feeders and an easy mark was an easy mark. Maybe he had an interesting blood type. When she leaned over him, he belched, the smell of alcohol and vomit thick on his breath.

"Oh for—" Not in a million years would she ever be desperate enough for that.

She pulled out a stiletto, and with a quick movement,

sunk it deep into the man's chest. A moist, choking sound spilled from his lips as she pulled it out and wiped it on her pant leg. She was glad she'd worn these dark leggings. Her blade came away cleaner than if she'd worn jeans.

Back out on the sidewalk, she paused at the next intersection. The scent Tracker had to live somewhere in the area—her people had followed the woman a few times, but they always seemed to lose sight of her here in Pioneer Square. What was around here, anyway? Slowly, she turned a circle, looking up at all the buildings that surrounded her, surveying each one. All of them were old, probably with a lot of history, so it wouldn't surprise her that the Tracker lived here. With their long life spans, vampires were attracted to such places, felt more comfortable, more at home.

And then she heard that sound again—faint, but slightly louder this time.

She cocked her head and tried to focus in on its precise location, while the taillights of a car disappeared in a distant intersection. Determined to find the source, she slipped into the street, over the tiny median with its spindly, leafless trees, and stepped onto the uneven surface of the cobblestone sidewalk. After passing a few darkened shop windows, she started to think that maybe it was nothing, that she just wasn't used to the indigenous sounds of the area, when something moved out of the corner of her eye, drawing her attention.

On the next block, the building seemed to—

Oh gods, it wavered a little—the edges going slightly out of focus like a mirage or 3-D movie. The movement was so subtle that if she hadn't been looking directly at it, she'd have missed it. Fascinated, she stood frozen in place and watched.

In the center, along a blank wall, the energy seemed to shift, displacing what she'd seen a moment ago. An ornately decorated entrance appeared, complete with twin gargoyle statues, two carved columns and a huge arched door.

Then there was that sound again.

Slowly, the door slid open and a man appeared. And if that wasn't shocking enough, as soon as he stepped onto the sidewalk and the door closed, the entrance disappeared—the outside morphed into just a plain cement-sided building again.

She sucked in a jagged breath. How the hell—?

The man wore a long black cloak that swirled around his legs. Old World and elegant, he looked as if he'd just stepped out from the gaslit streets of Victorian England. No one here, vampire or human, dressed like that any longer. Not even the old-timers.

A little thrill of excitement shot down her spine. He appeared to incline his head in her direction, but since she was still part of the darkness, she doubted he'd seen her clear over here. Light from a streetlamp shone in his jet-black hair and accentuated the shadows of his face. With his chin up, he had a regal air about him, like a prince, or someone important.

He turned on his heel and strode down the sidewalk at a fast clip. The amount of confidence and strength he exuded, combined with the fact that he chose not to shadow-move, compelled her to follow him and find out who he was. She stayed a good half block behind, hidden in the shadows.

She knew the Agency used highly advanced cloaking techniques. Was he coming from the Seattle field office? If so, then it stood to reason he was a Guardian or a member of the Council, but as she followed him, she realized that assessment didn't fit. He walked with the slightly superior air of someone at the top of the food chain who wasn't afraid to admit it. Moving with such power only came from being exclusively a blood drinker, and yet he didn't carry himself like a typical Darkblood either.

She turned the corner and he was gone.

Damn. Where did he go?

She could've sworn she'd seen him walk under the pergola and past the park benches, but he definitely wasn't here. Scanning her surroundings, she jogged under the domed walkway that snaked along the sidewalk. On the far side she again surveyed the area, but there was no sign of him.

It was as if he'd melted into the night.

Disappointed, she leaned against a lamppost to regroup.

A slight rustling noise came from somewhere above her head. Before her brain could register that it wasn't the sound of a pigeon or a seagull, the man dropped onto the sidewalk in front of her.

She stared, slack jawed, too stunned to say anything.

With eyes the color of obsidian glass, his intense gaze was almost tangible, hot upon her face. His cloak flapped wildly in the wind, as if it were alive, while his hair remained perfectly still.

The blood from her last feeding stilled in her veins. He was the most captivating individual she'd ever laid eyes on. When he opened his mouth, she detected the faint smell of Sweet.

"You follow me. Why?"

She wasn't prepared for the raw power of his voice and took a half step backward. "I'm looking for someone who lives in the area. Another vampire. She's an Agent and her name is Lily DeGraff."

Normally, she'd never admit this to a stranger, but this man was so out of place and had such an air of importance about him that she felt compelled to tell him the truth.

He smiled, close lipped and controlled, and pulled something from an inside pocket. With long, somewhat bony fingers, he handed her a black-framed picture. "Is this who you seek?"

She took it from him and held it up to the streetlight. The photograph was of an attractive woman with ultra-straight blond hair, who held the hand of a dark-haired, female youthling. Ventra's fingers gripped the frame tighter and she looked up at him excitedly. "Yes, I think so. But how did you know this is the woman I'm after? Where did you get this picture?"

"Why are you seeking a scent Tracker?" he asked, ignoring her questions and keeping control of the conversation.

When she started to answer, it occurred to her she hadn't told him that. "Do you know her?"

Amusement danced in his eyes. "We have never met. At least, not yet."

"Then how do you know she's a Tracker?"

"Because I am one, of sorts." He smoothed back his

hair, and that's when she saw what dangled from his fingernail.

She almost choked.

A prayer box.

This man was a blood assassin.

And fact that he wore this ancient relic could only mean one thing. His was hunting for his quarry.

She could hardly contain her excitement. He was involved in one of the highest, most respected levels of the Alliance. Making a good impression on him could be the key to her success. A positive word from him to the elders would do wonders for her standing within the organization.

Bowing reverently, she offered him her hand. "I am so honored to meet an esteemed member of the Order of the Red Sword." She told him her name, but he didn't reciprocate, nor did he take her hand. She straightened, clasped her hands behind her and tried to keep the disappointment from showing on her face. "You're looking for this Agency Tracker, too? Can you tell me why? Did she betray the Alliance somehow?"

He laughed and held out his pinkie finger. "This is not of her. But she will lead me to him. Again I ask, why are you seeking her?"

"We— I'm the new sector mistress up north. I wanted to start things off with a bang. Do something really special for the first Night of Wilding party I'm in charge of. In addition to getting the word out to the vampire public in untraditional ways, trying to reach more who might become sympathizers, I'd like to bring in a Class-A Tracker in order to more effectively and efficiently locate sweetbloods."

He steepled his fingers and nodded.

Encouraged, she continued. "Nothing brings in partygoers like the allure of Sweet. Preferably off the hoof, don't you think? I'm banking on the fact that vampires will pay exorbitant amounts for the chance to suck one dry. Also, I'd like to do a lottery of sorts. For every vampire guest you bring, your name will be entered into a drawing for a sweetblood. At the appointed time, I'll draw a name and the winner gets to take his prize. In front of everyone."

A hint of a smile formed on his lips. "Tell me more."

"We're constructing several viewing rooms that would house the most attractive sweetbloods we find. The plan is to drain the ugly ones and sell the blood as we do now. You may say there's nothing new about this plan— we've been draining sweetbloods for years—and I agree." She was talking faster, but she had no idea how much time she had to make an impression. "What I'm doing is giving our people a chance to have what they really desire. Taking a sweetblood. Live. Not from some vial. The beautiful ones will be kept in individual rooms to be sold to the highest bidder. Then everyone can watch while the winner takes possession of his purchase."

The assassin dabbed his forehead with a neatly folded handkerchief. She was thrilled to see the tips of his fangs protruding from his lips.

"I had planned to use her as bait," he said softly, almost to himself. "Then torture and kill her in front of the traitor. But this plan could fit nicely into my goals. I wonder what his reaction would be if he watched her transform into the very enemy he's been trying to destroy. Yes, this could be infinitely more interesting than just killing her."

Emboldened by his reaction, she asked, "Will you help me find her?"

"And how did you come up with this ingenious idea?"

She pretended not to notice that he hadn't answered her question. "I was inspired by the sex clubs in Southeast Asia, where sex slaves are bought and sold in those high-priced viewing suites. It gives the vampire population what they want in an exciting and titillating manner. Not only will it appeal to existing reverts, but I believe it will entice others over to our way of thinking. If this goes well, I can see it expanding into other major cities."

He laid a hand on her shoulder. "An impressive goal. I like the way your mind operates. Come. Let us discuss this matter further in the privacy of my suite. I would very much like to hear the details in greater depth. Shall we?"

Was he serious? "Yes. Yes, of course." She knew she sounded like an overexuberant puppy, but she didn't care. To have his support would be monumental. "Please, you haven't told me your name."

He slipped those long fingers into her palm and her inner thighs trembled.

He brought the back of her hand up to his lips, as if she were a lady. "I am Christoph Rejavik, and I am very pleased to meet you, Ms. Capelli."

"Ventra. Please. Call me Ventra."

CHAPTER FOURTEEN

LILY CLOSED THE FRONT DOOR of the Willow Run carriage house and leaned her forehead on the heavy wood. Thank goodness her parents were gone—especially her father. She'd thought the evening would never end. Dinner with him was never an easy affair. On the surface, he'd been polite enough to Alfonso, but beneath that crusty exterior, he was seething. She'd seen it in his eyes and she heard it in his snide tone.

With Steven in town for Zoe's recital, Lily's father had been pressuring her to resume her relationship, and he saw Alfonso's presence as a threat to that. A few times during dinner, she'd come close to having it out with her father, but Alfonso had nudged her under the table, discreetly stroking the back of her hand, calming her down, diffusing her anger until her parents finally left.

At least her mother understood. She'd offered to bring Zoe back to the main house with them on the pretense of watching a movie and sleeping there. Since Alfonso would be leaving for home before dawn, at least they'd have the carriage house to themselves. Her mother might be irritating and nosy sometimes, but she was also very perceptive.

"He's an old guy, set in his ways. It doesn't do any good to engage him." Alfonso came up behind her and kissed the back of her neck, sending shivers down her spine.

"But he's so—"

"It's not worth it, Lil," he said, turning her around to face him.

The bright azure of his eyes and the faint smell of the herbs he'd chopped earlier set her at ease, and she felt her shoulders relax under his fingers.

"He's just like my father," he continued. "Stubborn and convinced he's always right and that anyone who disagrees with him is wrong. You may never be good enough in his eyes, no matter what you do, just as I was never good enough for my father either. Maybe you need to stop looking for his approval and live your life the way you want to live it. Just don't screw it up, like I did." A dark cloud dampened his expression and he started to turn away from her, but she stopped him.

"You didn't screw up, Alfonso. It may feel like it because you surrounded yourself with Darkbloods for the last century, but that's not you. You were never one of them. And you've proved that over and over again."

Two deep furrows formed between his brows and his eyes raked over her face, studying her as if he was seeing her for the first time. "You don't know what I know. What I've seen. What I've done."

She grabbed him by the wrist and let her thumb caress his. "So tell me."

HE HESITATED AND LOOKED DOWN at their hands. Neither of them said anything for a full minute, the air heavy with silence.

He tried to let go, but she held tight.

What would she do if she knew the truth about him? Would she despise him? Would she accept him?

Maybe it was time to come clean, despite what she'd think of him. Hell, maybe it was better if she knew anyway. He was about to step out of her life, and this would ensure she wouldn't come back. He shouldn't care what she thought of him if it meant she would be safe. If she was horrified by what he'd done, by what he used to be, then maybe it would be for the best. She wouldn't want to be with him and that would keep her away.

He led her into the living room, which was filled with pictures chronicling her life with her family. Zoe as a pudgy baby. Zoe taking her first steps. Lily and Zoe laughing in a park. Zoe playing the piano. Yes, Lily deserved to know what sort of person he was, what kind of a man she thought she'd once loved.

One thing was certain. No matter what her reaction was, he would always love her—always wish things could've been different. That he'd made different choices back then, so that he was a different man now.

She sat on the overstuffed couch, tucking a bare foot underneath her, but he remained standing.

"What I've never told you is that many years ago I actually took an Oath of Loyalty to the Alliance and to Pavlos. I had to promise to uphold their covenants, promote their agenda and forsake all other needs that didn't correspond to…to the Overlord's. And I did…for a time. Not many members are asked, so it's supposed to be an honor. Since I was a friend of Pavlos's when the Alliance started, it was only natural that he would ask me to be a part of his inner circle. I put it off as long as I could, but finally I couldn't see any way to avoid it. It was during this time that I brilliantly entered into a relationship with a human woman, a sweetblood. I cared for her but had no intention of it getting too serious."

He ran a hand through his hair. "Jesus, just saying this aloud makes me ill. I'm reminded of my utter stupidity and gross lack of judgment."

She quietly waited for him to continue, but he wasn't sure whether to be relieved or not. Was she waiting to blow up? Was her disgust simmering below the surface? He couldn't look at her—didn't want to see it in her eyes. It really didn't matter what he thought or felt about it. She needed to hear this.

"It was made very clear to me that if I didn't take the Blood Oath, Jessica would be in danger. So I agreed, thinking I could fake it and figure a way out of the mess later. When it was done, a small piece of muslin soaked in my blood was placed inside a *shevala* for safekeeping and—"

"My God. The Order of the Red Sword." Her voice was soft.

He glanced over at her, expecting to see a hint of loathing or disgust in her expression, but all he saw was concern. "You've heard of it? It's rarely spoken of by name within the Alliance. Its members are revered and respected—feared, actually. None of the rank and file know much about them."

"It's the Alliance's version of Tracker Academy. Supposedly, they're experts in scent memories. Although their tracking skills are good, they're not quite as strong as a Class-A Tracker."

"Council propaganda, Lil. I've seen blood assassins at work. Their abilities are unmatched."

She stiffened at that slight, but he continued.

"As a result of being in this inner circle, I was privy to even more of the Alliance's monstrous ways. God, I was so naïve. Until then, I'd thought—hoped, actually—that they were engaging in and promoting harmless fun. Deep down, though, I knew the truth, but I chose to turn a blind eye toward it. Once I was inducted, things changed. I saw everything. Every fucking thing. I couldn't stand what they were doing and what they wanted me to do, so I left. That's when they activated my blood assassin for the first time. A killer named Christoph Rejavik."

"Couldn't your father have helped you?"

"I did speak to him and he…refused to help me. Rejavik tracked Jessica down and…" His voice caught again. He stood and paced on the other side of the antique coffee table littered with more family photos, including one he'd taken of Lily. They were on Coronado Beach, where they'd stayed for a few nights in the old glamorous hotel. The sun had just set, orange sky stretching out over the horizon behind her. She looked so happy then, so carefree. Not tense and worried as she was now. Too much information would do that to you, he thought.

"The woman. It was her, wasn't it? The one that you…" Lily looked like she was going to throw up. "You don't need to tell me more if it's too difficult."

"No, I want you to know this. You need to know what happened. When I left the Alliance—the first time—the assassin easily found Jessica. I'm not sure if it was because I did occasionally take her blood or if he followed my scent track there. The important thing was that he found her."

"And were you there, too?"

"No, at least I had the sense not to lead them to her, or so I thought. I was staying in a roadside inn. They found me later."

"What…what happened then?"

"They wore me down, exposed me to the sun for several days, embedded tiny silver spikes into my skin, then when I was at my weakest, most vulnerable point, Rejavik…" Alfonso's hands balled into fists and his nostrils flared. "He made me watch as he…fed…from Jess. Then, without sealing her wounds, he untied me."

The air inside the living room was stifling hot and he suddenly felt like puking. Before he drew in another breath, Lily was at his side, putting a cool hand on the back of his neck. Soothing energies coursed through him, loosening the tethers around his rigid exterior. He paused for a moment as she ran her hand down his arm and threaded her fingers into his.

He was stunned. This wasn't the action of someone who was disgusted. Maybe she wasn't rejecting him. Maybe she didn't find this as abhorrent as he'd thought she would.

"After it was over, I was…devastated. Couldn't stand to think what I'd done to her. When word got out that she was dead, drained of her lifeblood, my father and brother put two and two together. They confronted me and things between us got even uglier."

"And your mother?"

"My mother, who was always so idealistic, never thought I was capable of such…an atrocity. Little did she know, I was."

"She wasn't idealistic, Alfonso. What the assassin did was atrocious. You were a victim, just as Jessica was."

He stared down at their intertwined fingers, the current of her energies causing his arm to tingle, and he wasn't sure what to think. On the one hand, he was relieved she didn't think of him as some sort of a freak. On the other, it'd be better for her to be repulsed by his actions. It would make her want to stay away from him, and ultimately she'd be safe—which was the only thing that really mattered.

"But that's not all you're worried about, is it?" she asked.

"If they know about you, you're a target, Lil, just as Jessica was."

Lily was silent for a few minutes. "She was a musician, wasn't she?"

"Yes, she attended the Conservatoire de Paris."

"And a human."

"Yes."

"Hardly a trained Agency fighter, like me. Big difference."

"For godsake, don't you understand?" Hurt shone in her eyes, but he didn't care. "We're not talking Darkbloods here. We're talking a blood assassin from the Order of the Red Sword. I've seen their torture chamber and what they do in it. I can still smell its dampness, feel the claustrophobic atmosphere and hear the groans of the devices and the high-pitched screams of the victims. Rumor has it that one of their original members was a favored executioner for Vlad the Impaler, and after what I witnessed, I don't doubt that it's true. Not only are they killing machines, sent to destroy the traitor, but they're also trained to kill any loved ones as well. To teach others a lesson that betraying the Alliance will cost more than one life—it'll cost the lives of your whole family."

She started to protest, just as he knew the fighter in her would, but he interrupted her.

"Sharing blood makes you more vulnerable, creates a direct link to the assassin, as he has with me. He'd smell my blood in you and yours in me. He'd either use you to get to me or vice versa. Then he'd have us both. And since we know I can hardly keep from taking your blood, even a casual relationship won't work. Believe me, I thought about it, because the last thing I wanted to do was leave you."

"But we can face him together."

"Listen to me." He held her face in his hands. "We're not just talking you, Lily. What about Zoe? If he finds you, he finds her."

The competitive fight in her eyes faded as the enormity of his words sank in.

"You don't belong in this mess I've created," he continued, "and neither does she. I can't take that chance and endanger your life or the life of your beautiful daughter. Those are the risks, now that the assassin has been activated. Right now he's in Europe, but sooner or later, he'll track me back to the States. And when he does, he'll find me unless I'm on the move again. You deserve better than this. You deserve better than me."

She stood on tiptoe and kissed him. Her lips were soft, warm, as they moved against his. He kissed her back, and when his tongue brushed against her elongated fang, the resulting electricity went straight to his groin. How could she still feel this way about him after knowing everything? What he'd seen, what he'd done, what he'd promised—all were unforgivable. He'd tried to make up for that by feeding information to the Agency all these years, but nothing could truly nullify the horrible things he'd once done.

His joy in her reaction to him was bittersweet. He wouldn't be able to stay much longer.

"A man's worth isn't measured by what he does when times are good," she said, pulling away from him. Her voice was confident and clear, the set of her jaw determined. "It's easy to do the right thing when things are going well. It's how you act during the tough times that defines your character."

She laced her fingers in his and led him past the kitchen, down the hallway and into her bedroom.

"WHAT ARE YOU DOING, LIL?" he growled.

Noting that he came along willingly, she didn't bother to answer. He'd find out soon enough.

With one bare foot, she kicked the door closed behind them, took him to her bed and pushed him down on the mattress. Standing between his knees, she looked down into his face.

His eyes were crystalline, his lips slightly open as if he were breathing hard.

"Thank you for finally telling me the truth. I know how hard it was for you." Knowing all these details made everything so clear. Why he'd acted as he had. What he'd done. What he'd said. He had only wanted to protect her.

"I love you, you know," she continued, as she began to undress him. First his shirt, then his boots and socks. "I've never stopped loving you, even when you said you didn't love me back. I've not felt the same since you left. Nothing about me is as good as it was when we were together. I couldn't sleep. I couldn't eat. Even my abilities declined. Knowing all of this about you doesn't change my feelings. I knew you'd been through shit, Alfonso. I just didn't know all the details."

"Lily, I—"

"Shhh." He'd been so worried about her that it was her turn to serve him now.

After quickly lighting a few candles, she knelt down between his legs, eager to pull him into her mouth, to feel his body inside hers. She wanted him with an urgency she couldn't quite define. As she slid her hands up his thick thighs, he sucked in a breath through his teeth. She unfastened his jeans and belt, grasped the zipper pull and tugged it over the swell beneath it. Several inches of his erection extended above the waistband of his black boxer briefs. A delicious heaviness pooled low in her belly and she licked her lips.

"Lily, we can't. We shouldn't."

He must've seen the tips of her fangs.

"I won't take your blood if you don't want me to."

"It's not that I don't want it—thoughts of making love to you and sharing blood consume me."

"Then let's not worry about it. If it happens, it happens. You said yourself that the assassin is still in Europe."

Making love to him didn't always cause a blood need in her, but it almost always did in him. In fact, had they ever made love without him taking her blood? She didn't think they had.

And with that, she stripped off his jeans.

He let her.

The thin, sinewy cord of muscle traced along the outside of his abdomen and ended somewhere under the last item of clothing he wore. She hooked her fingers into the waistband of his tight boxer briefs and as she slipped them over his hips, he groaned. His erection sprang free, lying thick and proud up the left side of his belly.

He was amazing, utterly magnificent in the candlelight. He had propped himself up on his elbows to watch her. The flickering shadow and corresponding light accentuated the well-defined muscles of his stomach. The splayed-out ends of his hair brushed the tops of his shoulders, its golden color shimmering and catching the light with every movement. The pupils in his eyes had expanded, crowding out the blue until only a tiny ring of color was left.

He wanted her.

A burning, needful heat moistened her core as her body responded to what she was seeing.

She needed him. Oh God, how she needed him.

She dipped her head to take him into her mouth, but he stopped her.

"No, we make love tonight."

"That was my intention, but I wanted to do this first."

"If you do, I'll come before you've got your mouth fully over me. No, I haven't waited this long for you to do that to me. But I have waited for this."

He pulled her onto the bed and before she knew what was happening, he'd spread her knees with his hands and dipped his head between her legs. She had planned to be the aggressor, to show him that in spite of what he'd told her, what he was ashamed of and afraid of her knowing, she still wanted him as much as or more than she ever had before. It took a real man to admit his mistakes as Alfonso had, to devote his life to correcting them, and she loved him because of it. Words meant nothing—she wanted to show him with her actions.

But he obviously had other ideas.

His hair tickled the sensitive skin on her lower abdomen and inner thighs.

She held her breath, gripped handfuls of the sheets in her fists.

With his lips parted, he stared at the juncture between her legs as he slid his hands under her hips to tilt them up. She complied.

"You are so beautiful," he said huskily.

And when his lips touched her sex and his tongue flicked her sensitive folds, she let out a little shriek of pleasure and forgot all about being the dominant one this time.

Over and over, he pressed his tongue to her core, shrinking her entire world into this sliver of time and space. At some point, she'd slipped her hands into his hair and now she held his head in place. And when he slipped a finger—no, two—inside her, waves of glittering pleasure exploded outward. Her inner muscles tightened around him and tiny pinpoints of light danced behind her eyelids.

She felt him chuckle before the sound reached her ears.

"What?" she managed to ask as he drew his body up over hers. The air felt cool against her now that he'd moved his mouth away.

"That was easy," he said. "You came for me before I had a chance to do much."

"Since when has that been difficult?" she asked, and then she kissed him, tasting herself on his tongue.

"Ah, yes. So true."

Wait. Was he confusing her with another lover? Was that it? The heat of jealousy snaked along her spine and she gritted her teeth. Although it was impossible, Alfonso was hers. No one else's. No matter how many lovers came after her, she would make sure he'd never forget this.

She pushed his shoulders back and moved to straddle him as she'd done in the hospital, but he grabbed her wrist, stopping her.

Dark determination blazed in his eyes. "I will take you this way first."

With a pat on her hip, he urged her to roll to her stomach.

And she did.

Heat from his body covered her back as he came down over her from behind. She pushed up onto all fours.

"Because of my injury, I didn't think I would ever be able to make love like this again. On my knees."

A thrill tickled every nerve ending. He'd be able to penetrate even deeper this way. Dispersing the weight evenly on her elbows and knees, she waited to feel him push himself in.

Instead, she felt the brush of his hair against her inner thigh, and before she knew what he was doing, his tongue had found her center again.

She gave a little gasping moan. Her legs went boneless, and she thought she might collapse on top of him, but he held her up and continued his movements.

"Please," she begged. "I need to feel you in me."

"Like this?" He plunged a finger inside as well, shooting waves of pleasure down to her toes and up to her scalp, until every nerve ending burst into light.

"Oh God, yes. I mean no." He moved his finger in and out while she continued to writhe against his tongue. It was sheer bliss, but she wanted to share it with him. This was too much pleasure for just one person. "I want to feel your body filling mine from the inside."

The bed squeaked as he shifted. He pushed her knees wider and the head of his erection probed the inside of her thigh, seeking out then easily finding its destination. He didn't need to go slow—her body was ready for him now. But he didn't push all the way in. She started to rock back on him, but he held her still. Controlling her.

As he leaned forward, his body warmed her spine, his lips nuzzled the base of her neck. Oh God, would he take her blood again? Her gums ached, the tips of her fangs sharp against her tongue as she thought about taking his.

He slipped his hands down her forearms, laying his

fingers over the tops of hers, then covered her body with his.

Staking his claim on her.

Owning her.

Possessing her.

She felt his hips buck and his body filled hers completely.

ALFONSO EASED LILY onto her back, wanting to see her face as he pushed himself into her again. Her urgent need was obvious in the way her tiny white fangs creased her kiss-swollen lips. Just the thought of her taking his blood made him even harder. He moved in and out, pushing deeper each time, her luxurious silk covering every inch of him.

Everything about her was strategically placed to coincide precisely with what turned him on. Her breasts overflowed his broad hands, their perky nipples awaiting his touch. The soft curve of her buttocks fit his cupped palms. The front of her hip bones had that slight indentation for his thumbs to rest on.

And the chain in her belly button—

The diamond-encrusted arrow he'd bought for her several years ago was still attached to it. Although it had started as a joke, the thing served as a visual, if not tacky, reminder that her body was for him and him alone. He honestly couldn't believe she still wore it.

Then it dawned on him. How many other sets of male eyes had gazed on it since they'd been apart? Seen this arrow and thought it was meant for them? Had she worn it then, too? After he left tonight, how many others would see it?

She'd once told him he was the only man whose blood she'd ever taken. Suddenly, he needed to further distinguish himself from the rest. The lovers she'd had before him and the lovers she'd have in the future after he left.

He tried to ignore the gnawing feeling that tore at his heart.

Cradling the back of her head, he pressed her lips against his neck. "Drink from me, love. I can tell that you want to."

"You're…okay if I do?" Her words were muffled through her razor-sharp fangs, her breath hot against his skin.

With the assassin still in Europe, Lily wasn't in immediate danger. Its effects should be worn off by the time Alfonso was gone. But he didn't want to dwell on the fact that he'd be leaving soon. All he wanted to think about was this moment in time.

"Yes, I want it almost as much as you do." And before he finished speaking, he felt the sting beneath her soft lips and the pull of her mouth on his vein.

Exhilarated by her intense desire for his lifeblood, he wanted to shout to the world how much he loved this woman. How amazing and beautiful and strong she was and how lucky he was to have her desire him like this.

Using tiny thrusting motions so as not to disrupt her drinking from him, he moved in the same rhythm as her swallowing. Her inner muscles tightened like a vice around him, her nails digging into his backside.

She lifted her head from his neck. She had taken what she needed from him.

Instantly, the pressure in his loins increased. With one

powerful thrust, he seated himself more deeply inside her and sank his teeth into her vein. Her sweet, coppery smell filled his senses and flowed across his taste buds. A tiny moan of pleasure escaped her lips and he held her tighter. With every swallow of her lifeblood, shards of electricity shot through his veins and he felt the tiny, dark corners inside him instantly expanding. Her blood was transforming and made him feel more powerful than he had been only moments ago.

He could hold back no longer. In a blinding surge of pleasure, so intense he could've sworn his heart stopped for an instant, he released himself into her body.

CHAPTER FIFTEEN

"THE SEATTLE PERIMETER'S been breached."

Dom's words via the speakerphone hung in the air—a hollow, tin-can echo, blocking out all other sound in the War Room.

It took a moment before Lily could find her voice as people crowded in, taking seats at the mahogany table and standing in the doorway.

"When? How is that possible?" she asked Dom. Mentally, she raced through all the checkpoints in the field office but couldn't imagine any of them failing.

Before he could answer, Santiago swept through the doors, his presence taking up the unused space in the room as others scrambled to get out of his way.

"Everybody's here," he barked into the speaker. Poor Dom probably got his ear blasted on the other end. "So what the fuck happened? Have you been able to figure that out yet? What's Jackson's assessment? Talk to me."

The boardroom at Region Headquarters—called the War Room because of its cache of weapons stored behind lighted glass panels, which seemed more for show than anything else—was standing room only. The nickname hadn't seemed appropriate until now.

"Less than thirty minutes ago," Dom said, "security

noticed an unusual outage on the grid. Turns out the outer perimeter went off-line. Twice."

Lily absently bit at a chocolate remnant stuck underneath her thumbnail. She and Alfonso had shared the last of Xian's brownies when everyone was summoned here.

Someone leaned on the back of her chair. Alfonso touched her shoulder and left his hand there. All seven of the Agents not on duty were present, including a few staffers and medical personal who'd heard something had happened.

With bloodshot eyes, Kip stood quietly in the corner. He still looked like shit, but he was much better than the last time she'd seen him. He was walking and the hand tremors were gone, which was encouraging.

"Were the inner systems compromised?" someone asked.

"Do you know what they were after?" asked someone else.

"Is anyone at the field office now?"

"Does this mean the Region offices are vulnerable?"

"Why did—"

Santiago pounded a fist on the table. "Shut the hell up. Everyone."

Except for the squeak of a chair and a muffled cough, the room went silent.

Someone pressed a button, and with a low hum two panels in the wall parted, revealing a large screen. It flashed twice and suddenly, there was Dom, live from Australia.

The first thing she noticed was his tanned face. There was something about Mackenzie's blood, even after her transformation into a changeling, that made him less susceptible to the energy drain from the sun. Clearly, he'd been taking advantage of it down there. He looked good, even though his face was etched with worry and his hair looked as if he'd run his hands through it a few hundred times.

The special blood bond he shared with Mackenzie also triggered in him the ancient vampire ability to *vapor,* transforming one's corporeal body into a thick, blue smoke in order to slip through the smallest of spaces.

Even as a youthling before the Change, Lily had hoped those stories were true—that special abilities like that still existed among vampires, only to be awakened by the blood of one's true soul mate. But just like that wide-eyed girl who wished for a unicorn, somehow she'd never really believed the stories to be real. Her grandparents' bond was amazing enough. These were just legends and fantasies designed to enthrall children.

That was until Dom had shared, in confidence, that it had happened to him.

"Fortunately, it appears to have only affected the outer perimeter," Dom was saying, yanking her back to the problem at hand. "Preliminary reports from the security cameras and other checkpoints indicate the rest of the safeguards remained untouched."

"And Mackenzie?" Alfonso asked. "Where is she?"

Dom visibly stiffened at the sound of his brother's voice. Lily wondered when the last time was that they'd actually spoken a civil word to each other. Years ago? Decades ago? Maybe even a century ago?

"Santiago," Dom said, "I need a word with you privately."

"Bullshit. Now is not the time—"

"If not privately, then I'll come right out and say it. Did it cross your mind that this could be an inside job?" The words hissed from behind Dom's clenched teeth.

Although she had the utmost respect for Dom, this was too much. "An inside job? For godsake, you of all people know what he's done for the Agency. And until you pull your head out of your ass and stop thinking of only yourself, you'll never understand what he's truly sacrificed."

Alfonso's hand tightened on her shoulder, probably intending to calm her down, but it served to infuse her with even more conviction and determination to set things right. She reached up and covered his hand with her own, ready to give Dom a piece of her mind, but Santiago shut her down.

"Silence," he boomed out. "Everyone who is not a Guardian, get back to your duties. Out, all of you. Now. Kip, Tambra, Jonah, Caleb, take a seat. The rest of you, shut up. Alfonso," he added, pointing to the chair next to Lily, "sit your ass down."

When the room cleared out and only Guardians remained, Santiago slammed the door shut and spun back to Dom. His eyes blazed, the tattoos on his neck that ended somewhere within his hairline seemed suddenly more pronounced and menacing.

"Listen. I don't care what your relationship is with your brother, we need to mobilize every capable fighter. If you don't want to spend Christmas, Hanukkah, Kwanza,

Chinese New Year and National Secretary's Day with
him, that's your goddamn business. We've gone over this
before, and frankly, I'm tired of it. You know exactly how
the Council and I feel, so I'm not going to have it out with
you yet again. Since you and Mitchell are gone, we need
all the help we can get. Alfonso has agreed to step in as
a field agent—temporarily, that is, until you get back."

He paused for effect. "Dom? Do you understand me?"

"Perfectly," Dom said, cold fury flashing in his eyes.

"Jesus, I feel like a playground teacher telling two
youthlings to play nicely."

Lily doubted the rift between the brothers could ever
be repaired, but maybe they could learn to be civil. "Is
Mackenzie all right?" she asked, trying to get the conversation back on track, yet concerned about her friend
at the same time.

"Yes, Lily, thank *you* for asking," Dom said, making
it perfectly clear to everyone present that he was answer-
ing her question, not Alfonso's. "She's fine. The office
and the residential quarters went into lockdown. Sadie
took Xian and Mackenzie over to the safe house on the
island. They're on the ferry now."

"Chuck and Shirl's place?"

"Yes. They'll be safe there until we can get things
sorted out. My flight leaves in thirty minutes, so I'll be
there as soon as possible."

Relieved, Lily sat back in her chair.

Despite the fact that one of the Agency's most capable Guardians was with Mackenzie and they were on
the way to the retired Region Commander's residence,
she could see in his face that he was still freaking out.

Although Mackenzie was a changeling now, her blood-scent no longer enticing to vampires, she'd been a target of Darkbloods in the past. And with the baby on the way, Lily didn't blame him for being extra worried.

Stress apparently brought on Dom's ability to *vapor,* as he'd only been able to gather the energy to transform himself when Mackenzie was in danger. Kind of an adrenaline thing, he'd told her once. But given that he was so far away, she imagined he was feeling pretty damn helpless.

Maybe that was why he had such a short fuse with Alfonso. She knew that deep down, Dom cared about his younger brother. He had to—he was always asking about him.

"Jackson's already mobilized the teams," Dom continued. "I'm expecting a report from him any minute."

"If they only got through the first barrier, what was their reason for breaking in?" Tambra asked. "Did they get spooked and abort their original plans to get into the field office, or did they have something else in mind?"

"That's what we're trying to determine," Dom said.

"Where was security?" Caleb asked. "Didn't the intrusion trip the alarms and alert the field office?"

"For some reason, none of the alarms sounded. We're assuming the system was disabled somehow, but we'll need to run some tests to figure out what happened." Dom ran a hand over his face, and when he looked into the camera, his hard, angry expression had softened considerably from his earlier tirade, making him appear almost apologetic.

Was he feeling remorseful all of a sudden, having

questioned Alfonso's loyalties in front of the whole Region staff? Maybe Santiago's rant got through to him after all. He did have a tendency to behave rashly and blurt out things he regretted later.

"Hey, Lil?" His eyes didn't focus on any one spot; rather, he looked beyond the webcam, giving the impression that he was searching for something behind her.

"Yeah, I'm here." She knew he didn't have a video feed, only audio.

He drew a deep breath, as if he was gathering the courage to say something, then he stared straight into the camera. And in that brief moment before he spoke, she knew that it was going to be bad news.

"The security officer at the north entrance was killed."

It felt as though someone punched her in the gut. Her hands turned to ice. "What? Francesca? She's…she's dead?"

"I'm afraid so. I'm sorry, Lil. It appears that's where they entered the complex—through the residential section on that side. Jackson was the one who found her ashes."

The knot in the back of her throat made it difficult to swallow, let alone speak.

Lily recalled the last conversation she and Francesca had and the plan to get together after she returned. Francesca had moved up here several months ago, hoping to make it onto a capture team. She'd been working out hard, getting into the best shape of her life, attending a few of Lily's martial arts classes, and was thrilled when she passed the grueling physical. All that was left was the written exam.

Lily looked down at her fists, her nails digging into

the palms of her hands, the sharp points of pain mirroring the anger boiling inside.

Francesca. Gone.

Her knuckles were white and desperately needed to connect with something.

I'm gonna fry those bastards. Hunt them down, and pay them back for what they did to her.

Alfonso took her fist, peeled it open and laced his fingers with hers. His warm energy filtered up her arm into her body. It reminded her that she wasn't alone—he was with her—and together, they'd find out who was responsible. The anger wasn't gone, nor was the need for retribution, but it did infuse her with a sense of quiet calmness that made her feel even stronger and more capable.

"Francesca was a good friend of mine," she whispered to him.

"I'm sorry," he mouthed. "We'll find those responsible. I promise."

"We've got a team there now," Dom continued, "but they're having trouble picking up even the primary scent markers. Jackson's got them going floor by floor and condo by condo, but so far they've turned up nothing. In fact, they're actually not sure if it's one or two individuals. Before Agent Kerne left for the island, she went outside and tried to pick up the scent, but she wasn't able to detect a thing."

That didn't surprise Lily. Changelings' senses weren't as acute as a born vampire's.

"We'll send out others at nightfall to see if they can

pick up the trail, but they could really use you down there, Lily."

The knot in her throat turned into dread. She was going to have to come clean about her abilities. She couldn't let them think she'd be able to waltz in and it'd be business as usual. If only she'd told Santiago the truth earlier, she wouldn't be sitting here in a roomful of people who would soon know her secret. Despite how much she desperately wanted to keep this to herself, in good conscience, she couldn't cover it up any longer.

Not being forthcoming about it before had almost cost Kip his life. Although her abilities had improved enough to allow her to track him, she wasn't sure if things were completely back to normal or not. However, losing their respect would be easier to live with than risking someone's life again.

"Listen." She cleared her throat and tried to summon up the courage to tell them. Oh hell, just blurt it out. "You need to know that—"

"The north side. That's where your condo is located," Alfonso said.

For God's sake, she hated being interrupted.

She snapped her head in his direction, ready to rip him a new one, but when she saw the concerned look on his face, she hesitated.

"Because you live there, you'd have an easier time distinguishing the scents that belong there from those that don't," Alfonso said, giving her a pointed look.

He was protecting her, didn't want her to say anything, and while she certainly appreciated that, she couldn't lie any longer. Maybe he was so accustomed to covering things up, projecting a carefully crafted image, he couldn't accept the fact that she actually wanted to come clean about this. That all this hiding and lying had been taking its toll on her. He was good at secrecy, but she wasn't.

She glanced at the other Guardians, some of whom she didn't know well. Okay, maybe she wouldn't air her dirty laundry in front of everyone. But as soon as the meeting was over, she'd tell Santiago. This had gone far enough.

She squeezed his hand. *It's okay,* she said with her eyes.

He gave a slight nod, acknowledging her unspoken desire to get it out into the open, whether he understood her reasoning or not.

"Dom, do you know what the intruder's purpose was if he didn't try to get into the field office?" Caleb asked.

"Strangely enough," Dom answered, "we're not entirely sure whether he knew he was near the Seattle office or not since all those safeguards remained untouched. I know it's unlikely, and yet we can't discount that possibility. We need to consider everything at this point."

"Maybe they got spooked and aborted their plan," Tambra said, repeating her theory since it hadn't been addressed yet.

Dom nodded. "That's the more probable scenario. And yet, early evidence seems to indicate that the residential units may have been the target in the first place."

After the meeting concluded, Lily asked to have a word with Santiago and Dom. Alfonso started to leave, but she grabbed his hand. "I want you to stay, too."

Everyone filed out to start their preparations for leaving at dusk. When the door closed behind the last person, she cleared her throat and decided to just blurt it out. "For months now, my scent-tracking skills have been weakening. At first, I thought it was my imagination, that I might have a virus or something, but it was taking me longer and longer to track even the newest revert, and it's gotten progressively worse. It took me longer to find Kip than it should have, and he may have been taken in the first place because I wasn't able to detect that we were being followed. I should've said something sooner. That's why I'm not sure I'll be much help tonight down in Seattle. Are there any other Trackers you can pull in to help?"

She stiffened her spine and prepared herself for their reactions, keeping her eyes unfocused as she stared at an old, faint water ring on the table. She worried they'd now start looking through her, not seek her out, or talk *around* her, like her father did, rather than *to* her. Maybe she was brave enough to finally tell them the truth, but she wasn't brave enough to see it in their eyes.

"Bullshit," Santiago said. "You found that boy quicker than any one of us could."

"Only because Alfonso was helping me."

Alfonso held up his palms. "I did nothing. It was all her."

"Why didn't you come to me when you first suspected this was going on?" Dom said through the speakerphone.

"Because I love being an Agent and couldn't bear the thought of not being one anymore."

"You mean, you'd quit? Wait. You thought we'd fire you?" Before she could answer, Santiago stormed over to the wet bar, poured himself a finger of Chivas and knocked it back in one swallow, his Adam's apple bobbing once. "Good God, if I develop cirrhosis of the liver or boils on my ass, I'm blaming it on all three of you." He glared at Lily. "It pisses me off that you'd think I'd let you go just because you couldn't track any longer. You're an excellent Agent whether you're tracking or not. And furthermore…"

Dom coughed. She glanced at the monitor and saw him stifling a smile. He knew Santiago was about to launch into one of his famous speeches. They often joked that he'd been a football coach or motivational speaker in a former life.

Santiago pointed a finger first at Lily, then at Alfonso. "You and you make a great team. I've said that all along. Why do you think I've been busting my ass like I have?"

She glared at the monitor, but Dom's face remained blank.

"Listen," Santiago continued. "We're not always going to be at the top of our game, but that's what a team is for. You complement each other's strengths and shore up each other's weaknesses and together you'll go further than you would alone. All I ask, Lily, is that you do the best work you can do."

Yeah, and like a coach, he'd ride your ass if he thought you were slacking.

"After this is over, you should talk to Roxy, see if any of that New Age mumbo jumbo shit she's into will help. And if it would make you feel better," he continued, "I'll have a Tracker sent in from one of the other Regions. But until then, you're it, DeGraff."

She tried to ignore Santiago's jab about her mentor. Roxanne Reynolds may be unorthodox in her methods, but she was a skilled trainer, the best in the Agency.

"We'll walk through it methodically," Alfonso said matter-of-factly. "Like we did before. I know you can do it."

His hand felt warm against the back of her neck, and she wished that she could believe him.

ALTHOUGH NIGHT FELL EARLY this time of the year, the daylight hours seemed to stretch out forever. They considered crossing the border in a Daytran, but Santiago deemed it too risky. Large black vans with all the windows darkened didn't exactly give off innocent vibes to border officials. If the vehicle was searched, the Guardians sequestered in the back away from the sunlight would be discovered. They couldn't take that chance.

Traffic was still fairly heavy in downtown Seattle by the time Alfonso navigated the Panamera through the streets. The sound of tires rolling over wet pavement was loud with all the windows cracked open. Lily leaned her head back against the headrest, her eyes closed as she concentrated on all the smells of the city, a piece of her hair fluttering against her cheek.

He reached over and squeezed her hand. Without opening her eyes, she smiled at him.

He could really get used to a life like this. As Lily's partner. Making love to her, sharing blood like they used to, working assignments together. Not only did Lily want him to join the Agency, but so did Santiago. And although Dom didn't like it, at least he seemed to accept it. Alfonso had to admit it felt good to be a part of something rather than being on his own. He enjoyed the camaraderie, the banter with others who had the same goals as he did.

At a stoplight several blocks from the field office, Lily reached over and grabbed his arm. Her eyes glittered with excitement. "I've got something! Darkblood scent on the next street over. One is the same scent from the cabin where Kip was found."

"But we killed them all."

"Only the DBs who were present at the time."

Before he could protest, she jumped out of the car and pointed a thumb behind her. "Meet me down there. They were on foot." And with that, she slammed the door and took off down the sidewalk.

He quickly scanned both sides of the busy roadway. There was nowhere to park the car and the next street was a one-way in the wrong direction. He gripped the steering wheel, his knuckles angry white peaks around the stitched leather.

One of these Darkbloods had been at the cabin? Were they trying to find another Tracker to replace Kip?

And now, here Lily was, traipsing around on her own.

The light turned green, he punched the accelerator and the car shot through the intersection. He weaved in and out of traffic, earning a few well-deserved honks and one-fingered salutes. On the next one-way street, he found a narrow, angled parking spot and expertly maneuvered the car in.

When he realized there wasn't enough room on either side to get out, he pressed a button and the sunroof opened. In one easy motion, he pulled himself out, slid down the outside of the windshield and landed on the sidewalk. Lily would kill him if she saw him do that, he thought as he clicked the remote, closing the sunroof. Hopefully, one of these cars would have moved by the time they got back and she'd never have to know.

As if he had her on GPS, he zeroed in on her location several blocks away in Pioneer Square. She was stooping near a lamppost, her fingers touching the cobblestone sidewalk.

"They passed this spot about fifteen hours ago. One has a strong scent marker, the other doesn't. Not sure why."

A few passersby looked at her funny. He pulled her to her feet, cradling her elbows, which made it convenient for her to wrap her arms around his waist. "Damn, you're good. I can't smell a thing. But don't run off like that again."

She peered up at him with a smile that made his heart ache.

"One of them fed recently—a female. The blood scent is strong. And the other—" She inhaled deeply and bit her lip in concentration. "The other one, a male, had sweet-blood one or two days ago, but his scent is fainter."

"You sure they were together? Maybe you're picking up the scents of two individuals who were here at separate times. One last night and the other the night before."

"No, given that the deterioration of scent structure is exactly the same, I'm sure they were together."

"Impressive, Ms. DeGraff."

"Thanks," she said flippantly as she pulled away, but he saw the glint in her eye.

He stifled a laugh, recalling that a few hours ago she'd paid him a similar compliment, but they hadn't been talking about work.

The streets and sidewalks were full of people rushing to get home. Their annoyance with those who were just getting into the city was palpable. Alfonso and Lily zigzagged around the pedestrians, trying to move as quickly as they could without drawing attention to themselves.

Lily stopped outside the Pink Salon, a puzzled look on her face.

"What's up?" he asked.

"It's weird. Their scent continues north, but I'm picking up traces of one of them over there. If I'm not mistaken, the male spent some time in that pub across the street a few days ago."

Big Daddy's? Alfonso had a hard time imagining a Darkblood watching football highlights and shooting the shit with a bartender who thought she was a shrink. It occurred to him that if Lily was able to pick up that guy's scent from a few days ago, she was likely to pick up his, too. He'd better come clean.

"I suppose you can tell I was there recently as well."

"You were? When?"

"A few weeks ago."

She looked confused. "Why?"

"When I heard Darkbloods were looking for Trackers, I decided to check up on you. Make sure you were okay. I think the bartender thought I was stalking someone."

She raised an elegant eyebrow. "Well, you were."

"True. Listen, I'm sorry. I should've been up front with you, but I was afraid you'd think I doubted your abilities.

That I didn't think you were capable of taking care of yourself."

"Well, did you doubt my abilities?"

"God, Lil, I've told you. You're the most capable woman I know. But sometimes it doesn't matter how strong you are, how tough, or how amazing your scent-tracking talents are. You are a target and I worry about you because…because I love you. But that doesn't mean I'm not—"

With one hand, she grabbed the back of his hair and pulled him down. She kissed him. Hard. Then let go.

"No more sneaking around," she said, running the edge of a red-tipped thumbnail along her bottom lip, wiping off the smeared gloss. "No more lies."

He hesitated, then nodded. "No more lies."

They soon found themselves in the lobby of the old Edgemont Hotel overlooking Elliott Bay.

"I'm picking up a stronger scent leading down into the parking garage."

They followed the scent down to P3, but it became clear the Darkbloods had left by car.

"I'll alert one of the other teams and see if they can pick up the scent from here. Let's go check out the room."

Without too much effort, they located the empty suite on the top floor.

The elevator doors hadn't opened fully when the smell of blood grew heavy in the air.

She put a hand on Alfonso's arm, stopping him. "Someone's been murdered inside that suite." She pulled out her phone.

"Who are you calling?"

"Johnny Sinclair, a friend of Dom's who knows about us, is a detective with SPD. He also owns the martial arts studio that I teach at sometimes. He's a good guy. Just from out here, I can tell it was the two Darkbloods. A man and a woman. Same ones we've been trailing. They killed a young man. I'm guessing the body is in the bathroom. I'm pretty sure they left early this morning."

"Then they couldn't have gotten far."

"Maybe. Maybe not. They may have a Daytran."

After telling Detective Sinclair what little she knew about the events at the hotel, Lily ended the call before he could warn her to leave things to the SPD. Alfonso led the way back to the awkwardly parked car and got behind the wheel. It was time to head to the field office.

LILY STEPPED THROUGH the security checkpoints at the field office's north entrance and found herself blinking away hot tears when a stranger at Francesca's station motioned her through each step. Numbly she touched the thumb scan and inserted her key card, until finally she and Alfonso emerged on the other side.

The scent trail led straight to the elevator bank for the residential units.

"Only one came inside—the male. The female remained outside on the corner, probably as a lookout." She squatted, touched the floor in front of the elevators. "He took this one up."

The doors slid open and, as Alfonso followed her inside, she leaned close to the panel and inhaled. Once she filtered out all the other smells, the male's scent seemed to be strongest on the button for the ninth floor. She sniffed again. Definitely the ninth floor.

Her floor.

When the doors opened, she sprinted down the dark hallway, turned one corner and stopped right in front of her condo.

"He came straight here. That asshole was looking for me."

She felt Alfonso tense just behind her. "Just like when Kip was taken by mistake."

"We don't know for sure that it was a mistake," she said, retrieving her keys. "They might have been looking for anyone they pegged as a Tracker, and identified Kip."

"Or they could've been looking for the Council's best Tracker, who just so happens to work out of the Seattle field office. Face it, Lil, if you were planning something big and needed a bunch of sweetbloods, wouldn't you go with the sure thing by bringing in the best Tracker? I know I would."

She inserted the key into the lock and it turned. "Look, he didn't even jimmy it. The guy is definitely a professional."

Once inside, Lily walked around the condo, following the intruder's path as Alfonso quickly texted Jackson about the break-in. "He went in here—" she pointed into the kitchen "—and down there." She gestured down the hallway.

"I'll go check it out," Alfonso said and jogged toward her bedroom.

Lily followed the scent through the kitchen, where the

intruder had fingered all the pictures and artwork on her refrigerator. He'd circled around into the living room and paused next to her upright piano.

Just knowing some stranger had recently walked these rooms made her skin crawl. He had been standing in this very spot not long ago, looking at her things, breathing this air. Had he touched the piano keys? she wondered when she noticed the cover had been lifted. She always kept it closed. Had he moved through quickly or had he taken his time? Never had she felt so violated. No matter how much cleaning and scrubbing she'd do later, she knew she'd never be able to shake the horrible feeling that a stranger had gone through her things. One thing was certain: she'd not spend another day here.

At that moment, the door burst open with a bang. Instantly, her Glock was in her hand and she was taking aim. The first thing she saw was a colorful snake tattoo on a muscular arm and a hand holding half a sandwich.

She lowered the weapon. Jackson.

"Sorry, Lil, it's just me."

She holstered the gun. "Jesus. Don't you ever knock?"

Undeterred, he stuffed the sandwich into his mouth and disappeared into her kitchen. "We can't find any evidence that the guy broke into any of the other units," he called out. "I think yours is it, Lil." She heard the refrigerator door open.

"The DB was all over this place." She looked over the dozen or so family photographs on the piano. The black and white prints were in various frames that she and her mother had found and painted black. "He touched all my pictures."

"I'm sorry, Lily. Looks like they really want you. Good thing you weren't here at the time."

Alfonso emerged from her bedroom, worry plastered all over his face. "Your closet doors were open. I think he may have taken an item of clothing."

"DBs tracking the Tracker." Jackson barked out a laugh, but stopped when both Lily and Alfonso glared at him. "Sorry. I find it funny, that's all. You know, kind of ironic."

"Yeah, and we're both laughing." She turned to Alfonso and knew she was doing a lousy job keeping the worry from showing on her face. "The asshole took a picture, too. One of me and Zoe."

CHAPTER SIXTEEN

ALFONSO SAT AT THE FRONT of the boat while it plowed through the surf toward the tiny island. He slipped a hand inside his jacket and checked for the umpteenth time that his kunai were safely stowed away along with the rest of his weapons.

Yep, all there and accounted for.

He retucked a piece of hair under his knit cap and shielded his face from the spray of seawater, then glanced over his shoulder.

Lily was talking animatedly to one of the other female Guardians seated at the back of the boat near the motor. Although he couldn't hear what she was saying, he loved watching her gestures, her facial expressions. The passion she had for her work as a Guardian and for the Council's work instilled in him a tremendous sense of pride. He was proud of who she was, what she stood for and what she was capable of accomplishing.

Last night, Lily had tracked the DB scent from the hotel they'd found earlier straight to a boat launch at a seldom-used state park north of the city. No doubt the DBs were heading to the island location, getting ready for the Night of Wilding party. With dawn only a few hours away, they hadn't had time to secure a boat to investigate further. But when BloodySunday had received an all-important email from an HG friend, they'd determined this was indeed the location of the biggest Night of Wilding party. Tonight they'd had just enough time to assemble the boats before they had to leave.

If things went wrong tonight, Lily could get caught up in the middle of it all. Technically, she still was a target. Hell, if he'd had things his way, she'd have listened to him and stayed back at the field office.

But of course, she hadn't.

Although he'd tried.

And here she was.

Funny thing was, he loved it.

An endless series of waves, stirred up from the incoming storm, pounded onto the shore, muting any sound of the pontoon boats. The engines cut and the three skiffs glided onto a muddy, half-moon-shaped beach.

Alfonso was the first one off, followed closely by Jackson, who looked like he might vomit. His complexion was pale and a bead of sweat trickled down from his temples.

"Seasick, my man?" Alfonso relieved him of his heavy duffel bag.

"Guess you could call it that. I hate water. As in, really hate water."

"It's a bloody shame the biggest Night of Wilding party had to be on an island the year Dom's gone and you're in charge of the field operation."

"No kidding. I'd rather be back patrolling one of the other parties. Let someone else handle this one."

"Knowing Dom, he'd have made you come out anyway."

"Yeah, suppose you're right."

Alfonso reached around and caught the heavy weapons duffel Lily tossed to him, then he helped her off the boat, careful to set her down on the beach side of a wave.

After everyone else came ashore and the boats were secured, the Guardians scrambled over snags of giant drift logs and assembled near the rocky cliff face.

Moonlight peeked out from the heavy cloud cover long enough to illuminate a weathered sign arching over a set of rickety wooden stairs.

Welcome to Beacon Amusement Park est. 1901

How fitting that Darkbloods would use an old theme park as the site of their macabre celebration. It was an atmosphere straight out of Hollow Grave.

"Vel-comb," said Gibby, holding out a hand to Tambra as she climbed over a piece of smooth driftwood. "Come inside so vee can suck your blood. Vee promise that you'll only feel a leetle prick. That is all. Then, buh-bye."

Lily rolled her eyes as she unzipped a bag and strapped on her weapons. "Yeah, a very little prick."

"Good one, Lil," Jackson said.

"Touché, princess," Gibby said. "You're just upset because you haven't seen Mr. Skippy in a while."

"I've never seen Mr. Skippy, and, believe me, I don't care to."

"Would you chill for a change, Gibby?" Jackson said.

"Me? She started it."

A rumble sounded in Alfonso's chest. He stepped forward, his lip curled back, exposing the tips of his fangs.

Lily put her hand on his bicep. "It's okay, love," she said low enough that only he could hear. "He shoots his mouth like that all the time. I'm used to it. We all are. I just flip him shit right back and try to ignore him."

Some of the don't-fuck-with-my-woman tension slipped away, although he continued to stare at Gibby through narrowed eyes. Now the guy was joking around with one of the other females, who seemed to find what he said funny. Alfonso listened to the easy banter the others shared. They functioned as a family. They all were individuals who respected and cared for each other while working toward a common goal.

It had been so long since he'd felt like part of a family. Although he fought for the same causes as they did, believed in the same things, he had always done so alone. Was he even capable of working with a group? He wasn't sure if it was in his nature or not. Lily seemed to thrive on the camaraderie. But him? He just didn't know.

"All I can say," Lily added, "is there'd better not be any clowns up there. If so, Ima be a little freaked out."

"If I can manage the water," Jackson said, "you can deal with a clown or two."

She eyed Gibby. "Guess you're right. I already have."

Jackson wiped his sleeve across his forehead and cleared his throat. "Okay, listen up. The old theme park is located on the top of this bluff, facing the shipping lanes. With the storm coming, we don't have a lot of time. Their guest boats are already starting to arrive on the old boardwalk on the other side of the island. Sadie, Jonah and Gibby—you'll approach the park from the south. You'll need to wade through the sea arch located on the other side of those headlands."

"Sadie, me and you, girl," Gibby said, winking. "If you get scared, just hold on to me. Okay?"

"In your dreams." She adjusted her ball cap down low over her forehead, probably to keep from making eye contact with him and giving him the wrong impression.

"Guess I shoulda put my waders on," Jonah said facetiously.

"With the tide going out, the water will be shallow," Jackson said. He snapped shut one knife holster, then slid a knife into his ankle holster. "But don't come back that way. The tide will be turning in just over an hour, right, Cordell? If it's in by the time you come back and you get caught on the headlands, you'll be screwed. It's way too dangerous. Especially if you're bringing human victims out with you. The waves crashing through that arch pack quite a punch. You'll need to get back to the beachhead via an alternate route."

"You're right," Cordell said. "There are reports of people being swept out to sea at this very spot at high tide. Especially with gale-force winds and the turbulent surf conditions we have tonight."

"Why don't we helicopter them off the island?" Gibby asked. "Isn't the chopper standing by on the mainland?"

"It is," Jackson said. "But it's grounded due to the winds. Believe me, I'd much rather fly them out. We'll take them by boat first, before having our guy try to land the bird. He's good, but I don't know if he's capable of miracles.

"Tambra, Draven," he continued, "we'll be taking the north entrance. Just around the corner, there should be another old wooden stairway that leads to the top.

Lily, Alfonso and Caleb—you're heading straight up the cliff. There should be a series of caves past that outcropping that will lead you into the middle of the park, right, Cordell?"

"Yep. Straight into the old Cave of Mystery attraction."

"Watch yourselves in there, people. They've got a few live sweetbloods. So have your wits about you and don't forget your desensitization training."

"Any idea how many humans might be there?"

Alfonso cleared his throat. "From what I could tell on the game forum, quite a few wanted to come, but the invitations only went out to vampires who fit the moderators' demographic, although I'm sure a few humans will slip through the cracks and be in attendance."

"They're probably hoping that will happen," Jonah said.

Tambra snorted. "Yeah, no doubt."

"So you got invited?" Gibby asked Alfonso.

"Nope. Guess I didn't fit their profile."

"Hold on." Gibby looked up from strapping on an ammo belt, a confused look plastered on his face. "I'm coming in late here. How did you find this place if you didn't get an invite? I heard you tracked someone to the boat launch, but how did you know this was *the* party? I thought the location was under lock and key."

Alfonso pointed to Lily. "It was all her. She had the idea to reach out to a couple of gamers in the forums that we were pretty sure were vampires. My online persona got pretty chummy with a few of them who were loose enough with the information they shared about themselves. From that, we were able to find where they lived. Lily was prepared to track them to the party location when one of them emailed me asking if I was going."

"Bada bing," Gibby said, nodding his head appreciatively. "And here we are. Nice work, DeGraff." He gave her a high five and finished buckling his belt.

"Do we need to review our plans once we're inside?" Jackson asked.

"Nope."

"I'm good."

"So am I."

As everyone dispersed, Jackson clapped Cordell on the back. "Thanks, man, for coming when Shannon's been so sick. Is she doing any better?"

Cordell shrugged, rubbed the tops of this thighs with a pained look on his face. "We'll see. Glad you could use me out in the field for a change. Nice to get out from behind all those keyboards and screens."

Had the guy been hurt? Alfonso wondered. Out of habit, he flexed his own knee, but it felt just as strong as the other one now.

"He's a changeling," Lily whispered. "It healed his spinal injury, but he's never quite gotten used to having the use of his legs again."

A few minutes later, Alfonso, Lily and Caleb scaled the rocky cliff face and found the cave entrance. They shadow-moved easily through the pitch-black cavern and made it into the abandoned theme park well ahead of the others.

REJAVIK SNAPPED HIS FINGERS. "I want the hair pulled back on this one. It needs to be away from his neck. The clients need to see what they're bidding on and this is all part of the package. And this one needs her makeup retouched. Didn't you use waterproof mascara? You know they're going to be crying, but we can't have them drugged up. And that dress. Is that the best you can do? I wanted Grecian goddess, not trampy harem."

The cocktail glass in Ventra's hand broke, spilling ice water onto her strappy heels. One of her underlings handed her a napkin and quickly picked up the pieces.

She was selling a fantasy and the female's harem attire was part of it, as were the Roman gladiator, the Catholic schoolgirl, the fireman and the stripper.

Rejavik had taken over as if this were his own pet project. The guy was a regular Tim Gunn…with fangs. If he said *make it work, people,* she was going to totally lose it.

Calm down. Get a grip.

She inhaled a cleansing breath through her nostrils and let the anger seep out slowly, and as she dried her hands, the napkin came away red. With detached interest, she licked the deep gash on her palm and watched the edges slowly knit back together.

If things went as planned, tonight would be a big success, and Rejavik would point out her efforts to the Alliance. She'd get the recognition she deserved, and she'd have opportunities dropping into her lap. And she'd be richer…oh, God, would she be richer. As she fingered the sapphires dangling from her earlobes, her thoughts briefly turned to the matching bracelet that she didn't yet own. It would've been perfect with this outfit.

Next time. She'd be wearing it for the next blood rave

she organized. All she had to do was put up with this bullshit for a few more hours, then it would all be over, and he would be gone.

Oh hell, a few hours wouldn't kill her. She could put up with anything for a few hours. She'd done it before, and she'd do it again, if she had to. It wouldn't be the first time she compromised herself in the short term to get what she wanted in the long run.

She eyed the mascara tracks on the petite brunette. With rosy cheeks, porcelain skin and Shirley Temple curls, the girl looked younger than her seventeen or eighteen years.

Ventra's fangs, which had never fully retracted after the sweetbloods had arrived a few hours ago, stretched out from her gums until she had difficulty keeping her lips closed. It'd been way too long since she'd had any Sweet. It hadn't seemed right to indulge herself when they were saving any they could find for tonight's big party. Without having secured an Agency Tracker, they'd had to seek out these sweetbloods on their own. She'd been hoping they'd capture more, but she would have to make do with these. The precious liquid was worth far too much for her to waste on herself. At least not right now.

Rejavik, on the other hand, seemed to have no such qualms. He'd drained one of their hostages yesterday and looked to be about ready to do so again. On the opposite side of the staging room, he was leaning in close to one of the male captives, a little too interested in the whole process.

If he takes another one, I swear I'm going to rip his throat out.

She turned her attention back to the young woman, who was shivering uncontrollably in her thin muslin gown. Her scent was mouthwatering. Clearly, Ventra had been depriving herself for too long.

Personally, she didn't find the Goth goddess look as unappealing as Rejavik did. Not at all. It was basically an advertisement.

It said the girl was scared.

And everyone knew what that meant.

Ignoring the terror in the girl's eyes, Ventra advanced a step closer, brushed a hand over the springy brown curls. If only she could take a sip…

Caught up in the heady bloodscent combined with a perfume that had probably come from a T-shirt store in the mall, Ventra hardly noticed as fresh tracks of black seeped from the girl's eyes and quiet sobs shook her shoulders.

No, the thought was nice—very appealing actually, but she couldn't chance it. Someone would pay handsomely to drain this little morsel.

Ventra gave her one last head-to-toe as one of her people clamped a thick gold cuff around the woman's neck.

"Hold on, now. That's way too tight," Ventra said, running a finger under the collar.

Even as she cowered away from her touch, the girl snapped her gaze up in surprise, obviously thinking she'd found a sympathizer. Too bad it wasn't her comfort that Ventra was concerned about.

"Look here. It needs to be loose enough for access to the jugular. We need to consider the customers. Many don't feed off the hoof very often and they might only be comfortable this way. Old school? Maybe. But there's nothing wrong with that. I'm not a fan of these rigid collars. What happened to just a simple chain? They accomplish the same thing."

The girl sobbed and her knees buckled. Before she hit the ground, Ventra reached out, caught her easily by the elbow and set her back on her feet.

"Ask him," her assistant said, nodding his head toward Rejavik.

Ventra ground her teeth together when she saw Rejavik affixing a collar around the neck of one of the male sweetbloods. Figured. If the guy weren't so powerful, she'd have taken his ass down a few pegs by now.

The driving beat of techno music blared louder for a moment as the outer door opened, then closed. One of her most loyal assistants approached.

"Watch her, will you?" she commanded of the Darkblood attending the girl. "I don't want any unnecessary bruising until after the sale is made. Do you understand?"

"Yes, ma'am."

She turned to her assistant. "How's the crowd, Elan? I've been stuck back here for the past few minutes. Have the guests all arrived?"

"Yes, Mistress. The party barges were packed. The final boat docked a few minutes ago. For those who knew about the party but only contemplated coming, that last post in the HG forums must've done the trick. A couple of the boats reported picking up guests who tried to wade over to the island during low tide. The storm is pretty intense, and a few of them almost got swept away."

She laughed. "Eager fools."

"The prize of a sweetblood to the one who brings the most guests is brilliant. You're a savvy marketer, ma'am. You seem to have a knack for knowing exactly what people want and figuring out a way to give it to them."

She jutted out her chin. "Thank you, Elan. I try."

He continued. "We've got vampires from British Columbia, Idaho, Seattle, Portland. It's like they all came out of the woodwork for this party. Gotta love word of mouth. This is going to be the biggest, most talked-about Wilding party on the West Coast. You're a genius, ma'am."

That game had proved to be quite the find. If her future financial situation were to make it feasible, she might have to consider buying controlling interest in the gaming company. Casting a sidelong glance at Rejavik, she wished he weren't so preoccupied with that sweetblood so he could hear this.

"I certainly hope so. And is everyone enjoying the experience of going through the maze that leads them inside?"

"Oh yeah. With the calmer energies up here, they started off fairly subdued, especially when you consider what goes on in Mexico City."

They laughed knowingly. The vampire population down south was a wild bunch, although on the flip side, there was a much larger Council presence to deal with, as well as more Darkblood competition. Up here was a virtually untouched market, the opportunities boundless. Because the energies were calmer up here, she just needed to coddle and nurture the demand a little more than she did when she'd been an assistant down in Mexico City.

Elan rubbed his hands together, and his dark eyes glistened with excitement. "I just watched as one of our guys snatched a human out of the crowd and started feeding. What a great idea to have Darkblood plants in the audience to get things rolling. You should've seen the looks on everyone's faces. Those ones closest to the action were shocked as hell, but it didn't take more than a minute for a few of them to jump in."

She nodded her head, having expected and hoped for that precise reaction. "Their initial attitudes are much different here than down south, that's for sure. But I can see things are changing. How did it affect the other humans present? Have they panicked yet?"

"Nope. Because the maze is narrow, long and very dark, the humans ahead and behind couldn't tell exactly what was happening. I heard one of them saying it was a kick-ass haunted house with realistic special effects."

Things were all coming together perfectly. "Exactly the news I like to hear. See that it happens several more times along the route as everyone files in. I want blood-scent heavy in the air, and I want them to be stirred up and ready for the show."

"Yes, ma'am. They will be. By the time they're all inside, they are going to be *soooo* ready."

She glanced at the brunette pixie again.

"It should be a very entertaining show."

CHAPTER SEVENTEEN

ALFONSO STOOD WITH LILY and Caleb at the end of the tunnel, a piece of black painted plywood blocking them from going farther. Muffled voices and footsteps came from the other side of the wooden barricade. Flashes of light, timed to the beat of throbbing techno music, shone through several narrow gaps and cast eerie shadows on the rock walls.

"That must be the maze on the other side that leads to the rave," Lily said. All illicit parties like this had similar entrances, designed to slow down the cops in the event the location was discovered.

Alfonso ran his hands over the plywood to determine how sturdy it was. Given how much it wobbled near the center where two pieces met, he guessed it was only tacked up in a few places. Should be easy enough to pop loose.

"Do you think it's the only entrance?" asked Caleb.

"Main entrance, yes," Alfonso answered. "But raves usually have several exits. There's the main one here where people are screened before being allowed to come in. The rest of the exits will be obscured. That way, in the event of a raid, the elaborate maze will slow down the cops just long enough for many of the partiers to be able to escape out the back."

"I don't know where they think they'd run to since a bunch of boats brought them in. They're pretty much stuck here until the organizers decide it's time to let them leave." Caleb clicked his earpiece and turned away. "I'm going to report in that we're here and standing by."

"Will you at least promise you'll try to stay close?" Alfonso asked, pulling Lily into his arms. "If we're a team, that means we work together."

"I'll try, but it all depends on what happens once we get inside. Our primary goal is to get all the humans out first. If I see someone in danger, I'm not going to *not* help them because you're not right there. That's too limiting."

"Fair enough. You focus on the humans, and I'll deal with the Darkbloods by—"

A high-pitched scream permeated the loud music. Lily jumped from his arms and pressed her palms to the plywood.

"It's a human. A male. And he's right here on the other side. Quick. Several are feeding from him now."

With the heel of one hand, Alfonso popped a bottom corner of the plywood loose. "Hold the top in place, Lil. I'm going to try to slide him through."

Caleb was saying something about it not being time yet, but Alfonso ignored him. He wasn't planning to storm the place, just rescue this one person.

Hoping the guy wasn't a big man, Alfonso reached through the small opening and his hand closed around an ankle. He pulled the body out of the throngs of feet and legs, and punched away several clingers. Holy hell, it was like a fucking madhouse in there.

Once the body was completely in, he released the plywood and it snapped back into place.

"God, he's just a teenager," said Lily, as she quickly assessed his condition. "How did he get mixed up in this?"

"How does anyone?"

"He's still alive." Lily sealed the bite marks at his wrist and throat with a swipe of her finger. "Thankfully, you got to him in time."

"Caleb," Alfonso said, "you take him back to the beach. Cordell has medical equipment there."

"Me? Why do I have to go? You're not even—"

"Caleb, quit your bitching," Lily snapped. "Just get the kid down there. That's an order."

When Alfonso handed the boy off to Caleb, a muted male voice from the other side of the barricade caught his attention.

"Joe, man, where are you?"

It sounded vaguely familiar, but he couldn't quite place it.

Alfonso stooped down and pulled the plywood open just a crack. He saw a flash of red hair and Converse high-tops.

His eyes narrowed. The kid looked a little like—

Oh for godsake, it was Kenny, the boy from the computer store.

Guilt knotted into a tight ball in the pit of his stomach, and he rocked back on his heels.

How the hell was this possible? He'd wiped the guy's memory—he was sure of it.

He stared after Caleb, and it occurred to him that Joe must work at the computer store too.

Without too much effort, Alfonso could almost picture the kid wearing one of those kelly-green aprons and working the cash register next to Kenny. Although Kenny shouldn't have any memory of playing the game with Alfonso, this kid must've been watching and seen enough to find it online.

How long had they been playing it? he wondered. Probably from the very beginning.

He cursed under his breath. How could he have been so careless when he knew what was at stake? The back of his neck began to ache. Absently, he reached up and rubbed it.

He should have taken better precautions, checked to see if anyone at the store was watching them play the game. Or better yet, he should never have asked for outside help.

A nagging voice reminded him he'd never have gotten as far as he had without Kenny's help.

He ground his molars together as he reached for the plywood again. No one else was going to die because of his own stupid decisions. He'd get Kenny out of here too.

"What are you doing?" Lily asked, her eyes wide.

"Trying to fix a mistake I made. There's a kid on the other side who's looking for his buddy." He pointed a thumb in Caleb's direction. "I don't have time to explain things, but suffice it to say they're here because of me. And I'm getting them both out of this hellhole."

"Wait a minute. How do you plan to do that? There's no way you're fitting through that narrow opening. You planning to bust through now and blow our cover? The other two teams aren't even in place yet."

"No, but—"

"But nothing. Listen. I'll go. I'm smaller than you and can slip just as easily through the opening as that boy did."

And wind up smack in the middle of the throng of vampires and humans rushing to get inside? She couldn't be serious. "No. You're not getting separated from me."

But even as he said the words, he saw the determined set of her jaw and the fire behind her caramel eyes. Lily did what Lily wanted to do, whether he agreed with her or not.

"We're a team, remember? Each of us does the things the other can't do. You're big. I'm not. End of subject."

She knelt down, gave him a quick kiss, then planted herself in front of the opening, as if he'd never registered an ounce of protest.

"I'll slip through, grab the boy and be back in a snap."

"If he's not still right outside—"

"He is. Now, come on."

"You'd better have your ass back in here by the time I count to twenty or this plywood's coming down."

"Deal. You said his name is Kenny?"

"Yeah. Be careful, Lily."

Then, against his better judgment, he pulled back the corner and Lily scooted on her butt through the opening.

A BITING GUST OF WIND roared through the fir trees, stirring up the heavy limbs and making it hard to hear anything else.

Jackson climbed the last rung of the rickety ladder and pulled himself onto the roof of the Cave of Mystery attraction. The thumping bass of the electronic trance beat reverberated through his fingertips.

It must be blaringly loud inside.

He tested the footing. Seemed solid enough. He reached down to help Tambra and Draven.

Jackson loved loud, pulse-jarring music, and, from what he could tell, the DJ was spinning some awesome tunes. It would've have been a fun way to celebrate the Longest Night if Darkbloods hadn't been the organizers. And if killing weren't about to happen.

He found himself tapping a foot in time with the beat as readied his weapons.

He'd always felt at home inside a club. The abundance of human energy, which was easily accessible given the way most of them dressed, made it hard for him to leave. Drunk human women were clingy and never seemed to notice or care that he was a little touchier than normal. A quick high five here, a little kiss there, a rendezvous in a back room and he could tide himself over for another night without anyone being the wiser.

"Which way?" asked Draven.

Jackson pointed to a boarded-up window a few feet away. "There."

The music got louder as they carefully pried off the boards. When they climbed inside the dank and musty storeroom, the cloying smell of Sweet was thick in the air.

Instantly, he craved it, wanted to taste its sweetness on his tongue. His fangs elongated. His pupils stretched.

Fuuuck.

He put a hand on the windowsill to steady himself.

Having fed from an unsuspecting host less than thirty minutes before he'd stepped onto the boat, he didn't need more blood now.

Got it, Self? You're fine. Just chill out.

Recalling his desensitization training, he focused on everything else. The musty smell of the dust-covered room, the cobwebs on all the clutter, the clean soap smell on Tambra's hands from when she'd last washed them. Anything and everything except the Sweet.

His fangs retracted and his pupils shrank.

Christ, he hated surprises like that, especially since he wasn't feeling particularly strong after that vomit-inducing boat ride over here.

"Wow," Draven whispered. "That was intense. I totally wasn't ready for it."

"Me either." Tambra's voice was so soft he could barely hear her. "The wind must've carried the scent away when we were outside."

Although music drowned out most of the sounds, Jackson tiptoed anyway, around the wooden props, scenery backdrops and steamer trunks.

On the other side of a large Santa cutout, he spotted a rotted-out portion of the floorboards. Kneeling down, he peered through the hole into the room below.

Holy shit.

He wasn't surprised to see a sweetblood. He knew one had to be close.

But five of them? And what was with the costumes?

Including the guy at the door, he counted four Darkbloods in the room as well.

This couldn't be good.

He held up his hand. "Four DBs. Five sweetbloods. Tambra, call the other teams. See if they're ready. It's five minutes to midnight. I have a feeling they're saving these sweetbloods for something big."

"Shouldn't we do something now? We don't know how much time they have."

"No. We wait until the other teams are in place."

As he said that, a female sailed into the room below. Given how the others reacted to her, Jackson assumed she wasn't just an ordinary Darkblood.

She wore a formfitting, navy blue minidress with four-inch heels and a velvet cape that swept the floor as she walked. Her white-blond hair was messy in an eighties glam-rock kind of way.

With military precision, she inspected each of the sweetbloods, three women and two men, finally stopping in front of a young woman with curly brown hair and a gauzy white dress that reached nearly to her bare feet.

The girl put her hands over her face, but the female produced a thin cane and struck her arm. Obligingly, the girl dropped her hands, even as tears streamed down her cheeks.

An icy heat formed in the pit of his stomach and Jackson gripped the edge of the hole.

The female apparently liked what she saw because she grabbed a chain attached to a gold collar around the young woman's neck and led her out of the lineup like a leashed dog. She paused at the door, not far from where Jackson was looking down, and spoke to another Darkblood.

Despite the loud music, he imagined hearing the girl's sobs wafting up through the hole, and it stabbed at his heart.

She was a teenager, just a kid. No one deserved to be treated like this. This girl's luck would get much worse if they didn't act fast.

Lily's team was in place. Was Gibby's?

When he shifted his weight to ask Tambra, his boot dislodged a tiny smattering of dust. The breath caught in his throat as he helplessly watched it float down into the room.

Shit. If one of the Darkbloods saw—

The girl looked up, her wide eyes searching, and her gaze locked onto his.

His stomach tightened as if he'd just been punched, a roaring sound filling his head.

Although those eyes were much different, the emotion behind them was the same, reminding him of his little sister many years ago, when she, too, had pleaded silently for him to save her.

That was it. Enough with the waiting.

He put a finger to his lips. "Shhhh. I'm coming," he mouthed.

She sucked in her lower lip and nodded slightly.

Just like his sister, this girl was putting her trust in him. This time, he wouldn't fail.

He turned to Tambra. "We gotta go now. Are they ready?"

"Five more minutes. Gibby's team had a hard time getting through the old amusement park rides. Said it was like a minefield trying to get around and over everything. The moon made it too light to shadow-move very quickly."

The female jerked the chain and the girl reluctantly followed her out the door. She gathered up her dress, but it still dragged on the floor behind her.

"I'm not waiting any longer. Tell them I'm going in."

LILY TRIED TO KEEP PEOPLE OUT of her personal space, but there were so many crowding through the dark maze that they kept bumping into her.

In the flash of the strobe light, everyone's movements looked robotic, programmed. It struck her as fitting. These people came, wanting to be spoon-fed their entertainment, but ultimately, they were simply puppets of the Darkblood agenda.

Human blood and the scent of many heightened emotions filtered through her nose, but the strongest one, which came from a nearby human, was fear. She spun around, trying to get a lock on it.

When the light flashed again, she spotted Kenny's red hair just past a muscular guy in front of her. Kenny stood unmoving against the black plywood, a rock in a stream of water, searching the faces of the crowd filing past him.

"Kenny?" she yelled above the din.

She tried to elbow her way around the bodybuilder, but the guy grabbed her wrist.

"Hold on," he said, the coppery smell of blood fresh on his breath. "What's the rush? You. Me. It's a beautiful thing."

Oh please. She didn't have time for this shit.

In a basic Krav Maga move, she twisted her wrist, broke free from his hold and gave him a kidney shot with her elbow.

He doubled over and she sprinted to Kenny.

"Come with me."

"Do I know you?" he asked, his eyes narrowing.

"Nope, but you're looking for Joe, right?"

His guarded expression made it obvious he wasn't buying into this whole partying atmosphere. He clearly knew something else was going on. "Yeah, how'd you know that? Have you seen him?"

"He's back here. On the other side of this barricade."

"B-behind a barricade? What happened?"

"He…ah…went down. We helped him out of the crowd of people stepping over him."

"Is he okay?"

"He'll be fine."

Kenny blew out a sigh of relief. "He better be. It was his idea to come here, but this place is totally creeping me out."

Someone jostled her into Kenny. "He's a cute little morsel, now, isn't he? You saving him for later?"

The crowd kept moving and whoever had made the comment disappeared. She'd never been claustrophobic before, but this was ridiculous.

"See what I'm talking about?" he said.

Yeah, she did. "Come with me. We need to get you out of here."

Careful not to slog any of his energy, she grabbed his hand, and they slowly threaded their way upstream, fighting for every step.

Would Caleb have returned by now from taking Joe down to the boats? One of them would have to escort Kenny to the beach, too. She didn't like the idea of having to do it herself, but the cavern was too tricky for a human kid to negotiate alone, especially without a flashlight. And who's to say he'd even obey them, although she supposed they could mind-plant the suggestion. Could she help him down to the beach and make it back before Jackson gave the order to go in?

Just as she was about to rap on the plywood, she heard shouts behind her. Someone yelled, "Raid!" and people started running.

She turned her head just as gunfire sounded.

What the hell—? They still had a few more minutes till go-time.

The crowd surged backward, jamming her shoulder into the wall. She stumbled, almost fell. Immediately, the corner of the plywood gaped open and she shoved Kenny through. But before she could reach for Alfonso's outstretched hand, the crowd surged again and she was swept past him.

CHAPTER EIGHTEEN

IT WAS COMPLETE PANDEMONIUM when Alfonso burst into the maze, hell-bent on finding Lily. People, both human and vampire, ran in every direction. Strobe lights turned everyone into macabre automatons, their movements jerky, like old reel-to-reel footage. A terrified face here. Hungry, soulless eyes there. Although music blared even louder on this side of the panel, it couldn't drown out the screaming.

Bloody hell. Where was she?

The crowd had carried her to the right, so he bolted in that direction, only vaguely aware of the people he elbowed past. Once outside, everyone scattered into a few groups. He spotted Jackson near the skeletal remains of a wooden roller coaster away from the main crowds, ushering a group of humans through the tall, windswept grass. Bright, silvery light from the moon hampered his efforts to shadow-move as quickly as he would've liked, but when he arrived at Jackson's side, the eyes of the humans with him registered their shock.

"Have you seen Lily?"

"No, I thought she was with you."

"She was, but we got separated."

Why, for fuck's sake, had he wasted valuable seconds ordering Kenny down the tunnel when he should've gone after her instantly? If only he could've stretched out his hand a little farther, he'd have latched onto her. Could she have gone the other way instead?

"Dude, you need to chill. Lily's around here somewhere. She's pretty capable of handling things on her own, if you haven't already noticed."

"Yes, but—"

"Yeah, but nothing. Seriously, my man, she's around here somewhere."

Maybe the rising panic in his gut was clouding his judgment. He'd find her; she couldn't have gone far. He tried to settle himself enough to sense her presence, but all the commotion around him made it difficult. He had to remind himself that Darkbloods no longer needed a Tracker since the Night of Wilding party was over. Things would settle down soon after tonight.

With a sense that she was still inside, he pushed his way back through the confusing circular route with all its dead ends and wrong ways. The crowd had thinned out considerably. Most of the people were outside by now. When he got to the hole in the barricade that led to the tunnel, he was disheartened yet not entirely shocked to find she wasn't there. Lily wasn't the type of person to wait around while stuff was falling apart around her.

"Do you know how to get out of here?" asked a young human male, breathing hard. "I'm so friggin' lost—I've gone past this spot three times already."

One whiff told Alfonso this guy wouldn't last much longer. He wasn't a sweetblood, but he had a pretty unusual blood type, and getting out amongst all those adrenaline-hyped and energy-depleted vampires could cost him his life. Frankly, he was shocked no one had taken him yet.

"Get your ass in there," Alfonso told him, pointing to the jagged hole made by the missing piece of plywood. He gave him quick instructions to follow the tunnel to the top of the cliff, where someone should be there to direct him. When he stooped to shove the guy in, he felt a tickling sensation inside his veins and smelled the faint scent of lavender.

Lily.

She was inside the tunnel.

He exhaled a heavy sigh of relief. She was safe.

"There you are, love," she said from the other side of the panel. She gripped his hand, ready to haul him in. "Wondered where you'd gotten off to. Found another one, I see."

Although the compressed brick of worry had been lifted from his shoulders, a nervous energy still nagged at his insides, keeping him agitated and restless. He couldn't shake the feeling that something was still terribly wrong.

"Listen. Can you take him down to the beach? I'm going to go back inside. See if there are more stragglers that need to be rounded up."

Without waiting for her reply, Alfonso turned and sprinted deeper into the Cave of Mystery.

The maze opened up onto a large, cavernlike room, built at the turn of the century to look like a cave with a soaring three-story ceiling and curved rock walls. One wall actually was part of the basalt cliff face, and the rest were made to just look like rock. Fake stalactites hung from the ceiling, along with hundreds of twinkle lights.

A crackling noise hissed from the speakers, and beams of green neon flashed out a preprogrammed light show into nothingness. The unmanned turntables in the middle of the large stage skipped over and over. Behind it were several brightly lit glassed-in rooms with the curtains pulled almost all the way closed.

Viewing rooms.

Just like the sex club where Kip had initially been held. Had they planned to do the same thing here?

From back here, Alfonso saw that a microphone stand had been kicked over and lay next to an assortment of handcuffs, silk scarves and—

Shit. A length of chain hung from the ceiling over-head.

Kinky sex paraphernalia. Maybe couples were doing it out here on the stage instead.

A few individuals staggered along the perimeter toward the mouth of the maze, but since they were vampire, not human, he didn't feel the urgent need to help them. They'd made a choice to come here; let the Agency authorities round them up when they got outside.

"You guys really know how to kill a party," one of them said.

"Just when it was getting good, too," said another, sidestepping an overturned chair. "The show was about ready to start, and everyone was counting down to mid-night. Goddamn Agency assholes."

"Yeah, so bite me."

Once the two losers had left, the room was eerily quiet except for the turntable noise. The earlier unease he'd felt was even stronger, standing the hair on the back of his neck on end. He palmed his kunai and walked forward.

A flash of movement inside one of the viewing rooms drew his attention. Through a half-opened curtain, he saw what appeared to be an individual dressed in a long flowing cape leaning over a gurney-size table.

Holy shit. Someone was feeding from a host.

He bolted forward, his eye on the figure in the viewing room, so he didn't see the body on the floor until it was too late. He tried to jump, but the toe of his boot caught on the guy's foot. He stumbled, landing all his weight at an awkward angle on his bad leg.

Although he caught himself from falling, a sharp pain stabbed outward and he imagined all those internal stitches and pins popping loose. Gritting his teeth, he kept running, and when the neon flashed off, swathing the room in momentary darkness, he closed the distance to the stage and jumped up in one liquid movement of shadow.

A seamless piece of glass ran the length of the viewing rooms. Where was the goddamn door? He quickly scanned both directions, but couldn't find one. It had to be offstage somewhere.

Sheathing both kunai, he withdrew one of his guns, stepped back and took aim at the glass. But before his finger squeezed the trigger, the individual lifted his head from his victim, his teeth dripping with blood.

And Alfonso's heart stopped cold.

Although it had been more than a century before and the catacombs had only been illuminated by torchlight, it was a face he would never forget.

It was Christoph Rejavik, of the Order of the Red Sword.

His blood assassin.

Alfonso blinked once, twice. It wasn't possible. Rejavik was supposed to be in Europe. And yet, there he was, standing just a few feet away with the blood of an innocent on his mouth.

Lily!

Panic rose in his gut before he remembered she was down at the boats. Safe and away from the assassin.

It's just him and me. Right here. Right now.

A familiar wave of detachment washed over him as his body went on autopilot.

With the assassin dead and the *shevala* destroyed, Alfonso would no longer be easily tracked. He'd become just another Guardian, always on alert for Darkbloods and other reverts, but not the sole prey of a relentless, trained killer with one goal and one goal only. With his death, Alfonso could start living.

And Lily would be safe.

With the back of his hand, Rejavik rubbed his lips and stepped toward the glass. The tiny metal box, a seemingly insignificant piece of odd jewelry that had imprisoned Alfonso's scent for centuries, dangled from the man's fingernail.

Rage burned in Alfonso's veins as Rejavik peered through the glass at him. Ever since he'd so boldly betrayed the Alliance, leading to Pavlos's death, he'd known this day would eventually come. He just hadn't expected it at this time or on this tiny island in the middle of the San Juans.

Rejavik stared through the glass, his eyes unfocused and pitch-black from the thirst. It was as if he couldn't see where Alfonso stood.

How could that be? Had his assassin not tracked him here? Why was he not drawing a weapon?

Alfonso cranked his head around, looking for signs of a trap, but the place was empty.

It occurred to him suddenly that Rejavik truly couldn't see him. With the lights blazing inside the viewing room, Alfonso was invisible in the darkness of the cavern.

Narrowing his eyes, he quickly took in Rejavik's attire. The fucker was wearing a goddamn costume, because he was partying with the rest of the lowlifes at the Night of Wilding. The high-collared cape, the slicked-back hair, the frilly white cuffs. Except for the blood-tinged lips, which were the real thing, the whole getup was an over-the-top caricature of the vampire mythos.

Alfonso couldn't believe his luck—his blood assassin was drunk on Sweet. That could be the only explanation for why he hadn't scented Alfonso. He'd probably gotten caught up in the madness, as many did on the Night of Wilding.

And it was about to be his downfall.

A thrill surged through Alfonso's body as he took aim, and he knew he'd remember this moment for the rest of his life. He would soon be rejoicing at the sight of the man's body withering, then charcoaling before his eyes.

Rejavik lifted his head slightly and sniffed the air. A cold smile creased his face.

He might not see Alfonso, but he'd finally scented him.

With a hard set to his jaw, Alfonso squeezed off all

the rounds in quick succession, the sound reverberating like a machine gun in the huge hall.

The damn glass spiderwebbed but didn't break.

Startled, the assassin took a step backward, jostling the gurney behind him. His victim's arm swung down and drops of blood hit the white linoleum floor in rapid succession, puddling obscenely next to a discarded fireman's hat.

As Alfonso jammed in another clip, the assassin ripped off his cape, flinging the vestiges of the party behind him. He spread his hands over the shattered glass panel and looked for a way to go through.

Then someone hit a switch somewhere, illuminating the whole place with blinding incandescent light.

And Alfonso met Rejavik's now-seeing gaze.

They stared at each other for a moment until the assassin nodded and touched his lips in a fang-slang greeting. "So thrilling to see you again," he mouthed.

Rejavik cocked the heel of his hand back, preparing to punch the glass. Alfonso widened his stance and took aim again. As soon as the guy broke through, this silver bullet would give his brain a hi-how-are-you.

With his hand in midair, Rejavik's attention was drawn to something behind Alfonso, and he stopped. Hearing heavy footsteps, Alfonso glanced back to see several Guardians entering the cavern. The stage shook as Jackson rushed to his side, weapons drawn.

"Who the fuck is that? Oh Jesus, he's got the sweetblood we couldn't find."

"Just tell me Lily's back at the boat," Alfonso said through clenched teeth, not dropping his gaze from

Rejavik's. She needed to be off this tiny island. As far away from this monster as possible.

Rejavik leaned close to the glass and waggled his fingers, making the *shevala* swing wildly.

Yes, you asshole. You think you hold my life in your hands. But not any longer. This ends. Tonight.

Something stirred behind Alfonso and he heard several more Guardians approaching, but before his mind registered that it was Lily's presence he felt, the sound of her voice filled the space.

"Alfonso, love, there you are."

Panic vise-gripped his insides and a sour lump of bile rose in his throat. And when the assassin broke off his stare to look at Lily, Alfonso's blood ran cold.

"Get the fuck out of here."

With a slight smile, Rejavik surveyed the glass. It looked as though he was going to try busting through again.

"Hold on," Jackson said, clearly not getting that this was much more than a sweetblood draining. "Access to the room must be on the second floor. I'll approach him from behind."

Rejavik's gaze followed Jackson, then he took in the half dozen or so other Agents and slowly backed away. He was outnumbered, and he knew it. He reached inside his jacket, pulled out a stiff piece of paper, and set it on the body.

Then he disappeared out a back door Alfonso hadn't noticed until now.

"Stay here," Alfonso ordered Lily.

He tried to ignore the pain shooting through his knee

as he scrambled off the stage, looking for a stairway, a ladder, a door—but all he saw was a bunch of scaffolding, trash and fake rock paneling. He couldn't waste the time running through the maze again. The guy would be long gone by then.

He hauled ass down a hallway that seemed to be heading in the wrong direction but was his only option. His boots pounded out a lopsided beat along the hallway. As he approached the end, a mechanical rumble sounded from outside, getting progressively louder and higher pitched.

A helicopter? But it was too windy to fly the birds, wasn't it?

He threw himself at the heavy door, cranking the handle as his shoulder made contact, but the door didn't budge. Had to be blocked from the outside. However, nothing was going to keep him from Rejavik.

He took a few steps backward. Ignoring the tearing pain in his knee, he ran at the door full force, kicking it off its hinges and crashing onto the wet pavement. He sprang to his feet and saw a helicopter in the open area just beyond the derelict Ferris wheel. Rejavik was climbing aboard.

"No!"

Running forward, his arms and legs pumping, he ducked under a weed-covered portion of an old roller coaster track, hardly aware of the rotor downblast. The bird lifted off as he raced past the Ferris wheel. He stretched his arms up and jumped, vaguely feeling a snap in his knee, but the landing skids were just beyond his reach. A roar shot from his chest; wind and rain lashed his upturned face. His enemy had slipped through his fingers.

So close.

He was so fucking close.

And yet somehow, he'd allowed the asshole to escape.

The helicopter skimmed the tops of the trees, the repetitive sound of the rotors mocking him. No matter what he did or how hard he fought, the blood assassin would always best him. Always.

He pulled off his knit cap, wiped his face with his forearm and winced at the pain in his knee.

How could he have been such a fool?

The house. Rekindling things with Lily. Her blood.

Yeah, he was brilliant. Real fucking brilliant.

Through his incredible selfishness, acting on his shortsighted desire to live a normal life, he'd put everyone around him at risk. He never should have agreed to help out the Agency, never should have dreamed he could be just one of the guys.

Now that Rejavik knew he was here in the Northwest, there was only one thing to do.

Grasping his thigh, he turned to see Jackson barge through the broken door and beeline toward him.

Perfect. Just the guy he needed to talk to.

Jackson opened his mouth, but before he could speak, Alfonso cut him off.

"Jacks, man, I need you to do me a big favor. It's of the utmost importance."

"Sure, but—"

"First, I need you to take Lily somewhere safe, somewhere I've not been to. Don't take her to Region or to the

Seattle field office. Maybe out to the resort where Mackenzie is staying, since I don't know the location. It needs to have a top-of-the-line cloaking system and you need to cover your tracks."

"Okay, but you—"

"Next, you need to do whatever you can to mask the trail of the places I've been to with Lily. We were in Seattle, at my home near Bellingham and up at Region. Lily can give you directions to the house."

"I don't understand."

"Use those scent-masking crystals the Agency developed. Although they're not foolproof, they should weaken the scent trail just enough that when he comes across a stronger, more recent trail of mine, he'll follow that instead."

Jackson held up his hand. "Hold on. What the fuck are you talking about?"

"That guy in there? The one who drained the sweetblood? The one who's in that goddamn helicopter heading back to the mainland? He's with the Order of the Red Sword. My blood assassin. He's been on my trail since I betrayed the Alliance. I set up an elaborate ruse in Europe to make him think I was in hiding over there, but obviously, those efforts failed. And now that he knows I'm here, I must disappear again before he IDs anyone I care about."

Jackson frowned as he reached into an inner pocket and handed him a dog-eared photo. "We found this in the viewing room with the body."

Alfonso took it from him. With one look, his hands shook, a rushing sound ringing in his ears.

It was a black-and-white photo of Lily. Holding Zoe's hand.

Slow, sickening fear snaked up his spine and settled low in his belly. It was the assassin who had been in Lily's condo. Not some random Darkblood looking for a Tracker. The fucker had walked through her home, into her kitchen, her bathroom, her bedroom, her closet. Memorizing her scent.

"Lily? Where's she at now? Who's with her?" Alfonso could barely choke the words out.

"She's with Gibby and his crew. They're escorting the humans we found down to the boats."

Okay, so she was safe for the moment.

But not Zoe.

Sweet, beautiful Zoe.

A tingling sensation rolled in a succession of waves over his skin, growing more and more powerful, while Zoe's name drummed into his head like a chant. He felt suddenly detached from where he stood, and this time the detachment wasn't the familiar kind. He pictured Zoe, her chubby, heart-shaped face, her little fingers as she wrapped them around the medallion he'd given to her for luck.

"Dude, what the hell is going on? You're…you're fading." It sounded like Jackson was talking into a tin can.

But before Alfonso could respond, the roaring sound got louder, and the ground fell away from his feet.

CHAPTER NINETEEN

THE FIRST THING ALFONSO HEARD was the sound of a piano melody in the air, just before the ground solidified under his boots. A heavy velvet curtain was just inches from his face, and light spilled out through a narrow gap onto the dark wooden floor at his feet.

He stood from a crouch and looked around.

What had just happened? Where was he?

Track lighting hung far above his head along with another row of curtains. He took a few steps, reached out and touched a metal scaffolding. It was solid and very real. This wasn't a bizarre dream or hallucination.

He had teleported here. Wherever *here* was.

Good God. He really *did* have the ability. Just as he'd suspected. It hadn't been some alcohol-induced stupor that had made him think he had teleported to Lily's bed almost a decade ago. It hadn't been his overactive imagination, because somehow, he had done it again.

He was backstage, and from the sounds of it, Zoe was playing her piano piece. It was the same melody he'd helped her with.

Zoe.

He had to be at Region Headquarters in the small theater. Had he been able to teleport because he was worried about her?

Half hobbling, half sprinting, he made it to the wings of the stage and peered around the curtain. With her back to him, Zoe looked dwarfed sitting at a grand piano, her feet not touching the ground. She wore a pale blue dress, and long brown ringlets fell from a ribbon in her hair. The tricky part of the song was coming up. He held his breath, and sure enough, she nailed it.

Way to go, Baby Girl.

Lily would be so proud of her, he thought. Too bad she wasn't here to see this.

He glanced into the crowd of mostly parents and grandparents. Except for the children doing performances who would probably change their clothes later, everyone was dressed warmly in fleece and scarves, and held heavy winter coats on their laps. They'd be heading out to the bonfires afterward to continue the Longest Night celebrations. Lily's mother and father sat in the second row next to Steven Hastings, who seemed more engrossed in his phone than his daughter's performance.

Alfonso spotted Santiago standing near the back of the auditorium. Pain shooting through his knee, he dashed down a back hallway as quickly as he could, slipped in behind Santiago and vise-gripped his arm.

"What kind of fucking intel do you guys have over in Europe anyway?" he growled into Santiago's ear. Then he jerked him into the foyer, where he shoved him against the wall.

A mixture of shock and indignation registered on Santiago's face. "What the hell's going on? Where did you come from?"

"Your people in Europe screwed up. Rejavik is here.

At the Night of Wilding party. And he knows about Lily and Zoe."

Santiago's jaw dropped. It wasn't often the guy was speechless. "Rejavik is here? What the fuck are you talking about? I verified with Prague this morning, like I've done every morning since you told me, and he was still there. The Alliance is conducting training exercises and Rejavik was overseeing some of it."

"Someone over there is either lying, on crack or just an idiot, because the guy's definitely here and now Lily and Zoe are his targets." And somehow, his own safeguards had failed as well. As he quickly explained to Santiago what had happened at the party, people began filing out of the theater. He kept his voice as low as possible. "So you've got to put Zoe into lockdown along with Mr. and Dr. DeGraff. There's no telling what Rejavik will do. I'm not sure if he's flying straight here or if he plans to come later. You've got a Region bunker, don't you?"

Santiago nodded.

"Get them there and stay with them until you get the all clear."

"You've got my word, but what are you going to do?"

"I'm going to put an end to this once and for all."

He spun on his heel—and ran straight into Dr. De-Graff.

With narrowed eyes, she zeroed in on his knee, clearly noticing how much he was favoring it. He distributed his weight more evenly, but she wasn't fooled. "I see you've not been following my orders to take it easy."

"I…ah…"

"Come on. Let me take a look at it. The bonfires aren't scheduled to be lit for another thirty minutes."

"I don't have time. Santiago is—"

"Alfonso!" Zoe ran up behind her grandmother and hugged him around the legs. He winced, trying not to show how much it hurt. "You did come. I knew you would. The good-luck charm worked. I didn't mess up."

Hoisting her into his arms, he held her tight, thankful he had gotten here in time before anything had happened. Her baby fine hair was even silkier than Lily's, he thought as he brushed it away from his nose.

"Yes, I know, Baby Girl. You were fantastic, just like I knew you would be." He tucked his chin over her shoulder and spoke to Dr. DeGraff. "Look, I don't have time to explain. But you're all going to need to go with Santiago. He'll tell you what's going on."

Dr. DeGraff studied his face for a moment and Alfonso realized where Lily had gotten that nothing-gets-past-me look. Growing up with that mother of hers had to have been a bitch. No sneaking out. No monkey business. No wonder Lily was such a rule follower.

She patted Zoe's back. "Come on, honey, do as Alfonso says." Zoe wiggled out of his arms. Turning to Santiago, Dr. DeGraff said, "I'll be with you in a moment. I need to talk to Alfonso in private."

Aw, Jesus, he didn't have time for Twenty Questions and an angry lecture from his doctor. "I can't. I've got to—"

Dr. DeGraff poked a finger in his chest, stopping him. "Listen, you're going to give me five minutes, whether you want to or not. I just received some very interesting test results you need to be aware of."

Exasperated, he rubbed the back of his neck and tried to remain civil to Lily's mother. He didn't have time to explain how or why. Let Santiago tell her whatever he wanted to. It didn't matter to him. "I don't care about any test results. Frankly, it's the least of my worries. I've got to go. Now."

He turned away, wondering how he'd conjure up the ability to teleport again, but she grabbed the sleeve of his jacket, stopping him. The intensity in her eyes made him take a half step back.

"You might be interested to learn that you share a somewhat unusual DNA characteristic with Zoe."

He frowned. What the hell was she talking about? He didn't have time for this. Now that he'd ensured Zoe was safe, it was time for him to go.

"What I'm trying to say is that you are Zoe's father."

It felt as if someone had struck him with a hot branding iron. He staggered backward. A roaring sound rang in his ears. If the wall hadn't been there to prop him up, he'd have surely fallen to the ground.

His mouth moved, but he didn't know if he was speaking aloud. "Her father? Are you sure?"

Dr. DeGraff's expression softened, a hint of a smile on her lips. She tucked her hair behind an ear. "I've ordered another test just to be sure—it wasn't a paternity test I did before—but yes, I believe that you, not Steven, are my granddaughter's father."

He was hot. Sweaty. He pulled off his knit cap and

unzipped his leather bomber coat. "But how? I don't understand."

"Although I don't think you really need to hear the birds and bees speech from me, I'd have to imagine you and Lily were together...oh, about nine years and three months ago, to be exact."

He turned and pressed his hands to the wall, dipping his head between his shoulders as he tried to think. It had to have happened when he'd teleported to Lily on the eve of his departure. He'd been drinking heavily and had suddenly found himself in her bed. Groggy with sleep, she'd welcomed him into her arms, and they'd made love slowly, one last time, each sharing the other's blood. At nightfall, unable to find his car, he'd taken a cab to the airport and left for Europe, where he'd spent the next five years. That had to have been the night Zoe was conceived.

He was a father. Oh Lord, he was Zoe's father.

Movement at the mouth of the cave caught Lily's attention.

Alfonso hobbled out, a grimace on his face. Where had he been? She hadn't seen him in almost an hour.

She'd been helping human partygoers down the cliff, where they were loaded onto the boats and taken back to the mainland. They'd be debriefed and have their memories of tonight's events altered. Capture teams would assess the vampire partiers to determine which ones had killed humans and take appropriate action. The rest would be sent home, to be placed on the Agency's growing watch list.

Expression tense, Alfonso limped over to where she was standing with Jackson and pulled her close.

She wrapped her arms around his waist. His chest felt warm against her cheek, which was chapped and icy from the high winds on the beach.

"You thought you were out from under the clutches of my mother, but from the looks of how much that knee is bothering you again, you're going to be heading back up there." She hesitated when he didn't laugh. "You doing okay, love? You really shouldn't be putting any weight on it until she's had a chance to examine you again."

Alfonso gave her a remote smile before turning to Jackson. "You remember what I asked you before?"

Jackson had a strange look on his face. "Yeah, sure."

Something was up. She could feel it by the way he held her. She pulled away from him. "What the hell are you talking about?"

He ignored her. "Jackson, promise me that no matter what happens, you will not let her out of your sight. Not until this thing with Rejavik is over."

She put her hands on her hips. "Rejavik? What are you talking about? I'm not liking the sound of this already."

Alfonso turned to her, his forehead pinched with worry, his eyes grim and determined. "He knows about you, Lil. Both you and Zoe. Didn't Jackson tell you?"

Jackson held up his hands. "Don't look at me. I told her nothing. Figured you'd want to."

Alfonso pulled a bent, bloodstained photo from an inside pocket and gave it to Lily. "Rejavik wanted me to see this. To let me know that you and Zoe are not safe."

Her stomach clenched into a dozen tiny knots. It was

the picture from her condo. "It wasn't a run-of-the-mill DB who broke in, but someone from the ORS? Your... your...that assassin?" Her fangs threatened to break through at the thought of that monster invading her home. The one who'd killed her friend and was now—

Her eyes widened and her hands went cold. "Oh my God, he knows about Zoe."

But before she could make a move toward the mouth of the cave, Alfonso stopped her.

"She's safe, Lily. Zoe and your parents are safe. I've seen to that."

Relief rushed through her. God, she loved this man. "Okay, we track that asshole down and fight him together. I want a piece of this guy."

Jackson cracked his knuckles. "Yeah, I'm with you, Lil. He breached the Seattle perimeter on my watch. It's been too long since I charcoaled a DB."

"This isn't a fucking game," Alfonso said, his eyes an icy, dead calm. "Rejavik is no ordinary Darkblood. This battle is between him and me. It's not with you, Lily, or the Seattle field office. There is no *we*—only *me*. Through my selfishness, I've put you and Zoe and everyone I care about in danger. But it ends tonight."

"Alone? Are you crazy?" He couldn't possibly be serious, could he? Was he so accustomed to doing things on his own that he couldn't fathom working with a team?

"Yes, alone. This is my concern, and mine alone."

"If you won't let us fight him together, then we'll leave. Just the three of us. Me, you and Zoe. We'll go somewhere far away where he'll never find us."

"I won't let you do that to...your daughter. It's not fair

to either of you. We'd be forever looking over our shoulders. I was a fool to think I could hide from him in the first place, but to subject you and Zoe to that is something I won't do. And if he finds us—" Alfonso balled his hands into fists, the breath rushing out between clenched teeth "—he'll kill you and Zoe in front of me. Then and only then will he finish me off and fulfill his duty to the Alliance. Is that what you want, Lily?"

"Of course not, but—"

"I'm done running. It's time for this thing to end."

"Okay, fine. How do you intend to do that? You going to track him? You told me yourself you're not a good Tracker. I don't doubt your ability to fight him face-to-face, but in order to do that, you need to locate the bastard. You need me, Alfonso. Please, let me help you find him."

He pulled one of his kunai out and turned it over in his hand. As he rubbed his thumb over the rope grip, moonlight glinted off the blade, flashing light onto the dark walls of the cave opening. Those knives seemed to infuse him with a sense of calmness, she noted. He fingered them often when under stress.

"I plan to teleport in, using the *shevala* with my blood as a way to find him."

Her head snapped up. Had she heard him correctly? "What? You can…teleport?"

He nodded. "Lily, I think your blood activates the ability in me."

She was speechless and her bones felt like rubber. She clutched his arm to prevent herself from falling. He stowed the blade and pulled her close. If he was right, it could only mean one thing.

Enlazado por la Sangre.

Bound through blood, they were connected to each other on a deeper, spiritual level. Partners in the truest sense. Together they were capable of more than they were apart.

"How long have you known?"

"Just found out tonight." He paused. "I was able to teleport up to Region to check on Zoe. I could feel your blood giving me the strength I needed to transform myself. When I realized Rejavik knew about you and Zoe, I was afraid he was flying straight up to Horseshoe Bay to take her. As I stood out near the Ferris wheel, staring in the direction the helicopter had flown, something strange happened. My skin seemed to prickle with an odd energy. Next thing I knew, I was up at Region where Zoe was performing in her recital." His voice got quiet. "She's safe, Lily. Zoe is safe."

Lily's mind was numb, her spine tingling with nervous energy. "You...you saw Zoe's piano recital?" It didn't seem possible.

His eyes glittered. "She did a wonderful job. You'd have been so proud of her. I was."

Her heart thundered in her chest, so she took a few deep breaths to calm herself. The ability to teleport was an ancient skill, like Dom's ability to *vapor*. Could it really be true? "Have you ever done it before? Teleport from one location to another."

"Not sure. Maybe. Just one other time." He kept his eyes downcast, refusing to look at her. She tried to take his face in her hands but he pulled away. "Tell Zoe I'm proud of her and that even though I didn't get a chance to know her well, I…I care for her. Very much."

He sounded so fatalistic, so final. "You're scaring me, Alfonso. You can tell her that yourself. We'll go up there tomorrow night. I'll hear all about her performance and watch the video with her. We all can. All three of us."

He shook his head. "And, Lily, I want you to know that no matter what happens tonight, you have always been the most important thing in the world to me. The time we spent together was the happiest of my life, and despite the pain I put you through, I never stopped loving you." His voice got quiet. "And I never will."

He stepped away from her.

"Jackson," she said urgently, "will you tell him that the Seattle team will—"

Alfonso's physical form began to fade, the wall behind him suddenly visible on the other side.

What was happening? *Oh my God, no.*

She leaped forward, her hands going straight through him as his body disappeared into nothingness.

All that was left was the lingering smell of warm leather and an empty, ragged hole in her chest.

CHAPTER TWENTY

WHAT A COLOSSAL WASTE OF TIME this was. Especially since she had none to spare.

Lily shoved a sheathed knife into her already-packed weapons bag and prayed it wasn't too late, that Alfonso was still alive. What a fool she'd been, thinking she could talk Dom into classifying it as a field ops mission with the full support of the office. She should've just left straight from the island. Thanks to the cape Rejavik had left in the viewing room, she already had a lock on his scent.

But no, she'd been foolish enough to listen to Jackson, who'd convinced her that Alfonso had probably gone back to his place first before confronting his blood assassin. Dom had arrived from Australia while they were out on the island and was waiting for them back at the field office. She'd relented and agreed to go to Seattle, hoping to get full Agency support. Little good that had done.

After Dom's refusal, she'd threatened to go above his head to discuss the issue with Santiago, even though she was wasting precious time. Thankfully, Jackson and Sadie had stepped in, defying Dom's orders, and had agreed to accompany Lily.

Not that that had gone over well with Dom. The guy

had slammed the door so hard on his way out, a framed piece of artwork had fallen off the wall and shattered.

God, she hoped Jackson was correct, that Alfonso had stopped to prepare himself first, but in truth, she had no idea how Alfonso's teleportation skill worked. Was he able to teleport at will? Would he even be capable of going back to his home to ready himself for battle first? One thing was certain, if she hadn't actually witnessed him fade out, she never would've believed such a thing was possible.

He wouldn't have headed straight to Rejavik's location without making any advanced preparations, would he? It was like a never-ending debate. Did he or didn't he? If he was foolish enough to go in without a plan or any backup, he could very well be—

No, she wouldn't think that way, wouldn't let the pain of that possibility eat at her resolve. He was alive, she could feel it. She was positive. She'd find him and together they'd kill his assassin. She yanked open a drawer filled with ammunition and refused to let herself think the worst.

On the harried ride back to the field office, she'd called Roxanne Reynolds to see what she knew about ORS assassins. What the head of the Agency's Tracker Academy had to say hadn't exactly put Lily's mind at ease. In addition to being excellent Trackers who were easily able to pull up even the oldest scent memories, these killers could shadow-move faster than most vampires, and they trained for years in advanced torture techniques.

"Thing is," Roxanne had told her, "if he's got Alfonso already, chances are he hasn't killed him yet. He'd want to put him through hell first."

That was comforting.

"And, in my experience," she'd continued, "the assassin will take him to a place he's been to before. He'll have made preparations at the site, in anticipation of taking a captive. After all, that's what they're trained to do."

Lily shivered, but tried to keep the worry from her voice. "Thank you for the information."

"I tell you this, Lily, not to panic you, but to give you hope. Because it means that the assassin's trail, although hard to detect, will be slightly stronger than normal as you get closer, since it's a route he'll have taken several times before."

Lily snapped on a boot holster, jerking herself back to the present. She rubbed her forehead, trying to dispel the beginning of a massive headache. She sensed Alfonso was still very much alive, but whether or not Rejavik had him, she couldn't tell. He hadn't answered any of her calls or texts. She'd need to get closer in order to know for sure.

The far-off ding of the elevator sounded innocent enough, but as heavy footsteps pounded down the hall, getting progressively louder, a fresh wave of irritation and anger came over her. She white-knuckled the edge of the granite countertop and didn't look up when Dom stopped in the doorway.

"You heading out soon?" His voice had lost some of its earlier edge.

"Yeah, just as soon as I'm finished baking this cake."

"Listen, I'm—"

"Throw me another case of silvies." She didn't care to get into it with him again. Whether or not she found Alfonso, she was never coming back. She couldn't work for someone who wouldn't support the most important mission of her life. Dom could just go fuck himself and find another Tracker.

The drawer squeaked open and his fingers quickly skimmed over the ammo boxes until he found the right one.

"Got your mags loaded or do you want me to do that?" Without looking up, he reached for a pair of rubber gloves.

Had he come here to play nice now? Was that how it worked? She flexed her fingers, resisting the urge to put on a set of knuckles and punch something. Instead, she grabbed the box from him and jammed it into her duffel.

"I'm good."

Why had she thought she could talk Dom into coming with her to search for his brother? He was stubborn, unforgiving and pigheaded, and he would never change. At least Jackson and Sadie were going with her. She'd do it without Dom's help.

Only thing was, it hurt not to have his support. She didn't care that there was bad blood between the brothers. She'd figured that when she told Dom about her suspicions that she and Alfonso were *Enlazado por la Sangre,* he'd agree to help—for her sake if not for his brother's. But no. The guy hadn't even looked at her after she'd unveiled that little revelation.

He cleared his throat. "Listen. I came here to tell you I've okayed the mission. In addition to Jackson and Sadie, Mitchell will be joining you, and Cordell will provide real-time support here from the command center. If the storm abates, you'll have helicopter support from Finn."

She didn't look up. "Thank you."

Did she have everything? She surveyed the contents of her bag. Knives. Check. Guns. Check. Silver-lined handcuffs. Check. Brass knuckles, a half dozen high-capacity magazines, silver rounds. Check. Out of habit, she flicked her wrist, clicking her butterfly knife open and closed a few times before slipping it into her pocket.

"Geez, Lil, you could poke an eye out with that thing," he said.

She glanced at the *brindmal* coiled at his hip and gave him a cool smile. "Okay, Indy, thanks for the tip." He rarely went anywhere without that silver-laced bullwhip, so who was he to talk.

As she crisscrossed the shoulder strap over her head, her phone rang.

She looked at the screen. Damn. Not her mom again. Was something wrong?

"Mom, everything okay? How's Zoe?"

"She's still fine, but I really—"

"Mom, like I said before, I'm in a big rush. Don't have time to talk. Just keep Zoe there at the bunker until you get the all clear from—"

"Lily, stop. Would you just listen?" Her mother sounded frustrated, no doubt from the other two times she'd called only to have Lily cut the conversation short.

But Lily didn't have time for this. She could hear the recital details later.

"Mom, I—"

"There's something I need to tell you about Alfonso."

As her mother spoke, the ligaments in Lily's legs turned to rubber and she sank to the ground. She was hardly aware of Dom approaching and stooping at her feet, an obvious look of concern on his face. After she listened to what her mother had to say, she shut the phone, knowing her eyes and nose were probably red from all the sniffling.

"What's up, Lil? Is everything okay?"

She tried to center herself amid the storm of chaos brewing in her mind. She hardly trusted her voice to work. "Remember I told you that my mother was treating Alfonso's injuries?"

"Yeah. Both the new ones and the old ones."

"Well, she had to run a bunch of tests on him." Lily ran her sweaty palms over her fatigues, trying to piece together everything whirling in her mind. "It turns out Alfonso is Zoe's father, not Steven."

Dom rocked backward on his heels as if she'd slapped him, shock and disbelief written all over his face. "But how is that possible? Don't women know these kinds of things? I mean, you had no idea?"

God, you'd think so. She shook her head.

She thought about how Alfonso had treated Zoe compared to Steven, but longing for something wasn't the same as suspecting that thing to be true. Not only did she remember peeking in on Alfonso patiently helping Zoe with the piano, but she recalled how he'd spoken about her in the cave back on the island. He'd said then that he cared about her. He was talking about his daughter. Their daughter.

"Because Steven was from an influential family, my father adored him. I found out I was pregnant long after Alfonso had left. I just assumed the baby was Steven's. A perfect match, everyone said, so I tried to make it work."

"You made a gallant effort, that's for sure." Dom didn't say anything for a long moment. "This is unbelievable,

Lily. And the tests show he is Zoe's father," Dom repeated, almost to himself. He'd always been close to Zoe, to the point that she even called him Uncle. Now it appeared as though that nickname was reality. "And Alfonso knows?"

God—he did know. There had been something different about the way he'd looked in the cave, the flat determination in his eyes. It wasn't just the fact that he'd learned he had the ability to teleport—it was that he'd discovered he was Zoe's father. "Yes, my mother told him, but for some reason, he didn't see the need to tell me."

"He's not stupid, you know."

She snapped her head up. "What the hell are you talking about?"

"If he had told you, would you have let him go?"

"I didn't *let* him go."

"He probably figured you'd protest his going alone in the first place, but if you realized that he was Zoe's real father, you would've made it impossible for him to leave."

"Well, he did leave." Ignoring Dom's outstretched hand, she pushed herself to her feet. "He got his way and I'm left wondering what to do."

"If it were me, Lily, I'd have done exactly the same thing. He needed to do this alone in order to save his family."

"Stupid, stubborn Serrano brothers. Always thinking you know what's best for everyone without bothering to get input from those involved."

"We do know what's best when family is concerned."

She shook her head, grabbed her bag and hurried out of the weapons room. The thing bounced against her hip as she jogged to the bank of elevators. She punched the up button, and when the door didn't open immediately, she poked it again, over and over.

So Alfonso thought he needed to do this on his own in order to protect his family? If she weren't so pissed off, she would've laughed out loud at that Neanderthal attitude. Like hell was she going to sit back and wait for word that the only man she'd ever truly loved, the father of their daughter, the man she wanted to spend the rest of her life with, was dead. She didn't care if he thought she wasn't capable of taking on this fight with him. She was used to doing more than what others expected from her, and she wasn't about to stop now.

"We'll find him, Lil."

She spun around. Dom stood behind her, a black leather coat draped over his shoulder, his other arm bulging from the heavy bag he held, stretching the sleeve of his silky blue T-shirt. His eyes were the same color as Alfonso's, with the same deadly intensity, and yet, with his dark coloring, the two brothers looked very different.

He was ready for combat. Had he changed his mind?

He shrugged, juggled the duffel, obviously guessing her thoughts from her expression. "I keep it loaded in case of emergency. Comes in handy sometimes."

He was actually coming with her. A swell of gratitude surged in her chest. For Dom to volunteer to help her track down his brother was a huge deal.

"Thanks," she managed to say, despite the emotion clogging her throat. "You don't know how much it means to me to have your support."

Suddenly, all the terrible names she'd called him in his

office and the things she'd accused him of came crashing down around her. "I'm sorry that I—"

He held up a hand and shook his head. "Nope. No apology necessary. You were angry. I get that."

Fine, but she wasn't quite ready to just let it go. "Those things I said. That was wrong of me. I know you wanted to spend time with Mackenzie since you haven't seen her in weeks."

He didn't answer right away, just blew out a long breath and ran a hand over his ponytail. "Yes, well, I do want to see her. But to be honest with you, she was just as angry with me as you were when she found out I didn't authorize the mission."

Clearing his throat, he continued, "Although she didn't use quite the same argument as you did. And with this latest revelation…" He reached around her and stabbed at the elevator button a few times. "Let's just say that since I don't want to piss off a pregnant woman any more than she already is, I'm coming with you."

She bit her lip to keep from smiling. Yeah, right. Mackenzie couldn't make Dom do anything he didn't want to do.

That was fine. If he wasn't ready to admit that he did care about his brother and instead used his pregnant wife as a way to save face, who was she to argue?

All that really mattered was that she had his full support.

CHAPTER TWENTY-ONE

With a firearm in one hand, a kunai in the other and a multitude of weapons stashed under his jacket, Alfonso concentrated on the *shevala* and the ground slipped away.

It felt as if only a few moments had passed when the air grew suddenly still against his skin, smelling dry and faintly musty. He'd teleported somewhere indoors. Blinking a few times to adjust his eyes to the pitch-black darkness, he stood from a crouch and cranked his head around. Cement-block walls surrounded him on three sides and an open-beam ceiling cleared his head by only a few inches. Directly in front of him stood what looked to be the backs of several large bookcases, but upon further inspection, he realized they were fully stocked wine racks.

Okay, so he was in someone's wine cellar.

He rubbed a thumb along the rope-twined grip as he melded with the shadows and slipped between the shelving. A quick glance left and right. Just a bar-height table and four iron chairs. He was alone. Where the hell was Rejavik? He crept over the uneven floor toward a rustic wooden door on the other side of the table. The bastard had to be close.

If only he'd had the time to experiment with his new-found ability. He would've practiced exactly where his form took shape when he teleported to his target. He could've appeared outside somewhere, assessed the situation from a safe distance, then teleported the rest of the way in with a plan in place.

He heard nothing on the other side of the door. Could he have beamed in somewhere else by mistake? It shouldn't surprise him if he had, because, in all honesty, he had no idea how it worked. It just did.

He took a deep breath, concentrated, and without any effort, his senses easily homed in on the *shevala* again. No, he hadn't made a mistake. Rejavik was nearby.

Slowly, carefully, he pulled on the heavy door, hoping the damn thing didn't have squeaky hinges. It didn't. It opened effortlessly, without sound, and a faint rush of cool air from the room brushed past him.

He peered into a luxurious media room, complete with a large projection screen, reclining theater seats with cup holders, and velvet-draped walls. An old-fashioned popcorn machine stood in the back with a stack of red-and-white bags.

He smelled popcorn and—

Something niggled at the back of his mind, and the little hairs on the back of his neck stood up. By the time the movement of air settled around him, the faint smell of rotten meat registered in his brain.

He tried to spin around, but it was too late.

Silver-tipped spikes dug into his skin as cuffs snapped around his wrists from behind, immediately leeching the energy from his body. Panic shot through him like a jolt from a stun gun. He tried to focus on the emotion and teleport away, but the silver sapped his strength. He was as immobile and helpless as human prey.

Weapons slipped from his weakened fingers and clattered to the ground, and he didn't know how long his legs would continue to support his weight.

It was then that the vile face he'd been expecting to see became visible in the darkness.

"So wonderful you could join me, Mr. Serrano. And here I thought I'd have to come to you."

"LILY, ARE YOU SURE THIS is right?" Jackson asked as the team slipped through the wrought-iron fence in an exclusive Eastside neighborhood near Cougar Mountain. His breath fogged in front of his face.

Barely above freezing, the night was at its darkest, most coldest hour, but the damp wind, which found its way under every clothing layer, made the air feel about ten degrees colder. Lily went to zip her jacket further but it was already zipped as high as it'd go.

"I mean," he continued, "DBs usually hole up in shitty little houses in neighborhoods where people don't give a fuck what's going on next door. This place is like Wisteria Lane on crack. If I didn't already know where Bill Gates lived, I could easily imagine him living in one of these places."

Just to be absolutely sure, she fished out the small piece of fabric cut from Rejavik's cape and inhaled. Yep. The asshole was definitely nearby. The scent markers were the same. "I'm positive."

"How about Alfonso?" Dom put a hand absently on his *brindmal* as he surveyed what they could see of the houses through the heavy stand of Douglas fir trees. "Can you pick up his scent yet?"

"No, not yet." She watched as Sadie and Mitchell shadow-moved over to the guardhouse on the other side of the road. As a changeling, Sadie wasn't as quick as the rest of them. It was nice that Mitchell waited for her, rather than plowing ahead. Maybe he was trying to score tonight when this was all over.

Lily lowered her voice. "But that doesn't mean he's not here. If he teleported in, he'd leave no scent trail. One moment he's not here and the next moment, he is. Kinda hard to pick up a trail when there isn't one. I'll have to get closer to find out for sure."

She hoped to God he wasn't here. Between the five Seattle field team members, they should be able to take down Rejavik, but given what Alfonso and Roxanne had told her about the blood assassin and the Order of the Red Sword, she wasn't sure Alfonso could do it without backup. The thought of him being here—without her—made her stomach twist into knots. She needed to find him fast.

Rejavik's scent trail was fresh, no more than an hour old. Although she told herself it wasn't much time, in truth, she knew it was long enough. Five minutes was long enough.

They followed the scent to a huge Northwest contemporary at the end of a long driveway. U-shaped with a covered courtyard in the back, it had stacked slate columns, walls of windows and cedar-lined eaves. Some very wealthy humans lived here, but she didn't detect an active scent. Rejavik had obviously picked an unoccupied home.

"Snowbirds," Mitchell said. "How much you want to bet the home owners winter in Palm Desert or Scottsdale?"

Lily paused to pick up a golf ball half covered by crushed oyster shells in the bocce ball court. The logo was two turtles—a mother and a baby. "Or Oahu."

They split into teams. Mitchell and Sadie took the east entrance, Jackson and Lily took the west entrance, while Dom slipped through the shadows to the back of the property.

A restlessness stirred inside her. An unease that didn't match her strong resolve. It felt almost…external.

She rubbed the back of her neck but couldn't seem to shake the sensation—an unseen force pushing her away. Concentrating on it, she realized it wasn't actually *pushing* her away, it was *urging* her to stay away. Begging her to stay away. It was as if—

The wind changed direction.

Alfonso.

Her heart quickened and her throat swelled, making it an effort just to swallow.

He was here. In the house. Alive.

And she had sensed him *before* she detected his scent. He had communicated with her through his emotions.

Sniffing back her tears, since there was no time for dramatics, she motioned Jackson in behind her. As they sprinted toward the house, she tapped her headset. "Alfonso's here," she told everyone. "I've got a lock on him from somewhere below ground level."

If she smelled him, chances were so did Rejavik.

So they had to assume the worst.

Not knowing whether Alfonso could detect her or not, she pushed her thoughts out to him anyway. *Alfonso, we're here. All of us. We're coming for you. Just hang on and try to distract Rejavik, if he's with you.*

Sensing that he was in great pain, she had to force herself to think clearly and logically, when her heart was urging her to run in blindly and stop the hurt.

"Okay, people," Dom said, loud and confidently through her earpiece. "This is most likely a rescue mission, so be careful out there. If you get a clear shot of Rejavik, take it. But don't risk hitting Alfonso. There's no telling what's been done to him already or how much blood and energy he's lost. One thing's for certain. The blood assassin doesn't leave the premises alive."

CHAPTER TWENTY-TWO

THE KNIFE BLADE WENT DEEP. It pierced the skin near his shoulder and meandered slowly up his arm to his wrists, which were tied above his head.

Alfonso wanted to swing his legs up from where they dangled just above the floor, kick against the cement wall and break his restraints, but he barely had enough energy to lift his head from between his shoulder blades. Having lost count at ten, he no longer could feel the individual trickles of blood running down his back, probably because there were so many now.

"You know, Lord Pavlos and I were friends long before you met him in Paris that summer." Rejavik twisted the knife point a little deeper when he said friends, his breath hot against the back of Alfonso's neck.

"*Pavlos,*" Alfonso said, emphasizing his actual name, not the worshipful moniker employed by the Darkbloods, "was *never* a friend of mine." He was surprised he had the strength left to sound so caustic.

Rejavik continued as if Alfonso had never spoken. "You see, when my father lost his fortune in a series of business deals with members of the Night Brethren— excuse me," he said sarcastically, "the Governing Council—it was Lord Pavlos who stepped in and saved our family from financial ruin. Everyone else had turned their backs on us.

"If it hadn't been for him, my family would have been destitute and cast from our ancestral home, forced into servitude for one of the Council elite. Not only was he a great man with a clear vision of what our people could achieve in this world if we returned to the ways of our forefathers, he was a compassionate man as well."

Alfonso wanted to vomit. As if killing and preying on humans was compassionate. As if the Darkblood cause he fought for was a noble one.

Not sure if he'd spoken these sentiments aloud, Alfonso tensed what muscles he could in anticipation of another cut from the knife. When Rejavik continued his ramblings, Alfonso guessed he hadn't spoken after all.

"As a result of his kindness, I vowed to serve His Lordship in any way that I could and was both honored and humbled to join the Order of the Red Sword after my Time of Change."

"He used you," Alfonso said, "just as he used me. Both of us were a means to an end for Pavlos and nothing more. A way for him to advance his agenda."

Rejavik stepped in front of him, his eyes black with anger. "You are such a fool."

In the only physical response he was capable of making, Alfonso flashed his fangs. "Obviously. I was a fool to have gotten mixed up in everything. But then, so are you. We were both his willing victims. I was foolish enough to let myself get addicted to Sweet, and willing to do many terrible things I would never have done otherwise. And you allowed him to capitalize on the debt you felt you owed him. He wasn't a great man, just a great manipul—"

With a growl, Rejavik slapped Alfonso across the face, knocking his head back. Black spots formed in front of Alfonso's eyes. He tried to blink them away, but they remained, threatening to overtake his vision entirely.

"I never trusted you, you know that?" Rejavik said. "Not from the very beginning. I couldn't believe that the son of one of the founding members of the Governing Council would actually join our cause. I warned His Lordship, told him that you would deceive him and be an informant for your father. But he didn't listen. He thought that by having someone with your stature in our ranks, the movement would be further legitimized and our numbers would grow."

Alfonso felt nauseous. There wasn't a day that went by when he didn't wish he'd made different choices back then. To hear that his presence may have caused others to join the Alliance was almost too much to bear.

When he heard Rejavik take a few steps away, Alfonso squinted his eyes enough to see him unrolling a cloth bag on a nearby table.

"When we caught wind of your plans to leave the Alliance, I advised him to kill you. But he wanted to give you a second chance, to just send you a warning. I'm afraid it was his forgiving spirit that was his undoing." Rejavik ran a finger over the various implements stored inside the pouch and selected one.

Alfonso tugged on his restraints. "A warning? You motherfucker. She was an innocent girl, studying music at the Conservatoire de Paris, with no knowledge of our existence until you showed her what we're capable of."

"Ah, but you were playing with fire, weren't you, having a relationship with her in the first place? If you had left the sweetblood alone, that never would've happened. So it is because of you that the girl died."

Rejavik's words cut through him like the stab of another blade. He was right, of course. Thinking he'd recovered from his Sweet addiction but not wanting to test it too much, Alfonso had only taken Jessica's blood a few times and kept his true nature hidden from her. He'd been proud of himself and the restraint he showed, so at the time, it never dawned on him that his very presence was putting her in danger. He cursed the idiotic folly of his youth. As he recalled those thoughts and actions now, it made him want to reach back through time and throttle himself. No wonder his father and brother had been disgusted.

But in the end, the Alliance always caught up with him. Just as it had now.

A warm sensation stirred in his gut, and he closed his eyes. At first, he thought it was a new trickle of blood, but when it seemed to expand inside, heating his veins from his core to his fingertips and causing his skin to tingle, he knew that it wasn't.

It was Lily.

Oh Lord. She was near.

He pinched his eyelids tighter and willed her away. *Please, Lily, he'll kill you.*

A surge of adrenaline shot through him and, although he couldn't hear her thoughts, he felt her determination and focus as if it were a part of him.

Surely she hadn't come alone, he told himself. It would play right into Rejavik's plan. He prayed she'd brought backup—she wasn't foolish enough or brash enough not to, was she? A planner, a rule follower, she'd never attempt a mission like this on her own. Oh please, let him be right about that.

"You and I are very much alike, you know that?"

Alfonso scowled. Rejavik's sickly sweet odor, although much less pronounced than a regular Darkblood's, was still there just below the surface, the smell of the young sweetblood from the party still strong on his breath. And his eyes, gray orbs with obsidian irises, marked him as the bloodsucker he was.

"I'm nothing like you."

"Ah, but you are wrong, my friend. We are both driven to succeed at any cost, willing to sacrifice ourselves and give up a normal way of life for the cause we believe in."

Reluctantly, Alfonso realized there was a truth to his words. He had given up everything in order to right the wrongs he had made so many years ago.

"How's your woman, by the way?" Rejavik stepped closer and inhaled deeply. "You fed from her recently. I can smell her on you." He swiped a finger against the blood on Alfonso's torso and put it in his mouth. "And I can taste the sweetness of her blood in yours. Not only will she be easy to find because of it, but her daughter should be easy enough to locate as well."

A roar of rage ripped from his lungs and reverberated off the walls, his internal temperature cranked beyond boiling. He arched his back, kicked his legs, twisting, pulling at his restraints. Everything in the room blurred as he fought, the details fading into a red-tinged nothingness.

But the cuffs held. He continued to dangle helplessly in the unfinished storage room.

Out of breath, he was hardly aware of the sweat dripping from his forehead and stinging his wounds as his entire focus became pinpointed on the smug-faced assassin standing before him.

"You stay…the fuck…away…from them."

Clearly undeterred and with a faint smile on his lips, Rejavik looked mildly entertained and raised his eyebrows. "Or else…what? Doesn't look like you're in a position to do anything about it."

Dread filled every pore and Alfonso's body felt suddenly heavier. He should've just stayed away from Lily in the first place. It was a mistake to have inserted himself into her life again, thinking she wasn't capable of taking care of herself—that he could do a better job. Through his own goddamn arrogance, he'd put her in mortal danger. And now he'd put his daughter in danger as well.

Maybe he deserved to die for his mistakes.

But not Lily.

Or Zoe.

Oh God, Lil, if you can hear me, if you can feel me, get out of here. Please. Get away from him.

Alfonso wasn't sure what kind of affect his blood had on her, but if hers gave him the ability to teleport, maybe she could at least sense his plea. He hoped to God she could.

Out of the corner of his eye, he saw a thick blue-gray smoke seeping in under the door. Like an upside-down waterfall, it licked up the inside wall. A fire?

His throat suddenly became dry and scratchy; he couldn't seem to draw in a breath, the air suddenly devoid of any oxygen.

Instantly, he was taken back to the night when Pavlos had been killed, and he had almost died. Inside the lab, he had poured petrol onto the file cabinets and computer equipment, and set a match to them. As fire devoured the paper and the components began to melt, he'd watched, mesmerized, the thick smoke curling upward and accumulating on the ceiling.

It had signified the end of his life as a double agent. And he'd been hopeful, as Lily's face had flashed before him, that it would be a new beginning as well.

It was then that one of the guards had discovered him.

They'd fought, and although Alfonso didn't remember getting doused with gasoline, he must've been, because suddenly they were both on fire. He'd kicked hard to loosen the man's grip, felt a stabbing pain deep inside his leg. The guard had squealed in agony as the fire consumed him. With silver-weakened fingers, Alfonso had shed his burning clothes and the smoke had thickened.

Somehow he'd made it to the loading dock where his Daytran-outfitted SUV was parked just a few feet away. He'd dragged himself into the rig and had just cleared the building when the whole place had exploded. Never would he forget the smell of his own flesh burning. And it had all started with the smoke.

Rejavik turned toward him, pulling him back to the present. His black eyes sparkled with the promise of evil and he twisted a thin blade the length of a chopstick. With an eager expression on his face, he moved closer.

Alfonso sniffed, didn't smell anything burning. Yet. He stared over Rejavik's shoulder.

There was something unusual about the smoke. It

didn't seem to grow thinner as it spread outward—it had very distinct edges, with a finite beginning and end.

Almost like a contained entity.

Hell, that didn't make any sense. He must be getting delirious from the blood and energy loss. With a curious detachment, he watched as the smoke concentrated into a tighter mass.

It seemed to be taking shape.

Into—

Holy Mother of God. Alfonso choked.

This couldn't be happening. It wasn't possible.

The smoke *was* taking shape.

Into that of a man.

It was Dom.

His brother held a finger to his lips and reached for his hip.

Alfonso blinked, not believing he'd actually witnessed his brother *vapor*. He couldn't have spoken even if he'd wanted to.

He'd never heard of anyone being able to *vapor*. Like teleporting, it was an ancient vampiric ability recorded in the old tomes, but as far as he knew, it no longer existed in the population today.

Rejavik laughed, obviously thinking Alfonso was reacting to him and what he was about to do. "I wish I could tell you this will all be over quickly, but I'm afraid I'd be lying."

For the briefest of moments, Rejavik hesitated, his eyes narrowed as if he suddenly knew they weren't alone.

But before he could react, Dom flicked his wrist.

With a snap, the *brindmal* encircled Rejavik's neck.

Wide-eyed, his captor was yanked off his feet and landed hard on the floor.

It took too much effort to figure out what had actually happened, but relief rushed through Alfonso like a tidal wave. In the next few moments, he was vaguely aware of someone cutting him down, and the low murmur of several voices. The adrenaline that had kept him lucid seemed to have faded from his system. He couldn't keep his eyes open and fell like a rag doll on the floor. When the warmth in his gut increased, he knew that Lily must be near.

He expected to feel her touch him. He wanted to hold her in his arms to assure himself that she was alive and okay.

But instead what he heard was the sound of a boot making contact with a body. Hard.

He opened his eyes to see Rejavik curled up in a fetal position about ten feet away.

"That's for killing my friend," Lily said. She stood behind Rejavik, anger burning in her eyes, hands on her hips, fangs fully protracted.

Thunk. Rejavik's body jerked and he grunted again.

"That's for threatening my daughter."

The metallic sound of a blade being drawn echoed loudly in the enclosed space. Rejavik's eyes, as black as the barrel of a shotgun, bored into Alfonso's. Those same eyes that had witnessed his Blood Oath and watched gleefully as Alfonso had been forced to kill Jessica now looked terrified, but unrepentant.

"And this—" a flash of light glinted off Lily's blade "—is for putting my man through hell."

In a quick, downward motion, the sword hit its mark. Rejavik's mouth flew open, his jaw working with no sound. His body stiffened, then relaxed. As Alfonso watched, the skin on the assassin's face puckered and darkened as his body shriveled in on itself, curling inward, until, a few moments later, it was a useless pile of ashes.

For years he'd imagined what this moment would feel like—the day his assassin didn't exist, no longer a threat that prevented Alfonso from leading a normal life. A constant reminder of the terrible choices he'd made as a young man. He'd always pictured the guy's death would be a grander, more momentous occasion, the earth moving as the gates of hell opened. At the very least he'd imagined there would be the kind of huge-ass fire and explosion that had marked the end of Pavlos's reign. But the simplicity of this small room somehow made the event more poignant and powerful.

What had begun when he'd taken the Blood Oath in the dank catacombs under Madrid ended now in this claustrophobic storage room in Seattle. That part of his life was over.

He was vaguely aware of Lily's hands moving over him. Something tickled his face. Her hair maybe? The soft feel of her lips was on his cheeks, his eyelids, his temples. She was kissing him all over, the smell of lavender thick in the air.

"He's gone, love," she whispered.

And the last thought he had as he slipped into unconsciousness was that the woman he loved had saved him, and she was giving him a future.

CHAPTER TWENTY-THREE

One month later

JACKSON SPOTTED THE RED-HAIRED nurse—Carin, he thought her name was—over by the champagne fountain. She wore a flirty black dress that reached midthigh, strappy silver heels and a narrow scarf—purple, to honor the Serrano family.

Maybe she'd want to hook up again. He glanced at the purple flower on his lapel—they'd make a good pair tonight. He started to make his way over there, but a hand clapping his back stopped him.

"It's a good match, wouldn't you say?" Lily's father said as he surveyed the crowded room.

Jackson turned his attention to Dom and Mackenzie, who were still in the receiving line, showing off their new son before the christening ceremony began. They both looked so happy and proud, he thought, as they greeted everyone. Although having a family wasn't something he saw for his own future, he was thrilled for them.

"Yes, sir, they're lucky to have birthed such a healthy child."

"Indeed. But I'm not talking about them. I'm referring to my daughter."

Jackson followed the older man's gaze to the dance

floor. A three-piece quartet was playing some classical shit at the far end of the room. Not really what he'd call dancing music, but that didn't seem to matter to some people. Alfonso lifted Lily's hand, twirled her once, then pulled her close again.

Figured. Lily had always been into the slow stuff. Evidently, Alfonso was, too.

"I've never seen her happier," Jackson agreed.

"Any union that produces offspring is a good and sacred one."

Spoken like a true Council elder, forever concerned about their kind's dwindling fertility rates. Jackson remembered Lily telling him her father had said this about Steven as well, when they'd thought he was Zoe's birth father. Although Jackson respected Mr. DeGraff, he wasn't thrilled about shooting the shit with the guy. For good reason, he was not at ease around the Council elite.

Eyeballing Carin again, he drained the last of his gin and tonic. He was about to make some excuse to leave when Lily approached. Alfonso had gone to join his brother. She waved over Cordell and Gibby.

"Cordell, you know my father, don't you?"

Cordell reached out a hand and smiled. "Yes, it's nice to see you again, sir."

"And Daddy, this is Val Gibson. He's from the San Diego office, where he—"

"Please, call me Gibby." Val stuck out his hand.

Jackson noticed how Lily's shoulders stiffened at the interruption. She continued to smile, but it didn't entirely reach her eyes. Gibby was such a tool sometimes.

"Cordell," Jackson said, trying to change the subject,

"any luck tracking down the parent company that owns Hollow Grave?"

"No, not yet."

Lily turned to her father. "Cordell is trying to find out who has controlling interest in—"

"Sweetheart, can you get me a refill? I'm simply parched." Mr. DeGraff held out his empty highball glass to her and turned back to the men. "I'd like to hear more about this Darkblood computer game. I find it very fascinating."

"Hold on, Lily," Gibby chimed in. "Did you tell him how you tracked down one of the game's designers last week?"

Lily blinked, looking a little stunned. "Uh, no."

Gibson nudged Mr. DeGraff. "You gotta hear this, sir. It's totally kick-ass what your daughter did. The guy, a human, was apparently clueless about what the game was actually being used for, but his memory cap was pretty fried. The guy was a mess, right, Lily?"

Not to be outdone by his friend, Jackson piped up. "Honestly, sir, the Seattle office would be nothing without her."

Her father peered at her over the top of his glasses as if he were seeing her for the first time. Lily reached for his drink but he pulled it back.

"Tell me, daughter, before the ceremony starts. I'd like to hear more."

THE TINY CHAPEL at Region Headquarters overlooking Horseshoe Bay was packed. Old wooden pews squeaked in protest when anyone moved, and warm candlelight flickered off stone walls and pillars, creating a surreal glow over the faces of all in attendance. The smell of incense and scented anointing oil reminded Alfonso of when he'd been a boy and accompanied his mother to her devotionals.

Alfonso couldn't remember when he'd last seen the inside of a sanctuary—it may have been before his Time of Change. The traditions, like the lighting of the candles by the children, as well as the incantations and songs, seemed foreign and unfamiliar. But perhaps the strangest thing of all was that he didn't feel out of place here or as if he didn't belong, which, frankly, was what he'd been expecting.

Lily's mother, who sat next to him, patted his knee knowingly. "We're so glad you're with us," she whispered. It was something his own mother would have done. He flashed her a grateful smile.

Surrounded by these people, in this place, he felt like family, like he was one of them. For the first time in ages, he had a place in this world and people who cared about him.

Which was all that really mattered, he realized.

Lily stood at the front of the church wearing a lavender ceremonial gown, her straight hair shimmering like liquid gold. Seeing how beautiful she was, he knew he was one of the luckiest men alive.

He pushed his feelings out and shared a few of his emotions with her. She lifted her eyes to his and that little smile of hers warmed him up from the inside. God, he loved that they were empathically linked, sharing intimate emotions secretly amidst dozens of people. It was like having their own private language.

Making love and taking blood regularly from each other had strengthened their *Enlazado* link. He'd been experimenting with his newfound power, attempting to teleport to various locations, and he'd discovered that having a blood link—Lily, Zoe, his brother—at the target location helped pinpoint his focus. And Lily's tracking capabilities were now more acute than ever. Although only a few Agents knew about the special bond between them, word was getting out about Lily's extraordinary tracking skills and she was in demand all over North America. Being together caused each of them to transform into a better version of themselves.

And it was a damn good excuse for an active physical relationship. He recalled how they'd made love right before she'd put on that gown. They were a few minutes late because of it.

He glanced up to see Lily's cheeks flushed, her lips parted, and she shifted her weight from one foot to the other. Undoubtedly, she sensed what he was feeling.

Before he could think about it further, Zoe tromped down the aisle in her patent leather shoes and squeezed past her grandparents. With a heavy sigh, she plopped down next to him on the pew. She was determined and focused, just like her mother.

"Great job up there," he whispered to her. "Looks like you're an expert with the candles."

"How much longer?" She swung her legs impatiently back and forth.

"Not long now, Baby Girl." He draped an arm easily

over her shoulder. "I promise." His chest swelled with a deep sense of pride and contentment at the revelation that someone like him could have fathered such a perfect and amazing creature.

"You said that before I went up there."

If an impatient one, he thought, thoroughly amused.

"I know I did, but I'm serious this time. Look. Here comes the best part. Well, except for all the food and cake back at your grandmama's house later."

"Why? What's gonna happen now?"

"Your uncle Dom is going to hand baby Miguel to your mom, and the minister is going to bless him."

"How come?"

"Because they asked your mom to be the baby's eternal guardian."

"Why? What's that?"

"It was partially because of her blood that Auntie Mackenzie was changed into one of our kind, making it possible for her and Uncle Dom to have a baby. They are very grateful to your mom."

"But what's a *turn-all* guardian?"

"Eternal. It means forever and ever. If something happens to them, it will be your mom's duty to see that Miguel is raised in accordance with his parents' wishes and beliefs."

"They're going to die?" Zoe's eyes widened, a look of horror spreading across her face.

He squeezed her tighter for a moment, hoping to reassure her. "No, honey, no one's going to die. This is just a ceremony our kind has done for generations because babies are to be cherished." He studied her face, which now seemed so similar to his own. Her dimple. The shape of her dark-lashed eyes. The way her hair curled up at the ends without any coaxing. He prayed she would always retain her innocence, that she'd never experience the pain he had. God willing, he'd make sure she never would.

"Did they do that to me when I was that little?"

"I'm…I'm not sure, sweetheart." A lump formed in his throat. There was so much he didn't know about his daughter. So much that he'd missed out on.

She pulled herself up on his lap and wrapped her arms around his neck. As he stroked her hair, he was surprised to find how natural it felt to comfort her.

"I'm glad you're my daddy."

He blinked to clear the sudden blurriness in his vision. "Me too, Baby Girl."

Over the top of Zoe's head, he saw Mr. DeGraff looking at them. He must've been watching them, because he tipped his chin and nodded approvingly. Alfonso smiled back, closed his eyes and squeezed his daughter a little tighter.

When the singing stopped, he turned his attention to the front of the church again. As if on cue, Mackenzie unswaddled tiny Miguel and gave him to Dom. The child cried, his wails echoing loudly off the walls. A few people chuckled. The boy certainly had a healthy set of lungs.

Zoe covered her ears. "Man, he's loud."

Dom nestled his son to his chest, encasing him in his arms, and the child instantly stopped crying. Then, with tears glittering in his own eyes, Dom held his son up, in all his glory, for the whole congregation to see.

"It is with great honor that I, Dominic Miguel Serrano, present my son, Miguel Foster Serrano, to the world."

Everyone clapped, and a few people cheered and whistled. Alfonso expected Dom to turn to Lily now, as was protocol, but instead his brother's gaze met his own. He waited until the noise abated.

"Alfonso," Dom called out, "will you please join us?"

A hush fell over the room and all eyes turned in his direction.

He didn't understand. He looked around for guidance. What was going on?

Zoe slid from his lap and pushed him. "Go, Daddy."

"And bring your daughter, Zoe, my niece, with you."

With a heart pounding out of control, Alfonso grabbed her small hand and made his way to the dais in the front of the chapel. Jackson, Cordell, Sadie and Mitchell all watched from the other side of the aisle, smiling. Next to them, Santiago nodded approvingly as he walked past.

His feet felt numb, his legs like rubber, reminding him vaguely of the sensation he experienced before he teleported. Oh God, he wasn't going to disappear in front of everyone, was he?

Lily held out her hands and Zoe ran up the steps to stand next to her. "Nice job, love," he heard Lily whisper. Or maybe he sensed it.

Alfonso paused at the bottom step. Was he really supposed to be here? What was he supposed to do?

"Come on, Alfonso," Mackenzie said, motioning him up. She wore an ornately decorated gown in rich purple, the color of his family's lineage. "My son is getting cold."

He hardly remembered how he got to the top, just

that he made it somehow and was now standing in front of Dom.

His brother looked at him, his eyes still glittering with moisture, and he held the baby out—like an offering. Alfonso swallowed against the lump that was even larger now and felt as if he were on the verge of breaking down. A year ago, if anyone would've told him he'd be standing here right now, in front of the brother who'd wanted him dead but who was now entrusting him with the life of his precious firstborn, he never would've believed them.

With shaking hands, Alfonso took Miguel and held him gingerly, cupping a tiny bum in one hand and a dark-haired head in the other.

Dom whispered, "He won't break, A." Then he motioned for Lily to join Alfonso's side.

She slipped one arm around his waist and placed her other hand over his, and together they held the child. "I love you," she whispered in his ear.

"I love you too," he mouthed back.

In a booming voice Dom said to the congregation, "Will you, Alfonso Rafael Serrano, along with your betrothed, Lily Anya DeGraff, promise to raise our son in the manner we've set forth in accordance with the laws of our people and the traditions of our family? That in the event that something were to happen to his mother and me, you'd protect him and keep him as your own until the day the earth takes you back to its womb?"

"We will." Alfonso's voice was so thick with emotion that no words spilled from his lips as he moved them.

It was Lily's voice, strong and proud, that everyone heard.

CHAPTER TWENTY-FOUR

The next day

"I CAN'T HOLD HIM OFF much longer, you know." Lily set her cell phone on the dresser and walked back to the bed.

With nothing planned today and Zoe up at the main house with a friend, they had Lily's carriage house all to themselves.

"Santiago is like a dog with a bone," she continued. "But then, I'm sure that comes as no surprise to you. When he sets his mind to something, it's extremely difficult to shake him off of it."

Alfonso held the comforter up for her and she snuggled in beside him. "I know, I know. I'll talk to him later today."

"What are you going to tell him? Have you decided?"

"That I don't want to be a full-fledged Guardian right now. That's not to say I won't, because I have every intention of joining the Agency. But my duty is toward my family first. I have a daughter who hardly knows me, as well as a house that needs to be finished."

"Not to mention a soon-to-be wife who can hardly stand it when we're apart. We've got a wedding and a honeymoon to plan. I've been thinking, instead of having the reception here at Willow Run, what would you think about inviting everyone to your home overlooking the sound? It'd give Dom and Mackenzie a chance to see what you've done."

"*Our* home," he corrected her. "*Casa en las Colinas* is our family's home. Mine, yours and Zoe's. Do you think she'll like it there? If not, she can stay here and—"

Lily touched a finger to his lips. "I know she'll love it. She's been talking about it already, although I'm afraid Mom and I will need to do some shopping for bedroom furniture. Zoe has it in her head that she wants a four-poster bed."

"Then I will make her one."

"You'd do that, love? Make our daughter a bed?"

"I made us one, didn't I?" He remembered the painstaking detail he'd put into the carved headboard, imagining that one day, if he lived long enough to make love to Lily in that bed, he'd die a happy and fulfilled man.

With a casual ease, he kissed her and ran his hand over the soft curve of her hip. He noted that she wasn't quite as thin as she had been, and for that he was glad.

"But for now, I'll work as a freelance agent, doing special projects and filling in around the region wherever I'm needed, but I don't want to be put on a regular schedule. At least not yet. I want some time to adjust to my family and my new way of life. For the first time in centuries, I feel truly free, and I intend to take advantage of it."

Alfonso wrapped his arms around her and pulled her close. She smelled of lavender. He inhaled, holding the scent of her inside him for a moment.

Lily ran a hand over his head. "I've decided I like your hair longer. Not that I don't like it short, but I miss running my fingers through it. Promise me you'll grow it back out."

"Promise." As a symbol of all the changes he was making in his life, that he was a new and different man, he'd had his hair cut short. But for Lily, he'd grow it back out. After all, he lived to make her happy.

Her cool fingers reached down between them to cup him. He felt himself harden again, despite all the love-making they'd been doing lately.

He'd sworn he was going to just hold her, but parts of his anatomy had other ideas. He simply couldn't get enough of her. And he doubted he ever would.

She purred a sound of contentment against his chest. "Not tired of me yet? I figured I'd have worn you out by now."

"Never." He chuckled as he pulled her leg over his hip and slipped a finger inside her silky warmth.

"Not even when we're old and gray?"

"Nope, not even then."

He eased her onto her back and settled himself between her parted legs, that crazy belly button arrow of hers pointing straight down, just in case he lost his way. As if that would ever happen.

Poised to enter her welcoming folds, he looked into the eyes of the woman he loved, her blond hair spiraling out on the pillow beneath her. She'd given him his life, she'd given him his daughter and she'd given him his future.

Slowly, and with little resistance as she was so ready

for him, he pushed himself inside her. She arched her hips and he slid in deep, his lips fusing with hers.

And he knew that at last he'd found home.

* * * * *

Look for Jackson's sizzling story
TEMPTED BY BLOOD
An all-new sweetblood adventure
coming soon
from Laurie London and HQN Books!

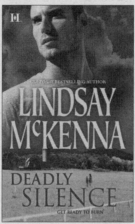

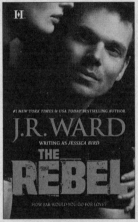

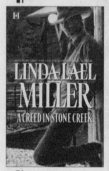

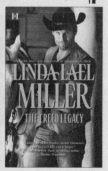

REQUEST YOUR FREE BOOKS!

2 FREE NOVELS FROM THE PARANORMAL ROMANCE COLLECTION PLUS 2 FREE GIFTS!

YES! Please send me 2 FREE novels from the Paranormal Romance Collection and my 2 FREE gifts (gifts are worth about $10). After receiving them, if I don't wish to receive any more books, I can return the shipping statement marked "cancel." If I don't cancel, I will receive 4 brand-new novels every month and be billed just $21.42 in the U.S. or $23.46 in Canada. That's a saving of at least 21% off the cover price of all 4 books. It's quite a bargain! Shipping and handling is just 50¢ per book in the U.S. and 75¢ per book in Canada.* I understand that accepting the 2 free books and gifts places me under no obligation to buy anything. I can always return a shipment and cancel at any time. Even if I never buy another book, the two free books and gifts are mine to keep forever.

237/337 HDN FEL2

Name	(PLEASE PRINT)

Address	Apt. #

City	State/Prov.	Zip/Postal Code

Signature (if under 18, a parent or guardian must sign)

Mail to the **Reader Service**:
IN U.S.A.: P.O. Box 1867, Buffalo, NY 14240-1867
IN CANADA: P.O. Box 609, Fort Erie, Ontario L2A 5X3

Not valid for current subscribers to the Paranormal Romance Collection or Harlequin® Nocturne™ books.

**Want to try two free books from another line?
Call 1-800-873-8635 or visit www.ReaderService.com.**

* Terms and prices subject to change without notice. Prices do not include applicable taxes. Sales tax applicable in N.Y. Canadian residents will be charged applicable taxes. Offer not valid in Quebec. This offer is limited to one order per household. All orders subject to credit approval. Credit or debit balances in a customer's account(s) may be offset by any other outstanding balance owed by or to the customer. Please allow 4 to 6 weeks for delivery. Offer available while quantities last.

Your Privacy—The Reader Service is committed to protecting your privacy. Our Privacy Policy is available online at www.ReaderService.com or upon request from the Reader Service.

We make a portion of our mailing list available to reputable third parties that offer products we believe may interest you. If you prefer that we not exchange your name with third parties, or if you wish to clarify or modify your communication preferences, please visit us at www.ReaderService.com/consumerchoice or write to us at Reader Service Preference Service, P.O. Box 9062, Buffalo, NY 14269. Include your complete name and address.

LAURIE LONDON

77544 BONDED BY BLOOD ___ $7.99 U.S. ___ $9.99 CAN.

(limited quantities available)

TOTAL AMOUNT $ _____
POSTAGE & HANDLING $ _____
($1.00 FOR 1 BOOK, 50¢ for each additional)
APPLICABLE TAXES* $ _____
TOTAL PAYABLE $ _____

(check or money order—please do not send cash)

To order, complete this form and send it, along with a check or money order for the total above, payable to HQN Books, to: **In the U.S.:** 3010 Walden Avenue, P.O. Box 9077, Buffalo, NY 14269-9077; **In Canada:** P.O. Box 636, Fort Erie, Ontario, L2A 5X3.

Name: _____
Address: _____ City: _____
State/Prov.: _____ Zip/Postal Code: _____
Account Number (if applicable): _____

075 CSAS

*New York residents remit applicable sales taxes.
*Canadian residents remit applicable GST and provincial taxes.